EXITUS

VOLUME II
THE CLIENT

By

David Slattery

First published in Ireland by Ds Books 2022

1

Copyright © David Slattery 2022

David Slattery asserts his moral rights to be identified as the author of this work.

PB ISBN: 978-1-7399137-3-1

EB ISBN: 978-1-7399137-4-8

HB ISBN 978-1-7399137-5-5

Cover design by: John Brady Design

Typeset in Adobe Garamond Pro by Coinlea Services

Front and back cover images: The Cabinet of Dr. Caligari image – Wikimedia Commons. Sigmund Freud image – Wikimedia Commons. Psychiatric patient image – depositphotos. Wizard image –gettyimages.

All are lunatics, but he who can analyse his delusions is called a philosopher.

—Ambrose Bierce

Part I

Philosophia In Tempore Tragicus Geekorum

Philosophy in the Tragic Age of the Geeks

Prologus
Prologue

The owner of the Frozen In Time Cryogenics Centre was unable to suppress a smile as the coffin slid behind the curtains. Business was booming. He had even hired an assistant: the thin replica who now stood beside him, studying his master's every move out of the corner of his eye. The owner knew his instincts were right, despite his many critics – above all, his wife, who had called his enterprise proof of his idiocy. In the way of all brilliant plans, it made complete sense when looked at in the cold light of success. Everyone who had either money or no imagination wanted to live forever. This one, Ernst Fischer – a philosopher with a bullet hole in the middle of his forehead – was going on the front of the brochure.

But it had been a close-run thing. Another week – two max. – and he would have been out of business. The stack of bodies piled four-high at the back of the freezer was defrosting by the time the electricity came back on. Whenever he did manage a fevered sleep, his clients appeared at the foot of his bed, threatening to melt. They gnashed their teeth and demanded their money back.

His fascination with what prospective generations would get

up to when defrosted had gotten him interested in cryogenics in the first place. That and studying his grandmother's body in the chest freezer in the garden shed when he was a child. His mother had made a ridiculous fuss because he had waited a month before telling anyone. What was the problem? She was dead. More proof in his mind that people were overly sensitive about the wrong things.

How would he spend all the money he was going to make? A new wife? Definitely. A new car? Ferrari. Holidays? Everywhere. He swiped the back of his assistant's head with the palm of his hand and told him to stop slouching. He would have to hire more sombre-looking staff. This one he could hide in storage.

Maybe he would even be featured in *Celebrity Hermit Magazine*? He could picture it now: a centre-page spread, stretched out beside the same model chest freezer in which his grandmother had first given him the idea for his frozen empire. Fortunately, her autopsy had been inconclusive.

I

Exim

Furthermore

Across the city in Saint Drogo's High Security Asylum for the Criminally Insane, Rik Wallace was thinking how a straightjacket that allowed for nose itching would be a humane advance in psychiatric medicine. He stopped wriggling and slumped on the rubber floor, feeling the energy drain from his limbs as if his big toe had sprung a leak. A congealing fog floated just above the surface of his consciousness. Why did that sadistic bodybuilding duty nurse always jab him in the left buttock when he had a choice of two?

He shifted his weight onto the other cheek. Ah, that was better. It was the same thing that set him off every time: the minor matter of denying having a wife and however many children were in that photograph that his psychiatrist, Professor Bentley Murphy, routinely handed him in illustration of his neglect of his domestic responsibilities that apparently reflected badly on his psychological maturity. The woman stared out of the picture with strong blue eyes that exposed a practised contempt for her audience. The children's faces revealed no evidence of age or gender: the kind of offspring one could find in any household, which is exactly what he told Murphy each time he took the photograph from the desk drawer. "I have never seen these people before in my life," he would yell in customary response. "They are impostors. I have no family."

"They are *your* family," Murphy would shout back, jabbing his finger in turn at his patient and at the domestic tableau. "Take him away," he would then command, slumping in surrender into his upholstered chair.

As usual, Rik would be carried out of the professor's office in the manner of a carpet thrown over the shoulder of the bodybuilding duty nurse back to one of a row of padded cells.

"My name is Rik Wallace," he would bellow over and over for the entire asylum to hear. He was sticking to his story.

"Yah, and I'm Elvis Presley," the predictable bodybuilding duty nurse would reply each time on cue.

In Rik's head The Pixies were now enquiring in song, perhaps with some justification, about the location of his mind when the sound of a key in the lock brought his thoughts back to his cell from the virtual canteen where he and the rest of the patients were stabbing each other with plastic forks to the rhythm of the music. Now what does that nurse want? he wondered. Back again so soon? It was difficult to distinguish the door from the surrounding wall because they were both concealed in buttoned-down quilting. A wire-covered fluorescent strip light screwed to the ceiling above his head lit half the windowless padded cell. A matching tube behind him blinked on and off with the crackle of a faulty starter switch. He doubted even Friedrich Nietzsche, who had set the standards for contemporary philosophical insanity, could have withstood such torture. He gritted his teeth. That brute of a duty nurse would ignore both his plea for an electrician and his vain protest that he could choke to death on the buttons that hung loose from the quilting.

As the door swung outwards into the corridor, a woman stepped into the padded cell. Rik recognised the mouth puckered around a burning cigarette – like an anus clasping a thermometer. The reflection from her black sunglasses broke through his consciousness like the edge of a spoon on the skin of a cold custard. "Pandora!" he cried, his surprise at the unexpected visitor immediately turning to dread as he remembered she had killed people. Now how many bodies were there?

"Hello, Rik," Pandora said in what she obviously imagined was a breezy, caring tone, appropriate to those she might encounter in a psychiatric hospital. But what came out of her mouth was her familiar, gravelly rasp. Rik remembered being too terrified to ask her age because her surface gave away no clue, having a resemblance to a mummified corpse.

Pandora's high heels punctured the floor of the cell causing her to totter and almost fall over, which slowed her advance on him.

"I am not Rik Wallace," he stammered – Pandora instantly succeeding in breaking his resolve where Murphy had failed. He shuffled his buttocks into the furthest corner of the cell, where he pressed his shoulders into the padding at the sight of the syringe in her hand.

"Of course, you are not," she said, showing her teeth in lieu of a smile. "I'm not stupid, Rik. I know what to expect in a lunatic asylum where no one is who they are supposed to be. I am aware of who you are not." She stopped, towering above him with the needle in one hand and the cigarette now in the other.

Pandora would not be distracted by such fine psychological distinctions as one's identity. She blew smoke while, no doubt, pondering where to jab him for the optimum effect.

"This is a non-smoking padded cell," he whispered.

"I don't see a sign," she said, studying instead the abstract patterns of bodily fluids decorating the quilted walls.

"It's behind your head."

She didn't move.

"I hoped—I mean … I *thought* you were dead."

As proof of her vitality, Pandora exhaled two cones of blue smoke from her cylindrical nostrils in the manner of a dragon.

"What do you want? What are you doing here?" he asked, instinctively shrinking further into the corner.

"Blah, blah, blah," she said. "You academics do love the sound of your own voices. *You* are coming with me." She squirted a thread of liquid from the needle to clear air bubbles as she bent over him.

"I'm not going anywhere. I may be insane, Pandora, but I am not crazy. I get three meals a day – when my arms are free – and regular medication to calm my nerves. All in all, I couldn't be happier; especially, if someone would fix that f—" Somewhere deep in his original-self of many selves ago he remembered that he tried to reserve swearing for the direst of circumstances. "—*light* on the ceiling. Institutional life suits me; in part, perhaps, because of the shock therapy and ice-baths. I don't want to return to the world with all of its complications and responsibilities. I like the regimented life of this hospital."

"Shut up."

"It's not that I have abandoned all hope of freedom. Not at all! I am desperate to be out of this padded cell where I have too much time to reflect on Nietzsche and his critics."

"I said *shut up.*"

"I would be grateful if you could escort me down the hall to the open ward where I can regain the embrace of the general uncomplicatedly insane population and the canteen where I can at least feed myself."

"Shut the fuck up! I'm not going to let you suck me into one of your pointless philosophical discussions." Pandora knelt on the stained, yielding floor in front of him. A smouldering cigarette protruded from the hand she clamped onto his kneecap. The other held the syringe, her thumb on the plunger.

"My life as a philosopher is over. Apart from the fact that the discipline struggles to have a meaningful role in the contemporary world. Sure, if this was the seventeenth century, I might be confident my ideas would find a discerning audience but—"

His narrative was interrupted by a high-pitched, hyena laugh from somewhere beyond the cell. Pandora and Wallace looked at each other for a moment. Then he started up again. "I am dedicated to pursuing my current career as a full-time lunatic here in this pleasant asylum away from real maniacs, like you, on the outside." He tried to press himself deeper into the padded wall, but the material used to cushion the mad had reached its limit of compression.

Pandora focussed the black plates of her sunglasses on his face. "We haven't met for— How long has it been?" she asked, shaking her head from side to side.

"It's been one year and ten months since my trial for the

people you killed. By the way, I noticed you didn't attend. Add on the time I spent on remand when you didn't visit either – that hurt – and I would say it was—"

"You haven't changed," she interrupted. "Still moralising; addicted to telling the rest of us how to behave. But as astonishing as it may seem, an urgent need has arisen in the outside world for a moral philosopher."

"I swear. I was only pretending to be a philosopher, but don't tell my psychiatrist. Besides, he will be disappointed if I disappear in the middle of my therapy."

"You were just unlucky to get caught running away from your responsibilities. It could happen to anyone. And you don't need therapy. There is nothing wrong with you."

"On the contrary, Pandora. I have had some of the finest psychiatric minds examine mine, and they are convinced I am extremely insane. I have at least one serious personality disorder because of my reluctance to form a domestic bond with a family, who inconveniently are not mine."

"I will never hear the end of it from Julie Progress if I don't bust you out of here; especially, since I lost my temper with your old colleague, Ernst Fischer, who was our first choice for our delicate mission. Progress is worse than you for non-stop talking. Start her going on a topic, especially something abstract and—"

"Oh, I remember Julie Progress."

"You should. You two were like this when you lived together on Love Street," she said, jamming the cigarette back between her lips to free her fingers to wrap one around another as an illustration of the intimate history of the couple.

"Aren't you and Progress supposed to be enemies? What

of your old feud between the Kantians and the Nietzscheans?"

"Oh, that's ancient history. Julie and I currently have a shared need to liberate you. She is waiting outside in the white van we rented for the purpose. On the drive over here, she kept prattling on about how she has to get back to her new boyfriend before he starts asking questions – it seems he doesn't like her leaving the house – as if I had nothing better to do than to break in here and knock you out. Pretentious bitch."

While aiming the syringe at his neck, smoke was diverted from Pandora's lungs into her mucus-lined trachea causing her to cough and plunge the needle into the padding on the wall just inches from his eyeball. As she beat the rubber floor with her palm, Wallace wriggled around her, threw himself onto his stomach and thrashed from side to side in the manner of a seal trying to build up momentum. When his chin reached the steel door saddle, he felt her hand close around his ankle. Rotating his neck, he saw the needle above her head, wrapped in her fingers like a dagger. "Not in my arse, Pandora," he pleaded. "Pick anywhere but there. Couldn't you knock me out with chloroform?"

"You watch too much television. Chloroform doesn't work. I experimented on Maurice Spencer for a whole week. I couldn't make him stop talking."

"Oh, how is Spencer?"

She clamped a hand over his mouth and broke the skin under his chin with the point of the needle. "At least this will shut you up for a while," she told him.

"I'll go with you. I promise. I'll be quiet. I will," he mumbled into her hand.

Some part of her hesitated in depressing the plunger all the way to the bottom. "Just a little prick," she said.

Wallace began to flap on the floor, yielding to the drug as it mixed with the cocktail of tranquilizers already in his system from the bodybuilding duty nurse's administrations, timed to exact intervals. Where was that oversized sadist the one time he was needed? His one regret was – when her sunglasses fell down over her nose during the struggle – that he should be subjected to the full horror of Pandora's tumescent, varicose eyeballs as his last sight on earth. Hopefully, hell – where he was confident he was headed – would have nothing to compete with that abomination.

II

Pericula Felix Pueritia

The Dangers of a Happy Childhood

Saint Drogo's High Security Asylum for the Criminally Insane was located in a fold in the landscape where two hills leaned against each other, overlooking the city's most desirable suburb, as if to remind any lunatic gazing through the barred windows of what they were missing in the world outside.

Flat-roofed, interlocking, shiny-glazed brickwork boxes housed the divisions within the institution. On the extreme right, a vertical box enclosed an unused gym where the few intrepid visitors could be relied upon to remark how surprised they were by the variety of equipment and its pristine condition. Indeed, on one occasion, the vaulting horse formed a useful focal point that allowed the visiting city mayor and his guests to pretend they didn't see the naked inmate dashing across the floor pursued by two sweating nurses.

At the opposite end, a horizontal box contained the canteen for unrestrained patients. In the centre, the glass front wall of the reception hall reflected the sunlight back into the eyes of those driving past the unmanned sentry hut five hundred yards to the front of the compound. Apart from the bars on the windows, the only other concession to security was a high, steel mesh fence suspended on wooden posts at twenty metre intervals that sagged here and there under a burden of rust. In the history of Saint Drogo's no one had ever broken out, or indeed, broken in. This state of affairs allowed the hospital management to conclude the inmates were a non-migratory variety of lunatic.

Yellowed lace curtains and sun-bleached velvet drapes hid the iron bars on the windows in Professor Bentley Murphy's office. The décor was chosen to signify a safe environment in which patients could reveal their innermost anxieties without fear of judgement. Other elements in this façade included wallpaper patterned with large flowers inspired by the paintings of Georgia O'Keeffe: colourful but calming. There were rows of reference books on shelves, wherein a patient might be tempted to research their symptoms. A hard-wearing brown carpet hid a Rorschach pattern of historic stains. All in all, it was the kind of room wherein a homicidal maniac might pause before bringing one of the matching set of heavy bronze fire irons on display in front of the reproduction Adams fireplace down on the professor's trained brain, for hopefully, a hesitation of a duration sufficient to allow him to flee.

The brown spiders that had established their webs in the intricate plasterwork on the ceiling cornices had observed enough therapy over the years to set up their own practices had there been a demand amongst their fellows. But experience made these arachnids free from any stress regarding the possibility of a duster ever reaching them.

Meanwhile a therapy session was underway in the professor's tranquil office.

"I know who I am even if no one else around here does,"

the person stretched out on the brown, leather chaise longue told the stern-looking man with the trimmed moustache and beard sitting in the upholstered chair behind the polished desk.

"I don't mean who *you* imagine you are *now*. You lunatics are all the same; jumping to the first wrong conclusion that comes into your head. I'll ask my question again," the man behind the desk said pedantically. "Who are you *really*, deep, deep down inside? The true *you*, trapped since childhood behind all those different faces you present to the world. You must discover your *real* nature because that is what governs how we turn out in life."

"Surely our parents and all the rest of them – nurture – have some role in it? Both nature and nurture together."

"Nonsense. That is a lazy compromise. It must be one or the other, and I am satisfied it's nature."

"Nurture."

"Nature."

"Nurture! Enough of this nonsense," Professor Bentley Murphy said, sitting up on the chaise longue by swinging his feet onto an almost invisible stain on the floor. "Come out from behind my desk and lie down here where you belong."

They passed each other on the track worn in the brown carpet between desk and couch for the third or fourth time that session. Murphy had lost count. The therapy resumed when the forensic psychiatrist had settled into the upholstered chair while his patient, Tiberius Lang, sat upright on the chaise longue with his left leg dangling over his right knee, waiting to move again.

"How can we know when we wake up in the morning that we are the same person who went to sleep the night before?

That is something that has bothered philosophers for centuries. If the finest minds in history cannot provide an answer, neither can you; even with all of your experience as a therapist," the professor said.

"We remember ourselves from the day before," Tiberius insisted.

"We recall someone, yes; but how can we tell it's the same person with the same nature? We assume we remember who we were yesterday. It may all be just an extended dream. Or a computer programmer could have planted our memories in our brains: some extra-terrestrial nerds amusing themselves at our expense."

"Whatever you say, I am confident a deep-down-inside-you *you* is in there that you have repressed," Tiberius said, tapping his temple with his index finger. "Look at the state of your fingernails. You are stressed out of your mind from all your repressing."

Murphy shoved his hands into his armpits.

"This couch evokes memories of my former clients," Tiberius continued, "which, you appreciate, I find disturbing. You don't want me to get upset, do you? Let me sit behind your desk again."

The threat of upset usually worked on the sympathetic – or was that *nervous* – psychiatrist. And so, they passed each other once more on the carpet.

"That basement in your head terrifies you, doesn't it, Prof? What monsters live down there in the undisturbed sludge? Oh, don't ever let them out. You need therapy, Professor. Talk is the best cure. Speak to me!" Tiberius demanded, striking his palm with a fist to punctuate his point.

If talking was a cure, the psychiatrist thought, this patient should be the sanest person on the planet. Professor Murphy's square, black-plastic glasses matched the colour of his hair, which stood up in an even dome as if he had been subjected to an electric shock before leaving for work that morning. The smile that almost never left the lips enclosing his perfect white teeth didn't climb all the way up his sallow face to his green eyes because it usually lost interest at his cheeks. He spoke with the practised, sedate tone he imagined would calm the heart of his wildest patient. His overall demeanour caused those who met him to imagine they liked him, when in fact, they felt sorry for him because they confused approval with compassion. His face inspired sympathy for unimagined tragedies being mulled over inside his spherical skull.

"Where were we in our analysis of *you* before you distracted me by discussing *me*? Go back to your childhood, again," the forensic psychiatrist said, reconciled to stretching out on the chaise longue where he sank into the yielding worn leather.

Tiberius put on a pair of round spectacles that magnified his watery, judgemental eyes. His bald pate provided ample space for an above-average-sized brain; his mouth a line between his beard and moustache that highlighted the yellowness of his teeth. His grooming was inspired by his uncanny resemblance to Sigmund Freud as photographed in the 1930s.

"I have told you a hundred times my childhood was idyllic. My parents were both cultured professionals who gave me an ideal start in life. The correct amount of discipline combined with constructive advice. They were enlightened people who were inspiring role models without setting unrealistic goals. They made me the free spirit I was before I got locked up in here."

"They were both child psychologists who published separate books with competing paradigms on how children should be reared," Murphy repeated from memory. "The last thing any child needs is a parent who imagines they know what they are doing. Admit it. It must have been hell for you trying to conform to their opposing hypotheses."

"It was easier than you suppose because I was a child prodigy. I was smarter than both of them. I read their books and articles on me when I was a toddler."

"So you say. Make something up, Tiberius. Lie to me about your childhood. We have nothing else to pass the time during these sessions because you are never being released."

"You go first."

"Nothing to tell. My childhood was happy." Murphy voiced the practised lie he told himself.

"A happy childhood?" Tiberius snorted. "That is what fucked you up. One needs a bad start in life if one expects to achieve anything worthwhile. A smart child should be able to ruin things for themselves while they are still young enough to take advantage."

The forensic psychiatrist sighed. "I am not 'fucked-up' as you clinically put it."

"You are. I've read your file." Tiberius raised his shoulders in an insincerely apologetic shrug at the forensic psychiatrist's startled look. "What? I have read everyone's file. You should lock those cabinets in the hall. The lack of security around here is scandalous."

While Tiberius squinted his eyes behind his round glasses, trying to imagine what might pass as a disturbing childhood,

Murphy took the opportunity to exercise his real psychological passion: reflecting on his own existential crises. Oh God, I am so bored I may have to kill myself before the next client comes in, he thought. How will I do it? Hanging myself from the chandelier as my predecessor did would show a lack of originality on my part.

He studied the ornate light fitting above his patient's head. Two of the electric bulbs were missing from where the rope had broken them off at the base. Maybe I could incite Tiberius to strangle me. One more homicide would not set his therapy back. I wonder if he throttles people on request? Childhood. Now that's something to forget, he reminded himself.

How does Tiberius always succeed in getting me to focus on myself, he wondered, disregarding the fact that self-reflection was his sole preoccupation when not planning his own end. He trapped a tear with the back of his finger as it escaped his eye. Tiberius may be mad, but he is a talented therapist, Murphy admitted to himself. He sighed so loudly that Tiberius stopped the made-up monologue on his childhood Murphy had been ignoring to study him with his most practised psychological gaze. "I should have killed myself last year on our asylum Open Day. That was my clearest chance," the psychiatrist lamented ruefully out loud. Murphy could hardly pass a pool of water on the road without feeling an irrational compulsion to throw himself in. If only he had time to work on his own problems.

Professor Bentley Murphy's regret at still being alive was interrupted when the door crashed open, and a man burst in dressed in a uniform one might expect to find on someone hired to deter shoplifters in a supermarket.

"Who the hell are you?" Tiberius Lang asked for

both of them.

"I'm the new security guard," the intruder said, fanning his fingers over his chest to call attention to his official-looking light-blue shirt. "This is my first day working here."

"Can't you see I am in the middle of a therapy session?" Tiberius asked. "You have interrupted us on the brink of a critical breakthrough. Months, perhaps years of delicate painstaking progress undone. I hope you are satisfied. What do you want?"

"I am sorry to disturb your confidential session," the security guard said without regret. "There has been an incident on the high-maintenance wing."

"What has happened now?" the mad therapist asked, deliberately sighing to signify his annoyance at the shortcomings in the order of things in the asylum.

"Someone has escaped."

"How did that happen?" Tiberius asked calmly, for his own education in security rather than out of curiosity.

"Who?" Murphy butted in, sitting upright on the chaise longue.

The security guard ignored him, addressing his answer to the dependable-looking gentleman behind the desk, who was just then composing the expression of trust he had perfected during years spent as a homicidal therapist. Amongst other effects, this involved polishing the lenses of his spectacles while he pursed his lips.

"Which patient—I mean, *client?*" Tiberius asked, ignoring the professor to demonstrate what he considered was the short-tempered response appropriate to the institution's highest authority on madness.

"Now, let me see." The guard consulted a clipboard, running his index finger down a column of names. "On the last count on that wing we had the Archbishop of Canterbury, Princess Diana, Hitler, three Napoleons, Richard Nixon, one Sigmund Freud—"

"That's Freud right there," Murphy said, pointing at Tiberius.

The security guard ignored the interruption, anxious to get through the unfamiliar list as fast as possible. "And one Rik Wallace."

"Three Napoleons? Are you sure our clients are so unoriginal?" Tiberius asked.

"I am. I read my briefing notes over breakfast with my wife this morning. The one who believes he is still married to Josephine is the one who walks around with his hand down the front of his trousers," the guard said, imitating the compulsion by shoving his free hand into his crotch. "Then there's the one who speaks with an unconvincing French accent, and the one who won't accept the outcome at Waterloo and wants to restage the battle."

"All three of them want that."

"According to my inventory we are one Napoleon light. The one with the accent."

"That's all right, then. He won't have gone far. We should try the bistro at the bottom of the hill," Murphy said.

"No. Wait. I'm wrong." The security guard turned the clipboard sideways. "I can't read my own handwriting," he chuckled. "It's Rik Wallace," he confirmed for the psychiatric patient who bore an uncanny resemblance to Sigmund Freud.

Professor Murphy sighed. "Whoever has gone, it's not

the one who calls himself Rik Wallace. Following yet another unproductive session with me, you will find him trussed up in a padded cell on powerful tranquilizers," he told the security guard from his position perched on the end of the chaise longue.

"It's definitely Wallace. The door to his cell was swinging open. I found this on the floor," the guard told Tiberius, holding out a syringe in the palm of his hand with its plunger depressed halfway.

"So, Wallace has escaped! What are we to make of that?" Murphy asked the security guard, who was wondering what concern it was of his.

"Anyone going to the trouble of breaking out of this place must be really mad." Tiberius laughed before his mood instantly changed to anxiety when he remembered Wallace was central to his secret scheme for redemption.

"You're the doctor," the security guard told him.

"He has been struck off," Murphy said. "And even then, he was never medically qualified."

"Why keep bringing that up?" Tiberius growled under his breath. "Damn Wallace," he said. "I was desperate to work with him. I mean, continue my counselling. Fascinating case, Bernard," he said, squinting through his ornamental lenses at the plastic nametag pinned to the breast pocket of the security guard's light-blue shirt. "It's rare to find someone like him in a secure clinical setting who presents such a diffused sense of identity. You won't appreciate this, but the investigation of the *other* is really a deepening of the exploration of the *self*. That is what attracts me to this profession: self-knowledge. Can you imagine how frustrating it is to find oneself with the whole jigsaw assembled in front of one only to discover that the most essential piece that makes sense of the entire pattern is missing?"

"Oh, I hate when that happens," Bernard said. "That's normal isn't it, to be annoyed when that happens with jigsaws?" He was terrified of being diagnosed as insane. Before he drove off that morning for his first day at the hospital his wife reassured him that psychiatric hypochondria was a normal response when starting a career in a lunatic asylum.

Bernard wore a peaked hat that didn't quite hide his bald patch because it sat too far back on his head. A pair of sculpted sideburns framing his cheeks gave the impression that his mouth was being squeezed into a pout by invisible fingers. His shirt stretched to ripping point across a spherical stomach held in place by a leather belt to which he had attached an array of accessories that hung around him like decorations on a Christmas tree.

"Yes. Yes. You are depressingly normal, Bernard," the insane therapist assured him. "But fortunately, Wallace isn't. We must get him back here at once because he is the final component in my magnificent therapeutic scheme. I had him right here in my hand, and you let him go."

Murphy stood up and approached the security guard. "Thank you, Bernard," he said, placing a palm on his chest and pushing him backwards towards the door.

Unconsciously the guard's hand fumbled for the can of pepper spray on his belt. His wife had handed it to him that morning, convinced he would be mad to turn up on his first day unarmed even if the conditions of employment they read through together the evening before forbade carrying weapons into work.

"That's enough, for today," Tiberius told Murphy, coming around the desk and trying to insert himself between the security guard and the psychiatrist. "Bernard, take this patient back to his cell and lock him up tight."

"He's the patient. I'm the psychiatrist, you idiot," Murphy protested.

He squeezed his eyes closed with his fists when the pepper hit them, screamed, and fell to the floor, the drool from his mouth adding to the pattern of stains on the carpet.

Tiberius and Bernard stood over him, looking down.

The security guard observed Murphy with the dispassionate manner of an experienced naturalist noting the curious reproductive behaviour of a rare species.

Perhaps I deserve this, Murphy was thinking somewhere in a serene place behind his burning eyes. Deep down I have never felt comfortable about my treatment of Wallace. Guilt. Yes, that is what I feel. Why did I do it? Despite all his loud protestations his willingness to submit to his fate annoyed me. I am just like him. I must fight back. We both must fight back. I wonder if one can die from pepper spray? The fleeting thoughts evaporated with his tears.

"Is he dangerous?" Bernard asked, describing a circle with his index finger at his temple while poking Murphy with the toe of his shiny shoe.

"Very," Tiberius confirmed. "Did you drive to work, Bernard?"

"Yes. I'm parked outside."

"Time cannot be lost tracking down Wallace. Where are your keys?"

"I have them here somewhere," the security guard said, searching through the items dangling from his belt. "It's the banana yellow hatchback. You can't miss it," he added as he handed them over. "Just one other teeny-tiny thing." Bernard held his index finger a fraction of an inch from his thumb hoping to illustrate the insignificance of the point he was plucking up the courage to make.

"What is it?" the homicidal maniac asked, taking the professor's Harris tweed jacket with the white plastic security-pass clipped to the lapel from the back of the door.

"Please don't lose your head. Promise you won't get mad, because it's my first day. My wife says all you psychiatrists are prone to hysteria."

"What is it?" the madman asked, coming as near to screaming as he had ever done in his life. "Spit it out. I'm in a hurry."

"In all the excitement, I forgot to mention. It appears another syringe was found."

"Where?"

"In the duty nurse's thick neck."

III

Leviathan

A Leviathan

The mansion stood towards the front of its extensive grounds, resting on the side of a rocky outcrop that sloped away from the city towards the coast. The original Palladian-inspired house was built 175 years earlier by a clerk who had become wealthy supplying dried goods to the armies on both sides of the most fashionable conflicts of the time. His son added walled gardens and stables with his father's money. His son, in turn, remodelled the building with the last of his grandfather's cash to include a ballroom stretching across the full width to the rear to facilitate his addiction to dancing. The cousin who inherited the mansion from the bankrupt dancer disposed of the contents at an auction held on the overgrown lawn. It took almost two years to shoot or find alternative accommodation for the clerk's collection of exotic animals which had gone feral after several generations running unchecked in the house and gardens.

Sightings by children of snakes under beds and panthers in the trees outside were not uncommon even after the house had been taken over by a religious order and turned into an orphanage where orphans were trained to strike the most sentimental poses for prospective parents in front of the original fireplace in the downstairs reception room. As time passed, the nuns clung on to outnumber their charges by five to one before finally quitting. Then the house enjoyed a short period as a luxury hotel, followed by a longer interval as budget accommodation for backpackers. The current owner, Randy Fortune – who gave his name to the building, Fortune Mansion - determined to restore the house, not to its original glory, but to a contemporary splendour as defined by the most in-demand architect on the planet.

Outside, the reinstated walled-garden with its symmetrical box hedging and regime of flowering plants gave the impression that their aesthetic harmony was natural and not the product of the imaginations of the gardening staff. Inside, some rooms were finished to the specifications of the now-dismissed award-winning architect, while others had fallen victim to the sudden and catastrophic moral malaise which ensued when the new owner's existential crisis struck without warning. A series of modern boxes constructed inside the original rooms left a network of hidden spaces, secret corridors, and irregular shaped gaps between the contemporary and old walls. Plumbing pipes, electrical cables, insects, mice, rats, and the occasional descendants of the clerk's original snakes occupied these areas. The household servants, who had been hired in quantity before ennui set in, used these crevices as short cuts from one room to another or to spy on their employer through holes drilled at eye level in the newly installed panels.

In the bronze glare from the setting sun, it was difficult to make out the separate shapes writhing amongst the silk sheets on the bed that stood in the middle of an empty cube behind the smooth expanse of a single enormous rectangle of glass. The three plasterboard walls vibrated to the strident bass piano cords of Radiohead's "Pyramid Song" blasting from the red spherical loudspeakers resting on the floor, built to produce sounds outside the range of human hearing. To a casual observer peeping through a hole in the wall, the scene in the bed might pass as a pair of walruses struggling on a beach to align their orifices in strenuous copulation. The one on top was indistinguishable in form from the one struggling underneath other than that this much bigger walrus, between grunts, was singing along to the music. Lyrics emanated from an open mouth like a bark, over and over again. Peering closer, it was possible to discern zips on their backs and brand names on the sleeves of these all-too-human monsters.

The upper wetsuit slowed and stopped slamming against the wetsuit underneath. It slid off to the side, twitching as the part of the song audible to the human ear faded out. The male wetsuit could be distinguished from its female counterpart by having a hole cut in the groin that allowed a condom-clad penis to penetrate the slit cut in the corresponding crotch of the female wetsuit that also had two circles cut from the front panels to expose a pair of breasts sheathed in transparent plastic. The wetsuits lay side by side on their backs, panting.

Julie Progress pulled off the rubber hood and released her long, flat, blond hair with a practised flick of her head. She was both conscious of her beauty and confident she was the most sexually intelligent person she knew. She leaned out of the bed to retrieve her still-burning cigarette from the antique Murano glass canoe on the floor that served as an ashtray. "You take minimalism too far, Randy. There is no place to hang my clothes in this ridiculous room," she said referring to her jeans, brassiere, blouse, tights, and knickers, where they lay in a heap beside the bed. Was that a common garter snake or a belt curled up beside her leather boots?

A film of moisture lubricated her skin beneath the rubber. "And nowhere to hang this ludicrous costume I have to wear for what you call having sex," she added.

"It's not my fault. You know I can't stand anyone touching me," Randy Fortune said as he stared up at the immaculate square of white ceiling framed by the elasticated edge of the hood pleating his face.

A spider affixed to the white plain above by the hairs on its feet would have a perfect view of the pair below, half-hidden in the crumpled sheets. But Randy was confident there was neither arachnid nor any other species of insect present inside the environmentally passive cubicles built into the old house. Of course, they could have crawled in through the spy holes – which Randy was unaware had been drilled into the walls – thus compromising the expensive air filtering system designed to allow nothing with a diameter larger than a micrometre into the rooms.

Randy pulled off his diving hood to reveal a head shaped like an egg, sloping to a rounded prominence, his sharp chin reflecting the point on his cranium. His eyes were too narrow and set too far apart for him to be attractive if he were poor. The tip of his nose hung down too far over his horizontal lips that no longer parted in a smile, while the frowns that might have decorated his forehead had migrated to the back of his neck. His misery was compounded by the fact that he suspected people didn't like him because he didn't particularly like himself anymore.

"Where were you this morning?" he asked.

"What did you say?" Progress asked, her thoughts coming back from wondering how to raise the topic that was preoccupying her. She never paid attention to what Randy said anyway. Before she met the billionaire, she couldn't have imagined proximity to wealth would bore her. She would have been horrified to learn it was intellectual rather than sexual stimulation she craved deep down inside the wetsuit. Even now, it was still just a nagging doubt, and with luck, she might never discover the full truth.

"I asked where you were this morning. You know I don't like you going out without my permission. In my position I can't—"

"I saw Rik Wallace," Progress said, seizing the opportunity.

"Who?"

"The genius I mentioned a million times. Typical, you don't listen. He has been released," she said, unwinding her prepared lie.

"From the loony bin?"

"We don't use that term anymore. It's a high-security psychiatric facility for the criminally insane. A fine line exists between sublime brilliance and prosaic madness, and psychiatrists aren't trained to tell the difference. In fact, being locked up is proof of Wallace's genius."

"You met him this morning?"

"I saw him in passing. We didn't have an opportunity to talk over the details, but I have told you already he is a world expert in values."

"Whose values?"

"Anyone's values. His. Yours. What does it matter for someone like you who has none? Of all the supervisors I ever had for my doctorate, he was the best."

She knelt on the bed and bounced on the expensive mattress in the excitement of giving way to her recollections. "He was unstable even back then when I first met him," she said, weaving extra strands into her web of dissimulation that she knew would be stronger for containing some truthful threads. "I told you we had a thing together. An intellectual affair: a meeting of minds."

"When was that?"

"At Candid Online College?"

"Where?"

"It used to be called CAT College – commerce, arts and technology? No?"

Randy's blank expression annoyed Progress.

"You own it. It's part of Fortune University. For fuck's sake! I work there. Don't you remember anything about my life?" She swung her rubberised feet onto the floor, stretched her arms behind her head, straining with her fingers inches from the strap attached to the zip running up the back of the wetsuit. Randy made no movement to assist her.

"You don't have to work or even go outside. Everything you need is here," he said.

"I am an economic prisoner. I have my own career to consider. At least pretend to be interested in other people's lives besides your own. That's why you are so unhappy. You are self-obsessed." She spoke from first-hand experience of the condition. "I teach philosophy there whenever I am in the mood," she added.

"What are you saying?" he asked, still stretched out on his back on the bed.

"I've told you a hundred times. I deliver the introductory psychoanalysis module and basic morality in the online diploma in reasoning and hairdressing at Candid Online College. Wallace inspired me, even if he didn't teach me much because he kept changing his fundamental beliefs; but that is the hallmark of a genius. He is the person you need to consult on how to build your futuristic moral order." Her fingers finally closed around the ends of the strap.

"What moral order?"

"The order you keep droning on and on about wanting to establish through an altruistic foundation for the benefit of humanity."

"Oh, that order! I haven't forgotten. It's just too depressing to dwell on it. Anyway, didn't you tell me some expert on someone called Immanuel Kant was going to help me discover the most effective way to do good?"

"Ernst Fischer? He's no longer available. You need to talk to Wallace. He knows all sorts of morality even the type that applies to the super-rich. You have to meet him."

The wetsuit sagged open releasing her breasts. She knelt in front of him again. "I am confident he will encourage you to feel morally good about your money. He can prove to you with philosophical arguments that it would be wrong to become poor by giving away everything you own, even in the event you weren't miserable as a result. Life's not all about happiness, you know."

"But there has to be a meaning to my existence other

than … stuff," he said, picking up one of his handmade shoes from the floor beside the bed and throwing it at the music system. "What is the point, if that is all there is?"

"Wallace will prove to you that your idea of right and wrong is for ordinary poor people. It doesn't apply to billionaires." She held up a hand to stop him interrupting. "I know you don't trust governments with your money, and you believe politicians are too stupid to spend it wisely if you give it to them as tax, and I know you believe you are above the law."

"I want to create my own society that will be superior to those that we have allowed to evolve by chance. Mine must be perfect. That's not too much to ask, is it?"

Progress dragged the wetsuit down over her thighs. "Society? What is society but a figment of the imagination of the disadvantaged like me? That's not you, Randy. You will never hear other billionaires discussing society. Why do you have to be different?"

"Hmmm, I am not so sure—"

"You can donate some money to save the environment. You could rescue a few trees and endangered animals. That's popular, and it will make you feel better," Progress said, peeling the wetsuit from her ankles and standing naked in front of him.

"I hate the environment. The more pollution, the less people will be left on the planet; the less skin for me to accidentally bump into. Watch what you are doing with your legs."

"Talk to Wallace."

"You can't imagine the challenges I experience being a billionaire."

"You could give me a few of your billions, and then I would

appreciate what you are going through," Progress laughed. "I could share your misery."

Randy Fortune didn't even smile.

"Why did you buy another college when you have so many already?" Progress asked, remembering what had sparked her indignation in the first place.

"Which one?"

"Why do I bother?" she muttered, pressing her nose into the armpit of her blouse before dropping it back on the floor. "CAT College, of course."

"I forgot I bought that one, but I do recall someone telling me that by having my own university, along with my television stations, music, films, books, phone apps – in fact, everything – I can implant my values into the next generation."

"Precisely. What values?"

"That's where my plan falls apart. I don't have any values just now, but I have everything in place to control people's minds if I ever discover what they are."

"But that's my *point*. Wallace is an expert on values. He will change your life. I am sure of it. He has that effect on people. For my sake, tell me you will meet him."

"I give up. You can bring him here, but I have a rule on morality: he has to be a good family man. Anyone who can't organise a harmonious domestic life has no business telling me what to do. He is a good family man, isn't he?"

"Where did this rule spring from? You're not a good family man."

"And that's why I don't know right from wrong. I want to meet his wife and children if I am going to rely on his advice."

"You haven't asked me about my family?"

"I ignore your advice."

"You make it so difficult to be pleasant to you," Progress said, covering her breasts with the palms of her hands and leaning over him.

"No. Noooooh, don't touch my face," he howled.

Progress turned away and crossed to the glass door of the bathroom, the soles of her feet sucking the marble floor. Randy studied her skin that was an exact fit for her back, buttocks, and thighs, as if it had been cut to measure by the famous tailor who made his suits before he stopped going outside. He rubbed his rubber hands across his ribs as if in pain. Her flawless skin embodied his problem. The nearer he came to his desires the further away he found himself. He hadn't always been allergic to skin. It was another price he paid for his wealth. There was a time when he was poor that he would have jumped off the bed, pressed Progress against the wall – there at the pair of holes beside the door frame – bunched her long, blond hair in his fist, buried his chest in the complementary hollows of her shoulders, and kissed her neck behind her ear – hard. He shuddered inside the wetsuit.

When Progress returned from the bathroom, she stood into her knickers and dragged them up the thighs that gave Randy so much anxiety. Did her belt move away from the bed of its own volition? "I'm starving," she said. "I wish we could go somewhere romantic. That bistro near Saint Drogo's asylum gets fantastic reviews."

"I can't."

"Why not."

"You know why not. I can't stand people around me. They have too much skin. Please put on your clothes."

Progress's fingers closed around the belt that she looped into her jeans. She couldn't relax. Randy and his rules! She had to consult Pandora urgently about finding Wallace's family.

IV

Dure Excitatio
A Rude Awakening

Rik Wallace pumped his arms up and down as he strode along the narrow street of tall buildings without a destination in mind. He wasn't cold despite wearing just shoes, socks, and a hat. Those around him, muffled up to their eyes in woollen coats and scarves, laughed and pointed to where his penis had been before it disappeared in the North wind. He rattled the handle on the locked door. He had to get inside because he was already late for the three-hour written examination in sanity he had forgotten to prepare for, remembering only a moment ago it was on today. He pitched head first into an elevator shaft when the door opened. Fortunately, he remembered he knew how to fly, so he flapped his arms. He was wearing a woollen suit that itched his skin. He cradled her bare belly in the palms of his hands.

"*Why did you run away?*" she asked without moving her lips.

"I imagine I panicked," he replied. He nodded towards her bulging stomach to indicate the source of even more anxiety on the way. "That is the horrifying thing about babies. They belong to themselves and not to their parents. You are letting another complete stranger into our lives."

"What are you talking about?"

"Your stomach! Aren't you pregnant?"

"I am not."

"You mean, I have been terrified all this time of another stranger invading my life, and it turns out you are" – he shook his head searching for a word – "*fat?*" She slapped him across the face with rhythm, as if measuring the interval between each smack with a metronome. First her right hand, then her left; then her right again.

"Wake up, Rik. Wake up."

His cheeks burned where a flat hand struck him with what he thought was the sound of a cork leaving a cheap bottle of champagne. It *was* the sound of a cork leaving a cheap bottle of champagne. Pandora's black sunglasses were inches from his eyes when he opened them.

Behind her, Casper Wall's thin, white face beneath his prematurely bald forehead now floated into view. Casper blinked as the foam flowed from the champagne bottle, which he held out in front of him with both hands, careful not to stain his navy tracksuit with a broad yellow band running down one arm and into the leg. Then, Maurice Spencer's face came into focus over Casper's shoulder: the same Spencer who no one could believe was an idiot because fools didn't come in tall, dark, handsome packaging.

Pandora scowled.

Casper licked his pale, thin lips.

Spencer grinned.

Wallace took in his surroundings through his streaming eyes. The sepulchral décor in the provost's office had not changed since his brief and troubled tenure there. The room had everything one might expect to find in a funeral home, including a hint of embalming fluid in the air. All that was missing was a corpse in an open coffin. Give him a few minutes, he thought, and he could oblige.

"Welcome back, Professor Wallace," Spencer intoned.

"Fuck, fuck, fuck, fuckety-fuck," Wallace said, abandoning his disdain for swearing. "I can't be here," he slurred. "Not again. Why didn't you kill me, Pandora?"

She was just then asking herself the same question.

But instantly, Wallace resigned himself – as usual – to whatever fate held in store for him. He tried to evaporate the iodine flavour from his mouth by dangling his swollen tongue between his cracked lips. "Pah. Whatever you filled me with is coming out through my system. I can hardly talk," he said, struggling to sit upright on the chair because he was still wrapped in the straightjacket.

"Good," Pandora said. "That is an unexpected bonus."

"You are lucky to wake up at all, if you ask me." Spencer said with a laugh. "You have been jabbed with a concoction of Pandora's own invention … twenty-three hours ago," he said, confirming his timings by glancing at his wrist watch. "It was her idea to knock you out. She was confident you wouldn't stop talking if you both just strolled together out of Saint Drogo's. Besides, she was the only one of us with the nerve to break in there to rescue you from psychiatry. I can't imagine how you felt being treated by those chemical reductionists who are convinced we are mere collections of molecules in a Petri dish to be altered this way and that as the mood takes them. They assign no role to the mind in modern mental health."

"Shut up, Spencer," Pandora commanded.

"I was having the most vivid dream," Wallace told no one in particular. "I wonder what it could mean? I was naked, and I couldn't find my penis."

A cat jumped onto his lap where it began to execute circles. "Get that monster off me," Wallace shouted, bouncing his knees. "Oh, it's you, Marlboro," he said, calming down when he recognised the cat. He was both surprised and disappointed to see the creature was still alive. "Did you hurt people, Pandora, while breaking me out?" he asked as the cat settled on his lap.

She inhaled on her cigarette. "What do you think?" she asked when filled with smoke.

"Untie me, for God's sake. Now Marlboro is digging his claws into my flesh."

"Come here, Marley. Leave that lunatic alone." Pandora lifted the obese cat into her arms. Did Wallace imagine Marlboro stuck his tongue out at him? He shook his head trying to dispel the remnants of Pandora's drug from behind his eyeballs.

"Naked dreams mean something, don't they?"

Ignoring the question, Spencer, Casper, and Pandora each raised a glass of champagne in a toast.

"To academic freedom," Spencer said, tilting the sparkling liquid against his lips.

"To modern technology," Casper said.

"To the status quo," Pandora said.

"Please untie me," Wallace groaned. "I need a drink."

"We will take off the straightjacket when you agree to work for us," Pandora said.

"Here? With you? No way. Leave it on," Wallace said without conviction.

"We need you," Spencer pleaded.

"I told you, Pandora, when you materialised in my padded cell, that I have quit philosophy for good. It's too dangerous," Wallace said.

"I have also abandoned philosophy because of the crisis in its contemporary manifestation," Spencer confirmed.

"What crisis?" Pandora asked, instantly regretting the question. She looked into her now empty glass before placing it down on the desk, silently vowing to drink more.

"Most of the stuff that philosophers – like I used to be – think about is obvious," Spencer said with the conviction of the recent apostate. "A child could tell them the answer. If a tree falls in the forest, and there no one there to hear it does it make noise? Of course, it does. What is the fucking problem?"

"The problem is you have no intellectual curiosity. For example, Renè Descartes's famous *cogito ergo sum* can be seen as an attempt to—" Wallace surprised himself that it was he who was saying this.

"Stop!" Casper shouted before Pandora could do so herself, clamping his hands over his ears and spilling champagne down inside the collar of his tracksuit in the process. "While you were away Pandora reminded us every day of the virtue of not thinking. Don't think. Just act."

"I agree," Spencer said.

"But your whole life was dedicated to contemplation, Spencer," Wallace said.

"Well, since I saw you last, I have become a disciple of Zen Buddhism. Since I discovered mindfulness, I realise thinking is a complete waste of time, except for that incident with Ernst Fischer where it would have been better had we paused for a moment to reflect on how—"

"But—"

"Shut up both of you, or I will have Horse settle this matter with his fists," Pandora said.

"Horse? That brute. Is he here?" Wallace asked, trying to swivel his head around in the straightjacket.

Horse sat in one of the cluster of armchairs arranged around the glass coffee table in front of the French doors that led out to the now overgrown private garden in the middle of which two white computer desks lay dead on their backs in the tall grass with their legs pointing to the grey sky. Horse was reading the sports supplement of a newspaper. His fingers swamped the pages. Was he wearing the same black suit, white shirt, and narrow black tie he had on the last time Wallace saw him – which was at the riot in the main quadrangle of CAT College? He looked up when he heard his name, studied Wallace and Spencer with an expression that suggested he was concluding it was not worth the energy to stand up, cross the room, and thump them both, before returning his attention to the incontrovertible proof of bias in the refereeing of Saturday's football derby.

"We are married," Pandora told no one in particular, holding out the fourth finger on her left hand to reveal a broad gold band beside a thinner one supporting a huge diamond. "It's useful for knocking people on the head," she said, rapping Spencer's skull as a demonstration of its efficacy.

"Ow, Pandora. I've told you before, that hurts. That's my brain you are battering. It's precious. I'm having it frozen when I die."

Pandora ignored the protest. "Our relationship is built on

the foundation of Horse's taciturnity. A silent man turns me on. That should leave you two in no doubt where you stand in my affections."

"I used to turn you on once upon a time," Spencer said.

"I am in denial on that subject. It never happened."

Spencer was already talking again, enthusing Wallace with his most recent belief system. "Mindfulness concerns real enlightenment and not the fake nonsense Western thinkers have been peddling for centuries. Buddhist wisdom is available to everyone rather than just a few elite scholars like you. Mindfulness is derived from the essential elements of transcendental meditation."

"Isn't that Hindi?"

"Hindu. Buddhist. Confucius. Tao. What difference does it make as long as it's not Western?"

"Please untie me," Wallace pleaded. "Or at least give me a drink. I haven't touched a drop of alcohol since I got locked up; except that one time the bodybuilding duty nurse tried to get me drunk in my padded cell."

Spencer ignored the request because his thoughts were still fixed on his own mindfulness. "Unlike you, I now have true insight into the actual nature of reality: the impermanence of life."

"Is that why you enrolled in a cryogenic storage facility?" Pandora asked, inhaling on a cigarette as if to underline her contempt for longevity.

"I am not stupid, Pandora. I am aware having my head frozen won't make me immortal. It will merely lengthen my life by a few centuries. Do you believe there is something after death, Wallace?"

"Hopefully, not. I imagine I will need a long rest. Can I please have a drink? Anything with alcohol will suffice. Please untie me."

"You can get pissed when you agree to co-operate with us," Pandora told him.

"What am I supposed to do?" Wallace asked, his will to resist diminishing with each non-alcoholic moment that passed.

"We work for the billionaire Randy Fortune."

"*The* Randy Fortune? The owner of Candid Communications?"

"That's the one. He bought CAT College. Casper here has done an impressive job transforming the place online."

Here Casper took up the story of the evolution of the college. "Can you believe it? We are now one of the most respectable virtual campuses on the Internet. Candid Online College – which is part of Fortune University, which, in turn, is a subsidiary of Candid Communications – is incredibly popular."

"I dreamt I could fly," Wallace said.

"And it is all thanks to you, Rik, for bankrupting the college in the first place," Casper laughed.

"I'll make us all gin martinis," Spencer volunteered, standing up.

"Our single tiny problem is that Randy Fortune plans to sell off his companies including Fortune University, and with it our Online College and use the proceeds to build a state-of-the-art ethical system for the benefit of mankind. He wants to give all his wealth away because he has convinced himself returning to the poverty of his youth will cure him of the moral crisis he is currently experiencing. Selfish bastard. You are going to stop that plan by morally talking him out of it because that is what you do best," Pandora said.

"What is wrong with him?"

"He is suffering from ennui," Spencer shouted from the drinks cabinet. "Can you imagine?"

"Do people still get that? I thought it had died out in the nineteenth century."

"It sometimes happens when you have too much money; when you are so rich nothing matters."

"I read in *Celebrity Hermit Magazine* – there was a copy in the waiting room at Saint Drogo's – that Randy Fortune is a recluse. How do you propose I am going to meet him in order to get this job to supposedly morally talk him out of giving away all his money?"

"Aha! Don't you suppose we haven't already thought of that? He might be a recluse but he sees Julie Progress because she is in a relationship with him," Spencer explained.

"What kind of a relationship?"

"She is having sex with him; what other kind of relationship is there?" Pandora asked, displaying evidence of pedantry that would have upset her had she been aware of it.

"I am sorry I asked."

"It was Progress's idea to bust you out so that she could introduce you to Randy Fortune. Now it's up to you to secure the post as his moral advisor."

"Why should I help you?"

"Because if you don't, we will throw you back into that nuthouse where you can rot forever."

"Yes, please throw me back. As asylums go, if it comes down

to a choice between here and there, I would rather become institutionalised in Saint Drogo's. Ironically, I was getting on fine in there insisting I am Rik Wallace. Apart from my left buttock, which is like a pin cushion."

Pandora leaned over him. "Listen carefully to this concrete, non-abstract, straightforward, and unambiguous proposition, Rik." She poked him in the chest with an extended bony finger. "Normally I would threaten to kill you, but I realise now having lost Ernst Fischer—"

"We didn't lose him. You shot him in the head," Casper clarified.

"Having *lost* Ernst Fischer," Pandora continued, "was counter-productive. And I don't care what Progress says, I was provoked. Imagine that pompous ass said our whole scheme was unethical. So – having also learned from that minor mistake – if you don't support us, I will kill your wife and children. Is there anything in that proposal that lends itself to more than one interpretation?"

"My wife is fat." Wallace sunk his chin onto his chest. "Would it make a difference if I told you they weren't mine?" It must be said that Wallace didn't appreciate at the time that her threatening his family and not him was perhaps proof of some level of repressed affection Pandora still retained for him.

"No, it would not," she snapped. "I am not a fool. You are bound to deny being related to them in order to protect them. That is what any loving father would do."

Spencer appeared at the desk with a jug of gin martinis in one hand and a stack of glasses held between the fingers of the other. "You might be wondering why Pandora is so concerned with maintaining the status quo. You see, Randy Fortune is too depressed to concern himself with the details of running his empire, and in particular, this corner of his empire," he said. "In the current situation we do whatever we like. We are authorities unto ourselves. He never comes here, ever. We have the revenue from millions of students so we are not going to give that up without a fight. If he gets his way, he might be poor and cheerful, and where would that leave us? Poor and miserable, that's where," Spencer said, recalling the lines Pandora had repeated to him over and over until he almost believed them. "Isn't that right, Pandora. Isn't that why you – I mean, we – want Randy to remain rich?"

Pandora looked at Spencer with pity, which was one of the expressions she kept to hand to illustrate her limited repertoire of practical emotions.

"I blame your parents for everything," she told him.

"That's not fair."

"But convenient. They had you, didn't they? It all started with them."

"I have no feeling in my arms," Wallace announced.

"Work with that," Spencer said. "In mindfulness, no feelings are superfluous."

"Pandora, if you are not going to untie me, can you please inject me again. Make it a lethal dose this time."

"Not until you agree to co-operate."

"Pour a martini down my throat, and I will consider your proposal. No olives."

Wallace concentrated on the ceiling while Pandora held the spout of the jug to his parted lips. Marlboro decided this was an opportune moment to pee on his lap as his contribution to what he thought of their visitor.

V

Venator

The Hunter

Professor Bentley Murphy's swollen eyes cried of their own accord as he sat with his elbows propped on his rosewood desk. His knuckles still throbbed from hitting Bernard the security guard under the chin as he helped him back on his feet after Tiberius Lang had made his escape in the Harris tweed jacket and the banana yellow hatchback. Bernard had abandoned his first ever shift at the asylum to go home to tell his wife the bad news concerning her car that she had loaned him for his first day, but the good news of how her pepper spray had been so handy, even if used it on the wrong person.

"Sit down," the psychiatrist said, executing a horizontal wave with his bruised hand to indicate Inspector Freddy Sullivan might sit on the worn leather chaise longue.

The policeman unbuttoned the jacket of the cheap, plain grey suit his mother had bought him in a buy-one-get-one-free sale, before balancing like a bird on the end of the elongated seat, ready to take flight at the first sign of being analysed. Despite his promotion, he was just as small and thin as ever.

"Thank you for getting here so quickly," the professor said, blotting his eyes with a handkerchief. "Photographs of our escaped clients have already been circulated to airports, ferries, train stations, etcetera."

"Clients? Loonies, if you ask me," Sullivan volunteered.

Murphy ignored the suggested classification. Since he had started chewing things in his office to spare his bleeding finger nails, he plucked a pencil from a tray of half-eaten exhibits and gnawed on its end like a rat. "I understand you are familiar with one of them. The one who insists he is Rik Wallace," he got out between bites.

"Oh yes, Professor. I am quite nostalgic about him because he was my first case."

"Yes, I know the details of your involvement in his arrest."

"He ran us round in circles before I nabbed him. In fact, I owe my meteoric rise in the force to Wallace. Before coming over here, I dug his fat file out of our archive to refresh my memory," Sullivan said. "There are all sorts of malfeasances in there. Off the top of my head, I recall impersonation, aiding and abetting, member of a criminal gang, conspiring before and after – and during – the fact, false representation, public lecturing without training or preparation—"

"That's not a crime," Murphy put in.

"Should be. Where was I? Traffic offences, desecration of bodies – both dead and alive – destruction of public and private property, disturbing the peace, inciting a riot, misrepresenting classical ideas—"

"Again, not illegal in this jurisdiction."

Sullivan ignored the interruption. "And traumatising men, women, and children. He has supernatural powers, if you ask me. He is able to control people's minds. He got to my governor back then, Inspector Jackson, who resigned from the force soon after. He had to, after paying for Wallace's hotshot legal team, who managed to get him locked up in this padded hotel instead of jail where he belongs. Wallace probably hypnotised him. His lawyer argued he never killed anyone himself, even if he got his disciples to do his bidding. But we have him this time. At last, we can pin a definite murder on him: the duty nurse's highly-tuned system shut down an hour ago in Saint Drogo's A&E from whatever was in the syringe found sticking out of his neck."

"I warned him he was overdoing the exercise. You can be too fit, you know."

"Do you think Wallace will strike again, now that he is on the loose?" Sullivan fished a notebook from his pocket as if he intended to document the psychiatrist's reply, which he didn't.

"Hard to tell because his is one of the most complicated cases I have ever dealt with. He may be insane in the classical sense because he did head up a gang of Nietzscheans who were at war with a rival gang of Kantians. However, he didn't respond to my standard treatments. I'm seen as a maverick around here, Inspector, because I don't sedate my clients. I believe in the talking therapies. Normally, I'm there for my patients. I try my best to even listen to them. But I made an exception for Wallace. He frustrated me, I suppose. I don't feel good about the way I behaved. You see, he refused to acknowledge who he wasn't and that drove me crazy. He denied being able to remember his family. I interpreted that as a classic case of repression, typical of the psychotic. He wouldn't accept that these were his," Murphy said, removing the much-used photograph from the top drawer and sliding it across the glossy surface of the desk towards

Sullivan. "I am impressed, Inspector," the psychiatrist added when the policeman picked up the photograph. "I can tell you have well-tuned psychological instincts from the way you tried to shock him into returning to his reality by confronting him with his responsibilities when you drove this wonderful family to meet him at the philosophy department at CAT College on the day of his arrest. We may never comprehend what those poor creatures suffered when he tried to run off on them."

"Thank you. I took courses in psychology at the police academy."

"It shows. Are you a family man yourself, Inspector?"

"No. I live with my mother, but she isn't really family, is she?"

"Possibly not, but a mother is the most important element in the formation of the psyche."

"I try not to think of mine."

"Yes, yes. That's understandable. But, as you know, your psychological ploy didn't work in this case because my client would never acknowledge these were his real family," Murphy said, leaning over the desk to point with a gnawed finger nail in turn at each of the faces in the photograph. "One of the most stubborn patients I have ever come across. God, some days I wanted to punch him. There was one occasion when I did, but it's best to forget about that now because —" Murphy was distracted when he noticed that Sullivan was turning red as he peered at the enchanting family portrait. "What's wrong?" he asked. "Don't you recognise them —*you* brought them to the philosophy department on that fateful day."

"Oh, those," Sullivan suppressed an embarrassed laugh. "At the time I was certain I had found the wife and kids the selfish bastard had abandoned. Killing people is one thing, maybe some of them deserved what they got, but mistreating little children makes my blood boil."

"Mine too."

"Listen, don't take this the wrong way, Professor, but the wife and children in this photograph aren't his." He placed the photograph on the desk.

"What do you mean they aren't his? Of course, they are his. You found them."

"I made a balls of the DNA samples. I was a rookie back then. I lifted hairs from a room on the sixth floor of the hotel instead of the fifth. Could happen to anyone. It's a scandal the way they don't properly clean hotel rooms." Sullivan now used the unrestrained laugh of the classical hysteric.

"You fucking idiot. You mean whoever he is, he isn't married to this woman?" Murphy shouted. He leaned across the desk to rap the photograph with the top of his index finger. "All the work I put into making him have false memories. My God, what have I done to his mental balance?" Murphy rubbed one hand over the other. He liked to hold his patients' hands in his, palm down, and massage the back of their wrists as reassurance that everything would be fine – for him. Something he wasn't even aware he was doing. When a patient wasn't within reach, such as now, he massaged his own hands, alternating one over the other. Sometimes he stopped a passing stranger in the street and rubbed their hands, a habit he couldn't break despite being punched on one occasion while asking for directions. The psychiatrist brought his palms to his forehead. He stood up and moved so fast the inspector was alarmed to find him around the desk reaching out for his hands. Sullivan jammed his arms down by his sides.

"Don't be so hard on yourself, Professor. If it wasn't this family, then it was a similar one. They are all the same: interchangeable. It doesn't matter because he is a hopeless case if you ask me."

"I am not asking you," Murphy shouted, before slumping down beside Sullivan on the chaise longue. "But under hypnosis he did admit that at least one of them called him daddy. They ran after him," the psychiatrist said, propping his face in his hands, his elbows on his knees supporting his sagging upper body. Then he began to rub his hands.

"I know. I was there. I saw everything. Fatherless children are like ducks: they will take to anyone in an emergency."

"But one of them looks like him," Murphy said defensively, standing up and picking up the photograph from the desk to point to the resemblance between the tallest child and his escaped patient. He sat down again. "Oh, I see it now. That's an example of classic parental transference. How could I have been so naïve? I saw them as his instant archetypal family that would fill some void that I projected onto him. Or at least you, Inspector, projected them onto him for me. It's a policing error, compounded by a classic Jungian blunder. Oh, such an elementary Jungian misinterpretation. I knew I should have stuck with Freud. I blame Carl Jung."

"I blame him too, Professor," the policeman said, happy to have a scapegoat, even if he didn't have a clue who Carl Jung was. "It could happen to anyone," he added. He shifted along the chaise longue, away from the psychiatrist slumped dangerously near him.

"No, it couldn't. One needs to be very experienced to make

a fuckup of this complexity. Why didn't you tell me this when he was first sent here?"

"It's not my business once the trial is over. Not guilty by insanity. That was a crazy verdict."

"It's always difficult for a jury to decide in cases where a defendant is familiar with the work of Nietzsche. I've said it before, there hasn't been enough research into—"

"He is as sane as I am, if you ask me."

"That is now a definite possibility," Murphy muttered. "Even at the time some suspected Nietzsche was feigning madness. Psychiatry is not geared to tell the difference between a genuine lunatic and a genius who imagines he is pretending. Oh my God, he probably is Rik Wallace after all."

"There is no justice. An electric chair or a rope would be too good for someone running off on his wife and kiddies."

"You just said they weren't his."

"That's not the point. It's the principle that counts. They could have been his. From what you are saying when he was hypnotised, he wasn't even sure they weren't. When his lawyer raised the possibility that he was crazy I said oh here we go—"

The psychiatrist ceased paying attention to the inspector, who prattled on with his hypothesis on the forensic abuse of mental illness as a defence. Murphy zoned out in the special way he had trained himself to concentrate on his own thoughts as he did when a tedious patient droned on about *their* problems while stretched out without a care in the world on the all-too-comfortable furniture in his office. He didn't consider he was ignoring his responsibilities, as such. Perhaps to the layman with a little knowledge, like Sullivan here, it might seem that way. Murphy did nod at pertinent points. He even enquired of them how that made them feel whenever he imagined he heard emotions being revealed or identified for the first time. He muttered uh-uhs at intervals to keep the monologue rattling along and rubbed his chin, signifying thoughtfulness. Maybe he should grow a beard like Tiberius Lang that he could stroke to enhance the overall empathetic effect. The layman might have described his behaviour as daydreaming or even neglect. He called it psychiatric listening, which was a specific form of inattention that was supposed to be proof against fatal levels of boredom. However, it wasn't working because he was bored stiff with people in general.

But, after this bombshell with the photograph, he reflected on what psychological damage he may have done to Wallace because maybe now he, Murphy, had to accept that he *was* Wallace? He wondered what impact tormenting the man to take responsibility for something that never happened had had on his brittle mind? In his defence, most of his clients had false memories whenever they claimed to remember anything anyway. Would he be struck off if it came out? He had pumped Wallace full of drugs because he couldn't remember his non-existent family? He zapped and froze him to no avail. At least he hadn't hypnotised him himself. He had hired that nice lady from the circus with the boa and the sequined monokini for that. Besides it was Wallace's own fault. He could have pretended to go along with the therapy like all his other clients, except of course for Mother Theresa. He should look on the bright side. This malpractice would be the ideal excuse he needed to kill himself if he were struck off. What was his problem?

His conscious self returned to the office from the cliff edge above the wild sea where he had been practising his leap into the comforting void. "Uh-uh," he muttered when it occurred to him that Inspector Sullivan had reached some punctuation point in his monologue. "How did that make you feel?" he asked, indifferent to the reply.

"How do you imagine I felt with everyone in the room staring at me?"

"Oh, yes. That would be a normal response. It's imperative, Inspector," Murphy said to change the subject, "that Wallace must not learn the truth about his fake family." "It could set him back psychologically. Please keep the details of both our escaped clients from the press. We don't want the public getting nervous."

"Ah, yes, this other one who escaped," the inspector said, referring to the face in the folded photograph he took from between the pages in his notebook. He consulted his almost illegible scribbles. "One of your security guards made a statement that this other maniac – the one who looks like Freud. By the way, is he a relative of the original psychoanalyst? You know, I studied psychology at the police academy," he boasted.

"So you said. No. He is not related, beyond thinking he *is* him. His name is Tiberius Lang."

"Anyway, as your security guard confirms he was here with you at the time …err … the duty nurse was stabbed in the neck with a syringe, that would make Wallace the only suspect in the nurse's murder. I'm sure Wallace did it. He is a maniac, isn't he? What further proof do you need?"

"We have a hospital full of maniacs. You have a photograph of Tiberius, and when last seen he was wearing my Harris tweed jacket and driving our security guard's wife's banana yellow hatchback. Furthermore, we know he is a therapist inspired by Freudian psychoanalysis."

"What does that mean?"

"It means he is extremely dangerous. Forget Wallace and concentrate on finding Tiberius before he throttles someone else."

"If it will stop you getting into a flap, I will assign my sergeant, Jones, to investigate Tiberius's whereabouts while I focus on hunting down Wallace. Say what you like, Professor, anyone who resembles Freud has to be harmless," Sullivan said, studying the photograph. "If you cannot trust a face like his, then who can you trust?"

"Now, please leave, Inspector, because I need to lie down here for a while and reflect on what possible irreversible psychological damage I have done to my client. Can you imagine how I feel about that?"

Sullivan stared into the rear-view mirror as the asylum grew smaller behind him. It was getting dark. He felt relieved to be driving away. Free. The place made him feel uncomfortable. So many lunatics gathered together in one building, and so many psychiatrists too. Surely that couldn't be right. He shuddered. Out of nowhere, the idea formed in his mind that perhaps one of those loonies had climbed into the boot of his car while it was parked in front of the asylum. They would, wouldn't they? If they were mad? Should he stop and check? No, that would be paranoid. He had read about paranoia on his police training course. But what if a maniac was hiding in there, and he didn't look, what then? They could crawl out through the back seat and strangle him while he was driving along. Maybe it was Rik Wallace, having concealed himself in the bushes waiting for an unsuspecting visitor like him to park. Sullivan swerved to keep the car on a sharp bend. Pay attention to the road ahead, he told himself, not behind. What is done is done. It doesn't matter that you fucked up the DNA tests. Wallace is crazy anyway.

He put his foot down on the accelerator while listening for unusual sounds from the boot.

"What about the duty nurse?" Bernard the security guard asked. His wife had sent him back to work, citing the psychological virtue of immediately getting back onto horses fallen off of.

"What about him?" Professor Bentley Murphy asked, in turn.

"Does Inspector Sullivan have a view on who killed him?"

"Thanks to your statement, he thinks Wallace did it. Sullivan is paranoid, if you ask me."

"Does he have a family?"

"A family? I think he mentioned a mother. But what is wrong with everyone around here today? Why are you all suddenly obsessed with fucking families? For God's sake, Bernard! That's not a straightforward topic. It goes to the heart of what psychiatry involves. Look at me. Every time I think about my -"

"I meant did anyone inform the duty nurse's family?"

"Oh, that. I don't know, Bernard."

Murphy reached out to grab the back of the security guard's hands. Bernard, who was still embarrassed over the part he played in Tiberius's escape, resisted the impulse to pull them away. He would spend a half hour washing his hands when he got home.

63

VI

Mutata In Educatio
A Mutation in Education

Life amongst the arachnids went along on the ceilings of Candid Online College much as it had done during the era of CAT College because the spiders weren't easily distracted from routine by pedagogic change. If they felt an impact from courses transitioning onto an online platform, as Casper Wall put it, they didn't say. Perhaps they missed the bustle of students coming and going from physical lectures. Since the sale of the college, the number of webs had increased along with their occupants because the cleaners had been dispensed with on the simple economy that virtual classrooms do not require dusting.

The straightjacket lay on the floor like a chrysalis shed to accommodate a changing form. Rik Wallace rubbed his arms in an attempt to restore the circulation, while Pandora was ready to grab him if he should try to run off on his wobbly legs. No one spoke against the soundtrack of rattling ice cubes and Maurice Spencer's humming to himself that his father may have had an undiagnosed gambling addiction way down in New Orleans as he concentrated on pouring cocktails. He placed a brimming glass in front of Wallace and retreated to the window with his own drink, from where he looked down onto the quadrangle outside.

"My arms don't work." Wallace explained, as he leaned over and stretched his lips towards the rim of the condensing glass.

"Times have changed in education," Spencer mused. He raised his own drink to herald his current favourite nostalgic conversation. "God, I miss the days when students rioted instead of all this studying in the library."

"Our library is online," Casper explained for no one in particular.

"Well, if we had a proper library, they would be in there," Spencer said.

"I blame contemporary parents who are victims of over-education themselves and want their children to experience the exact same misery that they had to go through growing up," Casper interjected. "Parents are unhappy unless their children are miserable in the same way they were when they were young. But that's not me," he said, tapping himself on his sternum.

The topic of miserable children put Wallace in mind of Spencer's imaginary daughter. She *was* an illusion, wasn't she?

"How is Samantha?" he enquired with rare spite. Perhaps he was unconsciously seeking revenge for the delay in getting a drink.

"I don't want to talk about her," Spencer lied, his eyes still fixed outside.

"I understand. Family is the greatest source of emotional pain."

"She is a huge disappointment to me, after everything I did to bring her up with the best possible set of values," Spencer continued, unprompted.

"Your values?"

"Yes, my values, that I believed in completely until recently. She doesn't even share my old values. I had such high hopes for her. But I am happy, I suppose, if she is happy," he said without conviction. "She says she is, but I doubt it. Who could be with that lifestyle? I hardly see her since she left home."

Wallace stopped himself from assuring Spencer that his daughter didn't exist. After all, who was he to lecture anyone on the ontological status of their family members? Instead, he diplomatically enquired where she had gone.

"She works as a programmer for Candid Communications. Ironically, we are not on speaking terms at the present moment."

"Why? What did you want her to be?"

"A philosopher or a dancer. Thinking is easier on a parent because a child can practise at home wearing their own clothes. I had to drive her to every ballet rehearsal. I even sewed her first tutu."

"She was arrested for breaking into Candid Communications' computer mainframe," Casper's disembodied voice continued the saga from under the desk to where he had slid from off his chair. "That's how she got the job. They hired her when she was released on bail."

"She is famous in the hacking community. Many people believe she is a virtual person: an avatar. Not real. Can you imagine that?" Spencer chuckled.

"I can't," Wallace lied.

Outside, a coloured assortment of vehicles was crammed onto the tarmacadam that covered the once-neat rectangular lawn so meticulously, if resentfully, maintained in the past by Jim the porter. A blue car was accelerating from the archway in the east wing, while a red car was picking up momentum from the west.

Wallace chanced standing up. When he found his legs would support his weight, he shuffled to the collection of bottles on the drinks cabinet where he swayed almost imperceptibly from side to side, while trying to decide what to try next now that he had regained the use of his arms. He settled on a half-empty bottle of Scotch to reinforce his pessimism. "Did all the students leave here after the rioting between the Kantians and the Nietzscheans?" he asked Pandora, as he made his way back to the desk with the bottle cradled in his arms.

"There are a few holdouts still here because they insist on finishing their degrees on a physical campus," she said. "I blame the literature, history, and theology lecturers for encouraging them. We had to shut down the philosophy department under public pressure. The police helped us to remove the students, along with Ernst Fischer, all of whom had chained themselves to the radiators. Spencer here redeployed himself into course design. I was sure Fischer would appreciate the opportunity to use his philosophy to help us, but he proved to be a die-hard Kantian right up to when I shot him."

Casper got his buttocks back onto the chair after a struggle that held Wallace's attention. Now he rested his face on the cool surface of the desktop. "We have banned both Kant and Nietzsche from every possible syllabus in the interest of impartiality," he said, dribbling out of the corner of his mouth. "We will have the place to ourselves when the few remaining holdouts have gone." Casper placed his palms on the desk with exaggerated deliberation and heaved himself into an upright sitting position. "The Internet has at least one advantage over everything that has gone before in education. We don't ever see our students. A perfect arrangement we are determined to maintain."

"But that's not all that's great," Spencer said. "While the bureaucrats at Fortune University perform the administrative tasks, we are free to implement educational reforms that will benefit all of humanity. We concentrate on the visionary stuff." Spencer spoke with such conviction that Wallace believed he believed what he was saying.

"Egg-xactly," Casper slurred. "We organize staff morale-boosting trips to egg-xotic resorts, invent fashionable courses, and have ourselves photographed singly and in groups leaning on the bonnets of fancy cars and lounging on yachts for our online cat-a-log."

"Randy Fortune is so rich, he doesn't know nor care what we cost," Pandora said.

"I suspect he doesn't even remember we exist," Spencer added.

"I don't even have a means of con-tact-ing him dire-egg-ctly," Casper concluded with satisfaction.

"Ours is an example of the symbiotic relationship found in nature where the well-meaning parasites keep the indifferent host functioning by doing the dirty work for them without them even realising it," Spencer explained.

"Someone has to be a parr-a-site," Casper said, repeating a phrase he used more often each day.

"A maligned though noble profession," Spencer confirmed, hardly paying attention to the conversation because he was now following the movement of the two cars outside.

"Online learning is the future," Casper slurred on. "My advantage is that I understand nothing about offline education.

That allows me to approach the problem with an open mind, free of prejudice created by prior knowledge. Ignorance is one of the most underrated assets you can have. What would Einstein have achieved if he knew physics before he started? Our virtual students are more satisfied than the flesh-and-blood ones who are always complaining. They expect to study only what they imagine they already know. But it doesn't pay to upset them – as we learned from the riots you organised," Casper gasped.

"I wasn't even there. I was only passing through," Wallace protested.

Everyone else ignored the correction to the collective memory that by now had established the myth of Wallace's central role in the rioting.

"Nowadays, instead of public violence, we focus on practical skills such as accounting, computing, of course, and human resource management," Pandora said, taking over the burden of narrating their recent history from the waning-again Casper. "We don't engage in that abstract thinking drivel with which you are so obsessed. We have over a million students studying with us worldwide. We had to knock two lecture halls together to create a space large enough for all the printers to keep up with the demand for qualifications."

"What do you do with the rest of the campus if all the students are online?" Wallace asked, uncorking the bottle of Scotch with his teeth.

"Now that was a real challenge. We couldn't just sit on this valuable real estate," Pandora said. She waved a cigarette in the direction of the window that still held Spencer's attention. "We discussed turning the college into a museum of learning where tourists could visit classrooms, what remains of the library, and exhibits showing how students used to study in bygone days: the primitive conditions they had to endure when you and your predecessors were in charge. But according to our market research CAT College wasn't around long enough to make a convincing transition to a museum. To appear ancient, we considered buying up wooden panelling, antique bookshelves, and desks from some of the old institutions that ironically are updating themselves. But instead, we paved over the lawns that took far too much time and money to keep trimmed, and turned the place into a car park."

Outside, Spencer saw but couldn't hear the impact of the red car's headlamp smashing into the blue car's fender just in front of the last free parking space through the glass.

"We make a fortune from suburban commuters," Pandora continued. "And income that Randy Fortune knows nothing about cannot hurt him."

This time Casper's forehead did make contact with the desk when he tilted forward. But he recovered enough to relate a revolutionary idea brought about perhaps by concussion. "Imagine a phone shaped like a hip flask containing alcohol that you can talk into and use to send naked pictures of yourself to strangers—"

"That is why the status quo must prevail." Pandora interrupted Casper, echoing her earlier toast. "We don't want any sudden changes at the top. The worst possible thing would be if Randy Fortune were allowed to pursue the dictates of his conscience. Your job is to convince him that doing the right thing is the worst possible thing he could do – and it definitely would be for us."

"Hear, hear," Casper said before his face fell forward with a crack so loud as it hit the desk that Wallace was confident that they wouldn't be hearing from him again.

"I'm not so sure that is the way of doing good works," he told Pandora.

In the car park, the driver of the blue car reached the front of his car first. The driver of the red car waved his fist and pointed to his broken headlamp.

"Haven't you ever wondered why you philosophers are so useless when left to your own devices? Leave the thinking to others. We will point you in the right direction. Everyone knows the difference between right and wrong until a philosopher shows up causing confusion. You are not here to confuse us – we know how you work. We are immune to your effects. But we recognise your unique talent for causing chaos wherever you go. So, your job is to confuse Randy Fortune. I am simply proposing you exploit that skill for our greater good. We want you to stir Randy Fortune up like you did us when you first showed up here when – you will remember – we were doing fine."

"Everyone used to complain all the time about everything when I first got here. I improved your lives. Casper said that the rioting that you unjustly blamed on me was a benefit to all of you in the end."

"Yes, Rik, we complained; but that is only a normal aspect of the human condition. Mindfulness teaches us to realize that when we imagined we weren't happy, we were; and therefore, what is the point in complaining if we are miserable because some time in the future, we will remember how content we are now without even knowing it?" Spencer drained his glass and glanced at his silent audience anticipating appreciative expressions, but not getting them. "What?" he asked when no one said anything, before answering himself. "I didn't say I was miserable now. I said that if I thought I was, I wouldn't be so—"

"Shut up, Spencer," Pandora commanded.

"I believe what you are trying to say is that, for you, the past was an improvement on the present because it's over," Wallace said. He was warming to what might be his first philosophical conversation since being locked up. He was surprised at how much he missed thinking.

"What I am saying …" Spencer said, continuing aloud a monologue he was having inside his head as he watched the knee of the driver of the red car sink into the groin of the driver of the blue car, who fell over sideways and scrunched himself into a foetus. "… is that life is full of unintended consequences."

"Stop talking, Spencer," Pandora pleaded, pouring another drink.

"We cannot comprehend how a single event impacts on another."

"Now I understand why I didn't want to be free when I was in Saint Drogo's," Wallace said.

"Horse, will you be a dear and take Casper home, or at least leave him in the corridor outside. He is distracting Marley," Pandora said.

"I have to take control of my own life, my own destiny. That is the key to mental wellbeing. I learned that much in the asylum," Wallace said. But no one was listening.

The red car was nudging the blue car aside to scrape into

the space. Just as the foetus got to his knees, a white car reversed out, two spaces down.

"Ten minutes with you, and Randy Fortune will agree to do whatever you say – which will be to abandon his selfish plan to give away all his money," Pandora concluded.

"Okay, is everyone's role in our enterprise clear?" Spencer asked, turning away to refill his glass.

"Absolutely not," Wallace said. "I haven't a clue what I am supposed to do to Randy Fortune."

"Good. Now that's sorted out, I suggest another cocktail to celebrate the unpredictability of life," Spencer said, leaning on the desk for stability as he passed by.

When Pandora's phone rang, she immediately pressed it to the side of her head and muttered repeated uh-huhs before hanging up. "That was Progress with an update from Fortune Mansion," she announced. "Had she carried out a little research in advance she might have saved us the trouble of busting you out." She sighed and pinched Wallace's sleeve to get his particular attention. "It now seems Randy is obsessed with your family, Rik. So, if you are going to work for him, you will need to track down your wife and kids. Look at it this way, now is your chance to take your domestic responsibilities seriously for perhaps the first time in your life."

"One teeny-tiny problem, Pandora. That wife and children, with whom everyone seems to be obsessed, would reveal to Randy Fortune – amongst other small details – that they are not, nor ever have been, related to me; because as I have been telling you over and over since you bust me out of the asylum, I am not who you think I am."

"Neither am I," Spencer volunteered as he struggled to pick

up a bottle. He placed a hand over his eye to maintain focus.

"But I am not who you think I am in a way that is different from the way you are not who we think you are and that makes all the difference."

"I'm warning you both," Pandora interjected. "Shut the fuck up. Just find this family, whoever they are and explain their responsibilities to them."

"I don't know where they live. I kept telling Murphy back at the asylum I didn't know them, but just because he thought I was insane, would he listen? No."

"This insane act won't work on me," Pandora snarled.

"You threatened to kill them, so you find them."

"Maybe I should track them down and take care of them to save us all this philosophical bother about their identity. That way, you could be a grieving widower. Randy would love that!"

"Forget I said anything. I'll find them," Wallace assured her. "How hard can it be?" Wallace did know enough to know he couldn't expect practical help from this lot.

On the ceiling of the corridor outside the provost's office a cluster of older, small black spiders were bored. They yearned for a return to the golden era when there was something to sneer at below. Nowadays there was little distraction from the singular monotony of reproduction and its attendant need to trap ever-increasing numbers of flies. When they reflected on it, which they did more often these days, what was the point? One generation replacing the next with nothing to show for the effort. What did it all mean? Why were they there in the first place and who remained in the college who could explain any of it to them? Not that they had ever learned anything from their proximity to class-based learning.

But wait. Who was this tottering out of the provost's office because Pandora had commanded him to go forth and confuse Randy Fortune? At least Wallace had the advantage of being confused himself. He, of course, didn't know what Murphy now knew, and in the absence of reassurance from such an authority confirming who he was, how could he be certain who he wasn't? He only had his imperfect memory to go on, and he knew what philosophers thought about the reliability of memory. There was practically an infinite number of people he might not be. But Pandora seemed confident. He could still taste the iodine on his tongue.

Without hesitation or thought, Rik Wallace climbed into the back of the dark green taxi that happened to be waiting outside the east wing of Candid Online College. Before he could even think where he wanted to go, the taxi took off and sped around the outside lane, throwing Wallace backwards.

VII

Auriga Benevolens
A Helpful Driver

The brakes of the taxi were slammed on so hard Rik Wallace tumbled forward, squashing his face into the headrest on the front seat, where his lips came in contact with what he hoped was chewing gum and not air-dried snot. The driver had almost missed the stop sign, halting at the last possible fraction of a second in front of the narrow archway to allow a banana yellow hatchback speed past into the car park inside. Then the taxi accelerated out through the arch that was once closed to traffic to maintain a scholarly ambience within, throwing Wallace backwards into the seat again.

He narrowed his eyes and washed his lips with his tongue, spitting whilst muttering curses on the driver. Then he caught sight of her eyes in the rear-view mirror. He recognized her at once, even though she was wearing an oversized peaked cap in a vain attempt to hide her beautiful face. "Della, what are you doing driving a taxi?"

"I have to make a living, like everyone else."

"What about the circus?"

"A producer commissioned my brother – the ringmaster, you remember him? – to tour the world making videos of circus acts in different cultures for social media. He fired everyone before he left."

"I'm sorry."

"Technology was bound to destroy our traditions sooner or later. We couldn't compete. I blame whoever invented the first computer. I miss the parties, though. The eighties were the best! Do you miss the parties, Rik?"

"Not the eighties! How long has it been? I haven't seen you since …?"

"That time I tried to hypnotise you at Saint Drogo's. I liked your psychiatrist. Or I felt sorry for him. He has sad eyes."

"He has the eyes of a sadist. What are you doing here? Are you following me?"

"I have a friend in customs who told me they are looking out for you at the border after your escape. I knew you would show up at CAT College sooner or later. Merely a matter of time."

"It's Candid Online College now."

She contemplated him in the mirror, taking her eyes from the road long enough to point the dark green taxi straight at an oncoming bus.

"Watch out," he screamed.

She adjusted the steering wheel inches from impact, throwing Wallace across the back seat.

"I'm impressed, Rik. I didn't believe you had it in you to organize a breakout. In fact, I am a little offended you didn't call me to lend a hand. When I hypnotised you I gave you a secret trigger phrase that, when you heard it, would cause you to dial a phone number for immediate assistance. Remember? Look into my eyes. No? Hippopotamus? Nothing? I can't believe you have forgotten already."

"Not a word we often used in Saint Drogo's, and if it had come up in casual conversation, I wasn't allowed to make phone calls anyway. Besides I quite liked it there. All I had to do was insist I was Rik Wallace, and they would have kept me forever. It wasn't my idea to escape. Pandora and Julie Progress bust me out against my will. Pandora wants me to help her stop the billionaire Randy Fortune, who is the current owner of Candid Online College, giving away all his money to worthy causes. She is worried the good times might come to an end for her. She says if I fail to morally confuse him, she will kill my wife and children. I told her that threat would be more effective if they were mine, but Pandora prides herself on not listening to me anyway. But if I am going to confuse Randy, I need to find some relatives because he likes his moral advisers to uphold traditional family values. I am guessing that is because he has no practical family values of his own and only embraces them in theory. You see it all the time. What am I supposed to do?"

"I could smuggle you abroad? I am sneaking a family of gorillas out of the port tonight. You could go with them. They might even adopt you. People don't appreciate how affectionate and loyal those creatures are. You won't catch them fretting over moral issues and who they are and aren't related to. Just tell me where you want to go and who you want to be when you get there and—"

"Thank you, Della. Your offer is attractive, but I have to stay here and sort out my life."

"That asylum has really changed you! Sorting out one's life is overrated."

They drove in silence listening to the Beatles sing "Let It

Be" on the radio. For the first time since leaving Saint Drogo's, he was beginning to feel hope. Maybe the drugs were wearing off. Perhaps it was his proximity to the back of Della's neck. He didn't care. Then he sang along. Della joined in. Shabby streets flicked by outside the window as the taxi sped on. Finally, Wallace leaned his head between the front seats. "Where are we going?" he asked.

"I suspected you might refuse to leave with my charming family of gorillas. I am taking you where you can find help with your mission, both moral and practical."

Ten minutes later, she pressed a button on the meter as the dark green taxi pulled up on a corner.

"I have no money on me. I have only these clothes I'm wearing," Wallace said, patting himself down.

"Typical. You can owe me. Get out."

VIII

Ex Improviso Matutinus Avis Rapit Vermes
The Early Bird Takes the Worms by Surprise

Tiberius Lang was the kind of maniac who enjoyed deploying all of his senses in pursuit of his prey. Through his buttocks he noticed the seat he had sat on in the provost's office between Pandora and Maurice Spencer was still warm from its previous occupant. He ignored the large gin martini Spencer placed on the desk in front of him beside the empty bottle of Scotch. "In my professional opinion, formed over years of vainly treating the criminally insane, Rik Wallace is extremely dangerous. He will stop at nothing to stay free. Under no circumstances should you approach if you catch sight of him. Leave that to me. Here is my card," Tiberius said.

"Did you find a parking space outside?" Spencer enquired.

"Err … yes. No problem."

"You are lucky. It is usually packed out there this time of the day."

Tiberius dealt two gold-trimmed cardboard rectangles from the stack he had printed an hour before with the name Professor Bentley Murphy followed by the qualifications MD, PhD, MBBS, MRCPsych, JD, DLFAPA and EW that he gleaned from the Internet. Perhaps he wasn't aware the card could have been interpreted by some in the psychiatric community as an unconscious over-compensation for his feelings of inadequacy at having no actual medical qualifications of his own. But his conscious self didn't care. He would show those charlatans what real sanity was. "If you do see him, ring that number anytime, day or night and I will send a team of armed police we regularly call upon at the asylum. They will know what to do."

"What's EW?" Spencer asked, impressed with the extensive list of accomplishments.

"Expert Witness."

"I don't have the memory for medicine," Spencer said. "Has anyone ever told you that you are the image of Sigmund Freud?" he added, unable to resist ingratiating himself with this man with the impressive gold-trimmed cards.

"Yes," Tiberius sighed.

"You're not related, are you?"

"No."

Tiberius moved his gaze from Spencer's neck where he felt it had lingered long enough to catch the attention of the woman in the black sunglasses blowing smoke at him, to rest his arctic eyes on the portrait of a woman above the drinks cabinet.

For her part, Pandora observed his shift in focus to the picture, along with the pulse that had begun to throb under his ear when Spencer referred to medicine. Out of nowhere, Tiberius's smell, the unique aroma that clings to institutions holding people against their volition, induced memories of school for which Pandora was unprepared. The recollection irritated her. To date she had proven to be made of psychologically resistant material. But was it because she was in the presence of someone who looked like Freud that she experienced a rare intimate revelation on the subject of herself?

She hated school. Even now, she felt exhausted by just the memory of the constant bullying and intimidation. It was ironic the smallest children were the fastest runners. That was, she supposed, an example of the balancing compensation of nature. She should have realised that when she was chasing the little shits around the schoolyard. Better to have used her brain than her lungs; smarter to have trapped them like mice. Pull yourself together, she told herself.

"That is our beloved dead provost, Patricia," she told Tiberius, wresting her thoughts from one past to another. "She was one of Wallace's predecessors. She was a saint. She broke her neck falling down the stairs. I am certain she was pushed by her husband."

"Such a gorgeous neck, too."

Patricia the provost wore a red academic gown with polka dots on the fur trim. Her hand rested on a book open on top of a waist-high marble column, a finger pointing to what Tiberius assumed was an edifying tract that he couldn't make out because it was rendered in a font too small to be legible from where he sat. The fingers on her other hand grasped her collar. The provost's sculpted blond hair was frozen in place in thick layers of oil paint. The young Patricia didn't smile because of the artist's prejudice that the gravitas appropriate to learning would evaporate at even a hint of humour. Tiberius studied the painting while storing away his impression that Pandora, apart from himself, seemed to be the only other perceptive person in the room. Just then the top of Casper Wall's head appeared above the edge of the desk.

"I thought Horse had put him outside," Pandora told herself out loud. "Where is Horse?" she asked. On hearing his name, Horse pushed his face through the French door leading to the overgrown garden and scrutinized the lunatic. He was holding Marlboro under his arm. Tiberius ignored the man bulging out of the black suit who had obviously neglected his brain in favour of developing his biceps to push a card in the direction of the drunken apparition who was trying to hold a chair steady while he climbed onto it. The subject of drunks turned his thoughts back to the bottle of Scotch. Something bothered him about the whisky. Everyone was drinking martinis; too many martinis. He recalled the dark green taxi passing outside as he arrived. Now there was a warm seat under his backside and a drained bottle on the desk. Wallace had been here!

"Did I just miss someone?" he enquired, waving his eyebrows at the whisky bottle.

"What do you mean?" Spencer asked, turning red.

"I am a forensic psychiatrist. I notice the little things such as an empty bottle and the straightjacket on the floor."

Spencer laughed with what even a novice psychiatrist would recognise as the onset of hysteria. "Oh that. No. That's nothing. Sometimes I drink cocktails out of bottles, and Casper here often needs to be restrained for his own good. Pressure of management," he lied, picking up the bottle and extracting the last drop with his tongue.

Spencer noticed his hand shook. He also noticed that Tiberius noticed it too. Oh God, he thought. I am lying to a brilliant forensic psychiatrist.

"You're nervous."

"Ignore him, Professor … err … Murphy," Pandora said, glancing down at the card Tiberius had given her. "What can you expect? He is into mindfulness," she added, considering this to be a more than satisfactory explanation for all odd behaviour. She glared at Spencer and gritted her yellowed teeth for their full Gothic effect.

"Oh mindfulness," Tiberius said, pretending to turn his thoughts away from the straightjacket with the crest of Saint Drogo's High Security Asylum for the Criminally Insane stitched onto the collar. "Are you interested in the science of the mind?"

The pedant in Spencer, who was never particular about the nature of his audience so long as he had one, launched into his familiar introduction with enthusiasm. "I used to be a Western thinker. But now I'm fascinated by Eastern ideas, especially mindfulness because it eliminates the age-old problem of the relation between mind and body. I would say I am more of a mind person than a body person, if I was forced to choose between them. Unlike Horse, there," he added, nodding towards the large man holding the cat.

Horse narrowed his eyes, trying to decide if this was a compliment.

"Ah yes. You are not alone in your obsession," Tiberius said.

"I can't believe there can be many," Pandora added.

"I find the mind endlessly fascinating," Tiberius continued. "I have a sideline in counselling. I am eclectic in my approach, including mindfulness. I use whatever it takes to reach my therapeutic goal."

"Which is what?" Pandora asked.

Tiberius ignored her to address Spencer. "I take on a few

private clients," he said, "every now and again, outside of my work at the asylum, but only whenever I come across a particularly psychologically nuanced intellect. I wouldn't work with an ordinary mind."

Tiberius poked the straightjacket with his toe while weaving his trap for Spencer. Perhaps he would have picked on Casper had he not been resting his forehead on the desk at that point – we may never know.

"I have this – let me call it an instinct – that you might be psychoanalytically distracting. Perhaps worthy of an article in a reputable journal?"

"Would you be willing to take me on? I mean, not that I have problems. I have none. But I do have an exceptionally complex mind, and I have a lot on it at the moment. In fact, I have often said I can't understand myself at all. Haven't I said that, Pandora?"

"Yes, and so have the rest of us," she growled. "Frequently."

"I'm not that competent," Spencer babbled on. "In fact, apart from mindfulness, I am talentless. My daughter, Samantha, says I'm not even a good father. Why am I telling you this?"

"Why indeed?" Pandora asked, blowing smoke at the ceiling. "Considering Spencer doesn't want to talk to anyone about anything, does he?" she snarled at him.

"I make house calls," Tiberius persisted.

"That's interesting. But as Pandora said, I don't need to discuss the problems that I don't have with anyone."

"You have my card."

"Do you analyse people in the evenings?"

"I enjoy working in the dark. I find it more conducive to

insight than the light."

"Your offer is tempting but, as Pandora said, I don't want to talk to anyone about anything."

"I understand."

Pandora picked up the straightjacket, squished it into a ball, and dropped it in the wastebasket, kicking Spencer in the shin as she passed his chair.

Tiberius stood up.

"I must be going," he said, satisfied with his performance as the forensic psychiatrist, Professor Bentley Murphy. "I have a busy schedule at the asylum making people sane again, assuming they were ever that way in the first place." He laughed in the manner of an actor playing a vampire in a black-and-white film and departed without another word.

"I am impressed with him," Spencer told Casper, who was snoring. "He may have restored my faith in Western thought."

Outside on the corridor ceiling, with these latest comings and goings, a group of arachnids, who had refused to move to the complex of webs overlooking the car park, were beginning to hope something meaningful was happening in the provost's office or anything at all that might put an end to the boredom of their existence since the college went online.

<h1 style="text-align:center">IX</h1>

Per Frons Judicare Librum
Judge a Book by the Cover

Rik Wallace saw the brake lights of the dark green taxi come on in the distance as it stopped on a corner to pick up a man in a long brown coat with his hand in the air. No point in running after Della now. He balanced on the uneven granite paving stones on the footpath, his legs still weak from whatever it was Pandora stuck in his neck. He looked one way and then the other, with his back to a shabby bookshop. Where could Della have meant him to go? Why hadn't he asked? Why was she always so cryptic?

Books. Books.

That must be a clue. He could blame books for everything that had gone wrong in his life as a moral philosopher. Even now, he wouldn't be in this mess if he couldn't read.

He turned around to examine the bookshop. A slice had been removed from the façade in which a pair of second-hand telephone-box doors opened onto the intersection of the two sides of the building forming a corner. The imperfections in the handmade sheet of glass in the large window to the right of the doors shimmered in the daylight, curving back in an elegant bend to meet the first upright wooden post holding the adjacent pane in place, and then on to the next, in all, three panes of glass. On the other side a diagonal crack ran from the bottom to the opposite top corner of the single large pane. Mouldy canvas awnings allowed the books arranged in the windows to fade at a genteel pace. The red doors contrasted with the rest of the shop front that sagged under layers of black paint. Above the canopy facing the main road, gold lettering spelled out the words "Second Chance Books". The next shop along was boarded up, as was the one after that.

A bell clanged above Wallace's head when he pulled on the door as instructed by the sign. He stepped inside onto worn floorboards that ran away from the sunlight to hide in the gloom against the back wall. The space was divided into narrow corridors by high shelves loaded with books that reached almost to the ceiling where nets of spider webs, black with dust, clung to ornate plaster cornices that were evidence of a once-glorious era in the shop's history. Rows of spotlights fixed on brass springs to the top of the shelves provided barely sufficient illumination to allow customers to make out the titles on the spines. Handmade signs were tacked to the timber frames indicating the genres, best sellers, historical, and rare editions, including buy-two-books-get-half-a-book-free offers. Other signs advised against eating, drinking or smoking in the shop and carried threats of dire consequences for wrongdoers. On a large blue sheet of cardboard, the use of mobile phones and cameras was prohibited. Browsing was discouraged on several pieces of fading brown paper. The signage seemed disturbingly familiar to Wallace.

He made his way further into the gloom in the manner of a just-blinded man navigating a busy road junction with his arms. Eventually, he found a woman perched on a high stool behind a counter which ran at right angles to the front window. She held a volume open in front of her face in one hand, while a cup of tea steamed in the other. Wallace hesitated in putting his foot down on the bendy floorboards, nervous that the columns of books teetering in front of her might collapse.

Suddenly, the signage made sense: bringing back memories of the library at CAT College. He recognized the large mushroom bob of hair that seemed to spring from the book cover and the soft woollen clothes. Had her skeletal features softened from her having put on some weight since he last saw her? No. It was the dust particles playing tricks on his eyes. She hadn't changed at all. She lowered the book to peer at the customer in clear annoyance at how difficult it was proving to have a good run at a chapter without interruption.

When Wallace stepped from the darkest alley of books into an isolated shaft of daylight, she smiled with the kind of relaxed expression an authoritarian might display when momentarily forgetting that order is maintained by scowling.

"It's Rik Wallace!" she exclaimed.

"It's the librarian," he said, as if exchanging an agreed code to establish their bona fides.

"You must come upstairs to meet my husband," she said, jumping down from the stool and coming around the end of the counter. "We often think of you." None of the towers of books inches from her elbows collapsed as she passed them. Swayed, perhaps – it was impossible to tell in the gloom – but didn't topple over.

The librarian made no effort to greet Wallace with a peck on the cheek or a handshake. Instead, she said, "I'll shut up shop," and disappeared down a tunnel of shelving to turn the sign on the door from "Open" to "Closed". The truth was that the librarian didn't miss her old job because she had come to realise in the second-hand bookshop that she could aspire to reproduce her love of order anywhere. In particular, she delighted in designing rules for books. Often, while writing her handmade signs, she reflected on the conundrum of whether it was more important to create a rule than to have it followed.

She startled Wallace by suddenly reappearing at the top of another passage. "This way," she said, indicating a narrow stair hidden behind the furthermost shelf of books at the back of the shop.

Rik Wallace could relax for the first time since leaving Saint Drogo's High Security Asylum for the Criminally Insane, deep in the embrace of the flower-patterned armchair beside the tiny iron fireplace in the small sitting room in the apartment above the bookshop. He had confided the details of his mission as he understood them to his hosts.

While the librarian pottered in the kitchenette squeezed into the narrow end of the rectangular space opposite the second of the sash windows, her husband sat in a matching chair at the other side of the artificial coals.

The librarian loved her husband, even if he wasn't the bibliophile that she at one time had hoped to marry. At least he tolerated books. Although, he ignored her innumerable regulations. Perhaps she loved him *because* he didn't obey her. He also paid no attention to the notes she stuck to the door of the refrigerator specifying the sequence in which the bottles of milk should be consumed; the comprehensive chart on the inside of the freezer box detailing the date each meal had been deposited therein and accordingly should be removed, defrosted for a specified number of hours, along with the length of time and temperature for reheating prior to its immediate consumption; the sign in the bathroom reminding patrons to put down the toilet seat; the list with convenient pencil attached on a string for noting provisions that needed replenishing. She didn't blame her husband. Instead, she reconciled herself to the fact that she needed a wider audience for her tenets. For this reason, along with her fondness for him, Wallace, the first visitor to ever penetrate their world as far as the apartment above the bookshop, was a welcome guest.

The retired police inspector rested his elbows on the arms of the patterned armchair, delighted to have a fresh audience for his favourite topic: how crime was not what it used to be. But Wallace was so at ease his chin nodded onto his chest, making it difficult to concentrate on what was being said.

"Technology has ruined the mystery of police work. Besides, most crime is online these days, and my computer is ten years old. It takes a week to send an email downstairs to enquire from the librarian what time lunch will be ready."

Wallace struggled to be sociable by at least opening his eyes, even if he felt joining in the conversation was beyond him. He called up a superhuman effort. "I remember the first time we met you were investigating me at CAT College. Even back then, you said it had been a long time since you thought it was the best time to be solving crimes."

"Yes. You are right," Jackson chuckled. His tall frame was folded into the chair. He had changed little since the last time

Wallace saw him. His permanent sad expression was in place, but his bald patch had expanded. "I suspect crime is less boring than police work. When you consider it, there is an infinite number of ways to break a law, and just one way to follow it. Anyone with a creative flair would choose to be a villain. Not a thug, mind you. In a choice between being bad or good, bad is less boring and more rewarding every time you're not caught. You can't argue with that. That's how I would encourage my children to behave."

"In that case, better for society you don't have any," the librarian butted in. "Tea?" she said, holding up a teapot to indicate its source.

Wallace covered the cup with his hand where it rested on the arm of the chair to indicate his lack of desire for a fourth refill.

Jackson reached out and took the librarian's hand in his. "I knew things would have to change if we were going to be together when I first saw my true love here in the library in CAT College. You must be the best you can be for the person you love, and in my case, that meant abandoning the law."

The librarian released her husband's grip and rested the palm of her hand on his bald patch in a habit that began when he first asked her to check if his hair had grown back. Jackson's head shrank into his shoulders at the touch while he curled his lips downwards into a smile. "It was obvious to both of us you weren't what you might call evil, even if we didn't know who you were," he told Wallace. "That's what I told the legal team I hired to defend you, and I'd say it again, even though the prosecutor said my opinion wasn't evidence. No one has to spend years and years studying the difference between right and wrong, because if we understand it at all, it's imprinted on our natures at birth. No one needs to read a book to learn how to swim, just as no one needs to go to college to tell the difference between good and evil. Doing a doctorate in swimming won't help if you fall into a river. In my opinion, a good person isn't capable of doing something wicked."

"That's why I tell Jackson he is wasting his time imagining he could ever be a real villain," the librarian told Wallace.

Jackson ignored the interruption. "For normal people such as the librarian and I, the difference between right and wrong is obvious."

"But a good deed can appear wicked to someone else?" Wallace said. He was becoming alert to the prospect of a philosophical debate.

"The librarian and I are moral referees. That's our current chosen profession. After all, we both have the experience. Imagine what I have come across as a policeman, and what she has seen in libraries."

The librarian shuddered on cue at a memory, perhaps, of long overdue books.

"We operate on a smaller scale than a professional do-gooder like you," Jackson clarified out of modesty. "After all, we are only amateurs."

"We try to right little wrongs," the librarian explained.

"Sometimes we have to bend the law, but so long as the appropriate people get hurt, we don't care."

"But who decides who these appropriate people are?" Wallace asked.

"We do," the librarian added from the kitchenette where she was now emptying the teapot down the sink.

"Mind you, it doesn't always work out the way we plan," Jackson said.

The librarian chuckled at a shared memory.

"You remember, dear; there was the case of that woman who came into the shop and begged us to find her son who was stolen when he was a baby from outside a supermarket? We advertise our services on a sign in the window. Did you see it on the way in? No? I put up a notice board with—never mind." Jackson smiled upside down at the recollection. "We thought it was a simple case of kidnapping."

"We were naïve back then." This came from the kitchenette.

"When was that, dear?"

"Two months ago."

"Imagine, after eighteen years the mother never got over it, despite having three other children. People are never satisfied."

"That should have been a clue to the kind of family we were dealing with, but we missed it."

"We set to work in our role as private moral detectives. Sooner than we could have hoped, we found the son a hundred miles from here."

"It was as if no one had ever bothered to look for him."

"It turns out that eighteen years ago, his brand-new mother had told her boyfriend, when she arrived home with a six-month-old baby after spending just two days away at the maternity hospital, that the child was his, and that he should do the proper thing and marry her. He did."

"There's another example of people having no common sense about right and wrong."

"Nor any understanding of rudimentary biology."

"I blame the schools."

Wallace squeezed the bridge of his nose between his fingers to stifle a yawn.

"The entire family was there eating dinner when we showed up to tell the son he had been the victim of a kidnapping."

"The parents, the stolen child, and a brother and sister – who were their own children or also kidnapped; we never found out and it was none of our business because no one had hired us to find them."

"I told you, didn't I, Jackson, that they looked contented for people with a terrible secret?"

"We told them why we were there while they were finishing off a homemade bread-and-butter pudding that the pretend mother said she baked herself."

"It looked shop-bought to me."

"It smelled delicious, but we insisted we couldn't stay."

"We said what we came to say, and told the son to pack his bags and meet us at our hotel – we insist on our expenses. From there we took him to his real home."

"Later we learned that the father—"

"—who wasn't the boy's real father of course—"

"—flew into a rage at the deception he had being living under all those years and killed his wife there at the dinner table."

"The son was so upset at having his up-until-then-idealistic domestic existence ruined that he burned down his new home within a week of arriving, roasting his three biological siblings to death in the process."

"They resented him showing up out of nowhere expecting an equal share of the family assets."

"It's impossible to please people, but you have to try."

"You must be familiar with the case because it was in all the papers."

"We were not allowed newspapers in the asylum, in case we got overexcited," Wallace said.

"Where would the world be if we all gave up trying to help people – which is the most difficult job in the world."

"Bound to make mistakes every now and again, dear."

"We will figure it out eventually. I am sure helping Rik to help Randy Fortune is the right thing."

"What happened to that kidnap victim you rescued is called 'unintended moral consequences' and is the best reason you shouldn't try to help anyone," Wallace explained, straightening up in the armchair and leaning forward into his theme. "That should be the subject of the first moral lesson I give Randy Fortune when I meet him. He is probably just a normal, sad, extremely rich person, who unconsciously wants to be talked out of doing some good in the world. But I do need assistance. Pandora's pragmatism doesn't even stretch to supplying me with a change of underwear."

"I can make you a fresh ID, a driving licence, credit cards, supermarket loyalty cards, whatever you want. We have a laboratory in the basement. What name will I put on them?"

"My own name."

"Which is what?"

He reflected on the matter while Jackson and the librarian waited for an answer. He sighed. "Make it Rik Wallace."

"That may not be the best idea. My old partner in the police, Freddy Sullivan, who is an inspector now, is bound to be looking for a Rik Wallace."

"I can't become someone else again. I have gotten too used

to being Rik Wallace. Once is enough for a drastic change of identity. Most people remain the same person for all of their lives."

The librarian stood between the two armchairs, drying a cup with a teacloth. "Your assignment with Randy Fortune should be easy because all you need to have are the higher thoughts you imagine you would have if you were worth billions."

"You mean do his thinking for him?"

"Exactly. Don't worry. You can be sure Randy Fortune is surrounded by people who perform all of his mundane tasks for him."

"I suppose he has people to take drugs and get drunk for him at parties. I would if I were as rich as him."

"Persuade Julie Progress to put you up at Fortune Mansion. There should be plenty room. Blend in as one of his many minions."

"You will be safe from Inspector Sullivan if you don't go beyond his garden walls and stay out of sight. Don't use the fake credit cards I will give you. Do you need transport?" Jackson asked. "I have a bicycle you can borrow, but take care of it because it cost me a fortune to buy it from the kid who stole it."

The librarian tut-tutted.

"What? That kid needed the money for a school uniform."

"You can stay here for a few days," the librarian said. "I'll adjust some of Jackson's clothes for you."

"There is one other teeny-tiny thing I need your help with."

"I'm sure nothing is beyond our powers," Jackson assured him. "What is it? Spit it out."

"It seems Randy Fortune is obsessed with family values. I

need to produce a wife and children for him. Could you track down the wife and children who showed up in the car with Sullivan outside the philosophy department at CAT College the day I was arrested and persuade them to co-operate?"

"Do you have anything we might use to help us find them?"

"Such as?"

"Oh, general features. Their ages; how many of them there are; boys or girls? That sort of broad detail."

"I don't know. I didn't have time to examine them in detail. As you know, I panicked and ran."

"Try not to be so hard on yourself. I'm sure that's a natural response," Jackson said.

"We are not judging you, Rik," the librarian added. "We wouldn't dare. We trust you, and if you ran away from your children, then maybe it was their fault."

"The thing is, I don't know any more whether or not they are mine. I was sure they weren't, but everyone else seems so certain they are; so how would I know? I mean, look at Spencer's daughter, Samantha. I always assumed she was a product of his imagination: a response to the trauma of his divorce. Turns out she works for Candid Communications. She is some kind of computer wizard."

"Traditionally, her ontological status was always in doubt," Jackson confirmed, remembering some of the philosophy he read while hunting down Wallace that, until that moment, he thought he had forgotten.

"Metaphysically, it seems she is as real as I—I mean, as you. So you see, I am not an authority on who is and isn't real. But whoever they are, Professor Murphy at Saint Drogo's has a photograph of my family in his desk drawer."

"Maybe we could break into his office," the librarian suggested.

"I will pay this professor a visit," Jackson said. "Leave it with us, Rik. Sorting out your family problems is a perfect example of one of those small things we can put right. Don't spend another moment fretting about it."

"What can go wrong, eh?" the librarian added.

Jackson linked his arm into the librarian's as they watched Rik Wallace doze in the patterned armchair in front of the fire, his legs stretched out, one ankle resting on the other. "I'm sure he will make a great father when we find those children," he said.

"He deserves some happiness after everything he has been through."

"It can't have been easy for him being locked up in an asylum, especially if there is a very slight chance he is sane."

"I suppose."

"What he needs is the healing powers of a devoted family, which is the best cure for an unbalanced mind. Funny, isn't it, how we have managed so well on our own."

Wallace snored his agreement.

"Hot chocolate?"

"Yes, please. With a large shot of Scotch," Jackson said. He held his thumb and index finger as far apart as he could to indicate the measure he had in mind.

X

Desidiosus Avis Rapit Vermes Inebrii
The Lazy Bird Catches the Drunken Worms

Inspector Freddy Sullivan and Sergeant Jones arrived outside the provost's office eleven minutes after Tiberius Lang had departed on the next leg of his psychological quest to find Rik Wallace. Horse opened the door to the police after Sullivan persisted in pounding on it with the side of his fist when he could hear raised voices from within. Pandora, Maurice Spencer, and Casper Wall were preoccupied with an argument on the merits of potential online courses. Squabbling was their approved form of market research.

"We must offer mindfulness programmes in our virtual psychology department," Spencer pleaded. "We will make loads of money, and people will benefit psychologically at the same time by being … well … more mindful. It's all good."

"We need practical courses," Casper said, now sober enough to speak. "We offer too much waffle already."

"Students love waffle. It's where the money is."

Inspector Sullivan observed the exchange of ideas in silence. No one paid him any attention when he cleared his throat. He also observed the overflowing ashtray, the glasses, the empty jug of martinis, and the drained whisky bottle on the desk without drawing any inferences. He marked his disapproval of drinking during daylight hours by lifting his sleeve and staring at the time on his watch. Meanwhile, Sergeant Jones was wondering if she should take notes.

The rhythmical nodding of Sergeant Jones's head was an unconscious means she used to acknowledge to herself that she was absorbing whatever her ears were processing because she remembered everything she heard. Despite many proofs of this hyperthymesia, her retention astonished members of the criminal world who assumed she forgot things, as they did. She even remembered Sullivan's name when no one else could. Her colleagues tended to overestimate her policing abilities because her undeniable capacity to retain the facts was balanced by the equal and opposite but less obvious incapacity of her brain to accomplish anything meaningful with them. Sergeant Jones had short, strawberry blond hair looped behind her ears and a creamy face with a rash of freckles as if an unskilled artist using an oversized paintbrush had spattered them on. Her thin, pink lips hid white teeth of which there were too many to fit into her compact mouth. Despite this she possessed an erotic gleam that, to date, seemed wasted on Sullivan, at whom she unconsciously pointed her breasts in an idiosyncratic salute whenever he addressed her. This was enhanced by the fact that being shorter than she, his face was opposite her chest. He responded with an unconscious thrust of his hips that would have horrified him had he been aware he was doing it. His mother too would have been scandalized, but fortunately for both of them, work was one of the few places where she didn't accompany him.

Eventually, when the twin black dishes of Pandora's

sunglasses swept over the pair, one staring at her, the other nodding with her head tilted to the side as if favouring her left ear, she shouted at her colleagues to shut up. Sullivan flashed his ID at Pandora so quickly he could have been showing her one of the photographs he took last summer on holiday with his mother. He shouted his name and rank, pointed at Jones, and shouted her name and rank in turn.

"Ah, Inspector Sullivan. Take a seat," Casper slurred, waving his hand at the space between Pandora and Spencer. "Sergeant Jones, you can sit here beside me," he said patting the seat of the chair beside him.

"Drink?" Spencer asked picking up a bottle from the middle of the collection on the cabinet under the portrait of the former provost and showing it to Sullivan for his approval.

"No, thank you, I'm on duty."

"Your face seems familiar."

"I was on the original Rik Wallace case when he was teaching here. It was *I* who nabbed him in the end," he boasted.

"Oh yes. I remember you now. You used to have a different colleague – a tall, bald chap in a crumpled coat. Miserable-looking fellow."

"Yes. That would be Inspector Jackson. He left the force."

"He ran off with our librarian," Pandora said. "I can't fathom what he saw in her. She wouldn't take my advice on wearing revealing clothes."

"We could close the library for good if those few holdout arts students would give up and go away." Casper voiced his long-held dream into Jones's fantastic ear, who filed away this ambition for the library in the vast archive housed at the bottom of her brain.

"What brings you back here, Inspector?" Spencer asked, as if he wasn't aware. He was determined to make up to Pandora for leaving the straightjacket lying on the floor. Still, he imagined it should be easier to lie to the police than to a forensic psychiatrist who was also an expert witness.

"As it happens, it's Rik Wallace again. He escaped from Saint Drogo's High Security Asylum for the Criminally Insane."

"It doesn't seem to be as secure as the title suggests," Pandora said, lighting a fresh cigarette. "We know all about the escape."

"You do?" the inspector asked.

"We do?" Spencer asked Pandora, turning red.

"Yes, we do. Professor—what's his name?" Pandora turned to Spencer, wagging her cigarette at him for assistance. "He gave us the details when he was here a few minutes ago. You just missed him."

"Oh yes, Bentley Murphy," Spencer confirmed, showing Sullivan Tiberius's card that he had placed in his wallet. "For a moment there, I didn't know what you were talking about, Pandora."

The policeman studied the gold trim.

"Yes, that's him," he confirmed. "What was he doing here?"

"He is hunting Wallace," Pandora said.

"I need that back," Spencer said, stretching out his hand for the card. "In case I have to contact him for anything … related to the case. Such as clues that occur to me about Wallace's whereabouts, or any sightings I may have." He aimed this excuse at Pandora rather than the policeman.

Spencer returned the card to his wallet while Sullivan took up a position looking out the window with his hands clasped behind his back in a pose his mother recommended from detective programmes on television. She said it would make him appear thoughtful. He observed a car at an awkward angle, half in and half out of a space in the car park below. "Hmmm, so Professor Murphy is off on some solo run after Wallace. Looking for all the glory himself, I assume. Bad form, if you ask me, when you can't trust a forensic psychiatrist to keep his nose out of police business. When the loonies are in the asylum, they are his concern; out here, they are mine."

"In my opinion, Wallace is harmless. These psychiatrists are always trying to make themselves more important than they are by exaggerating the dangers their patients pose to the public," Pandora said.

"Harmless? He is a dangerous lunatic."

"Don't worry, Inspector, Professor Murphy warned us not to approach Wallace if we see him, etcetera," Spencer said. "I don't imagine he will come around here ever again because we don't teach morality since the rioting; because it's too risky. He was fired, which is not an easy achievement, but technically, he was unavailable for work when he was locked up. In normal circumstances, a guaranteed job for life if you can stand it, but when you are doing life somewhere else, that does set a precedent." He laughed nervously.

Casper leaned back in the chair as his mind returned to the office from somewhere far away where he was running through a meadow filled with cornflowers, hand in hand with Jones. He hadn't decided whether they were wearing matching tracksuits. "I am prepared to celebrate the escape of an esteemed philosopher even if I don't understand what he drones on about. Thank God I chose technology as a career.

Champagne, Jones? No?" As he shifted closer to her, she moved an equal and opposite distance from him as if they were both magnetically charged.

"Where else can Wallace run to except here to his old colleagues? He has no money, credit cards, spare clothes, nor anywhere to stay, as far as I can tell," Sullivan said.

"Why didn't we think of that?" Spencer asked, glaring at Pandora.

"Of what?"

"He has no money. I hope he will survive. I mean, until you catch him."

"Survive? He is a dangerous lunatic."

"So you said. Obviously, he has accomplices: other dangerous lunatics, perhaps. Someone must have organized the escape from the outside," Pandora said.

"Have you gone mad?" Spencer shouted at her. "He would be crazy to expect help from anyone around here." He bulged his eyeballs in reproach.

"He is crazy," Jones spoke for the first time.

"I am confident Professor Murphy will be able to cure him when he catches up with him and forces him back into therapy. I got the impression he is an extremely competent psychiatrist. It's unusual to meet someone one feels one can confide in instantly. You know, tell them everything. Have you ever felt that way, Inspector?" Spencer asked.

"No, I haven't."

"Murphy has a list of qualifications as long as my arm," Casper told Jones, holding his out towards her as a practical illustration. "They are unnecessary, if you ask me. It's not as if he is dealing with electricity or machines or anything dangerous.

I can't understand the public obsession with a psychiatrist knowing what they are doing. I mean, the people they are dealing with are mad anyway. It's not as if they could *go* mad, if you see what I mean? They are already batty by the time he meets them. What is this obsession with qualifications?"

"I am an excellent judge of people because of my philosophical training," Spencer said. "I am never wrong. I trust Professor Murphy. He seemed calm and in control."

"You wouldn't recognise a homicidal maniac if he was standing in front of you holding an axe in one hand and your severed head by the hair in the other," Pandora said.

"That's not true. What about when you were arguing with Fischer about Kant? I said to myself then, now there's a—"

By this point the inspector, followed by the sergeant, had departed without saying goodbye, having decided there was nothing more to be learned in the provost's office. Outside in the corridor, in full view of the small, black spiders on the ceiling above them, and where they could still hear the sound of an argument through the door that Horse closed behind them, Sullivan turned to Jones.

"Well, Sergeant, what do you make of that?"

Jones revolved on her heel, pulled back her shoulders, pointed her breasts, looked down at his face, closed her eyes, parted her lips as a prelude to recite the conversation verbatim that he had found sufficient to endure once. Sullivan, familiar with the signs, stopped her before she could get underway by raising his hand.

"Never mind," he said. "Any leads on Tiberius Lang?" he

asked, changing the subject.

Jones searched her memory for relevant data.

"No, sir."

"Go and find something."

"There is one thing."

"Yes," he said with rising hope.

"You said he bears a resemblance to Sigmund Freud."

"Yes!"

"I will start there."

"And?"

"I will read Freud's books for a clue."

Sullivan's hope disappeared. "Investigate what you want. I am off to have words with Murphy about keeping his psychiatric snout out of police business."

Inspector Sullivan now had the small, black spiders' full attention as he waggled his hips at Jones, who responded with several thrusts of her bosom. Then they turned away from each other and strode off in opposite directions in the manner of a pair of birds mutually unimpressed with their innate mating ritual.

XI

Inertiorem Avis Rapit Vermes Crapulati
The Even Lazier Bird Catches the Sozzled Worms

Inspector Sullivan burst unannounced into Professor Bentley Murphy's office at Saint Drogo's High Security Asylum for the Criminally Insane. Bernard the security guard jogged in behind him. They found the psychiatrist stretched out on the chaise longue with a new tweed jacket covering his face. Bernard thought his boss was dead.

"Oh God, what has happened now? I leave him alone for a few minutes, and one of his patients—clients – one of those fucking lunatics – bumps him off. You wait here, Inspector, while I check his schedule to determine who was last in. I bet it was Mother Theresa."

"What is Mother Theresa doing here?" Sullivan asked the security guard.

"That is what we call her *nom de folie*," Bernard said with pedantic satisfaction. "We are proud of the tradition amongst our clientele in this hospital to assume the identity of eminent figures. Our wards are packed with celebrities from history. Interesting that Rik Wallace didn't assume a celebrity name. I mean who has ever heard of a Rik Wallace?"

As Bernard turned for the door, Murphy sat up, voicing his annoyance from under the jacket at being interrupted in the meditation on his woes during his brief break between appointments.

"My nerves are shattered since I started working here," Bernard confided to Sullivan before making his excuses to the psychiatrist. "I tried to stop him, Professor, but he insisted he had to see you," the security guard said in an obsequious tone he had been practising since Murphy punched him when he got back on his feet after being pepper-sprayed on the day of Tiberius Lang's escape.

"That's all right, Bernard. My concentration is ruined now anyway. He can stay."

"I forget why I decided working here would be a good idea. I must be mad. I will find a quiet unoccupied padded cell and lie down for half an hour," Bernard muttered to himself while leaving the office, wagging his head over and back at the continued revelations on the mysteries of mental health.

"Why were you at CAT College?" Sullivan demanded of Murphy as soon as Bernard had left the room.

"Where?"

"Don't pretend you don't know – the crumbling pile of stones where Rik Wallace used to teach. Why are you sneaking around behind my back?"

"Oh. The billionaire, Randy Fortune, bought that place. I read it somewhere. I can't remember. It's called Candid Online College now. What was I doing there?"

"Don't try to bamboozle me with your psychological questions. I assume you went there because you are aware criminals often return to the scene of their greatest crimes.

That's why I was there. What kind of a forensic psychiatrist are you? Couldn't you make yourself useful and construct a profile of Wallace instead of chasing him around his old haunts?"

"It doesn't work that way. I can't profile him because he is already my patient. I know him. Or, at least, I thought I did."

"I am not a fool. I saw your card with all of your qualifications. Over-qualified if you ask me for the crap job you do around here."

"I wasn't there," the professor said in the tone he had perfected for addressing potentially hysterical patients.

"You were so. I have three witnesses who saw you. They may have been drunk, but there were three of them. Don't treat me like one of your lunatics."

"Calm down, Inspector. I don't care where Wallace is. I was wrong about him. I don't believe anymore that he is dangerous, despite his involvement in those deaths at CAT College. He will turn up somewhere in his own good time. I am convinced he is harmless."

"You are going soft on madness. Next thing you will tell me I arrested the wrong person, and that he shouldn't even have been locked up. He should be free as a bird." Sullivan flapped his arms up and down as if he was going to take flight.

"Wallace should never have been sent here. He is as sane as you or – more accurately – I. Anyway, in my medical opinion, you are manifesting some form of obsession with him."

"Remember, Wallace is *my* case, Professor." Sullivan's face turned red in the effort to control his temper. "I arrested him when no one else would. I found his wife and children when no one else could. I—"

"You told me they weren't his," Murphy protested.

"That's not the point. I found them. Everyone thought he was innocent just because he was a professor of moral philosophy." Sullivan wagged his head from side to side to signify his contempt for the sceptics he believed surrounded him.

"Before you burst in here just now, I was contemplating my own misery. I used to believe I was despondent because of my childhood, and what my ex-fiancé said about my—never mind. But I realize I am not just depressed. I am disillusioned with the whole system. I'm fed up. I'm bored. Suffering from ennui. I'm sick to death of listening to all the non-stop introspection that goes on and on in this place. Everyone locked up in here is self-obsessed, if you ask me. Tiberius is right. People dwell on themselves too much. There would be less insanity if there were less thinking. It should be banned. Look at me." Murphy poked the inspector in the chest. "My brain won't stop processing information. I can't stop thinking: Analysing over and over. Do you know how that feels?" the professor shouted. Sullivan took an involuntary step backwards when Murphy made a lunge to grab his hands. "No? Why am I telling you this? But I should be grateful. At least you are obsessed with Wallace, which is a change from everyone else, who is obsessed with themselves."

"You are probably going mad from working here," Bernard said.

Sullivan jumped and clutched his chest because the security guard had come back in to the office unobserved and was now standing by the desk behind the policeman.

"What do you want, Bernard?" Murphy asked, calm again.

"Your next client, Mother Theresa, is waiting outside."

"I should go before I catch something," Inspector Sullivan said. He looked around as if he was expecting to see madness hanging in the air between them like dust particles.

"We should concentrate all our efforts on finding Tiberius. You are not taking the threat posed by that therapist seriously. What is your Sergeant Jones doing to find him?"

"She is reading up on Freud for clues.

"Reading Freud for clues? Have you assigned some sort of idiot to find Tiberius?" Murphy sighed.

"You are obsessed with Tiberius. You should talk to someone. Both Wallace and Tiberius would still be here if it weren't for your bungling in the first place. I blame you. Stay out of my case, Professor. I will lock you up myself if I find you have turned up somewhere else where you don't belong before I get there," Sullivan said. He waved his hands apart in a gesture of finality. "Stop interfering in my investigation."

When the inspector left, striding behind Bernard, slamming the door on the way out, Murphy lay back down on the worn chaise longue and covered his face again with the tweed jacket that he bought that morning on the way to the asylum to replace the one Tiberius wore for his escape.

Bernard the security guard opened the door a foot and slid his face inside. "Is everything alright, Professor?" he asked.

"I'm fine, Bernard. No need to fret," Bentley Murphy said from under the coat. "It's not your fault Tiberius escaped. I hold myself responsible. I never use restraints, ice packs, shock therapy, or ECT. None of it! Except on Wallace, of course. No wonder he ran off. Isn't it strange, Bernard, how he disturbed my usual equanimity? Why did I have him restrained and injected? Did he touch some nerve? I no longer even believe in institutions. Our lunatics should be out there in the community. I don't blame Tiberius either for escaping. In general, I support our clients showing some initiative even in breaking out, but not like this: not unsupervised."

"Mother Theresa is starting to become quite agitated."

"I'll be ready in a minute. I just need to put on my psychiatric face. It helps our patients when the therapist appears to be more composed than they."

Bernard closed the door with studied care. Strange, he thought, no lock on the outside. Shouldn't the psychiatrist be locked in for the safety of everyone else in this place?

Murphy turned his analytic mind to understanding the policeman. Perhaps Sullivan is suffering from a form of Fregoli delusion, he thought, believing that there are several versions of me out there trying to make his life miserable. Yes, that must be it. Maybe he thinks someone is pretending to be me. I could write a paper on Sullivan, with or without his co-operation. What symptoms is he manifesting in his particular case of Fregoli? Delusions – obviously – erratic temperament, hysteria, mood swings, and an obsessive fixation on unresolved past investigations in which he made fundamental blunders. Yes, that's it. It's extremely rare, but my diagnosis fits. The Rik Wallace case is playing on his conscience so much it has driven him to the psychotic delusion that impostors impersonating me are thwarting him. Maybe at an unconscious level he wasn't able to live with his unjustified promotion for supposedly solving the CAT College case, so he has transferred his sense of guilt at his unwarranted achievement onto Wallace himself, the object of both his success and failure. I must write this down before I forget it.

While considering sitting up to make notes, his thoughts began to return to his own sense of embarrassment at the treatment he had prescribed for Wallace, insisting over months of sessions he deny who he said he was and acknowledge the existence of a non-existent wife and children: straightjackets, injections, freezing water baths, hypnosis. Was it he who was obsessed with the ideal family he never had? Did he resent Wallace for rejecting a readymade household he had lost hope of ever having himself? But it wasn't his fault he ignored his patient's denial. Repression of false traumatic memories must be common, mustn't it? Perhaps the approach will have caused some form of inverse reduplicative paramnesia. How would that manifest itself now in Wallace? He might start to believe his wife and children are impostors, replaced by alien others, when of course he has no rational reason to believe they aren't; apart from the inconvenient fact that he has no memory of them simply because he never met them before in his life. Murphy worried that if Sullivan found Wallace and told him the truth concerning the family in the photograph, he would go insane, even if he weren't mad already when he first came to Saint Drogo's. The truth could send him over the edge. "I hope Sullivan never finds him," he said out loud. "Run Wallace and keep running wherever you are. Where is Sergeant Jones? I doubt she will ever finish reading Freud. Maybe I could persuade Tiberius to throttle me when I find him. God knows he owes me something for the hours of drivel he put me through in therapy. Perhaps if I can somehow undo the damage that I caused Wallace, it might make me feel better about myself. But what can I do? What can I do?"

After several minutes rubbing his hands together, he sat

up, crossed the room, and searched the desk for an unchewed pen. His taking of notes on Sullivan was interrupted by the sound of Mother Theresa breaking into the singing of hymns in the waiting room outside as her tedious familiar expression of impatience, exhorting her invisible followers to dance, wherever they might be located. "Oh, that fucking selfish saint," Murphy muttered, abandoning his notes.

XII

Ars Imitatur Vitam
When Art Imitates Life

Fortune Mansion was an attraction to nerds with technical innovations they wished to demonstrate to Randy Fortune if only he would grant them an audience. They congregated outside the main gates hoping to catch a glimpse of the billionaire: a futile hope since he had ceased leaving the house even in the back of his blacked-out limousine.

Rik Wallace pushed hard on the pedals of the bicycle Jackson had loaned him when he saw the gates standing open. He shouted his name at a guard behind the window of the prefabricated security hut as he pedalled through, but the man didn't challenge him because he was, at that time, snoring on a chair tilted on its back legs with his cap pulled down over his eyes.

Rik accelerated up the sloping drive with its slight bend, his front tyre slipping precariously on the gravel. He leaned the bike against one of the pillars at the top of the steps, which supported the portico over the double leaf door that gave access to the main house.

A grey-haired man wearing gold-rimmed glasses on a wrinkle-free face filled the vertical space when the right-hand panel of the door opened inward. This apparition supported himself with a white-gloved hand that gripped the closed leaf of the door so firmly Wallace was confident he would fall over if he let go. The man presented a stern but melancholic expression of the sort one might expect to find on an undertaker somewhat disappointed not to be officiating at his own funeral. He wore a black tie with tiny white polka dots over a white wing-collared shirt; a heavy waistcoat; black tails; and pleated trousers with fine, vertical grey stripes, crumpled at the ankles where they met gleaming shoes. A white triangle sticking out of his breast pocket picked up the collar and polka dots. The butler stared at the visitor, offering no evidence he was going to speak first. He seemed strangely familiar, and yet not.

Wallace cracked under his gaze. "Err … I'm Rik Wallace. Err … Professor Wallace. Retired; for health reasons. Would that make me emeritus? Okay, maybe I was never a real professor—why am I telling you this?"

"I couldn't say, sir," the butler intoned.

"Julie Progress is expecting me."

The butler rolled his eyes without lifting his chin. "Please follow me, sir." He let go of the door, rotated his upper body while holding his feet in place, and spun around – all without falling over – as Wallace looked on resisting an urge to reach out and grab hold of a spindly arm.

When the door closed behind them on a spring, Wallace saw he was in a glass box not unlike a security chamber in the entrance to a bank. His companion waited for a light on the glass door to turn from red to green to indicate an airlock had been restored before pressing it with a trembling finger. Wallace stepped after him into a large chequer-tiled hallway.

While the space lacked the grand furniture, old paintings, and exotic carpets Wallace expected to find in a house with such an imposing exterior, it did have an air of something macabre lurking behind the ultra-modern aluminium light fittings, most of which were in place above the restored picture rail from which portraits of the dried-goods manufacturer's family once hung.

As his guide shuffled across the black-and-white squares on the floor like a bishop in a chess game, Wallace took tiny steps to keep in synch. He hoped they weren't headed for the wide stairs that led up to a series of tall windows on the first landing because, at their current pace, he imagined attaining the summit would take what remained of the daylight. He was considering picking the creature up in his arms and carrying him, when a scream from above distracted him, causing him to collide with the butler.

Julie Progress silhouetted on the top step, then began to run down the middle of the white stone stairs with her arms spread apart in the manner of the lead singer in a 1940s Broadway musical, a professional smile fixed on her face. No one normal is ever that glad to see me, Wallace thought. She took the steps two at a time and leaped from the third from the bottom into his arms, where she covered his mouth with her lips preventing him from speaking – even if he had known what to say.

"Oh Rik. I missed you. I missed you so much," Progress told him with such enthusiasm he thought she might even believe she was being almost sincere. That or she was on medication for amnesia. She turned to the tall silent figure standing motionless beside them as Wallace placed her back onto the floor. "Thank you. You are dismissed," she said with a wave of the back of her hand. "That is the butler, Eustis," she whispered as the man began to turn away ever so slowly. "Isn't he fantastic?" she asked.

"A bit slow, perhaps; but he certainly looks the part."

"Oh, he should. He cost a fortune. He is not a real butler. He is an actor who played the role of a butler in a series of superhero films. Randy Fortune saw him in the second sequel and wanted him to work here: yet another example of his compulsive nature. Nothing is left to chance. Everything is supposed to be exactly as Randy imagines it should be when you have it all. That is, if he ever gets around to completing his vision. Some people call him a control freak, but that's because they don't appreciate how a super-rich mind should work."

"He played a butler to a superhero? He must have some secret powers of his own," Wallace said.

When Eustis stopped in his ponderous retreat and looked over his shoulder, Wallace thought he detected a flicker of concern on the butler's face, pushing aside his practised expression of serene melancholia. But it vanished as soon as he seemed to notice it.

"He doesn't have superpowers. He is an actor, Rik. He answers the door and does a few other butlery things; but he is worth the money, don't you agree, because he exudes bulterishness?" Progress stood on her toes to indicate her state of excitement. "Oh, it is so good to see you at last. I mean, awake. I saw you in the back of the van when Pandora carried you out of Saint Drogo's, but that was different."

"Good to see you too, Progress," he lied. But perhaps he wasn't displeased to see her, if he analysed his feelings; which he didn't.

"It's Doctor Progress now," she said, unable to disguise her pride.

"Congratulations. You finished your doctorate? And without my help?"

"At least, *I* consider it finished even if that stupid panel of assessors doesn't, just because those Neanderthals are too thick to recognise the validity of my arguments. My research consists of a unique blend of disciplines never before put together. Anyway, I will have Randy fire all of them and hire another panel made up of those who will appreciate my point of view if they don't eventually give in and abandon their dogmatic prejudices. They even said my introduction revealed evidence of a—"

"Can I stay here?"

"Of course. Where are your suitcases?"

"You might have noticed when I was unconscious in the back of that van that I had no bags with me. I have nothing. Well, I have a borrowed bicycle, and some socks and underpants in the basket, and this shirt," he said, plucking at the sleeve.

"Oh, don't tell Randy you have nothing because he would be sooooo jealous. He wants to divest himself of all his stuff." She threw her arms open. "I assume Pandora filled you in on your mission here?"

"Sort of. But she didn't tell me how you and Randy met."

"We bumped into each other – entirely a random event, I assure you – at a conference on twins that were separated at birth?"

"Who separated them?"

"That's not the point. One of the most important techniques we have for measuring the impact of nurture on human development is to track down twins, when they are adults, who were brought up in different social and economic environments. By comparing their resulting adult lifestyles – whether one of them is in prison for example – you can measure the impact of environmental factors on the way they turn out. So, you see, it's vital to separate as many twins as possible immediately after their birth, for the sake of our understanding of the human condition. But since enough don't part naturally, we have to help them along by bribing the mothers." Progress glowed with psychological pride.

"I appreciate the appeal such an experiment would have for *you*, but what was Randy doing at a conference on separated twins?"

Progress sighed. "He has always been interested in philanthropic research. But it used to be small-scale before his complete nervous breakdown. He funded many trailblazing psychological experiments back in the days when he was a normal rich person. He paid loads of mothers to give up one of their twin babies. Randy is fascinated with families, and how our parents shape who we are. He believes that working out the impact of nurture will help future generations to have the opportunities he enjoys."

"But apparently he doesn't enjoy them, because he is miserable now."

"Randy is convinced that his wealth is a result of his unique environment. He keeps changing his mind, but his last great scheme was to invest in reproducing the exact social conditions he grew up in, which he imagines made him successful in the first place. That plan fell apart when he couldn't find an exact younger version of his parents to function as the basis for an experimental family he wanted to set up on a remote farm under the supervision of a hidden team of psychologists. But it doesn't matter as long as his schemes are relatively cheap – like his model farming family – even when you include the cost of the litigation. Just make sure you don't propose anything too expensive. We won't miss a few hundred million here and there, but he must hold onto his billions. If he says black, you say white. That is what philosophers do, isn't it? Just be your normal confusing self. I won't even tell you what to say or think because you are better at being you than anyone else."

"That's more or less what Pandora said."

"That is why we bust you out of Saint Drogo's in the first place."

"That, and because Pandora lost her head and shot your first candidate, Fischer."

"Be yourself, Rik. Is that asking too much? But remember, the most important thing: we don't want him interfering with Candid Online College unless it is to fund a scholarship, maybe in my name."

"But you live here in this mansion with a billionaire so why is Candid Online College important to you?"

"Right now, it's the only place where I can find a job."

"Doesn't Randy give you money?"

"I'm not some sort of prostitute, Rik. But no, he doesn't give me as much as he should, considering what I have to do for him. He is very tight for a billionaire."

Wallace studied Progress. Her smell was familiar. He stopped his mind wandering to her naked shoulders, her— She looked contented, or at least more relaxed than he remembered.

"Do you love him?"

"I love his money, which is an integral part of his nature; so, yes; I suppose I do love him. I can't imagine what my feelings for him would be if he suddenly became poor. Ordinary people who behave the way he does are tedious, but his wealth allows him to be eccentric, which is an attractive characteristic in a billionaire."

"You appreciate this will end badly?"

Progress ignored his doubts. "Don't be nervous when you meet him. He is a normal person, same as you or I, except he is worth billions and billions. Come on," she said, linking her arm into his. "I will find you a room. Preferably something with four finished walls."

As they turned towards the stairs, Progress pulled at his sleeve to turn him to face her.

"By the way, I assume Pandora told you about Randy's obsession with your family."

He nodded.

"How is your search going?"

He sighed. "Jackson and the librarian are working on it."

When Eustis the butler reached the corridor that ran parallel to the staircase, he seemed to dematerialise into a wall panel. But, by then, he was confident Rik Wallace and Julie Progress weren't looking his way as both had lost interest in him, being deep in conversation as they climbed the steps together.

XIII

Periculum In Tedium
The Danger of Boredom

Tiberius Lang parked Bernard the security guard's wife's banana yellow hatchback in the shadow of the high hedge bordering the front garden of the address that Maurice Spencer had given him on the telephone. He opened the glove compartment, removed a fistful of cable ties, and shoved them into the pocket of the Harris tweed jacket he stole from Professor Bentley Murphy. He believed it was best to be prepared because it was difficult to predict where a therapy session might lead. Cable ties were ideal for prolonging the agony of his clients: justice for the tedium they usually put him through; and when their eyes popped out of their sockets, it was the nearest they came to an expression of insight. He laughed.

Tiberius was proud of the fact he could never be accused of pragmatism. He hadn't focussed on accumulating a wealthy, neurotic clientele as his prosaic peers had done. The one utilitarian act in a career he liked to describe as sentimental was to accept the inheritance of a hysterical, heirless spinster. Following his arrest, the police had confiscated the country house, the cars, the paintings and furniture, the doll collection, and the boat: the lot; all on the assumption he had acquired them with menaces, which was nonsense. The hysteric had loved him with the intense passion only transference can instil in an admirer. For God's sake, he had earned everything he got. He even shoved his tongue down the old bag's throat at least twice. They took it all away, except the secret Swiss bank account and the penthouse in Sigmund Freud's name.

He sat in the car trying to control his breathing. He swallowed to repress the excitement. He would not allow the adrenalin rush he experienced whenever he began a therapy session with a new client to be his real motivation in counselling. Healing wasn't just about the thrill. He had been mortified when the judge called him a homicidal maniac. The memory still caused him to blush. The pleasure in killing was not the main reason he counselled people. It was a serendipitous side effect. He was after an elusive truth, too sublime for a mere judge to comprehend. But Tiberius was aware he was running out of both time and energy. He was no longer a young graduate filled with enthusiasm. Constant disappointment in those who had come to him for help had blunted even his fanaticism a little. He needed to find someone soon who would stretch his formidable powers of empathy to beyond that point any of his previous clients had achieved. Where were the case studies on which Freud had built his selfish reputation? He still hoped to come upon that diamond-mind sieved from the slagheap of humanity: the one person whose anxieties, neuroses, terrors, and compulsions didn't blindly follow the tramlines of undergraduate psychological convention. What he liked to call an individual: the most overused concept. He had learned this much – the ones who claimed to be unique were farthest from it. He was drawn to those eccentrics who imagined their obsessions were normal. How long was it now since he last thought he had found such a rare creature? There was the client with boanthropy, who couldn't believe her family didn't share her conviction she was a cow. That lasted a record five sessions, but chasing her around her living room proved too tedious in the end.

During his therapeutic training, his mentor advised him to build his reputation as a counsellor on the typical and not the extraordinary client: the everyman, not the only man. That fool took longer to go than the others. He seemed to have had less need for blood in his banal brain than the average person. Typical pedant.

Tiberius gripped the steering wheel. He resolved aloud to the empty car that he would not strangle Spencer. Surely, he told himself, he would let him go in exchange for revealing Rik Wallace's whereabouts? After all, he was fair-minded, wasn't he? When he caught up with him – which he would do – he was certain Wallace would prove to be that elusive case study for whom he searched his entire professional career, not even interrupted by incarceration: the client who would redeem the human race, including all those who made the ultimate sacrifice along the road of this psychological pilgrimage. His conviction was not based on mere hope but on the certainty of necessity. Wallace had to be the one because who else was there?

But that was in the future. What of now? Tiberius's first impression was that Spencer displayed the worrying symptoms common in self-absorption. But then anyone who sought out his services was de facto not the one he was looking for. Spencer was too keen. He would have respected him had he never gotten in touch. That was why Tiberius was both relieved and discouraged when he heard Spencer's voice on the phone. The most appealing clients were the ones who were somewhat reluctant to discuss themselves. They might wait several days before phoning, and when they did, they might not launch straight into their problems on the phone without even the preamble of a hello. But he hadn't yet worked out how to compel someone into counselling apart from kidnapping them, and even those cases hadn't gone to plan.

Inside the banana yellow hatchback, the humane fragment of Tiberius's unconscious hoped Spencer would prove to be distracting despite the inauspiciously prompt phone call. A different part of his mind given over to cruelty that fingered the cable ties in his pocket was confident he would disappoint. Yet again, he made a familiar bargain with himself.

"You can have him if he bores me," he told his savage-self.

"Deal," his savage-self answered before his several selves climbed out of the car together.

The Spencer who opened the door was wearing a tracksuit.

"I am grateful, Professor Murphy, you coming here this evening at such short notice to analyse me in person. But don't tell Pandora because she doesn't appreciate therapy. The professional body governing our counselling courses at Candid Online College is debating whether or not therapy on the Internet counts as real; so until they make up their minds, it's safer to unload in person."

"What professional body is that?"

"There are several, but I can't decide which one to recognise. I keep changing my mind. Let's do this in the sitting room," Spencer said. With unconscious temerity, he turned the back of his neck to the analyst.

"Wherever you are least comfortable," Tiberius muttered at the retreating tracksuit. He followed Spencer down the darkening hall. "Are you sure you live here alone?" he asked.

"Yes, I'm sure."

"You remember what I said on the telephone? It is vital for the success of my approach that we are not disturbed."

Spencer sprawled on the sofa, draping his feet laced into unused running shoes over the armrest nearest to Tiberius. These were his latest props in his theoretical commitment to exercise. His arms were folded behind his head. A brimming glass of red wine to fuel his thoughts stood on a low table within easy reach.

"Did you decorate this place yourself?" Tiberius asked, studying the interior as a potential external manifestation of the mind confined behind his client's thick skull.

"Yes. I chose everything: the wallpaper, the furniture, and the carpet. People say I have great taste."

Tiberius thought the room could function as an advertisement for a design catalogue. He was surprised to discover so many shades of beige were available in so many finishes on so many surfaces. "What else do they say about you?" he asked.

"People don't understand me," the teenage self in Spencer whined. "I thought for a while Rik Wallace understood me, but he didn't."

Tiberius almost shouted for joy. Unprompted, less than a minute into the session, his client had mentioned Wallace. If he would just tell him where he was, he could end this now. Patience, he commanded himself. To Spencer he said, "Uh-huh. How does that make you feel?"

"It makes me feel annoyed. Fortunately, I use my mindfulness techniques to—"

"Err … where is Wallace now? Have you seen him lately?" Tiberius interrupted to head off the danger of a treatise on the benefits of mindfulness. Before Spencer could reply, Tiberius leaped to his feet when a dustbin lid crashed to the ground outside, spun on its rim like a cymbal, before coming to a stop. "Who is that?" he shouted.

"The neighbour's cat. Look, I know why you are here."

"You do?"

"You want to help me explore how I can tell whether or not I am really happy?"

"Oh, yes. You are very perceptive. That is exactly why I am here," Tiberius lied.

"I may be only fooling myself that I imagine I am happy now, but I worry how I will feel if I discover later that I am mistaken."

"Do you think about yourself a lot?"

"Not all of the time. I do have other things to occupy me now that I am an important course designer in a virtual college that is an integral part of a global online university that, in turn, is a subsidiary of a communications empire. And, of course, there's my mindfulness training and thinking about taking exercise."

"Yes. There is always that," Tiberius sighed.

"I practise remembering what I am trying to forget. Or is that what I'm trying to remember? Anyway, it involves overcoming the duality imposed on our experience by Western reason and replacing it with the superior insights of

Eastern thought."

"Duality?" Of their own volition, Tiberius's fingers groped for the cable ties.

"Yes. Duality. Apparently, there are all sorts: Ontological, epiphenomenal, predicate and, of course, Cartesian. I assume you are familiar with Renè Descartes. You remember? Cogito something or other – I think therefore I am?"

"*Cogito ergo sum.* Yes, I have read all of his books."

"Oh, I read a summary of his ideas online, but I can't say I understood any of it except that he is a typical example of the Western imposition on us of a crude mind–body separation. I use meditation to escape from all of that nonsense. Wallace believes we can't simply abandon the foundations underpinning our own thought processes to embrace alien Eastern mysticism we don't understand and that bears no relationship to our own culture. But I disagree."

"Ah, so you were *recently* discussing Descartes with Wallace? When was that?"

"Why do you want me to talk about Wallace? Why can't I talk about me?"

"Well, since you are acquainted," Tiberius blustered, "Wallace could be a way of exploring yourself, but one step removed. Some of my clients find it less intimidating to express themselves by blabbing about other people."

"You are disappointing me, Professor. I expected subtler insights from you. Those clients you refer to usually employ strangers as psychoanalytical intermediaries. For example, I could relate the entire conversation with the person I met on the train this morning to fill up the space between us with talk, and at the same time, avoid saying anything pertinent about myself. It allows me to talk non-stop but say nothing. I am aware of that common psychological ploy. But that won't work here because we both know Wallace. Oh, it's always been Wallace this and Wallace that. Wallace, Wallace, Wallace. This is supposed to be my session."

I know we know him. Why else do you think I am fucking here? Tiberius asked himself. Do you imagine I want to hear your thoughts? I would rather stab myself in the head with a screwdriver than—"Yes, of course. I'm sorry. Go on," he said out loud, instantly tuning out.

Since his escape from Saint Drogo's High Security Asylum for the Criminally Insane Tiberius's thoughts kept returning to the evenings spent sitting with his ear pressed to the door of Wallace's cell on those many occasions when Murphy had him restrained, listening for some psychological hint as to the nature of the person at the other side of the padding: a scream; a laugh; a cough; any tiny clue. Why had Wallace run away? They could both still be comfortably locked up together. Ah, but when he eventually caught up with him, Wallace would end this protracted engagement with counselling: bring closure to the long, drawn-out process. He shuddered at using that word "closure", but such was his state of desperation what could he do? First, he had to find Wallace. Therefore, he must stay focussed on the task at hand. Anyway, after he had finished analysing Wallace in the ultimate therapy session ever, he would make him pay for this time spent with Spencer. "Go on," Tiberius said, coming back to the room having plucked the word "Wallace" from the background noise. "Where were we?"

"I said Wallace isn't a real philosopher, even if he understands a lot more of it than me."

Tiberius's cramped fingers loosened their grip on the cable ties in his pocket. "But Wallace reflects deeply on the world, doesn't he? I have read his file. Perhaps he is just another casualty of reading Nietzsche in earnest. After all, Nietzsche went mad, probably from reading back over his own notes. Wouldn't that alone make him a real philosopher?"

"Not at all. If anything, Wallace thinks too much, and mostly about the wrong things. Besides, he doesn't have my intellectual training that was designed to prevent me taking ideas too seriously. Except mindfulness, but that is different. He doesn't even have the kind of shallowness that comes from the rigour of a proper education."

Nietzsche would never have run, Tiberius lamented to himself. *What wouldn't I give to have had him as a client?*

"You won't catch me reading Nietzsche." Spencer interrupted his thoughts. "Besides, Wallace abandoned him for Immanuel Kant. That is what caused all the trouble at CAT College."

"Kant? You mean he is a Kantian?" *A stab of anxiety that perhaps Wallace wasn't the ideal client after all. No, impossible! He would not entertain doubts. Doubts were for the followers of Descartes, and he wasn't one of those!*

"Who knows? He keeps changing his mind about everything. Why am I telling you this?"

Headlights from a car passing on the road outside swept over the beige wall behind Spencer.

"Do you mind if I close the beige curtains?" Tiberius asked.

Spencer took a slug of the red wine. "Even though Wallace is a fraud – and who isn't when you consider it – you, me, everybody: we are all engaged in deception."

Tiberius tightened his grip again on the cable ties.

"But after what happened with Ernst Fischer, Pandora said we were desperate; so we hired Wallace. I'm still not convinced Fischer would have worked out in the long run because of his blind commitment to Kant. Wallace is more flexible. Despite what she says, I think Pandora secretly admires Wallace, but since she is incapable of expressing her emotions in a conventional way like you or I, you can only tell she cares for someone if she isn't actively trying to kill them. Neutrality is affection for her." Spencer laughed.

"This was when you hired him in the past at CAT College?"

"No. I mean, in the present at Candid Online College," Spencer clarified. "Ooops, I don't imagine I was supposed to tell you that. It's a secret. Okay, you are good, Professor," he said covering his lips with his fingers.

Tiberius held his breath.

"Technically Casper Wall hired him because he is nominally in charge," Spencer added. "But he does whatever Pandora tells him because he is terrified of her, just like the rest of us."

Tiberius examined his watch while pretending to absentmindedly rotate it on his wrist as a sign of thoughtfulness. Patience, he counselled his psychotic self. Spencer was leaking information.

"It's not easy being me, but I am willing to dredge up unpleasant memories and confront them. That's what mindfulness has taught me. My wife left me because she said I was too self-absorbed. Me? She was the one who kept going on and on about herself, constantly asking me how I felt about her. No self-awareness whatsoever. She left me without giving me any hint she was unhappy; though afterwards, she said she told me a hundred times, but apparently, I didn't hear her; which is a lie because I would have remembered that, wouldn't I? Our daughter, Samantha, takes after her mother. It's as if she isn't even related to me. She moved out of this house. I miss her."

"Does she ever visit?"

"She turns up whenever she needs to wash her laundry, borrow money she never pays back, and devour whatever is in the fridge. She says she can't stand me because I am a control freak. Me? I only ever wanted her to be happy. What else would a normal father do? I hoped she would become an academic or at least a ballet dancer, but she became a computer programmer at Candid Communications just to upset me because she knows that computers are the antithesis to everything I believe in; because – unlike mindfulness – they provide the answers only to the questions that aren't worth asking in the first place. Could there be a career further from philosophy than a programmer? I don't think so." He took a slug of wine. "She comes here when she thinks I am out because she doesn't want to meet me."

"Did you tell her you were out this evening?"

Spencer ignored the question. "She doesn't talk to me. I'm entitled to tell her how I feel, considering everything I have done for her. It wasn't for me. It was all for her. I drove at least a million miles over and back to ballet lessons. How else is she supposed to appreciate the sacrifices I made for her if I can't tell her? I'm a normal parent."

Tiberius's struggled to take in the words flowing out of Spencer's mouth without screaming. Meanwhile, in his pocket, his fingers fluttered in excited anticipation of taking matters into their own hands if they didn't receive a green light from his brain soon.

"Shut the fuck up," he shouted at last, getting to his feet.

"Isn't swearing at your clients unethical or against counselling guidelines? Which approach did you say you espouse?"

Tiberius clamped his hand over Spencer's mouth.

"Shut the fuck up," he shouted again. "Don't you ever stop talking?" Spencer's teeth sank into the fleshy part of Tiberius's palm between his thumb and index finger as his other hand groped for the cable ties in the pocket of the Harris tweed jacket. Don't do it, Tiberius's rationalist-self pleaded – not out of clemency, but from the pragmatic concern that Spencer hadn't yet revealed where Wallace was hiding. For the moment, reason seemed to prevail against emotion, but surely it couldn't last, because he wasn't a pragmatist.

Tiberius slumped into the beige armchair that matched the sofa on which Spencer had been struggling seconds before. He wiped his brow with a starched handkerchief he had found earlier in the inside pocket of the professor's jacket. "I'm sorry if that took you by surprise," he said, while gasping for breath. "It's part of my experimental analytic technique that hasn't been approved yet for widespread distribution amongst the counselling community. It's designed to …err … shock the client into revelations they might not otherwise make. You are one of the first to benefit from it."

Spencer had lost his words for almost a full minute before he found them again.

"Well, yes, I appreciate family is a traumatic subject, even for a psychiatrist. Have you children, Professor?"

Tiberius had sieved every word he heard in the session for

the tiny nuggets of psychological gold. "Tell me why Pandora made Casper Wall hire Wallace," he demanded, determined not to be distracted again.

"But I want to talk about meeeeee," Spencer wailed.

XIV

Conventis Mentium
A Meeting of Minds

Rik Wallace spent his first night alone in Fortune Mansion in a white cube with a bed and a chair. Next morning, he lingered in a different cube, waiting for his host. The parquet floor shone in the morning sun pouring through the restored sash windows in the south-facing wall. Outside, the trimmed symmetrical patterns of box hedging, with five-pointed stars inside circles inside squares, provided a distraction. By contrast, there was nothing in the room, not a crack, blemish, nor crooked line to engage the imagination of the DIY enthusiast in Wallace.

He turned, sensing rather than hearing a presence behind him, when Julie Progress skated across the floor on canvas slippers. "Rik, this is Randy Fortune," she said, holding an upturned palm in front of a pale, bald figure coming in behind her, also wearing canvas slippers. Both were dressed in plain white cotton jumpsuits of a style last worn by those depicting future societies in seventies made-for-television films. Wallace stretched out a hand in greeting. "Pleased to meet you, Mr Fortune," he lied.

"I don't shake hands. I can't tolerate the feel of skin on skin," Randy said, joining his own as if in mute prayer.

Wallace clamped his fists to his sides to keep them out of the way. Why doesn't he wear gloves if he is so bothered, he thought? Rich bastard. What does he imagine he might catch from me? Perhaps a little humility, he concluded.

"I imagine you are wondering why I am not wearing gloves," Randy said.

"No. Not at all," Wallace lied again. "What you wear in your own mansion is not my business." He tried to configure his face to appear as if he was processing his thoughts, pausing before speaking to give an impression of gravitas, as he imagined a billionaire might expect when making the acquaintance of a philosopher. He was desperate to fit in. Perhaps that compulsion even outweighed his fear of Pandora.

"I understand Julie told you all about me," Randy said after a full minute, during which both Progress and he stared at a grimacing Wallace with matching expressions of curiosity.

"Only that you need my help to give away all of your money."

"You have no idea how unhappy my wealth has made me," the billionaire said. He plunged his hands into his jumpsuit pockets.

"I'm broke, and I am miserable, if that is any consolation?"

"Not really. Poor people generally don't have feelings, and those who have don't appreciate how lucky they are; and the poorest, if they had sense, would realise they are the happiest of all. The penniless should welcome death because they are leaving nothing behind them. But someone as rich as me, imagine giving all that up? I can't bear the thought of dying with so much money. I remember when I was badly off – I didn't realise how contented I was."

Progress glided between them on her canvas slippers. "I keep reminding Randy that being poor without ever having been rich is easier than living in poverty when you have experienced billions. Didn't Buddha say something about our not being able to step into the same river twice?" she asked, as she floated away.

"That was the Greek philosopher Heraclitus," Wallace corrected her. "Are you a Buddhist, Mr Fortune?"

"No."

"Not into mindfulness?"

"No."

"At least, that's something."

"But not being able to take everything with me is just one of the many reasons I want to be broke when I go. I need some worthwhile cause I can give my money to so I can die happy. Can you assist me with that?" Have you had any thoughts at all on how I might disperse my wealth?"

"I have," Wallace lied again. It had been quite a while since he had an opportunity to string so many lies together in such rapid succession. He was almost enjoying himself.

"Well? What are they?"

Wallace inhaled. "You could give all of your money to someone you trust, such as Progress here; or your butler, Eustis, and then if you changed your mind, you could ask for it back. Consider it a holiday from your wealth."

"I distrust everyone."

"Give it to your children. You trust them, don't you?"

Randy squinted at Wallace through suspicious eyes. "That's a strange comment coming from a family man. I don't have any children, but if I had, I don't imagine I could trust them. Are you sure you are married with children?”

“Yes, yes,” Wallace stammered. “My wife and children are on their way. They should be here any minute— I mean, day— week.”

No children! Wallace may have found something in common with the melancholic billionaire. “But it’s not too late. You can still have children and give your money to them,” he said.

“I couldn’t stand the thought of having sex without wearing a condom. My aversion to feeling skin anywhere on mine stretches to every part of my and other people’s bodies. Ugggh.” Randy shuddered.

Wallace struggled not to make a face. “You could donate your sperm to a surrogate mother. I am confident there would be many volunteers. For example, Julie here?”

“What? Fuck you, Rik. I’m not having children with him, even if he does give them all his money. I have a career to consider, and my figure.” She executed a pirouette.

“How would I tell if she is the right breeding stock?” Randy asked, ignoring the outburst.

“Breeding stock? Fuck you too, Randy. I’m not a cow.”

“Family is the one value I believe in. You think me a hypocrite, but I couldn’t have children with just anyone,” Randy said, ignoring the outburst again.

“I’m not just anyone,” Progress protested. “What’s wrong with me? I’m beautiful, intelligent, healthy, and sane. What more could you want? You would be lucky to have one of my babies.”

“I would need to select the biological host after meticulous screening, but genetic science is in its infancy. One company

I interviewed said they couldn't guarantee I could return any children that proved unsatisfactory."

"Unsatisfactory?" Progress shouted. "You are not having any unsatisfactory babies with me," she said, for once heedless of the poor economic pragmatics of her objection. She skated to a window. Outside, she saw the head gardener mime his frustration at his daughter who was kneeling in a flowerbed. He was obviously arguing over the tulips she was planting for the spring. She wanted an all-black arrangement, while he was holding out for yellows, reds, and pinks.

"Anyway, you're not a satisfactory role model even by your own prejudicial standards?" Progress said. She was still angry at having her breeding potential impugned. "You're weird."

"I'm perfectly normal," Randy protested, demonstrating a lack of self-awareness appropriate to the super-rich.

"There is the skin-touching thing," Wallace pointed out, wondering why he could hear himself supporting Progress.

"And the dust allergies; the aversion to moving faster than walking pace; the intolerance of body hair; the Styrofoam phobia; spiders; and that thing you do with yogurt—" Progress said, counting on her fingers.

"Adopt a huge number of children to spread your money thinly, and thereby put less pressure on any one of them to be satisfactory," Wallace interrupted, with a new plan.

"It would be impossible to provide security for so many because they would be targets for kidnappers. It's no use. They would all go off the rails together."

"Well, your wife, then?"

"What about them?"

"Give all your money to your … err … wives."

"Which one?"

"Any one of them; all of them; how many are there?"

"Too many. They already have more than they can ever spend – and their lawyers. You are wasting my time, Wallace. Don't you imagine I have thought of these ideas already? Where are the brilliant morally beneficial proposals Julie promised you would have?"

Wallace refrained from pointing out he couldn't undertake serious moral reflection without a drink.

"He is boring me," Randy told Progress, who was by then on the move again, gliding past the window. "Will you please stand still? You are making me dizzy. You told me he was some kind of genius."

"He is only getting warmed up. That's what philosophers do. They need to have a practise run at a problem before saying anything intelligent," she said, stopping in front of him with her arms held out in the manner of a skater at the finale of her performance.

"Wait, wait, I have another idea," Wallace said as if in proof of Progress's hypothesis. "Give all your money to a church," he blurted as if guessing the solution to a puzzle that Randy had set him. He hated puzzles. "Religious people understand better than anyone, including me, the nature of good deeds," he said looking around in vain for a bottle of anything liquid. There wasn't even a shelf in the room.

Progress scowled while kicking him in the back of the leg with her canvas shoe as a reminder he was supposed to be persuading Randy *not* to give his money away. She is so unsubtle, Wallace thought.

"Any idiot could make a better world than God did. I can't

follow commandments written by someone whose work I find inferior."

Wallace stopped himself interjecting with a theological point on vanity. Randy was still talking.

"I wrote to the Pope to tell him that, if I was going to give my money to his Church, it was reasonable that I rewrite five of the current ten and add maybe four additional commandments. I would settle for three, but I didn't tell him that. My commandments would spell out the details. *Thou shalt not kill* – what does that mean? Meaningless without a list of valid exceptions. And what relevance is *Thou shalt not covet thy neighbour's wife* supposed to have? I have no neighbours, and if I did, I would encourage them to covet all of my wives."

"What did the Pope say to that?"

"He wrote back to thank me for my offer but turned me down. Apparently, I'm not God. I get that criticism all the time. I don't have delusions of power. I *am* practically omnipotent."

"We have laws to cover the grey areas in the commandments. That's what the courts are for," Wallace said.

"I can afford to stay in court forever contesting every law. I could hire God to defend me."

In his panic, another suggestion came to Wallace.

"Give your money to the most wretched people on earth. Divide your wealth up between the poorest billion in the world. Puff, it's gone, and you have made a billion people happier."

"Can you imagine how many petitions I receive every day from the poor asking for my help? I couldn't meet them all, even if I wanted to, because there are too many. I have people who ignore them for me. Don't you understand rudimentary charity? The poor can't be trusted to spend even the smallest amount of money wisely. They would blow it on drink, or drugs, or gambling, or tracksuits, and giant television screens."

Ah, drink. Those lucky, poor people, Wallace was thinking.

"Within an hour of my donation, most of them would be back to where they were before – broke."

"Give it to politicians who know best how to distribute it amongst the most needful."

"This isn't getting us anywhere. Politicians would spend it making themselves popular with the poor by buying them giant television screens and tracksuits. Now can you appreciate the predicament in which I find myself? Not so straightforward, is it, to give away all of my money? I must be desperate to have allowed Julie to persuade me to talk to a philosopher. This supposed genius she was raving about last week never showed up, and now she says you are the best moral authority money can buy. What are you proposing to charge me for your advice?"

"I don't want your money?"

"That is a first. I assume you are either very bad at your job or very moral; not that I have come across the latter type before."

"It doesn't work that way. You can't buy right and wrong."

"Yes, he can," Progress said. "You aren't the only moral authority around here. My doctorate is pending. If you won't interfere in his business, then I will."

Randy ignored her.

Progress thought the billionaire made her angry. But it wasn't anger she felt. She was jealous of his money: an understandable psychological mistake by someone whose qualifications were pending.

"I am confident whatever Julie said I could do for you,

I can't. Despite our acquaintance, I am certain I am not the person she thinks I am." He almost surprised himself because, for a change, this wasn't a lie. From over Randy's shoulder, where she was attempting to execute a camel spin, Progress scowled at him and shook her head. Wallace ignored her. "Besides, as you have all the money, and I have none, that proves you are smarter than me. You don't need the advice of a poor fool."

"People confuse being rich with being smart. I'm supposed to be smart because I'm rich. I had one great idea involving clothes hangers, and even then, it wasn't mine, and I didn't realise how good it was at the time. I haven't had another original idea since – even someone else's. After that, everything was easy. Money makes money, and I used that to buy companies that make money. That doesn't make me intelligent. But you're clever, Wallace," Randy said.

"He is?" Progress asked, coming to a stop.

"Yes," he said, addressing his remarks to her. "He has probably worked out that people are always trying to ingratiate themselves by telling me how fantastic they are, so he has decided to use inverse psychology on me because of his training."

Progress smiled and nodded her approval.

Wallace decided it was time to try straight-up reasoning.

"Philosophers are not supposed to use inverse arguments," he lied.

"It's all the same to me. Do you imagine I am stupid enough to fall for people pretending to tell me the truth?"

"I don't reflect on these things as much as you seem to," Wallace lied again.

"But you said you are poor. At least, that's something."

"These days I am a leading authority in poverty. Look at me. This is everything I possess in the world: nothing. And I have nowhere else to go," Wallace told himself, not realising he was speaking aloud.

"I envy you. Helping me is both a moral and practical necessity for you. A loneliness hangs over you that reminds me of me. That, and you are cheap. Do you want the job?"

"It would be a distracting experience to work with a philanthropist, someone who loves humanity. You are the first one I have ever met."

"I didn't say I loved anyone. I hate people. So much skin." Randy shuddered. "I am not a philanthropist. I just want to give away my money for my own selfish reasons."

"I have much to learn about charity," Wallace said. "Is there a button I can press to reveal a hidden drinks cabinet around here? No? Pity."

"Okay. You are hired. You are now my official moral advisor. Your job is to help me become as poor as you."

In celebration of the first phase of her elaborate plan falling into place, Progress executed circles around the perimeter of the room, her hands clasped behind her back.

"Don't you have an entourage, or something, who accompany you everywhere doing your bidding?" Wallace asked, his eyes following Progress.

"I have no one now," Randy said.

"You have me," Progress shouted, as she glided past.

"No one," he confirmed. "I am the loneliest person on earth."

"Except for other billionaires," Progress corrected.

Wallace was wondering how anyone could feel lonelier

than he did at that moment, and he was broke.

"But you are fortunate, Wallace. You are poor, but at least you have your family," Randy said. "You are hired as my moral advisor, pending your wife and children meeting my approval, of course. Let me know the moment they get here. I am dying to meet them."

"So am I," Wallace lied.

Progress was asking herself in song – as David Byrne once did – my God, what had she done?

XV

Parva Spe
Little Expectations

Rik Wallace watched the sixteenth-century navigator's terrestrial globe, suspended in a circular mahogany frame in the library, turn on its axis. As it slowed, he propelled it on again with the tips of his fingers, almost catching them in the graduated brass plate indicating longitude that followed the surface of the planet. He was envious of the people who built this graceful model of Earth because, for them, the world still had unknown territories and peoples yet to be discovered. They could hope something worthwhile lay over the next unexplored horizon. Nietzsche's prophecy seemed to have come to pass for Wallace because everything that had been brought into the light of Western reason had lost its lustre.

He couldn't stop his thoughts as the globe spun on. Why was he so pessimistic? Was his host's ennui contagious, he wondered? Something they both caught from the walls of the old mansion still standing long after it had fulfilled its original function, like an ancient patriarch decaying in a hospital bed, kept alive on a ventilator at the insistence of squabbling relatives desperate to postpone the disappointment they suspected would be revealed in his will. Wallace looked around at the bare oak shelves that lined the walls between the ceiling-height windows. The librarian wouldn't be happy here. Where were the signs? Where was the collection of valuable editions with which any vain billionaire should want to surround himself? But he forgot that even rare books attract dust. When Wallace heard laughter and raised voices beyond the door, he decided he needed to find the source of the joviality as an antidote to the gloomy mood into which he had so precipitously descended in this empty library.

Outside in one of the few formally decorated corridors, the walls were covered in gilded portraits of men in military uniforms captured in dark oils, some leaning on swords, others astride horses; and women who squeezed their breasts out of colourful taffeta ball gowns as eye-level advertisements for their merits as potential breeding partners. Wallace knew from Julie Progress that Randy Fortune acquired these pictures from the sale of the assets of a variety of financially distressed aristocrats.

He came upon the source of the commotion when he turned the corner. Eustis was propped with his back against the wall between a pair of pictures opposite an open sash window. He was smoking a cigarette. A maid leaned into the corner where her shoulder made contact with the hand-painted wallpaper. These two stopped laughing when they caught sight of him. The maid passed her cigarette to the butler, holding it upright by the filter, and vanished through a papered panel that became invisible again when it closed behind her.

"Smoke?" Eustis asked, pointing the still smouldering cigarette at Wallace.

"Sometimes," he replied, taking it and placing it between

his lips, tasting the lipstick on the filter.

His head swam. Unlike most of his fellow inmates at Saint Drogo's, he hadn't taken to chain-smoking for peace of mind. In fact, he had quit when he was sent there.

"Welcome to the show," Eustis said, standing upright and executing a 360-degree pirouette on his heel. He held out his arms. "Everything here is an illusion. Who are you in this elaborate production of a super-rich freak?"

"I am not an actor. I can only play myself."

"What do you mean *yourself*? No one is themselves."

"I am afraid I am merely me," Wallace lied.

Eustis smirked. "You're fucked if that is to be your approach to surviving around here," he said, grinding his cigarette butt between the sole of his polished shoe and the waxed parquet floor at the edge of the handmade carpet running the length of the corridor. "Behave as you think a billionaire would expect you should, and you will be fine. Easier than you might imagine. You told me when you arrived you are an ex-philosopher; is that the role you will play?"

"I think I have been hired as Randy's moral advisor."

"Make the most of it. This is the best gig I've ever had. There are few lines to remember; no rehearsals; no opening nights; no reviews – only guaranteed work."

"Isn't the traditional role of the butler to have done it?"

"Done what?"

"The crime."

"What crime?"

"Whatever crime occurs. What kind of a butler are you? Don't you watch television or read books?"

"Listen," Eustis said, grabbing Wallace by the front of

Jackson's shirt which the librarian had adjusted for him – the green one Jackson objected to giving away. "Fuck this up for the rest of us, and I will kill you. That will be the crime."

Wallace held onto the butler's wrists.

"No need to get violent. Believe me, I am desperate to fit in. I am not here to make any drastic changes. Julie Progress has persuaded herself that I am the best person to convince Randy to hold onto his money for moral reasons, despite his current intention to give it all away. There is a possibility that her scheme might not work, and he will ignore my advice that is supposed to confuse him. But listen to me, I am confusing myself just thinking about it. It would be best if I just kept my mouth shut."

Eustis assessed Wallace in silence. He shook his head to clear the confusion. "Just don't ruin my life's ambition that I am achieving here for the first time ever?"

"Which is what?"

"To live as a poor man but with money."

"What does that mean?"

"It means having the ambitions, hopes, and motivation to improve both my life and the lives of my wife and children without either the anxiety of poverty or the hassle that's involved with being rich."

"Oh, you have a wife and children. Do they live here with you?"

"They are downstairs in the kitchen?"

"Lucky you."

"They are actors like me. I hired them to fulfil Randy's fantasy about blissful domestic life. But if they were my real family, then I would want the best for them."

"I know what you mean."

"I have no desire to be Randy Fortune. His life is hell surrounded by sycophants, thieves, and liars like Progress and me. And now you, whatever you are. I want to share in his wealth without the responsibilities and anxieties that go with it." For example, look at this watch," Eustis said, raising his arm and pulling up his sleeve so fast that Wallace ducked, imaging he was about to be hit. The butler revealed a diamond-encrusted glass and platinum dome on his wrist. "I'm persuading Randy to give it to me. Right now, I have it on loan. It's worth half a million."

"What does it do?"

"It tells the fucking time," Eustis said. He sighed deliberately. "When this longer hand is pointing to twelve, and this shorter one is at four, that means it's four o clock."

"Does it tell the time in twenty other locations or at the bottom of the ocean or on top of a mountain?"

"No, it tells me the time *here, now.*"

"What do you think of *my* watch?" Wallace asked, holding out his wrist enclosed by a faded metal strap and matching circle.

"Impressive. What's that worth?"

"An ex-policeman gave it to me. He said he paid a kid a fiver for it. It tells the time *and* the date. That's twice as useful as yours."

Eustis nodded his head in admiration.

While Wallace was wondering how to reassure the butler his mission was doomed anyway, especially as he, Wallace, was too stupid to have thought of hiring actors to play his devoted family, his thoughts were interrupted by the sound of an engine outside. Below the window, a black-leather-clad woman was wobbling down the gravel drive on a pink Vespa 50. A huge rucksack on her back threatened to topple her over. The ends of her long, straight, black hair fluttered from under her helmet in the breeze created by her reckless speed.

"Who is that?" Wallace asked, studying her through the second from bottom of eighteen rectangular panes of glass.

"Oh, that weirdo. Her rocket is still steaming somewhere here in our extensive gardens, pointy end in the grass, where she came down from outer space. She is one of Randy's computer wizards. If you ask me, hackers are even further removed from reality than—what did you say you used to be?"

"A philosopher."

"Yeah, one of those! Listen," he said grabbing Wallace's shirt front again, "you can be whatever you want so long as you don't ruin the status quo for the rest of us. Anyway, what am I worried about? Since you are here without your family, Randy won't even allow you to confuse him or whatever it is you are hoping not to do. Oh, forget it," Eustis said, letting go of the shirt in frustration.

Before Wallace could reveal his own plan to find a family, Eustis had moved away, getting into character by shortening his stride after a half dozen lengthy ones. He wasn't frustrated by Wallace. It was the computer wizard who was driving him crazy. She never returned his texts; ignored him while he stood for hours in the corner with a drink balanced on a tray on his aching arm; never asked him to deliver anything to her room late at night. Yes, she was definitely the source of his exasperation.

Wallace looked out the window again in time to observe

the rider still upright on the pink Vespa 50 pass through the main gates and jink around a ragged entrepreneur who crossed her path. The computer wizard had mastered the art of balance.

XVI

Sordidati Lauandi
Dirty Laundry

Samantha Spencer parked her pink Vespa 50 beside the hedge that ran along the side of her father's drive, separating him from his nervous neighbours. When she saw his second-hand Saab parked in front of the garage on the other side of the house, she wondered why he was home on a Wednesday. He should be at that creep Pandora's place, getting drunk and doing whatever it was he did there with her now that she was married to Horse. She had refused to attend that wedding, offering as her excuse her moral objection to formally witnessing *that* particular form of human congress. She squeezed a spontaneous image from behind her eyes of Pandora and Horse in bed with her father wedged between them. "I should consult someone for a cure for my lurid imagination," she muttered to herself.

Maybe her father had reformed and left the car behind, deciding for once not to drive home pissed? She weighed up the pros and cons of turning around and leaving, not risking finding him inside. In favour of flight was avoiding the lecture on her latest tattoo, springing plant-like from under the grimy collar of her once-cream blouse. "How can you expect to find a responsible job with flora painted onto your face?" she could imagine him whining. She mimicked his peevish tone and accompanying facial expression for her own amusement. It's a spider's web. And it's my neck not my face. Basic anatomy. Arse–elbow, you know? And the spider is down here, she would say, lifting her blouse over her bare, flat breasts to annoy him. She would be unable to resist, even though, officially, she wasn't speaking to him. Why did she let him provoke her? Don't show me, he would wail, covering his eyes while retreating from the room, only to return immediately as if he had an important afterthought that just couldn't wait. This would be to inform her how her tattoo would ruin his life, if destroying her own didn't bother her. Meeting her father would cause annoyance she wouldn't be able to shake off all the way into the following day.

Against retreat would be the need to find a laundry open at this late hour. She had already rotated all of her underwear in the rucksack on her back at least twice. But even she had some limits, because by now, most of her knickers were brittle with encrustations in uncomfortable places. She would also need to wash socks, tights, tops, and at least one skirt in case called upon to make a presentation. The straps of the rucksack bit into her shoulders, urging her to consider her bodily comfort for a change above her psychological wellbeing. She made up her mind when she could almost feel the sensation of the crotch of a clean pair of knickers between her thighs. She inserted the key in the lock, turned it, and pushed against a modest pyramid of mail on the floor inside the door. She removed one earphone, in semi-curiosity.

"Hello. It's me, Sam. Anyone home?" she called out in warning, as much for her own sake. She was still haunted by a childhood image of her father in a spacesuit mounting Pandora on her hands and knees in the hallway, naked, save for her sunglasses and a cigarette dangling from the corner of her narrow mouth.

She switched on the light, scooped up the post, and placed it on the hall table. She walked to the end of the corridor, turned into the utility room and switched on another light. She swung the rucksack from her back onto the tiled floor in front of the washing machine. She might have heard the laundry sigh in anticipation of a swim in warm, soapy water had she not replaced the earpiece when she emptied the bag through the porthole. In her ears Eminem was promising Rihanna that if she tried to leave, he would tie her to the bed and engage in an incident of pyromania involving their shared accommodation.

In the darkened kitchen, she studied her food options in the golden glow from the fridge. She made a face while smelling an open package of processed meat slices: the odour made her resolve to become a vegetarian someday. She picked up a microwave meal, squinted at the date, and weighed the risks. She decided against it. Instead, she settled on a block of cheese in a plastic wrapper. She found two slices of stale, though not yet mouldy, bread in a tin box on the worktop. She applied a dollop of mayonnaise to the bread with the casual moves of an experienced bricklayer, gluing them to opposite sides of the cheese. She stretched her mouth wide and crammed a corner inside. She chewed and made a face. It needs onions, she told herself as critical culinary feedback, with no intention of adding them to her construction.

She turned off the music in her headphones. She jumped

at a sound from behind the door she had just come through before registering it as the washing machine moving through the heavy-soil cycle. "Take it easy, Sam," she muttered through the bread and cheese. "What is wrong with you?" she asked herself. "I am scared of meeting *him*," she answered. Reasonable, she nodded in agreement, still chewing. She glanced at the clock above the kitchen door and calculated the wash would take ages. She had enough time to catch a film on television. With the sandwich gripped between her teeth, she left the kitchen, crossed the hall and pushed open the sitting room door. The curtains were closed. In the pitch-blackness, she groped on the wall for the light switch. The bulb came on with a pop.

Someone was sitting upright on the beige sofa with a head at least twice as large as Samantha would expect to find on a normal person. Not that she would stereotype people by head size because she wasn't judgemental on anything relating to normality. With her upbringing, she couldn't be, could she? Except when it came to Pandora's sex life.

From her work with computers, Samantha's mind was in the habit of making connections between things without rushing to register their meaning. She liked to input the separate components individually before processing possible solutions.

The skin on what she took to be the face was purple and the eyes bulged from their sockets with an expression of acute attention to the blank television screen. Had it switched off the channels after witnessing the single most compelling broadcast in the history of television?

Was there room for her to share the couch with this creature?

Was this an inflatable sex doll her father forgot to pack away? If so, where was Pandora?

Why was it wearing a tracksuit?

Who would wear a cable tie around their neck in such a way that it constricted the passage of blood?

She opened her mouth, and the cheese sandwich dropped to the carpet; where it rolled over once before settling in front of the left toe of her black biking boots. She extended her two arms out wide because she needed both to deploy her most operatic scream as her brain completed its computations.

THIS THING WAS HER FATHER!

Part II

Usus Et Abusus Frigus
On the Use and Abuse of Refrigeration

XVII

Fides In Futuro
Faith in the Future

The sunlight refracted into its constituent colours as it passed through the stained-glass windows on the south-facing wall where biblical scenes outlined in lead recalled a time when the space was a chapel for those who believed in an afterlife. It now served as the departure lounge for well-intentioned humanists, indecisive agnostics, and those, such as Maurice Spencer, who hedged their bets on an afterlife by subscribing to the services of Frozen In Time Cryogenics. The expansive room was empty, except for a single row of consolable mourners anxious for the ceremony to end. The red silk curtains lurched towards each other as they closed in front of the coffin that contained Spencer minus his head – that was in a plastic bag in cold storage. Despite never believing he would actually die, he had made a will stipulating the music to be played on the unimaginable occasion of his funeral. That song now started up without warning: "One Day I'll Fly Away".

Samantha Spencer's father was dead. She couldn't move beyond that fact to wonder who might have killed him. She was angry with him. He was weak, always giving in first. She could rely on his resolution cracking within minutes of her storming off in a sulk. Her strategy of ignoring him was predicated on her knowing he anxiously waited for her to make contact. She would no longer be in control of their relationship now that, for once, he had taken the initiative by dying.

While she knew her father had loved her, she wondered if he had liked her. Strange, she hadn't thought about that until now. She had always assumed he did. It was too late to ask him. Was it easier to love someone rather than like them? You could love someone you didn't even know. Did anyone love her now that her father was gone? Certainly not her mother. Why couldn't she have picked her parents? Why was she stuck with the idiots who were there beaming down at her when she was born? It was so unfair. She imagined a market stuffed with parents – tied up, gagged for good measure, hanging upside down like turkeys on a stall. She would never have selected hers: the mother who abandoned her and the father who embarrassed her. But who would she have chosen? Maybe rock stars? Maybe Randy Fortune?

She did love her father. But she didn't like him. How could she? The vanity; dressing-up; his friends; his ideas; the stupidity of those ideas?

The music stopped, interrupting her meditation on her loss. As Samantha stood up, a tall, sombre man in black, who was lurking at the back, glided across the new carpet to hold her hand as if she was a bird who might fly away if all the stained-glass windows hadn't been rusted shut. Despite her grief, she felt social in part because she had changed her knickers for the ceremony. She told herself it was out of respect for her father's memory. She matched this with a black lace brassiere she was surprised to find in her drawer in her old bedroom at her father's house, having no memory of ever having purchased it. Her unconscious self would not have allowed her to acknowledge that she enjoyed the attention of being the principal mourner, since her mother, surprisingly averse to hypocrisy at a time like this, had decided not to put in an appearance.

"What is the point?" she asked no one in particular, sniffing into a crumpled tissue. Mascara ran down her white face in vertical black lines, putting the recently hired cryogenics undertaker in mind of a zebra.

"I don't know. I don't know," he murmured, in the insincerely sympathetic tone he practised every morning in the bathroom mirror since he got the job, taking her question to be the kind of platitude that passes unregarded as yet another existential observation typical of funerals. His job – which he had taken over from the owner of Frozen In Time Cryogenics, who now seemed to spend all his time on holiday – was to officiate at the cremation of the surplus body parts not destined for the main freezer.

"Death can take any one of us at any time," he murmured to Samantha. "That is why our motto is 'Better to Be Frozen In Than Out'," he added, glancing down at the banner on the brochures he held in his hands. "I appreciate that the next of kin are upset when their loved ones are called away suddenly, especially in cases of murder—"

"Or sex games gone wrong," Samantha added.

The undertaker ignored the suggestion. "—however, your father was prepared. He opted for the 'head only' discount, even though we assured him the entire cadaver was just thirty per cent extra. But he did avail of our two heads for the price of one special offer. He named you as the beneficiary, so you should have no anxiety when your turn comes."

"I know how much he looked forward to coming back with his own head sewn on to the body of an athlete when someone invents a cure for death ..." She smiled at a memory and blotted her nose with the tissue. "He used to say how great it would be to be alive again when everyone on earth would be mindful. Oh, I hope his brain hasn't been damaged beyond repair. Can you imagine his disappointment if he can't remember a line of any of the hundreds of books he read simply because some thoughtless monster restricted the flow of oxygen to his brain at the final moment?"

"The model of brain he had wasn't up to the abuse he put it through cramming it with all those philosophical ideas," Pandora put in from over Samantha's shoulder. She had been eavesdropping on the conversation. She continued without encouragement. "You have to look on the bright side. It will be a good thing for those around him in the future if his mind isn't fully functional. Hereafter, if people are sensible, they will have outlawed thinking by the time Spencer is thawed out." Pandora lifted her black sunglasses and dabbed her varicose eyes with a handkerchief that Horse had passed to her for the purpose. He was supporting his wife through her ambiguous ordeal by holding her up with two fingers fastened to her elbow.

Samantha and the undertaker winced at the sight of the twin grey egg whites with bloody red yolks that were her eyes.

"Oh dear," Pandora said. "I never imagined I would be this upset at his passing. I may even miss the twaddle he spouted on the decline of Western philosophy and the corresponding rise of that mindfulness nonsense. It's not the same when there is no one to act as a constant reminder of how sensible one is by comparison."

"I know what you mean," Samantha said.

"What do the police believe happened to him?" Pandora asked, despairing of ignoring the policewoman, Sergeant Jones, who was pushing her bust in and out behind the undertaker.

"Inspector Sullivan believes your father's ex-colleague, Rik Wallace, bust out of Saint Drogo's High Security Asylum for the Criminally Insane with the express purpose of killing him because he was jealous of Professor Spencer's reputation." Jones repeated the motive from memory.

"Reputation for what?" Pandora asked, still drying her eyes with the handkerchief.

"Moralizing."

"It would account for why Wallace was locked up in a lunatic asylum in the first place if he was jealous of Spencer," Pandora snorted. A smile almost formed on her sphincter lips.

"That's not fair," Samantha protested.

Everyone ignored this as a classic example of the sentimentalism common amongst the bereaved at funerals.

"Inspector Sullivan is an idiot," Pandora said. "Wallace might be a maniac, but he wouldn't hurt a fly. Strangling Spencer is not his work."

"Have the police ruled out my theory, which is a sex game that went wrong?" Samantha asked Jones.

"Can you specify what you mean?" Jones asked as her ears started recording.

"My father had unusual habits. Some of them he shared with Pandora here. I am considering counselling, but who would believe some of the costumes I have seen those two pulling off each other while growing up in that house? Therapists aren't trained to deal with that sort of thing. By the way, where were you Pandora the night he died?"

"Don't be ridiculous. I loved your father both platonically, and in that other way," she said, shaking her fingers at Samantha, as if dismissing some sticky memories. "I was at home with Horse. Wasn't I, darling?"

Horse nodded.

"Don't you have any credible suspects apart from Wallace and me?" Pandora asked Jones.

Before Jones could reply, the undertaker interrupted to hand a brochure to Pandora, Horse, and the sergeant in turn.

Samantha was wondering if Wallace could really have been jealous of her father. Perhaps he was a genius, after all. It was possible. Especially now he was dead.

"You might find comfort in our services if you are acquainted with homicidal maniacs," the undertaker was saying. "We have group deductions. We also have many second-hand parts in storage. For example, we have lots of eyes, in a wide range of colours. You can buy a pair in contrasting shades. Yes, we have lots of eyes," he repeated.

"Go away," Pandora growled, lighting a cigarette.

"Lungs. We also have fresh lungs. We take bookings." He was so desperate to impress his employer by generating new business he didn't consider the horror of a decomposing Pandora without her sunglasses appearing at the foot of his boss's bed in the middle of the night when he was back from holidays. However, his instincts for promotion, being more discerning, caused him to pluck the brochure from Pandora's fingers just before she turned away.

XVIII

Exponens Phrenesin Aut Exponens Phrenesin

Psycho Analysis or Explaining the Lunacy

Professor Bentley Murphy was interrupted while researching the diagnosis and treatment of mercury poisoning. He slammed the book shut, cleared his throat, and waved Inspector Freddy Sullivan into the office. As soon as Tiberius Lang was back in custody, he promised himself he would apply his undivided attention to ending it all. As for Rik Wallace, he hoped never to lay eyes on him again.

"Sit down, sit down," he said, pointing to the hard-bottomed plywood chair in front of the desk that Bernard the security guard had rescued that morning from a skip in the car park to provide himself, and visitors of course, with an alternative to the chaise longue.

Sullivan sat down as instructed while Bernard, who had shown him in, stood with his back to the wall, hands clasped together across his spherical stomach in the manner of a sentry ready to intervene at the first evidence of erratic behaviour on the part of the policeman. Bernard was hoping to make up in any way that might present itself for spraying his boss with pepper on his first day. He fantasized about demonstrating his loyalty with the Taser gun on his belt that replaced the spray can the professor had confiscated.

"You can leave now, Bernard," the psychiatrist told him. "I have the emergency buzzer you installed under my desk here if I need you," he said, groping for it with his fingers. "Ah, found it." Mother Theresa, praying in the waiting room outside, covered her ears with her hands and swore when he pressed the button.

"Make sure you hit it at the first sign of trouble. It would defeat the purpose of my security measures if you find yourself lying paralyzed on the floor unable to summon help with a maniac standing over you brandishing an axe."

Paralyzed. Murphy lingered on the comforting thought, imagining himself on his back on the carpet with a patient, or perhaps even this policeman, looming over him with a syringe filled with mercury.

"I'll try my best if the need arises," he said without enthusiasm.

"I suppose you heard, Rik Wallace has struck again," Sullivan said by way of introduction.

"Struck what?"

"Strangled his ex-colleague, Maurice Spencer. It has been all over the papers."

"Sit down, Inspector." A file in blue cardboard covers sat on the desk between the psychiatrist and the policeman. "Your record keeping is a disgrace, Professor," Sullivan said, picking it up and opening it. "From these notes from his sessions with you how am I supposed to determine who Wallace really is deep down inside?"

"That, Inspector, is not the result of poor note-taking but

human nature. There is no one single self. There are layers of identity. We are all fractured selves, and that is what those files reflect," the psychiatrist said.

"Speak for yourself, Professor. I'm not fractured," Sullivan replied with naïve conviction.

"I've been reading up on madness," Bernard said, butting in. It seems he hadn't gone after all. "It's a fascinating subject. Freud was a genius. Not our one, but the other one," Bernard clarified for the policeman. "It's amazing when you think about it, which I admit I had never done before coming here to Drogo's, but how can we know who anyone is? How can I know who I am? That question makes me giddy. And my wife at home – who the hell is she? I don't recognise her since I started working here. She has changed."

"Indeed, who are you, Bernard? Someone obsessed with weapons?" Murphy mused out loud, staring at his overloaded belt.

"I wonder how people in history knew who they were, before passports and driving licences were invented?"

"That's an intriguing thought, Bernard. We might make a psychiatrist of you yet. I suppose they had to rely on a close circle of friends and family to remind them," Murphy said. "Your relationships define who you are: mother, father, brother, cousin, friend, boss, wife, etcetera. In your case, husband, for example."

"Therefore, it follows the less friends and relations you have, the more identification you need," Bernard concluded, smiling at his own insight.

"Precisely," Murphy confirmed. "Consider me. I have neither friends nor family since my only sister joined that enclosed order of nuns when our mother took off in a hot air balloon and was never seen again. How am I supposed to know who I am?"

"But if a person went to a big city or abroad where they knew no one—?"

"In that case, I imagine they could become anyone," the professor said in answer to the unfinished question.

Inspector Sullivan twisted his neck to glare at Bernard behind him. "Even if we don't know who he is, I can tell you why Rik Wallace strangled Maurice Spencer," the policeman said. He snapped the file closed to signal his satisfaction with his theorising. He leaned back on the rickety legs of the rescued chair to count off his evidence on his fingers as Bernard waited for the chair to collapse under him.

"One," he said, raising an index finger. "He is a maniac, and that is what they do."

"So is Tiberius Lang," Bernard said, saving his boss the trouble.

"Yes, I'll give you that but, two—"

He held up another finger ignoring the inconvenient point and spun around to confront the security guard, placing unreasonable torque on the spindly legs of the chair. Bernard winced in anticipation of a tragic accident.

"Wallace calls to Spencer's house to discuss something philosophical, either spontaneously or by appointment. We don't know nor care how these things work. Picture the scene: two philosophers in a room together; the lethal cocktail of a few glasses of wine and a debate on morality on planets in outer space or whatever nonsense they discuss. Things turn violent, and Wallace strangles Spencer with a cable tie. That is how philosophers have settled disagreements for over two thousand years. Wasn't Socrates the first to be killed in ancient Greece setting the pattern for the rest?"

"But the cable tie is Tiberius's modus operandi when killing his victims," Bernard said, chopping the air with the edge of his hand to illustrate his logic.

"Of course," Murphy put in. "Tiberius said something about why he uses cable ties while he was droning on in one of our therapy sessions, but I wasn't paying attention. A tiny clue to the inner workings of the psyche, Bernard, is always revealed during analysis; but you have to be able to concentrate all of the time. It has to be Tiberius, but why did he kill Spencer?"

"Leave the police work to me. Wallace is trying to throw suspicion onto Tiberius. He learned all his methods when they were locked up here together. I am sure they exchanged notes. I'll tell you what I told Sergeant Jones when she raised the same point with me after Spencer's funeral: Tiberius couldn't be so stupid as to strangle Spencer using his own technique."

"He is mad. He can't help it," Murphy said.

"Thank you, Professor, for helping me out with that point," Bernard said.

"You are welcome, Bernard."

"Three," Sullivan said, holding up another finger. "Wallace helped Tiberius to escape in order to deflect attention away from his own murderous rampage."

"No. I can't accept that because it was my fault Tiberius escaped," Bernard protested.

"Four," Sullivan said, holding up a fist. "You only believe it was your fault when in fact Wallace hypnotized you. That's what happens in an asylum. Ask the professor, here."

Murphy tried but failed to tune out of the conversation. By now he was wondering if he could drink himself to death. Would Bernard stop him if he lunged for the bottle of whisky in the bottom drawer of his desk? But if he was not to be allowed to focus on his own problems then he must contribute to the discussion.

"Tiberius is psychotic. He lost contact with reality a long time ago; if, indeed, he ever had any. Wallace is neurotic, which makes him similar to the rest of us, and even that may be my fault. I am worried I may have caused him to experience an episode of inverse reduplicative paramnesia."

"I haven't come across that in my reading. What is it?" Bernard asked.

"Never mind. I'll explain it to you some other time. Inspector, I even thought you were suffering from Fregoli delusion."

The policeman shuddered.

"That sounds serious. I won't end up in here, will I?"

"Not if I have a say in the matter. Besides, I have abandoned that diagnosis. I am starting to believe that Tiberius may be impersonating me."

"Why would he pretend to be you?"

"Why indeed? What could he gain by passing himself off as me? It sounds crazy, but remember, he is insane. I must think. What have I learned from him during our therapy sessions, apart from his obsession with natural selection, and his fantasised idyllic childhood? What else is there? Inspector, you said I was looking for Rik Wallace at Candid Online College."

"Don't deny it. You were there."

"That is where the victim Maurice Spencer worked.

Tiberius was there, pretending to be me. But why? What did I want? Of course! It's because I am hunting Wallace."

"You are? Why?"

"That's it. I need—I mean, *Tiberius* needs to find Wallace. What does he want with him? Oh, it's obvious," Murphy shouted, bringing his fist down into his palm. "He is obsessed with the goal of analysing him," he added, answering his own question.

"I'm confused," Bernard said.

"Inspector, we must find Wallace before Tiberius does, or he will end up with a cable tie around his neck like Spencer. Find Wallace, and we will find Tiberius."

"So, Professor, are you saying that if I agree with you that Tiberius was impersonating you, then I don't have this Fregoli delusion thing?" Sullivan asked.

"That's what I am saying. Either I am correct, or you are mad. Take your pick, Inspector."

"I need to mull this over," Sullivan said.

XIX

Nisi Mundi
Saving the World

The members of the proposed Foundation for Universal Caring and Kindness Unlimited sat in no particular order around the circular mahogany table set in the centre of one of the largest unfinished cubes in Fortune Mansion. It seemed all were equal in this philanthropic enterprise. A cold bottle of mineral water, condensing beside an inverted glass, formed wet rings on the polished surface in front of each.

Water everywhere and nothing real to drink, Rik Wallace lamented to himself.

"Shouldn't we put the kindness before caring?" Julie Progress suggested. She was sitting on his left.

"Why?" Randy Fortune, opposite, asked.

"It would be less vulgar—"

"She means more *fashionable*," Maxine interjected.

She was next along after Progress.

To make this observation Maxine had ceased squeezing her oversized lips in and out in front of a Fabergé hand mirror while coating them in red lipstick. She was the star of music videos watched more for her state of undress than her singing. "Are we some sort of secret society?" she asked. "Monica and

Francine will be so jealous when they find out. They are not in a secret society because they would tell me if they were."

Wallace wasn't paying attention. He was preoccupied with the water bottle in front of him, which he acknowledged was a disproportionate source of annoyance. But then he had spent countless days locked up inside gulag Fortune Mansion, searching high and low for anything containing alcohol. He consoled himself that it wasn't that he had what could be described as the conventional problem of drinking to excess: his trouble was that he couldn't lay his hands on a single fucking drop.

Across from him, Randy sipped water with what Wallace understood to be the smug piety that springs from self-sacrifice. There was something seriously wrong with this billionaire, he thought.

Then there was Bené, an ageing rock star, who up until five minutes ago when he first came into the room, Wallace believed had been dead these last ten years from an overdose of unexpectedly pure heroin. Before sitting down, Bené boasted to Maxine that he owed his improbable smooth-faced appearance to nowadays sticking a syringe in his face rather than his arm. While telling her this, he laughed with the sound of a hyena getting its tail caught in a car door. From the way he related his current commitment to legumes it could be deduced he was now a manic vegetarian: a development that was positively received by his fellow philanthropists. It seemed to Wallace he had substituted one compulsion for another. He overheard Bené telling Progress that a meat pie had almost killed him.

Next, there was a prematurely-grey-haired man Wallace didn't recognize. He was wearing a pink discount shirt and red tie and was sitting beside the girl with black hair and matching lips. He didn't recognise her as the one under the helmet he had seen through the window wobbling down the drive on the pink Vespa 50. She was glaring at him with obvious hostility. What was her problem, he wondered? Why would anyone so oddly beautiful ever need to appear so angry?

He scowled back at her as he swallowed a mouthful of water.

Randy cleared his throat and tapped his pen against the side of his glass.

"I want to thank Professor Rik Wallace for inspiring me to set up this foundation that has allowed me to bring together those on our planet most qualified to decide what is best for humanity. He impresses me even before I have met his beautiful wife and four children, who I am positive, will be everything the family of a moral authority should be."

Progress was mouthing "four" at Wallace while holding up the same number of fingers as if to remind him how many he should supply.

Wallace felt sick.

"Once he has absorbed your ideas, he will provide a synthesis of your separate suggestions to show us the collective moral way forward."

"Ooooh, a synthesis. I want one of those in my next video," Maxine said while monitoring her lips as they exercised in her hand mirror.

"What's Maxine doing here? She isn't a good family person. According to Celebrity Hermit Magazine she's been married at least ten times," Wallace blurted to Progress.

"She's obviously not a hermit but she is a celebrity. The

rules don't apply to her."

"Perhaps we should start with science," Randy suggested in an attempt to deter Maxine from elaborating on her creative plans. "Everyone here knows the host of his own popular physics show on television," he said pointing at the man in the bargain pink shirt and red tie. "He needs no introduction."

"Who the hell is he?" Wallace whispered to Progress.

"Shush," she whispered back. "I am pleased to say I know nothing about popular physics, including its practitioners."

"He will give us his expert opinion on how investing in science could save humankind, while keeping in mind that I don't want to save many of them because there are loads of us already."

"Thank you, Randy. I won't waste your time because we are all important people here," the popular physicist said, looking at each of the faces around the table in turn before stopping at the girl with the black hair and black lips in a contrasting white face. "Well, almost all," he added. "Let me get straight to the point. I propose this foundation builds ships to colonize outer space. I estimate that with an investment of approximately three hundred billion now, you could transport everyone here in this room and their families to Jupiter in say, fifty years, give or take a decade. Imagine it, Randy, on Jupiter you won't have to deal with people."

"Or oxygen," the pale, black-haired girl muttered.

"What is she doing here?" Progress asked, voicing the popular physicist's thoughts.

"Samantha Spencer is a computer genius. We will need her to programme whatever we decide," Randy said.

Samantha stuck her pointy pink tongue out at Progress.

Samantha? Maurice Spencer's imaginary daughter! Wallace gazed at her in wonder. Her smell seemed to confirm her reality all the way across the table. He was both attracted and repelled by the odours that evaporated from her skin: a combination of decay, sweat, soap, cheese, and strategically applied antiperspirant.

Rik Wallace was walking on the gravel paths between the patterns of box hedging in the garden. The perfume of flowers competed with Samantha's scent, confusing the bees. He was holding the petite white hand that protruded from the rigid cylindrical leather sleeve of her biker's jacket, designed to protect the rider from a fall from a machine with a far bigger engine than that of the Vespa 50. They were squeezed together when the path narrowed where the points of two hedge-stars converged. She moistened her black lips with the tip of her pink tongue. Women didn't throw themselves at his old cautious self. But he was Rik Wallace now. For some reason he didn't understand, they hurled themselves at him.

"Kiss me quick," he gasped, leaning towards her while she bent backwards, away from him, coyly keeping her face a constant tongue-length from his.

"I can't."

"Why not?"

"We must be sensible. We work together on the FUCKU."

"I thought we decided it was to be called FUKCU."

"Whatever — we can't let spelling or our emotions get in the way of designing a platform to manage goodness. We would lose our objectivity."

There was no evidence of breasts under the grey T-shirt topped by a greasy ring that formed a collar sticking here and there to her skin. In her long leather boots, she was taller than he, obliging him to gaze up into her pale blue eyes.

"*We have nothing in common. I hate philosophy,*" she murmured, her lips closing on his cheek.

"I hate computers. I don't even have a mobile phone. Pandora doesn't want me calling anyone for help. Not that there is anyone I could call except perhaps my psychiatrist or Della." What was the word that was supposed to trigger the memory of her number? I can't remember. Oh yes. Hippopotamus!

"*We are different ages. Different heights.*"

"Opposites attract. Besides you smell wonderful."

"*Do I?*" She lifted her arm and pressed her nose into her armpit. "*I can't smell myself.*"

"Yes, you smell – interesting. People are obsessed with washing away their natural oils."

"*I agree.*"

"*You evoke a hint of vintage car seat leather and vegetable stall. Kiss me.*" The arms holding him away began to bend like a pair of steel struts experiencing metal fatigue. Her lips parted as his face closed to within a tongue-length.

"What is that cow doing here?"

Wallace was back at the round table in the stuffy cubical. His eyes moved down Samantha's solid arm and along her black-painted index finger pointing at Progress.

"I am taking notes," Progress said in explanation of her role.

"Why Jupiter? Why not Mars?" Bené asked the popular scientist.

"That's a good question. It's because everyone with money is going to Mars. It will be crowded in fifty years' time. I'm thinking perhaps a nice quiet moon, such as Ganymede – off Jupiter. Imagine the opportunities in real estate. You would make a massive return on your initial investment, Randy. I have shares in a company my brother-in-law set up selling plots of land on two of the moons and a central section on the planet itself. A Japanese consortium got in ahead of us for the other moons, but most of those are only asteroids. There will be demand for shops, houses, schools, swimming pools, cinemas, and hospitals; not to mention the mining rights. You can make billions on the Chinese tourist business alone."

"I want no return on my investment," Randy said. "When I sold all my properties – except this place – my important paintings, furniture, boats, planes, and helicopters, I got a better price for them second-hand than I paid in the first place. It's hopeless. I can't lose money."

His audience feared Randy was on the point of bursting into tears.

"No need to panic," the popular physicist added, wiping sweat from his face with the sleeve of his cheap pink shirt. "There's plenty worthless real estate out there in the solar system. Uranus will never be a fashionable destination. We can go there if you like."

Randy stared into the distance as if assessing whether living on some far away rock would give him the peace of mind he craved.

"Can't argue with someone with no values other than their

own self-aggrandizement," Bené the badly ageing rock star said, seemingly out of context.

While Wallace was interpreting this statement to mean Bené was acquainted with Progress, Randy asked to whom he was referring.

"Your popular scientist, here," Bené said. "He only wants to popularize physics on other planets. But don't despair, I have a superior plan that will meet your needs."

"Congratulations on your latest record," Samantha interrupted.

"Oh … err … thanks," he said. He was experiencing confused pride, though the Botox in his face prevented him manifesting the emotion.

"How many decades ago was that?" she added, smirking.

Bené cleared his throat. He ignored the question to focus on remembering his prepared speech. "The lads in the band and I have been doing some reading. According to Camus morality is made to appear complicated by political and religious authorities in order to confuse us."

"Is that a group?" Maxine asked.

"Albert Camus was a goal keeper and a philosopher," Wallace answered for Bené.

"For Camus morality is simple: stick up for your friends, be brave, and play fair," Bené said, concentrating on not being distracted.

"I have no friends," Samantha said.

"I hate sports," Progress said.

"I'm a coward," Wallace added, to complete the demolition of Camus's opinion.

Bené tried to make a face. "My band members and I follow

Camus in keeping it simple. We are not philanthropic novices. We have already combatted all sorts of diseases all over the planet. I estimate that with three hundred billion we could wipe out death in fifty years. I guarantee it. You will have all the patents on the best cures and saving lives attracts great tax breaks."

"I have already spent a fortune saving tax," Randy told him.

"But if no one dies, the planet will become even more packed. Randy can't tolerate crowds, even small groups like us," Samantha said.

"Her again," the popular physicist muttered. "That is why we will have to go to Jupiter. Give me the three hundred billion."

"He hasn't got that much money," Progress said. "Have you?"

"I have thought of that, smartass," Bené told Samantha, ignoring the scientist. "We will introduce mandatory sterilization to stop people reproducing. We can roll out a snipping programme in the poorest countries first," he said while making a scissors action with two fingers. "Naturally, we will have to allow a few elites to have babies: for example, those with musical genes."

Rik Wallace stood on the surface of a moon of Jupiter with Samantha. They were naked because they were ready to make a baby. A green leafy tattoo sprouted from the black pubic hair flowerpot between Samantha's thighs and spread out across her skin in search of the sun burning over her shoulder. A spider made its home in a web strung between her breasts and her chin.

"Kiss me," Wallace pleaded, trying not to breathe in, not because of her bodily odour but because he was afraid there might be no atmosphere. Maybe he would pass out in her arms. He didn't care. "Imagine, I didn't believe you were real," he said. He ran his fingers through her greasy hair before unconsciously wiping them on her flat chest.

"*Maybe I'm not real. You philosophers have trouble distinguishing between fact and fantasy.*"

"That's a problem for metaphysicians, which is a different branch of the discipline from mine. They don't know what is real. Epistemologists can't say what is true or false."

"*I can't tell what's right or wrong.*"

"Between us we have all the important areas covered. It's marvellous the way I can discuss anything with you. Have you considered becoming a therapist?"

Samantha vanished into a cloud of green gas rising from the surface of the moon.

"Yeah, the nasty people won't be allowed to have babies," Maxine was saying.

"Congratulations on your latest music video," Samantha put in.

"Thanks. Did you enjoy it? Go on. Tell me the truth. I can take it."

"No."

"Bitch. My idea is to remove all of the nasty people from the planet, thereby making extra room for the rest of us."

"Remove them?" Randy asked.

"Yes. The world will be fantastic when there are no nasty people like Jonathan – my latest ex-fiancé – living here," she said, pointing her gold lipstick holder at her host.

"What's your plan for spending all of Randy's money?" Samantha enquired.

"I haven't got one yet. Besides, that's not my job. Randy asked me to lend my face to his campaign," Maxine said. She spread her fingers in front of her eyes in overlapping fans before pulling her hands apart. She smiled for the camera that wasn't there.

"I have it," Samantha said. "We could put all the nasty people into rockets and send them to Jupiter. Is that an example of a synthesis, Professor?" she asked Wallace, smirking.

Our first lover's tiff, he thought. He smiled at the idea.

Wallace hoped Samantha imagined she loved him the way he imagined he loved her. It didn't matter that she didn't know him. In fact, if only she admired him before getting to know him, he would stand a better chance. Chance for what, he asked himself? He couldn't say. A vision of a wife appeared before him. She waved her fist in his face, surrounded by a swarm of children clinging to her eighteenth-century dress. When he asked himself why his wife was appearing to him in historical costume, he concluded that his fantasies were shaped by alcohol deprivation.

"We could start by rounding up Jonathan, his friends, his family, and all of his fans. Monica could decide, and Francine. Oh, I love her music," Maxine was talking.

"Would your celebrity moral police force wear uniforms?" Samantha asked.

"Oh, I didn't think of that. We could ask Ramiro to make

our costumes. He is a genius. I just love his work." She clapped her hands together. "Did you see his Milan collection? But he might refuse to design anything for the mass market, which is any number greater than one person. Wait, wait, I have it. The good people would wear Ramiro, and the nasty people would all be sent into outer space wearing other labels. I'm sure he would go for that."

"Could I volunteer to leave Earth with the nasty people?" Wallace asked Maxine to ingratiate himself with Samantha. He thought it might have worked because she, just then, stopped a smile from forming on her black lips, but only after he saw its first hints lift their corners. She does love me, he thought.

"Hmmm. I have to think about this. Let me text Monica." Maxine rummaged in her oversized handbag.

"I have another synthesis. You are all fucking mad," Samantha said.

"It's insensitive to refer to psychological states such as madness when someone here has been locked up in Saint Drogo's High Security Asylum for the Criminally Insane until recently," Progress said, waving her eyebrows in Wallace's direction.

"Wow, man. You were in Saint Drogo's?" Bené asked. "Our drummer spent six months in that place after our Let It All Hang Out World Tour."

"Shut up," Randy shouted, bringing an instant silence to the democratically shaped table. Maxine's fingers stopped moving above the screen on her mobile phone. Then he spoke just above a whisper. "In the beginning, when I first became staggeringly rich, I was naïve – perhaps like all of you are now. I thought doing the right thing was straightforward, like Bené here or Camus or, what's his name – the popular physicist. But now I suspect it is hopeless." His voice faded, causing his audience to lean over the table, straining to hear their sponsor's words. But Randy had nothing further to say. He put his face in his hands and sobbed.

Just then Wallace decided he liked the billionaire. Perhaps he recognized something of himself in the melancholic hunched over the table, crying. He would help him. He told himself his decision was not because he had fallen in love with Samantha and wanted to impress her with his goodness. No. It wasn't that. It was because he wanted to do good. His wife and children would have to take their own chances with Pandora.

Sensing some change in the emotional atmosphere in the room, Samantha, in turn – as if unconscious psychological threads linked their psyches – felt she hated the person who may have murdered her father less than she should. She knew Wallace from the hours her father devoted to gushing about his brilliance; from newspaper accounts of his lengthy trial; from peeping through a hole in the wall at him when he was undressing in his room at Fortune Mansion. But, technically, only twice because the third time she didn't open her eyes. Well, maybe, four times. But was *he* aware who she was?

"I am not surprised you are depressed because, in my experience as a professional moralist, humanitarian acts only make things worse," Wallace said in an attempt to cheer Randy up. But he was directing his words at Samantha rather than the billionaire. "However, one shouldn't stop trying to help others just because it's impossible. Altruism works in theory. Camus is partly correct. If you reflect too much on the practical implications of kindness, you turn it into something it's not."

"Altruism?" Maxine asked.

"Living in the interest of others," Bené explained.

"Do people do that?" Maxine giggled at the novel idea.

"Ethics is too difficult even for the greatest philosophers in history. The smart ones, such as Hegel, tried to keep as far away from it as possible. They stuck with a speculative metaphysics that is easy by comparison. Even Hegel's practical philosophy is abstract. Thinking opens up a chasm between our minds and the world. It's the same with love or poetry," Wallace said. He was still addressing Samantha at the other side of the table. "No one should be allowed to study those subjects. Love changes if you analyse it. It's Heisenberg's uncertainty principle."

"Wow. I'm impressed. You understand Heisenberg?" the popular physicist asked. "We covered his work on our fifth show."

Oh no, Wallace fretted. He was losing her attention. How could he turn the conversation back to the subject of himself, for Samantha's sake?

"Heisenberg?" Maxine asked.

"He invented quantum mechanics."

"It sounds complicated. Is it a type of electric car that's good for the environment?"

"In a way, yes."

"Maxine is too thick to appreciate the aesthetic appeal of quantum mechanics," Samantha said.

"Imagine, Maxine, a cat in a box on the back seat of your electric car. The cat is in a state of quantum superposition because he might be dead or alive; we can't tell," the popular physicist explained.

"Is the cat sick? My cat died."

I am acquainted with a cat I wish would die, Wallace thought, remembering Pandora and forgetting himself, and then immediately regretting his lack of sympathy for Marley.

"In a way, yes, the cat is sick because poison in a glass jar and a radioactive substance is in the box with the cat. The jar breaks if an internal monitor detects radioactivity, releasing the poison that kills the cat because, metaphysically, the cat is linked to a random subatomic event."

"Who linked him?"

"Schrödinger. He is Schrödinger's cat. You can't say whether the cat is alive or dead unless you peek inside, and of course, if you open the box then it wouldn't be the same thing, would it?"

"I suppose the cat would run away. I would."

"Who mentioned the stupid cat or Schrödinger?" Wallace asked. "I referred to Heisenberg to make a simple point."

"No. The cat wouldn't run away."

"You could shake the box and listen for a meow."

"Someone should find out if this is legal?" Bené said. "Man, I've gotten into trouble with experiments that weren't strictly above board. Can happen to anyone. I have the name of a great lawyer Schrödinger could talk to."

"He's dead. It's a thought experiment. Philosophers such as Wallace here do them all the time."

"Cruel bastards," Samantha said.

"Why are you looking at me like that? I didn't do anything to the fucking cat," Wallace protested. He instantly regretted swearing.

"The point is that quantum mechanics tells us that the cat is both alive and dead at the same time. Yet, if you look in the box, you perceive that the cat is either alive or dead, not both alive and dead."

"Did Schrödinger make a living out of this nonsense?" Bené asked.

The popular physicist was not to be deflected from his pedagogical mission.

"The cat is both dead and alive if you don't see inside the box. This poses the question of when quantum superposition ends and reality collapses into one possibility or the other."

"Do many people watch your show on television?"

"Forget the bloody cat. Doing the right thing is *doing*, not thinking., You will mess up whatever it is you are supposed to be thinking about if you think," Wallace interrupted. He was desperate to regain Samantha's sympathy. "Act. Don't think. You start with a simple question, say – what is the difference between right and wrong? It seems easy, but you make your first mistake. In order to say something sensible, you start reading a book, and you soon realize you don't understand what you are reading; so you find another book to understand the first one. Before you know it, you have read a pile of books, and you are so confused you become convinced you should sign up on a course where you learn all of the theory. You find yourself participating in discussions, and maybe even in extreme cases, attending conferences. Then after twenty years you can't remember what the question was you had in the first place. And then you die without achieving anything. Books should be banned, and life is meaningless."

"Yes. You die unless someone kills you first," Samantha said.

"Don't listen to him, Randy," Progress interrupted. "Unless

he means, don't try anything. You have experienced too much pain doing the right thing. You should stop now."

"Mindless altruism is the only way Randy can achieve peace of mind," Wallace told Progress. "Nothing he has tried has worked for him."

"That's not true. There are still cars, boats, watches, and houses he hasn't bought. And drugs. There are all sorts of pioneering drugs on the Internet you haven't tried. Oh Randy, don't do the right thing," Progress pleaded. "At least talk to Bené's drummer first."

"I have it," Wallace exclaimed, bringing his hand down flat on the table with a detonation that ended the pleading. Everyone stared at the sweating thinker. Randy had even removed his face from his hands to look at him.

"From where does inspiration spring?" Wallace asked no one in particular. Perhaps since now they knew he had been in a lunatic asylum no one dared to interrupt, and so he continued. "For some, it comes from science or spiritual meditation. For others, it is the outcome of an abstract thought experiment."

"What is he saying? Is he on drugs?" Bené whispered.

"What is your great idea? Spit it out," Progress demanded.

"What you need is a moral system that works only in theory. Let me help you build the first theoretically coherent moral framework. Immanuel Kant was unsuccessful, but he didn't have your money, Randy."

"Kant?"

"Oh God, Rik. Not Kant," Progress pleaded.

"Is he dangerous?" Bené asked.

"Who? Kant or Wallace?"

"Either. Both."

"Even the mention of his name makes Progress nervous. because she blames him for the rioting that caused the parents to pull their children out of CAT College. He did his thinking in the eighteenth century," Wallace explained.

"Oh, that's okay then," Randy said. "Don't worry about Kant, Julie, because he was around before computers."

"That's it," Wallace interjected. "Build a moral system based in artificial intelligence that will make judgements for us and end, once and for all, anyone ever having to decide what is right and wrong in a particular case: an automated process we can apply without thinking. Let computers get the headaches for us."

Samantha stood up. "We could start a social networking site dedicated to promoting random altruistic behaviour. Users share stories of unplanned kind acts they perform and their followers provide moral approval by clicking a heart button. The greater number of hearts you have, the kinder you are."

She does love me, Wallace thought. To hell with my children! They will forgive me for betraying them if Pandora doesn't kill them before they are old enough to understand why I did it.

"And … and … when someone reaches a million hearts Randy gives them a million quid." Maxine put in, getting into the spirit of the proposal.

"Great suggestion," Randy said. "That way I can get rid of loads of my money."

"It's supposed to promote kindness for its own sake," Samantha objected.

"Kindness in theory," Wallace added.

"Exactly, a complete waste of my money," Randy said. "I

love it. We will call it KindFace."

"I want the first profile. Oh, imagine the publicity. I will have the first ever KindFace page," Maxine said. "I will go down in history as the most – what was the word? Thank you, Bené – *altruistic* person ever. Wait till I tell Monica. She will be so pissed off."

"Samantha, as you have the technical expertise to make this work, and Professor Wallace has the moral knowledge, I propose you create this together," Randy said with rare enthusiasm.

"I don't want to work with him."

"Why not?" Wallace asked.

"Because you killed my father!"

Samantha's face turned red under the heavy white make-up. There, she had said it. She hadn't planned to, but it was out now. She couldn't take it back.

"Oh, that's nasty," Maxine said. She broke off texting Monica and Francine to examine the homicidal moralist for any hint of madness she missed earlier. "I knew it. Anyone who will do that thing to a cat with a jar of radioactive face cream is only a tiny step away from killing actual people. My cousin Kelvin was the same. He used to pull the legs off spiders; so the day that minibus full of tourists went missing, the police drove straight to his house. Okay, they found them in the pub, but that isn't the point."

"I did not kill your father."

"Liar. Liar and strangler."

"What do you mean? Spencer was strangled?" Wallace pleaded.

"Don't pretend you don't know. He was your friend, and

you killed him."

"Oh God. Spencer. Strangled? What happened? Progress, why didn't you tell me?"

"I didn't want you to be distracted from your mission."

Progress turned to Samantha. "He couldn't have killed your father because he was here with me at the time."

"You killed him because you were jealous of his intellectual powers. He was a genius," Samantha cried, ignoring the alibi.

"Jealous? Your father was a moron. Oh God – Samantha, I'm sorry. I have waited all my life to meet – I mean, I thought you weren't real. I thought he had made you up. You are real."

"Do you want to pinch me?" Samantha asked, holding out her arm to Wallace. "Is that the way philosophers establish whether or not people are real? Ouch."

She withdrew her hand, rubbing the red spot that appeared on the back of her thumb where he had squeezed her flesh between his fingers. "I hate you."

Wallace thought there was something deliciously chilling about being rejected by this enigmatic woman.

Now they were back in the garden amongst the ornamental hedges. *I forgive you, Rik, for killing my father. I could have done it myself because he was so annoying*, Samantha whispered, holding his face between her white hands. He would have pleaded innocence to the crime, but he didn't want to upset the mood. He wanted her to think well of him, whatever that might be.

"I am confident you will make the perfect team to build KindFace," Randy said. He smiled for the first time since Wallace met him.

"It's going to be huge," Maxine confirmed.

"I'll feature it on my television programme," the popular physicist said.

"It's going to be a hit," Bené said.

Progress had imagined, for a moment there, that Wallace had gone over to the other side and wanted to help Randy. But now she was unsure what to think because he seemed to have achieved an unexpectedly satisfactory level of moral confusion. Well, at least, *she* was bewildered.

She scowled at him because she wasn't going to let him know how she felt. What was this unfamiliar feeling rising from her stomach that grew in intensity each time she looked at Samantha Spencer? Why did a pasty-faced hacker make her feel angry? She told herself she wasn't jealous. After all, her boyfriend was a billionaire with an aversion to touching people. What more could she want?

Eustis looked around: slowly. He ducked through a door under the marble stairs when he saw the hall was empty. Inside, he switched on a light; pressed on a panel at the far end of a narrow room containing mops, buckets, and cleaning fluids; turned on another light; closed the panel behind him; and squeezed himself around a water cylinder to emerge into a wider space. He pressed a switch to extinguish the bulb over his head, before removing a wine cork jammed into the wall. Samantha stood by the bed removing her rigid leather jacket. Hah. As usual, he knew she knew he was there, so he was in for a show. She sat down on the bed and pulled off her biker boots, one at a time, dropping them onto the floor. She lay on her back and pressed her nose into an armpit. "Oh, she loves me," Eustis growled.

XX

Diversos Rationes
Conflicting Theories

Jackson followed Bernard the security guard – and now devotee of Freudian psychoanalysis – down the corridor of Saint Drogo's High Security Asylum for the Criminally Insane towards Professor Bentley Murphy's office. A cleaner, wearing light green overalls to signify his sanity, buffed the blue Marmoleum floor with a white woollen mop. The shine amplified the orchestra of squeaks produced by the soles of their shoes. Bernard guided him past Mother Theresa in the waiting room belting out the chorus: *"Bringing in the sheaves, bringing in the sheaves. We shall come rejoicing, bringing in the sheaves."*

He stood aside, pushed the office door open with the flat of his hand, and told Jackson to go straight in because the professor was expecting him.

Mother Theresa stopped singing to protest she had been waiting there all morning for just one glimpse of the psychiatrist within.

"He doesn't care about you," Bernard told her, unable to resist the recent growth of pedantry coinciding with his intellectual interest in madness.

"That's not true. He told me he loves me."

"I am confident that is an example of counter-transference. I haven't read that chapter yet, but I know typical transference is where you have redirected your feelings from a significant person in your past onto the professor. You need to stop that."

"Fuck you," the saint said before resuming her song.

In the office, they found the psychiatrist standing on the recently installed plywood chair. Bernard cleared his throat to drown out the racket from outside. But his boss seemed engrossed in studying the chandelier dangling from the ceiling.

"Someone supposedly sane to see you," he shouted by way of introduction, handing up a plain card on which the word "Jackson" was printed above a phone number.

Murphy climbed down without explanation and commanded his visitor to occupy his empty chair behind the desk while he perched on the plywood one. "No credentials, eh Jackson?" he asked, studying the card.

"No, Professor."

"No issues with just being yourself?"

"None."

"That is refreshing in my business. Tea, Jackson?"

"Yes, please."

"Bernard, will you ask Mother Theresa to break off singing and brew us a pot of tea. We will have a couple of slices of her delicious lemon cake to go with it. You must try it, Jackson. Inimitable flavour."

Murphy transferred himself to the chaise longue as Bernard departed on his errand. "It's my version of immersion therapy that I started here at Saint Drogo's. I predict fame for the hospital and a ground breaking article for me if it works.

If not, my successor can attempt something else. What use is a life without risk? Eh? Don't you agree?"

"I don't understand what you are talking about, Professor."

"The tea and cake."

"Risk?"

"I have assigned menial tasks to some of our patients on a trial basis."

"The security guard, Bernard, is one of your patients? No wonder you have so many escapes."

"No. No. Not Bernard. He is a real guard. The woman you passed on the way in the blue headscarf singing hymns is my patient. Mother Theresa."

"Why is she locked up in here?"

"We call her Mother Theresa because of her obsessive concern for the poor. She poisoned her family because she thought they were too prosperous. Oh, don't worry. I know what I am doing. She will never be fit to be released back into the community if we can't trust her to accomplish something as simple as making tea, will she? Besides she can't get strychnine in here. Bernard has all the keys to the secure pharmaceutical cabinets. You are safe. How can I help you, Jackson?"

"I was the police inspector who worked on the original Rik Wallace case at CAT College. These days, I am a private vigilante, righting wrongs. Where are you, Professor, in your investigation of Wallace? And don't ask me where he is because that is covered by client confidentiality."

"Where am I? Wouldn't I just love to know? I was asking myself the same question before you showed up. Where are any of us? You could pick any philosopher at random and they would give you a different answer to that conundrum. It would be easy to conclude that they are all wrong, wouldn't it?"

"Err … I suppose it would."

"But perhaps each one of them is addressing a different question. Imagine someone thinking Hegel, or Husserl, or even Adorno were concerned about the same kind of doubt."

"Indeed. Imagine that."

"We don't appreciate that what we don't know is not all the same sort of thing. Where am I, indeed?"

Jackson hoped the psychiatrist wasn't dangerous.

"Imagine thinking the realists and the idealists, deists, theists, and atheists have anything in common, even in the way in which they are confused on where they are in their lives? However, I suspect the realists and idealists are the same deep down. Don't you agree?"

"I definitely agree." Jackson lied to humour Murphy. A line of sweat broke out where his last strand of hair clung tenaciously to his scalp.

"With Husserl, we are concerned with meaning being revealed through a study of the structures of consciousness that is close to my own profession. I feel I am not wasting taxpayer's money reading him. And then if you take Adorno, you are looking at human suffering. A genius, even if he is a bit out of fashion these days. Somehow, suffering has lost its appeal in the contemporary world."

Jackson unbuttoned his jacket. "It's roasting in here. Can I open a window?" he asked.

"I'm afraid not. Security risk since the escapes."

"Escapes? You mean there was more than one?"

"Yes, practically a stampede. Well two. It hasn't been in the newspapers, but a therapist, Tiberius Lang, escaped with

Wallace."

"A therapist? Why would a therapist need to escape?"

"Because he was insane."

"Insane because he escaped?"

"Forget I said anything. Open the window if you like."

"My wife and I are worried about Wallace since his friend Maurice Spencer was strangled to death."

"Oh, yes. That was an awful business. Inspector Sullivan believes Wallace did it."

Jackson kept his opinion of his one-time assistant to himself.

"Clearly, Tiberius Lang, the therapist who escaped with Wallace killed Spencer during a counselling session," Murphy continued. "Tiberius had a penchant for strangling his clients when he had a practice."

"Aren't they trained not to be judgemental?"

"They are, but sometimes it is impossible not to form an adverse opinion when you hear some of the things on the minds of even normal people."

Bernard, pushing the door open with his buttocks, carried a tray into the office and placed it on the edge of the desk. He began to pour steaming liquid from a large circular porcelain pot into two cups of an almost matching pattern.

"Will you join us for tea, Bernard?"

"No thanks, Professor; my wife gives me a flask in the mornings."

"Bernard's wife may have an obsessive-compulsive disorder manifesting itself as a morbid fear of psychiatric facilities: a form of dementophobia. She needs help. I have asked him to bring her in for free treatment – one of the perks of the job. We value our employees and their families."

"I told the Professor here she said she wouldn't put a toe past the fence, not even for the Christmas party. Her cousin visited his mother in one of these institutions for a half hour on a Sunday, and he is still there – twenty-two years later." Bernard put the pot on the desk when he finished pouring and stomped out of the office to emphasize the strength of his wife's prejudice.

Jackson sipped the tea, his tongue searching for any unfamiliar flavour.

Murphy drank a mouthful without milk or sugar, swallowed, and waited several seconds before repressing the almost unfelt disappointment that he was still conscious. "Where were we? Ah, yes. I suspect Tiberius will go after Wallace next. This is a complex case," the professor said, leaning back on the chaise longue and elevating his feet, one ankle resting on the other. He interrupted his treatise to chew on a large slice of cake sitting on a chipped plate balanced on his stomach beside the cup and saucer, paused to swallow, looked around the office for a reason unknown to Jackson, sighed, and continued talking.

"This cake tastes so moreish. You must ask for the recipe for me," Jackson lied.

"Mother Theresa says the ingredients are a family secret handed down from one generation to another. Although, as she is here because she has wiped out the last lot, the secret may die with her." Murphy laughed at the irony. "Now, where was I? Oh, yes. Tiberius is a tragic case. He is a victim of psychology. Believe it or not it can happen. His parents were both psychologists in competing paradigms: one a behaviourist and the other a psychoanalyst. Can you imagine two less compatible perspectives?"

"No, I cannot imagine, but my reading in that field is limited. When I first met my wife, who was a librarian at the time, I borrowed weighty books that I lied to her were for my research into Wallace. I was trying to impress with my supposed erudition. But I soon realized I should be myself. You are storing up trouble if you have someone fall in love with a false version of yourself."

The librarian had warned her husband before he left home that morning that he should not enter into a conversation on or even remember anything at all to do with his own childhood while interviewing Professor Murphy. By saying nothing he could hope to remain in control of the situation. "I didn't have a childhood," he said out loud.

"That is quite unusual. Most of my clients have had one. Without even consulting my notes, I am certain they were all children once."

"I came into the world fully formed, the way I am now. It happens," Jackson said voicing the lines the librarian had prepared for him.

"Ah, you are a product of spontaneous generation?"

A scream from somewhere interrupted his thinking process. Murphy chewed on a mouthful of cake, listening. He continued when he heard the reassuring sound of running feet. "I have heard of your sort, but I have never met one before," he said when satisfied a chase was underway outside. "Thought-provoking; convenient; disappointing, Jackson. Anyway, I can't imagine what bitterness lay beneath that veneer of domestic bonhomie Tiberius's parents deployed to pretend they didn't hate each other with all of the bitter intensity typical of rival perspectives on human nature. They wouldn't be normal if they hadn't. God knows what they could have seen in each other, one being an analyst and the other a behaviourist? He claims he had a perfect childhood, but that is classic denial; which is understandable as he struggled to cope with home life. In my business, if someone tells you something, you can be certain the opposite is true. Would you like another piece of cake, Jackson?"

"Yes, please," Jackson said, trying to hide the slice he was now pretending to eat in his pocket.

"Classic paranoia?"

"What? I mean who?"

"Tiberius Lang."

"Oh, yes."

"Naturally, his parents pressured him into following in their footsteps, but which theory was he supposed to espouse: behaviourism or psychoanalysis? Can you imagine a more pernicious predicament?"

"I can't," Jackson lied. He no longer cared what he was saying. He studied the slice of cake and wondered what Mother Theresa had put in it. If not strychnine, then perhaps some of her own medication prescribed to prevent her putting strychnine in cakes?

"Professor, what did you say was wrong with Mother Theresa?"

Murphy ignored the question, being in full analytic flow on another case. "The conflict unhinged Tiberius both emotionally and intellectually, and this manifested itself in an obsession with Wallace. I didn't think it was important at the time, but reading through his scant case file since his escape, I noted that during one session he told me he was searching for the ideal client; because it's obvious – don't you see, Jackson?"

"No. I mean, yes. Yes, I do see, but you see it clearer than me. Tell me what I see." Jackson ran two fingers across his forehead. Did he have a fever or was that steam from the tea?

"He believes that Wallace is the incarnation of *the* client who will ultimately help him resolve the methodological predicament foisted onto him in childhood: a crisis representing the displaced act of choosing between his mother or father, rather than anything in the approach itself. You might consider his parents unimaginably cruel to put him through that, but at least he was given a choice – which I wasn't. Parents are bastards, Jackson. Don't you agree? The world would be better off without them? What attracted you to the police force?"

The question took Jackson off guard. Why had he ever wanted to enforce the law? Was it his sense of fairness? And was that the same lure that had ultimately turned him away from it? Only idealists like this Tiberius maniac and he could experience such disillusion. Where was the meaning he once got from solving crimes? His original desire to do the right thing remained with him still.

He remembered the physical bulk of his father beside him and above him. He was eight. "Trust me, I know what is best," his father said. "Shoot him as he runs towards you. He won't know what hit him. He will die happy. It's not fair on anyone to keep a dog that's gun-shy. We can't afford to feed a creature that doesn't contribute. He is not a pet." Young Jackson squinted down the barrel of his gun, Biscuit coming into focus on top of the end sight, the duck between his teeth producing a smile on his golden face. Biscuit was not a pet. He wasn't allowed to lie in the bottom of the bed with his stomach warming the soles of Jackson's feet, but he did it anyway. He wasn't allowed to clamp his teeth into Jackson's wellington boots and drag them out from under the chair when Jackson arrived home from school to signal his desire to run with him through the fields behind the house. But he did it anyway, heedless of the resentment he was storing up in the adults. He wasn't allowed to sit on Jackson's feet, laughing, under the table in practised anticipation of a half-chewed piece of chicken landing in front of his nose.

"Shoot," his father commanded. "For God's sake, shoot before he gets all the way back here." Young Jackson felt a hot tear run down his cheek and across his trembling fingers grasping the stock of the rifle. His father sucked in air between his teeth, swore, raised his gun and fired in a single smooth motion that would have impressed a drill sergeant. Young Jackson did learn from that life lesson what betrayal on a friend's face looked like.

"I forget why I joined the police," Jackson lied, remembering his wife's advice. He wiped away a tear with his sleeve that he hoped the psychiatrist didn't see. Thank God he is lying down looking at the ceiling, he told himself, surreptitiously glancing over at the psychiatrist. "As I told you already, I didn't have a childhood: nothing before the age of thirteen."

"Pity. Good God. I even allowed Tiberius to change places with me during our sessions. Do you realise what that means? I enabled his psychosis."

Jackson mopped his forehead with a handkerchief he pulled from his pocket, causing a slice of half-eaten cake to roll onto the desk. I'm dizzy, he told himself, struggling to focus on the hand he held up in front of his eyes, wondering whose it was.

"Are you alright, Jackson?" Murphy asked, his psychological instincts working even while he continued to stare at the ceiling.

"I'm fine," Jackson lied. Keep lying, he told himself.

"Tiberius blamed what he regarded as his own inadequate intellect for not coming up with a synthesis of behaviourism and psychoanalysis when he should have recognized it as the fundamental structural incommensurability at the heart of psychology and – indeed – parenting. I'm a very insightful psychiatrist, Jackson, but usually only after it's too late to benefit my patients. I realise now a straightforward timely reading of Thomas Kuhn's *The Structure of Scientific Revolutions* would have set Tiberius right. How much needless lunacy could be avoided if people read the right books? But that is a question for another session, eh, Jackson? You will be coming back?"

"Definitely," Jackson lied. But now he was worried. The professor wants me to come back for extra emergency sessions. What is wrong with me? I thought I was normal until a minute ago. Oh, God. I am going mad. What is in this tea? He peered into the cup.

"Good. I find you make an excellent sounding board. Are you sure you are not hiding a deep mind from me? Imagine Tiberius chose counselling as a possible compromise to his unsolvable dilemma," Murphy laughed. "I always say the choices that are easy to make when we are young are the hardest to live with when we are older. Don't you agree, Jackson? God, how naïve even a homicidal maniac can be? There is a lesson in this on the dangers of relativism and eclecticism, as well as a scholarly paper. Excuse me, while I scribble a few notes.

Sometimes I frighten even myself." Murphy sat up.

I am terrified, Jackson confirmed to himself.

"Tiberius killed Spencer as the first step on his route to Wallace – there's another case I worked out too late – that much should be obvious even to Inspector Sullivan from a simple interpretation of the displaced impulses, let alone the overwhelming circumstantial evidence." Murphy brought his palm down onto his thigh to punctuate the analysis that was exhausting his visitor. The sound brought Jackson back to the office from the padded cell where his imagination had already confined him.

"You should worry about your friend … err … client, Wallace, because he is in the gravest danger. Tiberius sees him as the embodiment of the ideal neurotic. Hah, it's a simple case of sublimation. I am ashamed to say I should have seen it ages ago."

The psychiatrist was standing, waving the teapot in front of Jackson.

"I have had enough," Jackson pleaded. Of what he didn't specify. He straightened up in the upholstered chair. "I came here to get information on Wallace's family," he told the psychiatrist. "I promised I would help reunite him with his wife and children."

"Now that brings us on to something embarrassing. I lost my usual composure that defines my general approach to all my clients because I may have been antagonised by aspects of my own behaviour that I subconsciously saw in him. Ourselves, Jackson, often repel us. I thought Wallace was deliberately frustrating me by lying about who he was and repressing memories of his family. Anyway, that was before I discovered

Sullivan screwed that up."

"What do you mean by screwed that up? Is that some psychological terminology?"

Murphy put the teapot on the desk and lay back down on the chaise longue.

"No. It's a straightforward blunder. There was a mix-up with the DNA and hotel room numbers. Didn't Sullivan tell you?"

"No. I had left the force by then."

"Anyway, who knows who Wallace's family are or if they even exist? Wallace may be too rational for his own good. A normal patient would have agreed that he was who I said he was. But not with too much enthusiasm, mind you, which I would have seen through. Just the exact amount required," Murphy said. He rubbed his fingers against his thumb as if sprinkling salt onto his prone stomach. "It's not an excuse, but I would have had something to work with if he had been a little mad when he got here. I might be better off myself if I was a little madder too. Please tell him I am sorry for what I put him through in therapy when you see him. Raking up all that sludge from the bottom of his psychic pond: sludge, it seems, that wasn't even his. I never want to meet Wallace again. I mean, who wants to be confronted by their glaring mistakes walking around on two legs. My priority is to find Tiberius before he strangles anyone else in his search for Wallace."

"So, how am I supposed to find his real family with no leads to go on?" Jackson wondered aloud. Despite the librarian's warnings he decided it was time to talk. Perhaps he could mention his recurring dream about the bag of kittens his father made him drown when he was nine.

Jackson flipped over the "Come In, We're Open" sign as he rushed through the red telephone-box doors of the second-hand bookshop. "Get out, we're closed," he grunted at the lone customer browsing a shelf of books on extra-terrestrial travel.

The librarian put down the book she had been reading when she saw her husband's face, that for once, was not wearing the upside-down smile he put on whenever he caught sight of his wife. "What's wrong?" she asked, climbing down off the high stool.

"I got some disturbing information from Rik Wallace's psychiatrist, Murphy. It seems that idiot Sullivan isn't the only one looking for him. Another escaped maniac, Tiberius Lang, is also on his trail. His parents drove him insane by making him choose between divergent approaches to psychology that he was unaware at the time were incommensurable because he hadn't read Thomas Kuhn. That means that Hegelian classic triad of thesis, antithesis, synthesis could be wrong."

"Are you aware you are babbling? I warned you not to mention your childhood to that psychiatrist. Not one word. You didn't tell him about your father, did you? You promised me you wouldn't. Did he make you take something?"

"Mother Theresa's lemon drizzle cake and lots of tea. A classic case of Freud's theory of psychodynamic abnormality where psychosis is caused by an unresolved childhood conflict."

"Is that what he said you have?"

"No. Not me. Tiberius Lang. Okay, maybe me too."

"You look green. You're sweating."

"And it seems, even though he denied it all along, Wallace isn't aware he wasn't married to that pregnant woman with the children Sullivan brought to CAT College to confront him. His psychiatrist told me in the strictest confidence that the pressure he put Wallace under to recognize them as his may have driven him around the bend. In other words, he was as sane as you or I when he was carted off to Saint Drogo's."

"Even I appreciate that, and I don't know anything about Hegel or Freud."

"Shouldn't we warn Wallace that Tiberius Lang is after him?"

"He has enough on his mind with his current responsibilities without worrying about some maniac hunting him. Did you tell him where Wallace is?"

"No. No. I don't think so. Anyway, he doesn't want to meet Wallace ever again because he can't face being confronted with his psychiatric mistakes. I told him everything else though. He said I need to go back as soon as possible for at least twenty more sessions."

"Wallace is safe from Tiberius Lang in Fortune Mansion."

"Oh, what are we going to do? We have no leads on his missing wife and children. We don't even know if they exist."

"You are overreacting. One family is much the same as another. Surely those we can find will suffice if we can't find the real ones. Wallace is not your average parent obsessed with having the right children around him all the time. Human individuality is overrated. I can't understand the fuss. There must be tons of files on missing people back at the police station. No one would mind you borrowing a few. Trust me, relatives are interchangeable, especially if you can't remember them. What can go wrong?"

"After just one session with Murphy I'm starting to think

families can be tricky. I need to think it through, but first I have to go upstairs and throw up. I'm sure Mother Theresa poisoned me. Call a doctor, a real doctor, not a bloody philosopher or a psychiatrist."

XXI

Olet Aemulatione
Smells Like Jealousy

Rik Wallace spun the ornate globe in the empty library in Fortune Mansion with the tips of his fingers as he waited for his true love to appear on the other side of the planet. He passed the time imagining their first moments alone together. She would fling herself into his arms.

"Kiss me," he would say, crumpling her against his chest.

She would resist for a demure second, holding his beating heart back with her palms. *"I can't kiss you because I am still in mourning for my father. Perhaps we should wait until tomorrow before surrendering to our feelings?"*

The aroma of a rancid, second-hand leather biker's jacket stung his nostrils like chilli. She was standing in front of him when he looked up. He held his breath.

"I don't care what Randy says, I refuse to work with you because you killed my father," Samantha told him.

Her eyes sparkled with irritation. His shone from suffocation.

"Not that again. Even if I did kill him, which I didn't, that shouldn't stand in the way of our relationship because you hated him."

"That might be true if we were in a relationship, which we never will be. Besides I stopped hating him after he was murdered. But I admit he did annoy me while he was alive," she added, in what he interpreted to be a softening of her hostility towards him. "That is normal, isn't it?" she added, her temper already running low.

"Who cares what anyone says, I think you are normal."

"Well, you are not." Her anger was returning.

"Your father was my friend." He worried that if this conversation continued he might voice something fatal to the love that he felt was blossoming between them. He couldn't tell the difference between a real and an imaginary emotion when it came to desire. He thought he had better change the topic. But he didn't. "Your father retreated into Eastern meditation to embrace something untainted by the contemporary world."

"I should have tried harder to understand him when I had the chance, but he annoyed me so much I wanted to strangle him. Oh, God, I shouldn't have said that."

"Isn't it funny how understanding people is easier when they are dead?" Wallace said. He was happy. At least they were still talking. He wanted to ask if he died would she understand him?

Let's not discuss your father, he thought. At least not while we are falling in love. The topic reminded him of Freud – the real one; not Tiberius Lang – and of the many differences between Samantha and him. His face was in an invisible cloud of digested onions. He squeezed his eyes shut and blinked them open again. "Have you had any thoughts at all about our KindFace project? Have you had any ideas about kindness?" he asked, reluctantly switching from the affairs of the heart to the prosaic topic of work.

"Well, yes, I did," she said, softening to her favourite subject. "Once I start analysing a programming challenge such as this one on the relationship between morality and technology, it's hard to stop."

"You are so pragmatic."

"Women are more practical than men."

"So, you admit men are more romantic? We fall in love easily."

She remained silent on her side of the planet.

You wouldn't have practical thoughts if you loved me, he wanted to tell her. Nor would you eat onions.

She spoke. "What contribution do you propose to make to the moral aspects of my programme? You don't have a clue, do you?"

"I do have clues," he lied. "But I am bound by the secret code of philosophers not to say what they are."

"What code?" she snapped.

He pulled in his elbows as his imaginary Samantha tickled him under the arms to get him to tell. Perhaps he had gone so long without a drop of alcohol, he was finding it harder to tell the difference between who Samantha was and who he wanted her to be. But wasn't alcohol supposed to cause that kind of disorientation in the first place? He was confused. Maybe he loved both versions of her: the real and his imaginary? Maybe they were one? Or maybe it was the effect of withdrawal from the drugs pumped into him at Saint Drogo's. Could Murphy's treatment have been working all along because he didn't feel any more insane – however, that might feel – than when he first got out of the asylum. He barely remembered who he had been pretending to be or who he was supposed to be now.

"What code?" Her shouted question brought him back to planet Earth that was beginning to slow on its axis. He clamped his hand over his nose when assailed by the smell of a pungent cheese. "The code shared by those who know the meaning of life," he muttered through his fingers.

"Oh, that," she said, obviously disappointed. "I thought for a moment that, unlike every other philosopher, you had a useful programmable idea. You are as bad as my father."

"God, you are obsessed with him," he told her.

"I wouldn't describe it as an obsession. He has been murdered, and you are a suspect."

"So are you. You practically confessed. You said you wanted to strangle him. Freud believes every woman falls in love with her father," he added before she could think of anything to say.

"That's Jung's Electra complex. It's similar to Freud's Oedipal complex, but for girls," Samantha corrected him.

"Aha! You are interested in emotions and not only heartless computers?"

Samantha sighed.

"I had to read my father's books because there was nothing else in the house except all the crap he collected on human consciousness and S&M. Jung was a moron, same as my father used to be when he was alive, and just like you are now."

At that moment Julie Progress, who was outside with her ear pressed to the door straining to hear what was being said, lost her balance and fell into the room. She picked a pellet of fluff from the carpet as if that had been her true purpose all along in stretching out on the floor. "Eustis told me I might find you in here," she announced, getting up off her knees. "What are you doing? Aren't you supposed to be programming?" she asked Samantha.

"We were trying to find inspiration," Wallace said as he accelerated the globe with the tips of his fingers as it came to a stop. "We were discussing Jung's Electra complex," he added.

"Isn't that where daughters fall in love with their fathers?"

"We are discussing our project, KindFace," Samantha said, pushing past Progress, who clamped a hand over her nose. She slammed the door behind her.

"I doubt she is right for you," Progress said.

"What do you mean?"

"She is not your type."

"What is my type?"

"Someone who smells fresh."

"She doesn't believe in washing away her natural oils and minerals. You are jealous, aren't you?"

"I am not. She stinks."

"You used to be a slob before you started living with an eccentric billionaire."

"Well, she is also a nerd."

"Yes, but an attractive one."

"Have you had your eyesight tested since you got out of that asylum?"

"My eyes are working fine."

"You should be ashamed of yourself. You are married with countless children."

"You didn't care about them when we were together."

"That was different. I was unaware of the orphans you had abandoned."

"I have been having dreams about you."

"What am I wearing in these dreams?"

"Nothing. The picture of your beautiful body must be burnt into my unconscious to materialize whenever I close my eyes."

"You are sick. How do I behave in these naked dreams?"

"You are in bed with me."

"Go on."

"You are on one side, and Samantha is on the other."

"Stop. Enough. I'm not sharing your deranged fantasy with her. Listen, Rik. You can trust me. I got you out of that horrid asylum, found you this great job confusing Randy, and accommodation in this fabulous mansion—"

"You did that for yourself – and Pandora."

"I'm telling you as a friend that she is not your type."

"You mean you believe she likes me?"

"Your mind is muddled. You've been in a lunatic asylum. You're a rationalist, Rik. Ask yourself why you were locked up in the first place. It's because you are crazy. Samantha would be mad to be attracted to you."

"Maybe we are both unbalanced. That could work, couldn't it? It would be ideal if we were both unstable in the same way – or even in complementary ways."

Progress couldn't come up with a reasonable, or even an unreasonable, response. She settled on, "Keep away from each other." She turned on her heel and departed.

Wallace was thinking that if Progress was jealous, then maybe Samantha did love him. Well, he was nuts, wasn't he?

XXII

Causa Et Effectus
Cause and Effect

Tiberius Lang was aware he was a victim of his own impatience. A few more minutes tolerating Maurice Spencer's self-indulgent drivel and he would surely have discovered Rik Wallace's whereabouts. But all was not yet lost. Casper Wall would tell him why he hired Wallace and where he was now. Casper leaned forward in the leather office chair and pushed the crystal decanter towards his guest, skating it across the expansive polished surface of his desk. "Help yourself," he said, sliding a cut glass after it. "I didn't expect to have another visit from Rik Wallace's eminent forensic psychiatrist so soon. You must be worrying about my mental health."

"Do you need counselling?" Tiberius Lang asked.

"Definitely not."

"Are you sure? None of us is that normal."

"Nothing in here needs fixing," Casper said, tapping the side of his skull. "I am technical. Same as a computer, I have no feelings." He dismissed a call on his mobile phone.

"No feelings? You are lucky," Tiberius said, genuinely impressed.

"Maybe not ordinary feelings. But I do have an

uncomfortable sensation in my chest that goes down my side and into my groin when I picture Julie Progress sitting where you are now. Is that normal?"

"That depends on who this Julie Progress is!"

"She used to be Wallace's girlfriend. Didn't he mention her in his extensive psychiatric sessions with you at the hospital? Most people blame his insanity on reading Nietzsche but, if you ask me, she is the reason he ended up in your asylum. At least she drives *me* crazy."

"Ah, yes," Tiberius said. He pretended to consult his notes in the tiny book he removed from the inside pocket of Bentley Murphy's Harris tweed jacket. The coat had become one of his minor compulsions, along with the banana yellow hatchback. "You say she *used to be* Wallace's girlfriend. Has that relationship ended? Do you think he might want to rekindle the flames now that he is free?" So, here was yet another person he might analyse in the event Casper frustrated his patience.

"I am not sure, but with Julie the past tense is the most common in her relationships. Though I am looking forward to a time in the near future when she will remember me fondly as one of her exes. Do you do relationship counselling, Professor? Help people to impress the ladies; advise them on how best to unleash their hidden attractions. That sort of thing?"

"You should try a dating site on the Internet." Tiberius scribbled notes in the unlined page balanced on his knee. "It might prove vital for Wallace's sanity if you can tell me every detail about this Julie Progress person. Is there anything at all, even some insignificant teensy-weensy thing that might provide a psychological breakthrough in my understanding of her, such as the colour of her hair – or her address?"

"Oh, that's easy. In the mornings here in the office when we gather for a strategy meeting and the sun lands on her head at just the precise angle, her hair is the colour of gold with lines of copper and I can't concentrate on— But I dare not tell you where she lives because that's supposed to be confidential."

"I am a therapist. Everything I hear is confidential."

"In that case, what's the harm? Julie persuaded me to hire Wallace for a special task. I'm not paying his salary, though. She is in cahoots with Pandora – the last time you were here you met her—" Wall said. He formed circles with his fingers and held them in front of his eyes as an aide-memoire for Tiberius. "Bloodshot eyes? No? Oh, you wouldn't have seen them under the sunglasses. Lucky you. And cigarettes? Puff, puff?"

"Yes, I remember her," Tiberius said, suppressing a shiver when the memory crystalized as a tread of ice in the marrow in his spine. He wondered if Pandora would make an engaging client before dismissing the idea with an imperceptible shudder. He remembered the black sunglasses focussed on him like a stereoscopic camera. But he was desperate to find Wallace – desperate.

"Are you sure you won't have a drink?"

"No, thank you. Hired him to work on what?" Tiberius almost shouted, before composing himself again. He needed all of the very limited capacity for patience he had developed as a therapist to keep Casper focussed.

Casper sighed. "I am surprised. You are supposed to be the high and mighty forensic psychiatrist. Isn't it obvious to someone of your experience why I would hire Wallace despite what happened here the first time around?"

"Yes, it's obvious," Tiberius lied. "But I would rather hear it in your words: your interpretation of the case. By the way, don't you consider it a little early in the day for drinking—what is that?"

"Port."

"Port?"

"Not just any port, but the finest vintage. No. Now is a good time," Casper confirmed, consulting his watch by holding his left wrist steady in front of his eyes with his right hand. "Everything you observe around you here is a wonderful collective dream," he said, spreading his arms wide to encompass the office, the building, and the car parks beyond. "Candid Online College." He stopped to lean across the desk to retrieve the neglected decanter and refill his own glass.

Tiberius was waiting for him to continue without a prompt, but he cracked first. "I know where I fucking am," he growled.

"I know you know where you are, but what you would imagine a normal person would know is that giving away all of your money would be an alarm clock."

"Alarm clock?"

"Waking us up from our fantasy."

"Is Wallace rich?"

"Not Wallace. For a psychiatrist you are quite slow, Professor. You must be aware people don't enjoy waking up."

"How does Pandora imagine Wallace can help you avoid waking up?" Tiberius asked, naïvely hoping Casper may have a rational answer.

"I imagine it must be much the same with insanity."

"What is?"

"Madness creates further madness. Like money and rabbits."

"What are you saying?"

"Drink. Finest port rabbits can buy."

"You are completely pissed."

Casper ignored the observation. "You understand Wallace from his time at your asylum. He is able to confuse anyone, and as Pandora says, bewilderment stymies action."

"Completely pissed."

"Or was that Spencer who said that? At least, that is what someone says. People in universities overuse the term, but Pandora is a genuine genius. We are very fortunate to have one here. Most colleges would be lucky to have even half a one. She says Wallace's powers of confusion almost worked on her."

"Can I get you a coffee?"

"No. I am a genius too. Always have been. Child prodigy, you know. Technical intelligence. So, let me see: that is two geniuses; three if you throw in Wallace's genius for confusion."

"I was a child prodigy too."

"What field?"

"Emotional intelligence."

"Not the most useful talent, but now that poor Ernst Fischer and Maurice Spencer are gone, we have a few openings here in the college. Are you interested in teaching, Professor? No experience needed because we are online. You don't even have to meet the students," Casper laughed.

"Teaching? I'd rather remove my eye with a cold spoon."

"That's the attitude I hope to find in our online lecturers. I can fix you up with an office. We have loads of room here. You could teach something in forensic psychiatry. That would be popular. You must be acquainted with many criminally insane persons you could persuade to make cameo appearances.

They could give their side. I am sure there is an imbalance in favour of the perspective of the sane person on the courses our competitors offer. Our students would love that."

"What?"

"Yes. It will be huge in pedagogical circles. Poor Spencer was into mindfulness, but injections are where it's at," Casper mimicked holding a syringe to his neck. "Our students are interested in learning everything they can about drugs. And straightjackets," he added splashing his drink across Tiberius and the wall while wrapping his arms around his chest to illustrate restraint. "And electric shock therapy," he said. He shook his head and rolled his eyes in imitation of a convulsion that for a second Tiberius thought was real. "Don't forget to put plenty of volts on your syllabus. Yes, technology is the future, Professor."

Tiberius waved a hand in front of Casper's face.

"What did you hire Wallace to do?" he asked, surprisingly calm.

"What do you imagine? Isn't it obvious? We hired him to philosophize. It's the one thing he can do. He is with Julie Progress. I don't know what she sees in him. I hope he is causing maximum confusion."

"More than you are?" Tiberius wondered aloud. "Where is Julie Progress?" he asked, remaining composed, hoping to track down his quarry by increments. "Where can I find her? It is too complicated to explain to you in detail why I must find her to maintain Wallace's mental balance so just tell me where she is. Please."

"Okay, but only if you promise to tell her when you see her that, in your professional mental opinion, she and I are the perfect psychiatric couple."

"I promise," Tiberius lied with enthusiasm.

"Okay, so I will tell you, but I am going to stop after that because I have already said too much. Then I will clam up like a clam. Oh, you're good," Casper said, wagging a finger. "I suppose it's all the psychiatric training you have gone through. Getting people to talk. Blah, blah, blah! But as you say, everything is confidential. Drink? You haven't tried this port. It's an exceptional vintage. It's surprising what I can afford to spend on booze since I became provost."

"Where. The Fuck. Is She?"

As Tiberius's hand closed around the cable ties in his pocket, there was a knock on the door. His fingers sprang apart as a line of people began to stream in.

"Is that the time?" Casper asked himself, squinting at the doubling screen on his mobile phone. "Oh, I forgot I have a marketing meeting for our newest online business courses. Boring, but someone has to sleep through it," he laughed. "You should stay, Professor. We would value your opinion."

Tiberius stood up, put away his tiny notebook, and walked out without saying goodbye, his fingers opening and closing on the cable ties in his pocket. In the hall he kicked the wall in frustration. "So fucking close," he snarled.

XXIII

Bonum Est Non Loqui
It's Good Not to Talk

Pandora closed the S&M subscription magazine she had been flicking through, unable to give her undivided attention to the articles. "I can't concentrate," she said, throwing the magazine across the coffee table as proof of her distraction. Horse sat opposite in one of the pair of matching floral armchairs in their sitting room; those seats annoyed her because he had bought them from an online catalogue without consulting her. He was knitting, his tongue protruding from between his teeth in concentration at a tricky row, terrified of dropping stitches again. He placed the almost-finished hot-water bottle cover on his knees and began stretching out its corners with his chubby fingers, forcing the wool into a shape bearing some resemblance to a bottle. He held his head sideways, appraising his craftwork. The woollen rectangle sprung back into a sphere the moment he let go.

She snatched up the receiver when the phone rang. Jackson, whom she hadn't heard from in ages, was hysterical. Between something about lemon cake, Mother Theresa and tea she deciphered that an escaped lunatic Tiberius Lang who bore an uncanny resemblance to Sigmund Freud strangled Maurice

Spencer and now wanted to strangle Rik Wallace. Jackson also passed on the gossip that Wallace's family that she had threatened to kill weren't his. She hung up without speaking.

"So, Horse, dear, Jackson – remember him? Yes, we haven't seen him in ages. Yes, typical he only rings when there is a crisis, but that's the way people are. Anyway, it appears the real Professor Murphy, who interestingly was not the one we met at the college is convinced the fake psychiatrist, Tiberius Lang – yes, I am sure it was him because Jackson said Murphy said he was the image of Sigmund Freud – strangled Spencer and is searching for Wallace to throttle him too. I knew Spencer couldn't resist an opportunity to talk about himself with the first therapist that came along. I appreciate they don't all have the same qualifications, but his being a lunatic doesn't necessarily put him in a position to help anyone with their emotions, does it – even Spencer? It's a disgrace. That high-security asylum is like a sieve. How are ordinary people supposed to sleep in their beds at night when they can't keep dangerous psychopaths locked up?"

Pandora's predatory instincts were on alert now there was another predator so close. She didn't welcome the competition.

Horse pushed his index finger through a hole in the middle of the hot-water bottle cover and made a face. He sighed and began to slide the stitches from the needles in preparation for starting again for the fifth time that day.

"I could have done without this complication. I have enough problems without having to think. You know I cannot stand thinking," Pandora shrieked. "Everything is falling apart around me. All I ever wanted was to make the best possible home for us, and for that to happen, things must go on the same as they always have done. No changes. No innovations. Feel that heart," she said, lifting herself from the seat and clamping Horse's palm onto her breast. "That is the beat of a conservative. Imagine that greasy-haired Ernst Fischer with the dandruff – ugh – lecturing me on Kant after all I've been through. What was I thinking allowing Julie Progress to persuade me to spring Rik Wallace from that nuthouse? I must be out of my mind. Wallace is barely out of that asylum, and Maurice Spencer is dead. Wallace is supposed to be disturbing Randy Fortune's peace of mind, not mine. What have I ever done to deserve this?"

Joy Division on the radio agreed she had lost control.

Pandora lit a cigarette to aid her reluctant thinking process. "Maybe I should tell Wallace about Tiberius. After all, I made him help us by threatening to kill his children, and now I discover they aren't even his. I'm no expert, but I imagine, in general, people would benefit from knowing whom they are and are not married to. Remember, Horse, you and I are happily married to each other! I can't imagine anything more horrible than suddenly finding myself responsible for a swarm of snotty infants. I wouldn't sleep at night worrying that they might appear at the end of my bed. He must be conflicted not knowing whether he should hope I kill them or not. But they were the only thing with which I could think to blackmail him. I am ashamed, Horse. I do have a conscience. I should have threatened to kill him not them. That would have been ethical, I think. But look at the mess killing Fischer got me into, and I didn't even get a chance to threaten him. I am the first to admit it: I don't understand ethics. Should I warn Wallace, or should I wait to see what happens? He might run again if I tell him there is a maniac after him and that would undermine our future in Candid Online College. You are aware how much he likes running away from his responsibilities. But he might get killed if I leave him in the dark, and that would also ruin our plans. Oh God, this is an example of what that idiot Spencer would call a moral dilemma. Why isn't he here the one time he is needed? Calm down, Pandora, you are overreacting."

Horse held her hand while she sobbed on his shoulder.

Pandora blew her nose when she ran out of tears.

"I don't want you ever to see a therapist. There is nothing to talk to anybody about, Horse. We are deliriously happy. Anyway, Tiberius Lang will never find Wallace. How could he? Only Casper Wall, Julie Progress, you, and I know where he is. Oh darling, the news is starting on the television. Turn up the volume."

The newsreader gulped in air to fuel her relating that day's developments in a conspiratorial shout when the hysterical music died down. "Today," she bellowed, "the reclusive Randy Fortune announced he is setting up a foundation dedicated to determining how best to give away all of his money. Unconfirmed social media sources close to the eccentric billionaire said that he had put together a team of expert celebrities and at least one prominent controversial moral philosopher to help him decide where his money should go."

"Unconfirmed social media sources? That's that idiot Casper Wall," Pandora snarled. "I hope Tiberius Lang isn't watching this. Do maniacs watch the news?" she asked, as if she wasn't living proof that they do.

She reached for a cigarette with one hand and for Horse's occupied hands with the other. "What is wrong with me,

Horse? I am not my normal self. Look at me. I am shaking. I must be seriously ill. I appreciate I say that every week, but this time I am certain it is something terminal. Tiberius must know Casper knows where Wallace is, having interrogated Spencer. I have to warn Casper before that madman catches up with him. He has such a skinny neck. Imagine, for such a high-tech guy, he never answers his phone. But he is always in that bloody office. Never goes home, wherever that is. I am driving over there now. Mind the cat, and don't answer the door to anyone."

On the floor, Marlboro was bored with the lack of attention. He pushed a surplus ball of wool from Horse's miscalculations for his project over and back with his paw. He was wondering what he could try next to amuse himself. He tucked his claws under his chest and closed his eyes. He was bored with taunting Horse. But it had been distracting while it lasted knowing Horse wouldn't dare kick him while Pandora was present. It wasn't his fault he needed a diversion. After all, he was the only cat on the street suffering from Feline Attention Deficit Disorder. So there! Marlboro stuck his tongue out at no one in particular.

"I told him nothing, Pandora. Not a single word. No-thing," Casper Wall said, pressing his finger to his mouth. "You know me. I am the embodiment of reticence. He didn't extract a syllable. A secret is safe with me. I am a tomb; a vault; a crypt; as silent as the grave; as—"

"Shut up," Pandora screamed.

"Okay. I might have told him that I have feelings for Julie Progress, but you can imagine what happens in a typical psychiatric session. They are trained to extract information from a stone. One minute your lips are sealed," Wall said, miming zipping his mouth closed. "And the next you are singing like a canary, spilling your darkest fantasies."

"You have feelings? For Julie Progress? You? Feelings?"

"That hurts, Pandora. I didn't realize it until I explored my unconscious self with the Professor. It's not my fault. He could make a rock self-aware."

"He is not a psychiatrist, you idiot. He is a fucking lunatic."

"All psychiatrists are mad if you ask me. You would have to be, wouldn't you? The things they must hear in those asylums. And if you weren't nuts when you started in that business you would be after a few sessions with the kind of people they must meet every day."

"Such as you, you mean?"

"What do you think – Julie Progress and me? Can you picture us together? He promised to put in a good word with her on my behalf. Or would Sergeant Jones be a more suitable match? Just because I work with machines doesn't mean I can't recognise when someone is attracted to me."

A miniscule dark freckle on her arm distracted Pandora. But maybe it wasn't a freckle. She placed her burning cigarette on the edge of the desk, raised her sunglasses onto her hair, and squeezed the blemish between her thumb and index finger. She brought her arm as near to her bloodshot eyes as she could. It was a melanoma. Her arm, at least, would have to come off. That would leave her just one with which to pummel Casper. She would consult a doctor if those fools could be trusted. She would ask Horse for a second opinion when she got home.

"Did he ask where Julie Progress is?"

"Who?"

"You are such a poor liar, Casper."

"Here, Pandora, have a drink. Check this out," he said as he took his mobile phone from his pocket. "I am working on an application for people like you who worry too much. It's called an Anxiety App. It gives you a menu of typical worries. You select the appropriate one. For example, worrying what other people think about you – that's popular. Then you press this tab where it says how you feel. Here, you try it," he said, stretching his hand with the phone towards her.

Horse says control is the key to defeating anxiety. I have to take control of the situation, Pandora told herself. But how can I predict the random consequences of my actions? I blame Fischer. I wouldn't have palpitations now if he had agreed to help me.

"Did he ask where Progress is?" Pandora repeated the question.

"Yes, he wanted to find her. Maybe he fancies her. I don't blame him. I still fancy her even after I got to know her. But Jones pointed her boobs at me. You have boobs. I don't. What do you think that means, Pandora?"

On the ceiling of the corridor outside the provost's office quite a crowd of small black spiders had gathered to watch the comings and goings below, perhaps word having got around the webs that it was now the place to be. But then they didn't have mobile technology to distract them from their fatuous existence. They watched in silence as Pandora emerged, looked one way then the other, straightened the front of her jacket, fired up a cigarette, and strode off. They waited and waited, but Casper didn't appear.

Sometime the following morning, a secretary entered the office carrying files. There was a scream. The secretary came out without the files and ran down the corridor calling for help. Yes, the spiders agreed: it was the most distracting place in Candid Online College to hang out.

XXIV

Quod Est Manifeste Falsum Indicium
An Obvious False Clue

Sergeant Jones shuffled her buttocks on the unyielding surface of the chair. She was sitting at her boss's desk. Inspector Freddy Sullivan was on the other side staring at the blank computer screen to give the impression he was experiencing deep thoughts. On the wall beside his head a cork noticeboard carried wanted posters, mixed in with health and safety notices, and out-of-date announcements of police family-day outings. These pages were pinned on with coloured tacks. The jacket of his conservative grey suit hung on the old-fashioned coat stand he inherited from his predecessor that constituted the only other furniture in the room apart from a row of neglected filing cabinets.

Freddy sipped coffee from a paper cup and flicked through the blank pages of his notes, while Jones broke off tiny pieces from a scone sitting on a paper napkin balanced on the edge of the desk and fed them into her mouth.

"Any trace of this Tiberius Lang fellow?" Freddy asked, finally despairing of anything else to say. He blew on the hot liquid in his cup to signify his pretend indifference to the reply. Jones remained silent while nibbling around the edges of the scone.

"I might let you have a go at catching a notorious gangster such as Rik Wallace after you net a small fish like Tiberius," Sullivan said.

Jones stared at the scone, which had fractured into several equal-sized crumbs, preoccupied with which one of them she should shove in her mouth next. She hated when that happened, preferring to work her way around the edges, or when that proved impossible, as now, up from the smallest pieces to the larger ones.

The silence irritated Sullivan because it meant he had to think of something else to say.

"Here is the way I see it, Jones – from the vantage point of my greater policing experience. Wallace killed Maurice Spencer. Why would I believe that, you are wondering? Everyone else thinks Tiberius did it because he uses cable ties to kill his victims. I have learned from solving many important crimes that nothing is self-evident in police work. Nothing is, Jones. And if anything was – say, for the sake of argument – *obvious*, then it is obvious Wallace is pretending to be Tiberius. Forget speculation. Examine the facts, Jones. They were in a lunatic asylum together, so Wallace knows how Tiberius thinks. Why would Tiberius practise his own modus operandi on Maurice Spencer? You can't say, can you? But I can. Because it wasn't him. He might be mad – which I doubt – but he isn't stupid, is he? Have you asked yourself why there was no forensic evidence of Wallace at Spencer's house? Did that not strike you as odd? No? You haven't, because you believe he wasn't there. Am I correct? Use your head, Jones. I'll tell you why no trace of Wallace was found at the crime scene. It's because he cleaned up after himself, that's why. Wallace is engaged in a copycat killing. And I can prove it. First, he knew I would be on to him the minute he escaped from Saint Drogo's where he killed that poor harmless duty nurse, and second, he is also aware that I would know his every move, including the ones he would know I couldn't know. We are dealing with a super-intelligent criminal maniac. You can be sure Wallace has thought everything through in advance. You have to think like a criminal mastermind if you want to catch one." Inspector Sullivan tapped his forehead. "We don't have to agree with him, Jones, but we can respect his criminal professionalism."

"A witness reported seeing someone resembling Sigmund Freud speeding out of the college in a banana yellow hatchback on the day Casper Wall was killed. That would fit Tiberius's description," Jones said while trying to dissolve a piece of scone in her saliva.

Sullivan sighed.

"The Casper Wall case? What are you trying to say, Jones?"

"Isn't it probable that the same person killed both Casper Wall and Maurice Spencer?"

"Yes. Maybe."

His almost agreeing took her by surprise. "If you accept that Tiberius killed Casper Wall, then it follows he—"

"So what you are saying, Jones, is that you have already dismissed the idea that Wallace disguised himself as Freud and rented a yellow car?"

"Err ... I didn't dismiss that idea because it didn't occur to me."

"No, it didn't, did it?"

Jones wasn't to be so easily distracted. "But if your theory is correct, and Wallace is copying Tiberius, then why didn't he strangle Casper Wall with a cable tie?" she asked, removing a currant from between her teeth with a flourish of her fingers.

Sullivan placed the coffee cup on the desk so that he could press the sides of his forehead together with both hands to demonstrate his frustration with the naivety of his sergeant. "I admit that even I was surprised that the autopsy showed a mobile phone had been rammed down his throat. I was expecting to learn he had been strangled, same as Maurice Spencer. But after a moment's reflection, it was obvious to me why Wallace didn't resort to a cable tie this time. Do you know why, Jones?"

"No."

Freddy Sullivan sighed, again. "Because it would be obvious that he was copying Tiberius. Two in a row? Come on, Jones, remember what I said: Wallace is a criminal genius. Could it be a co-incidence that two of his ex-colleagues are killed so soon after he escapes? No, Jones. In police work there are no co-incidences. Maurice Spencer and Casper Wall both worked at Candid Online College, and they both knew Wallace. He had the means because he has killed before."

"I read his file. His original conviction seems doubtful."

"The jury didn't think so."

"They found him insane after fifty-seven days of deliberation. They were cracking up themselves by then."

"There, you have said it yourself. He had a motive that probably only makes sense to him because he is insane. He had opportunity because we have no idea where he is. Motive and opportunity, Jones."

"Why are you obsessed with Wallace, sir?"

"You would have to ask a psychiatrist, Sergeant." His lips smiled, but his eyes remained serious.

Jones studied the contents of the paper napkin. She decided to change her approach to the problem because this was getting her nowhere. It was best to be flexible. She crammed the largest piece of scone between her teeth in one go. She spoke with her mouth full. "I finished reading the standard edition of Freud's complete works without finding a single clue as to Tiberius's whereabouts. Will I start into the non-standard editions?"

Sullivan resisted telling his sergeant what he thought she should do with Freud's books. Instead, he stood up, thrust his hips twice in her direction, turned, and gyrated out of the office. Jones licked the micro-crumbs from the napkin and threw it onto the floor – there being no need for a wastepaper basket in the inspector's office.

XXV

Canis Dormiens Calcitandro
Kicking a Sleeping Dog

Jackson propped his brand-new black bicycle, designed to appear old-fashioned in a contemporary sort of way, against the rusting railings enclosing the shabby semi-detached house at the bottom of the slope that formed a cul-de-sac in the neglected housing estate. The librarian closed up behind him, carried down the hill by the momentum. She hopped off the saddle and stopped the front wheel just inches from the back of his legs. She was still smiling in delight at the sensation of the wind rushing over her helmet of hair. Her bicycle matched her husband's, except it was an actual old model.

"Did you bring the locks?" he asked. "I'm sure there are bicycle thieves in this neighbourhood."

"There are thieves everywhere," she assured him, lifting the pair of heavy chains out of the basket attached to the wide handlebars.

By the time the librarian had chained the bicycles together, Jackson had already strolled up the broken path through the garden that was a studied display of unrestrained flora: unchecked by mowers, rakes, and inspiration from Saturday afternoons spent at the garden centre. If the neighbours complained, the local bees did not. They bounced around the profusion of daisies, buttercups, and dandelions scattered through the tiny meadow that had begun life as a neat rollout lawn. He pressed the bell on the horizontal plank that divided the upper panel of brown opaque patterned glass from the unpainted temporary plywood that occupied the bottom half of the front door. Almost at once a short tube, mounted on a semi-circular disc at eye level on the doorframe, extended and retracted before rotating in search of whoever it was had woken it from its sleep. It stopped its agitated motion when pointing directly at Jackson's face.

"Yeah. What do you want?" a voice from the speaker in the aluminium plate under the camera asked.

"We are here to see Ellen Dubois," the librarian said, materialising over Jackson's shoulder, sending the camera into a hysterical whirring in and out in an attempt to focus on this second face. The tube settled on Jackson again.

"What do you want with her?" the intercom asked.

"It concerns her missing husband."

"What about him?"

"We found him," Jackson said.

Silence from the intercom!

The tube retracted a half-inch, as if in thought.

"Why were you looking for him?"

"We are part-time private vigilantes," the librarian explained.

The tube rotated as if raising a sceptical eye brow.

"Is he looking for money from me?"

"Not at all. On the contrary he is working for a billionaire."

"Wait there. Don't move."

A second later, a shadow appeared behind the brown Pilkington glass and Ellen Dubois stood blocking the open doorway – as if Jackson and the librarian had even considered entering the house from which a strong smell of ointment, cooking oil, and methane gas was then escaping. She was shaped like a handmade sausage that was constricted with twine at the ankles, knees, and waist. But not at the neck, where her chin dangled from a face made fatter by a cheap, too-short haircut. She rested a plump, proprietorial hand on the head of a boy who came up to her elbow.

"DNA mix-up or not, he is an exact replica of Rik Wallace," Jackson whispered to the librarian, unable to suppress his excitement.

"I have never been able to spot a resemblance between any child and any other human being," the librarian whispered back.

A smaller, plumper, red-faced boy appeared from behind his mother's hip. She put her other fat hand on his shoulder to hold him in place.

"No. I stand corrected," the librarian muttered. "This one is the image of her."

"He is not well," Ellen Dubois told her visitors, with undisguised pride in her son's medical condition. "He has spent months in hospital, and no one can tell us what is wrong with him. He has a delicate constitution, same as me. We attend the same consultants. We are even on the same medication, which is handy if one of us runs out."

"I assume these are your children. Aren't there supposed to be more of them?" Jackson asked, trying to see around the rotund woman.

"There's her," Ellen Dubois confirmed, rotating her eyes skywards to indicate the thin girl in plastic sunglasses with green lenses standing behind her in the shadowy hallway. She was wearing a filthy, blue dress with her tiny feet pushed into the top of a pair of what Jackson assumed were her mother's high heel shoes that he could not imagine ever taking the strain of the load of their intended wearer.

Ellen Dubois detached herself from her children to rummage in her pockets. "We all have asthma," she said setting fire to the end of a cigarette and blowing the smoke over her visitors as if disinfecting them of whatever germs they may have picked up in the outside world.

"Isn't there another? A fourth? There was a report you were pregnant when you showed up at the college?"

Pain ended Jackson's line of enquiry when the librarian kicked him in the back of his leg.

"I don't know what you are talking about. Anyway, three is my limit. I couldn't cope with more. Ruin my figure, it would. Besides, between the trips to the hospital and the truancy officers banging on the door every morning, I don't have the time. That's the lot. Three."

"Shouldn't the children be in school now?" Jackson enquired, looking at his watch.

"You caught us getting ready to go to the hospital."

"We mustn't stop you," the librarian said as she stood aside.

"No point at this stage because I expect those doctors will find nothing, as usual. They are useless. I'm better off on the Internet than at the A&E at Saint Drogo's. My husband is working for a billionaire, you say?"

The librarian tried to pull Jackson by the sleeve away from

the door. "Let's find someone else," she muttered.

Jackson shrugged her off. "Is this him?" he asked, handing her a photograph of Rik Wallace taken after he was arrested.

Ellen Dubois glanced at the picture before handing it back. "That's him."

"Are you sure?" the librarian asked.

"Sure, I'm sure. He's my husband."

The librarian took the photograph from Jackson and handed it back to Ellen Dubois. "Is this the man the police said was your husband?"

Ellen Dubois ignored the picture to hold the librarian's eyes in hers. "That's him."

"Did the police tell you they muddled up the DNA found at the hotel?"

"I learned biology from the Internet. I had to with our shared medical conditions," she said, indicating with a nod at her children, now filling the door beside her. "DNA is overrated. Too much scientific mumbo jumbo going around these days, if you ask me. Imagine the DNA in this lot," she said waving her cigarette in front of her like a wand. She laughed. "As the wife, I am best qualified to say who is and isn't my husband. Look at them," she said, gesturing to her stair of children. "They are the spitting image of him. This one has his nose, that one his hair, and tell me they are not his ears. What further proof do you want?"

The librarian thought the tiny girl could have anyone's features under the layer of jam, cereal and – was that yogurt? – that clung to her face. And she didn't favour her brothers who bore no resemblance to each other.

"Let's go to the next house on our list in search of a possible match," the librarian suggested to Jackson.

"At least she is willing to admit she is married to him. That's a better start than we could have hoped for. Let me ask you this one question," he said, addressing Ellen Dubois while holding onto the librarian's arm to prevent her taking off down the path. "Are you willing to be a loving wife to the man in that photograph and a devoted mother to these … err … creatures, who in theory could be his children?"

"Which billionaire did you say he works for?"

"Randy Fortune."

"Hah. I knew it. Ran-Dy Fuck-Ing Fort-Une," she repeated, emphasizing the separate syllables. "He is my husband, and I am his loving wife. You love your dad, don't you?" she said slapping the top step on the back of his head.

The boy smoothed his hair into place and kicked his mother in the shin.

"Bastard. I mean, *ungrateful child*. But what he needs is the influence of a rich father. Listen, while you are here, you couldn't loan me some money, could you? As an advance on whatever I can squeeze out of what's-his-name?"

"Rik Wallace."

"So, that's what he's calling himself these days. Yes. I mean him. I'll pay you back when I meet … err … Rik. I am being evicted just because I can't pay the rent on this dump. You are lucky you caught me in today. I wouldn't be here if you had called tomorrow. It must be fate. I'm sure Rik wouldn't want his family to be homeless. If I know him – and, don't get me wrong, I do – he wouldn't want his darlings sleeping on the street."

The librarian was unable to make her eyes turn away from

the slug of green snot that was crawling from the middle child's left nostril, over his lip, and down into his mouth from whence a pink tongue poked out to scoop it inside.

"Jackson," she gasped. "Jackson, give me a handkerchief, quick."

She managed to shut her eyes. She inhaled, trying to keep the contents of her stomach in place.

"Here," she said. She handed the child the crisp white cotton. "Wipe your nose before I faint."

"I have to inform you, err … Mrs Wallace, that I—"

"It's *Ms* Dubois. I kept my own name when I married—what's-his-name?"

"Rik Wallace."

"I'm an independent woman."

"I am allergic to children," the librarian continued.

"Allergic?"

"Yes. I can't stand them."

Ellen Dubois was sound asleep between the clean sheets on their bed in the one bedroom in their tiny flat above the bookshop. The librarian would have liked to turn onto her side, but there wasn't room to adjust her position on the narrow inflatable mattress that occupied the space on the kitchenette floor between the cooker and the refrigerator without forcing Jackson to move in synch. A few feet away at the other side of the serving counter, the three children were asleep under a pile of blankets and overcoats on the cushions from the matching armchairs that the librarian had pushed apart as far as they would go. Their three heads were inches from the artificial coal fire.

"Are you awake?"

"Of course, I am awake. How could anyone sleep with that noise? What is she doing in there?

"Snoring."

"She doesn't sound human."

"Don't let her bother you."

"Why would the racket she is making while sleeping in my bed, the non-stop talk when she is awake, her obvious Munchausen's syndrome, the less obvious Munchausen's syndrome by proxy, and the constant self-medication bother me? And she emptied the refrigerator. We should have given her the money to find a place to stay. Sometimes you are too stingy for your own good."

"Rik would want us to protect her and the children."

"He doesn't have a clue who she is, and vice versa. I am certain she doesn't know him. We promised Rik we would find *his* wife and children. Not this lot."

"We specified *a* wife and children. We cannot be held responsible for a technical misunderstanding if he inferred they would be the ideal ones, who by the way, only seem to exist in Randy Fortune's imagination. Besides, Sullivan thought she was the right one at one time. That has to count for something."

"I'm too tired to argue with your ridiculous logic. I knew we should have started with missing persons and not with the lot Sullivan turned up. I didn't record the exact conversation we had with Rik. But I do recall we didn't say what we would do with them when we found them. It's not as if children are real people. They don't have strong opinions on anything. They have to go."

"Go where?" Jackson asked, loudly.

"Shuiiiissssssh. They will hear you. They have to go. *Away*," she whispered.

"We can't kill them," he whispered, his lips right beside her ear. "They have just gotten here."

"Who said anything about killing them? We can't kill children. What do you think I am? A monster? All I am saying is we could smother them."

"Let's try to sleep on it, and see how we feel in the morning."

They held their breaths to listen.

The sound of a plank of hardwood splitting along its length came out from under the bedroom door.

"That is not natural," the librarian said as tears welled in her eyes. She blinked and stared at the tideline on the ceiling where a semi-circle of light from the streetlamp outside lapped over and back in the wind. The spiders in the corners looked down on the couple with schadenfreude. They could have told them this would happen.

"We can't let her turn up at Fortune Mansion. You heard her. Every second word out of her is *billions*."

"We just have to rehearse her in what to say, that's all."

"What about the children? How are we going to train them?"

"Nobody listens to children anyway."

"Besides she ignores all of my rules," the librarian added.

"I ignore your rules," Jackson said.

"Yes, but that is different. I can nag you. I can't say anything at all to her, but she starts crying and wheezing and clutching her fucking chest. Bitch. They all have to go."

She made a karate motion with her hand in the restricted

space, landing a chop on Jackson's leg.

"Ow."

"Sorry."

"It's only been half a day."

"They *have* to go."

"We can't put them out on the street. What would we tell Rik? Not with the state the middle one's in. He is at death's door."

"Oh, for God's sake. You are worse than her. Nothing is wrong with any of them. They are as healthy as a herd of oxen."

"You saw that rash on her buttocks when she was climbing into bed."

"Yes, to my regret I did look. They have to go."

God, she needed to adjust the pillow on which both their heads were propped at an awkward angle.

"Move your hip."

"I can't."

"They have to go," the librarian murmured, losing hope.

They stared at the ceiling forming their separate unvoiced thoughts. The dark can be a fertile environment for the germination of emotions and plans.

I feel sorry for Rik, Jackson thought. He is alone in the world. He needs someone like Ellen Dubois. She will be perfect for him. Thoughtful, caring – well, she must have some qualities. Anyone is an improvement on no one.

I feel sorry for Jackson, the librarian thought. He has never discussed having children. How could he since I keep telling him how much I hate them? I suppose I could make a sacrifice for him. How hard could it be?

I feel sorry for the librarian, Jackson thought. I am certain she would love children if she sought treatment for her allergy. She could make an appointment with Professor Murphy. She hated herself as a child. Yes, I'm sure that's it: the tiniest amount of self-awareness would cause any child to hate themselves. Funny how easy it is to make sense of people using just basic psychology. What could Murphy have been doing all those years in college?

Rik is better off on his own, the librarian thought. He is too independent to be burdened with the responsibility of children. And they would be safer away from him.

A lot can be said for Rik's single lifestyle, Jackson thought. With children around he wouldn't have time for his own ideas. They would cramp his style.

I have no sympathy for Rik, the librarian thought. He is too self-obsessed to make a good father or husband. And, if he is unhappy on his own, so what? Anyway, family is the main source of misery. That's the nature of domestic responsibility. It doesn't suit everybody. I feel sorry for myself.

I feel sorry for myself, Jackson told himself.

And no, Ellen Dubois isn't better than no one. Anyone, except perhaps Rik, could be a better parent for those children, the librarian thought.

Maybe a parent could choose the child if a child cannot choose their parents. That makes sense, doesn't it? Jackson thought.

"What are you thinking?" the librarian asked.

"Oh, nothing," Jackson lied.

"Me neither," the librarian lied in turn.

"Let's not make any rash decisions concerning Ellen Dubois and the children until tomorrow."

"Okay, good night."

"Good night."

Was it the sound of timber splitting or the wheels in their brains spinning that kept them both awake until dawn? Maybe. But it was the splash of cold milk that the middle child spilled on the librarian's face while making his breakfast that woke her up.

XXVI

Ratio In Histrionem
Method in Acting

Pandora shuffled along behind Eustis as he slid the soles of his shoes over the smooth tiles of the hallway of Fortune Mansion. She wore a tailored, wide-pinstriped, double-breasted suit. In place of a clutch bag, she gripped a packet of cigarettes.

Pandora rolled her eyes behind her black sunglasses and grimaced at the butler's back, resisting an impulse to push him aside as he climbed onto his toes to press down on a gold handle with both hands, and lean into the ornate eggshell door panel of one of the many empty rooms on the ground floor. Inside Julie Progress strode over and back, wearing a track into the priceless Persian carpet.

"Thank you, Eustis," Progress said, shoving the butler backwards with the palm of her hand pressed into his chest, before closing the door in his face.

When Eustis put on a pair of headphones that hung on a hook and pressed his eyeball against the spot of light that appeared at eye level behind the wall, he saw Julie Progress pacing in front of her guest.

"This had better be important. I told you Randy Fortune is a hermit. He doesn't receive visitors. Did anyone apart from the butler and that crowd of entrepreneurs outside the gates see you arriving?"

"No. You are overreacting as usual. I had to come here because I couldn't talk on the phone. You can never tell who might be listening." Pandora scanned the room with the radar dishes of her sunglasses. "Jackson phoned me. He was hysterical. Your foolproof plan is unravelling. A real homicidal maniac, Tiberius Lang, is on the loose. It seems Rik Wallace's psychiatrist tried to poison him."

"Wallace? Why would a psychiatrist poison his own client?"

"No, you idiot. Poison Jackson! I met him at Candid Online College with Maurice Spencer and Casper Wall. He was pretending to be Rik's psychiatrist."

"Jackson?"

"No. Tiberius Lang."

"The one who poisoned Jackson?"

"No. That was the real psychiatrist! The pretend one resembles Sigmund Freud. Pay attention, Progress."

"I'm confused, Pandora."

"Me too," Eustis muttered his agreement behind the wall.

Pandora hesitated for what may have been the first time ever in her life in the act of lighting a cigarette. The morning's routine bout of coughing that accompanied her opening her eyes each day was on her mind. Even by her standards that particular episode had drained her and the gobs of phlegm weren't the usual shade of green.

"Are you sure you are all right, Pandora?"

Pandora pushed aside her niggling concern about her health in favour of her immediate one. "Jackson rang me – several times. He is hysterical. He said Wallace's real psychiatrist believes his relationship to his imaginary family is vital to his mental health."

"How does the psychiatrist's imaginary family involve Rik?"

"No. Rik's family aren't real. Rik may have developed some form of inverse false memory repression syndrome from his psychiatrist's efforts to force him to remember the woman who isn't his wife. Is that much clear?"

"The real one?"

"No. Not the fucking real one! The family that Inspector Sullivan produced at the philosophy department aren't his. The pregnant woman that chased him through CAT College wasn't his wife."

"She was pregnant?"

"No. Jackson found her! Turns out she was fat."

"I hate when that happens. You mean Rik isn't married."

"Who knows? But not to her."

Behind the wall, Eustis was feeling relieved. "In the absence of an ideal family joining Wallace, there would be no convincing Randy to change his ways," he muttered. Wallace would be thrown out of Fortune Mansion, which was good because he had seen the way his beloved Samantha gazed at Wallace and he at her.

"So, who the hell is he going to bring here to meet Randy Fortune?" Progress asked.

"Jackson says the mother seems to be willing to be married to Wallace if she can get her hands on some of Randy Fortune's money."

Eustis felt a pang of anxiety under his butler's waistcoat. People had no principles. Wallace wouldn't be thrown out!

"I have been trying to think this through, step by step," Pandora continued. "We learned from the trial that we still don't know who Rik is, but we do know that the real wife – assuming she exists – of the person he isn't may be living on a tropical island with the compensation she got from the hotel when she believed her husband had fallen off the balcony. She won't make a fuss because she would have to give back the money if she agreed Rik was her husband and that he is still alive –which he isn't – that is, assuming that her real husband, whoever he was, is the one who is dead. Are you following me?"

"No."

"Me neither," Eustis concurred. "He was beginning to conclude eavesdropping was overrated.

"We also know that this family Jackson has installed in his flat aren't his," Pandora added.

"Whose?"

"Wallace's."

"I see. But he's not the husband who is dead."

"Shut up. But Randy Fortune doesn't know that he didn't abandon that woman."

"Which woman?"

"What difference does it make who he fucking abandoned? Whoever it was he thought he ran off on, I suppose." Pandora rubbed the back of her neck. "You should understand these things better than me. Isn't all this family bullshit metaphysics or something? Don't you have a doctorate?"

"It's pending. I hope you feel bad now about threatening to kill his imaginary children."

"I do. Especially since he's unaware they don't exist. That doesn't seem right, somehow."

"Stick with not having principles, Pandora," Progress said. "It's morally more acceptable for the rest of us. I will tell Rik when I see him that Jackson has located his fake family," she lied. She was thinking why she should allow that smelly bitch Samantha to sink her unmanicured nails further into Rik's flesh. By keeping him in the dark, he will be racked with such feelings of guilt over his non-existent children he just might stay away from her. "I read in the paper that Casper Wall was found dead in his office with a mobile phone rammed down his throat," Progress said.

"Oh, that."

"And it was reported someone bearing a close resemblance to Sigmund Freud was seen leaving the college around the time he was killed. That must be this escaped maniac you mentioned."

"The one you helped to break out of that ridiculous asylum while I was liberating Rik. You said you would wait in the van. The moment my back was turned you bust someone else out at random."

"I don't know what you are talking about. I stayed in the van all the time except for a few minutes to make faces through the canteen window. Oh, my God," Progress gripped Pandora's hands, which annoyed her because she had decided to fire up a cigarette at that moment. "Am I safe? This loony may be after me too. First Spencer, then Casper. I'm next."

"Pull yourself together and leave go of my hands. Tiberius didn't kill Casper. I did."

Eustis suppressed a shout.

Pandora's radar sunglasses swept the room again.

"What was that noise? I heard something behind the wall

over there."

Eustis held his breath.

"This place is crawling with rats," Progress said.

A rat passing by Eustis's feet might have felt he was being picked on – again. Why did *he* have to carry the burden of all human sneakiness? Well, maybe not all. The snake wasn't comfortable either with the adverse propaganda that clung to his species. Those pandas got off scot-free because they couldn't breed with the effortless efficiency of rabbits. The rat had too many offspring to get himself mentioned on the endangered species list. Maybe he should give up sex for a month? No. Not worth it. Humans were strange creatures, and it was frightening to imagine that at any one time you could be sure there was one within two yards of wherever you were standing. He shuddered and scuttled off.

"But why did you kill him, Pandora? Poor Casper didn't deserve that."

"Yes, he did," Pandora said while flicking the flint on her cigarette lighter. "He was a blabbermouth. I did it to protect you and Rik. Well, that's not completely true. He was annoying me. I haven't been my usual imperturbable self recently."

"I suppose someone being annoying can be a moral justification. But why is this maniac who resembles Freud chasing Rik?"

"Who cares why? Motivation is overrated."

"There must be a reason."

"Jackson said the psychiatrist treating him had a theory."

"You appreciate I am interested in the mind. What did he say?"

"It seems that when Tiberius was a child his parents who

were both psychologists made him—"

"You're right, Pandora. What does it matter why? Just get to the point."

Behind the wall the butler was disappointed not to learn more on what the psychiatrist said had inspired this particular maniac.

"Tiberius is a therapist. He wants to analyse Rik, and then kill him."

Tiberius is hunting Wallace? Now that is curious. The insane is definitely a tiny community, Eustis told himself.

"We must warn Rik."

I must tell Tiberius, Eustis told himself. My, my; it will be good to see him again after all these years. Or will it? However, Tiberius could permanently solve his problem with Wallace sticking his moralising nose in where it didn't belong – which was Samantha's gripping aroma. He inhaled with his eyes closed, imagining the tangy smell of cheese.

"Rik is safe here. No one can circumvent our security. Besides, I have enough on my mind trying to keep him on track convincing Randy of the moral need to abandon his philanthropic plans without his being distracted by worrying that some mad therapist is chasing him for a counselling session."

Eustis opened his eyes, regretting he had nothing on him with which to make notes.

"I'm worried because we don't know what, if anything, Spencer or Casper Wall told Tiberius," Pandora said.

"Oh, I doubt if a topic other than themselves came up."

"Maybe, but make sure nothing happens to Rik. He has kind of grown on me against my will. Like a tumour," she added as an afterthought, letting slip something of what was on her mind. Perhaps her life-long obsession with medical afflictions was manifesting itself in hypochondria. Or maybe this time she was dying. "Anyway, we are unlikely to find anyone else after what happened to Fischer. It's not as if we have a long list of go-to moralists."

"I should never have allowed you to talk me into your infallible plan in the first place."

"The entire scheme was your idea. I remember your exact words – 'This is a simple uncomplicated plan guaranteed to—'"

"Never mind who came up with it. There will be plenty opportunity for recriminations afterwards. Please don't light that cigarette, Pandora. This room is wired to go up like a rocket if anything larger than a fucking milli-micron particle type thing gets in here. I'm sure smoke will set the alarm off. Pandora, I'm begging—"

Eustis clamped his hands over the earphones on his head as a siren went off.

XXVII

Rebus Familiae
Family Matters

The pair of Dobermann dogs who featured as the main deterrent in the security night shift at Fortune Mansion had retired under an overhanging bush that they had learned from experience provided shelter from the rain. This was a few minutes before seven in the evening when their handler passed through the encampment of entrepreneurs outside the main gates on his way to the pub at the bottom of the hill. Just after midnight they were in the habit of resuming a display of vigilance when they saw him staggering back up the drive. In between, they slept because it wasn't as if they were being paid.

A flashlight, shining a few inches in front of his face, dazzled Tiberius Lang before he could check himself for cuts and rips when he climbed down off the barbed wire fence that surrounded the grounds. "Get that bloody light out of my eyes. I can't see." Tiberius worked his gloved fingers into his sockets.

Eustis switched off the torch.

"Who are you supposed to be?" Tiberius asked through a watery blur. "I don't recognise you in that disguise."

"It's not a disguise. It's a costume. I *am* an actor, remember?"

"My God, despite appearances you haven't changed. What

role are you playing now?"

"I am Randy Fortune's butler, Eustis." He made a slight bow as introduction.

"It has been a long time. Let me take a look at you, brother." Tiberius held him by the shoulders at arm's length, and studied the moonlit face. "So that was you I saw in our film club at the asylum."

"What did you think of my performance?"

"You seemed convincing enough, but then I am no expert in butlering."

"Okay, let's get down to business, Tiberius. You got the message I left on your answering machine at your penthouse."

"I drove straight here in that car," he said waving at the banana yellow hatchback parked at the other side of the fence. "How did you find out I was looking for Rik Wallace? Who told you?"

"Let's just say the walls around here can speak. I have a job requiring your peculiar talent. I want you to kill Rik Wallace before his fake family shows up, and together they ruin everything." Eustis reasoned that a family issue would be more likely to engage the curiosity of an analyst, rather than his real motivation – which was his desire to rid himself of a rival in love.

"What do you mean *fake?*"

"I don't have time to explain, and even if I did, I can't explain because I don't understand it myself; but his family are not his. It's surprising how often that can happen. You can discuss it with him before you throttle him. That's what you want, isn't it? After that, you can climb back over that fence and continue with your insane life."

"You are every bit as judgemental as the judge at my so-called trial. I can't imagine what you heard, but I don't want to kill Wallace; I want to analyse him." Tiberius pulled off his gloves, one finger at a time.

"From what I understand about you, that amounts to the same thing. Suit yourself. Analyse him and then kill him."

"That might not be possible. I may be reformed, but I won't know until I meet him. I have to get near him to know for sure. I am on a – call it a psychological – pilgrimage to discover who I am. I need to find myself and resolve once and for all my inner conflict. I am convinced I must be on the right subconscious path because here you are having contacted me about Wallace at the very time I am searching for him. That cannot just be a co-incidence. It's a sign."

"A sign? You really are disturbed. And no, it wasn't a co-incidence; it was a phone call."

"You can never tell for certain with such miraculous events. Yes. I'm inclined to call it a miracle. Don't look so astonished. According to Carl Jung there are incidents that don't fit with the Axiom of Causality that dictates everything has to have a cause: a prejudice so beloved of physicists and butlers."

"And all other sane people."

"However, you cannot deny our auspicious meeting is meaningful in a deep Jungian way we can't explain, even if you did leave me a message on my answering machine."

"But you're a Freudian. You even look like Freud. You despise Jung."

"That's irrelevant. All analysts hate each other."

The butler sighed. "Enough philosophizing. As your older brother I command you to assist me in my mission to kill

Wallace."

"Older by three minutes."

"Minutes, hours, years, what difference does it make? I am still the elder. You have to obey me."

"I'm not taking orders from you. I've only ever met you three times in my entire life."

When a light came on in an upstairs window Eustis led his brother further into the gloom under a tree. "Ah, the past," he said when they had blended into the darkness of the branches.

"You remember the first time we met on our eighteenth birthday?" Tiberius asked.

"It's all a bit of a blur."

"It should be because you were drugged for most of the evening."

"That was also the first time I met that pair of psychology lunatics – your mother and father – when they surprised me with our reunion in the laboratory in the basement of your creepy home."

Tiberius grabbed his brother around the throat. "I've told you before. I won't have you denigrating their memory with the crude label of psychologist. One of them was a behaviourist and the other an analyst. It may not be important to you, but the legacy of our parents is sacred to me."

Eustis gripped his brother's wrists.

"They were *your* parents, not mine. You were lucky. At least they fucked you up in an interesting way, while that slob of a mother who sold you for research an hour after we were born had no imagination when it came to my neglect."

"There should be a law against selling people."

"There is. She needed the money."

"At least my parents would never have sold me on after they bought me."

"Why did you kill them if they were so sacred to you?"

Tiberius relaxed his grip on his brother's neck. He dropped his arms to his sides. "They were getting old. I couldn't stand by and watch them decline. All parents become their children's children. You wouldn't understand because you weren't there in the front row for that joint paper they presented in Geneva on telepathic gerbils. I knew they would want me to prevent them embarrassing themselves further. Their reputations were their single consolation in the ever-decreasing academic circle in which they circulated."

"You will be pleased to learn your biological mother is still alive and embarrassing herself within her ever-widening circle of bookies."

Tiberius ignored the reference to biology. He was concerned only with his psychological identity. "You must get me access to Wallace. I need to explore his mind and mine it for those insights that I know will contribute to my quest to discover who I am: a task that will require several days of undisturbed deep probing."

"Impossible."

"Minimally, ten one-hour sessions without interruptions or toilet breaks."

"Can't be done."

"Five minutes?"

"I'll try, but you would have to assume a role above suspicion, which won't be easy because Randy Fortune is in paranoid full-retreat from the world."

"I have many talents. I could be a musician come to write

him a ballad on my ukulele."

"No way, I remember you singing at our birthday party."

"I thought you were unconscious."

"Unfortunately, not at that point in the evening."

"Or a poet to compose a verse; or an artist to paint his portrait."

"They have all been and gone. Randy has ennui. He has lost interest in life in general and the arts in particular. Much easier if you went in there now and strangled Wallace while he is asleep in his bed upstairs and leave again immediately. That's his room on the corner."

Tiberius looked up at the rectangle of yellow light. So near! His objective was a sheet of glass and a ladder away. "Do it yourself if you are so desperate to be rid of him," he said.

"I would, but I can't take the risk."

"You have the same chance of being caught as me."

"It doesn't matter if you are arrested because you are supposed to be locked up anyway. Besides, it's not just that. It's the emotional uncertainty. I can't risk strangling Wallace and then discovering that I feel no guilt afterwards; or worse, regret. That would make me as mad as you. You must be aware that sort of thing runs in families. I would prefer you killed him because you already know you are mad. I can't gamble with my sanity."

"Why do you want Wallace dead?"

Eustis paused before replying, having rehearsed a little lie. "He is doing an excellent job persuading Randy Fortune to squander his wealth on a ludicrous moral networking platform, and that's even before his fake lovey-dovey family have gotten here. Randy Fortune will be broke, and I will be out of work if Wallace keeps coming up with such spectacular ideas. The butler is bound to be the first to be laid off in a financial crisis. Can you imagine how stressful the life of an actor can be? You therapists have it easy. No reviews; no waiting on tables between roles; no wondering if you will ever work again.”

“You had a great acting career. All those films. You must be rich enough to retire.”

“For a therapist, you don’t understand people, do you? I need something to give my life meaning. Everyone does. It’s a natural instinct. I have found that here.”

“There is a woman involved, isn’t there? The only time you ever call me is when you hope to get rid of a romantic rival.”

“No. I need to know what Randy Fortune is going to do next.”

“I am a therapist not a fortune teller.”

“Wait, I have it.”

“You do?”

“You are a genius, brother.”

“I concur.”

“What is the one thing your most depressed clients never lose faith in, ever?”

“The brilliance of their analyst?”

“That’s not it.”

“I give up. What?”

“Superstitious nonsense: the more incredible the belief, the better. In fact, the more depressed, the likelier they are to fall for the first charlatan that comes along. They unconsciously believe what they consciously say they don’t believe. Or at least they hope that, this one time, it’s the real thing.”

“I’m impressed, brother. What have I in mind?”

Tiberius asked.

"Randy Fortune is extremely depressed, which calls for an extremely talented charlatan. I will be a classical magician from the past to reveal the future. A wizard," he added with a flourish of his arm.

"Do you know any magic tricks?"

"I once played a magician in a television series. I remember a few tricks with cards. How difficult can it be? All I need is a hat, a few rabbits, and a wand. I can advertise for an assistant: some bimbo who can distract the audience while I perform my sleights of hand. Then you disguise yourself as me, Eustis the butler. After all, under this muck, I am identical to you. That will allow you – as me – to get close to Wallace without him suspecting anything. I will play the wizard. You analyse Wallace, and then kill him, but without implicating me, the butler. I will go back to being Eustis, and you go back to being you, the escaped maniac. Simple."

"It would be simpler if I disguise myself as you now, go in there, analyse him for a week, then kill him if I have to, and escape while you hide out at my penthouse."

"I'm not going to let you be me for a week unsupervised. Are you mad? Don't answer that. Are you even familiar with what a butler does?"

"How hard can it be?"

"No Tiberius. You would fuck everything up for me here. I remember patches of what happened in your parents' basement."

"I can help you with those memories when this is over."

"No, thank you, Tiberius, considering you were the cause of most of them."

"Maybe I could help with this woman you are so obviously lying to me about. I could get her to fall in love with me – I mean, you."

"Keep away from her."

"This is going to end badly, like the last time. I can tell."

"You were always the pessimist, which complements my optimism. You are my alter ego, brother. Three minutes. Three tiny minutes is all that separates us," the butler said, holding up two fingers and a thumb in the dark.

"It's a lifetime," Tiberius said.

One of the Doberman dogs beneath the bush opened an eye, studied the two men in animated conversation under the tree, before closing it again. Plenty time to bite either or both of them if he wanted to, he thought. But only if he wanted to, which he didn't, because it wasn't after midnight yet. He knew this, not through some canine instinct for telling time but because his handler hadn't yet come staggering through the gates, singing.

"Tell me more about this woman you are trying to impress," Tiberius said, wrapping an arm around his brother's shoulder.

"She smells really interesting."

"Smell is a start, psychologically speaking. Have you told her how you feel? No? Well, that's something. She doesn't know you even exist, does she?"

They turned away together from the sleeping dogs and strolled out from under the tree towards the ornamental garden, arm in arm.

The Dobermann could have checked to determine exactly how long he had left to doze if he wore a watch, but he didn't, so he found it difficult to relax, unlike his brother who was snoring, legs twitching while dreaming of sinking his teeth into the buttocks of an entrepreneur fleeing in slow motion from his fangs.

XXVIII

Aestus Complexionem
An Emotional Dilemma

Sometime after midnight in a room above the garden where the Dobermann dogs now circled the fence around Fortune Mansion feigning vigilance, Rik Wallace lay in the middle of the bed between a half-naked Samantha Spencer on one side and a naked Julie Progress on the other. How had it come to this, he wondered? What was he doing with both when the contrast between the two women could not be starker? One was dark; the other fair. One was bony; the other voluptuous. One smelled of WD-40; the other of Chanel. Was he attracted to extremes?

"Say you love me, Rik," Progress purred, pressing her compact curves against him in the manner of a cat begging for a scratch under the chin.

"You have many wonderful attributes."

"Such as? I insist you list them. Tell me specifically. Otherwise, you are merely patronizing me."

Wallace leaned back, all the better to assess Progress, using Samantha as a knobbly pillow. "You have a great figure."

Progress hit him on the arm.

"Ouch. You are strong, ambitious, focussed, independent-minded when you want to be, popular even if no one likes you, successful, organized, cunning, jealous, vain and lazy. Is that enough?"

"*No. Keep going.*"

"On the deficit side, you are selfish; so perhaps it is ironic you are trying to help me to help Randy Fortune to be kind."

"*Nonsense. Kindness has to be self-centred, because if you don't know how to be kind to yourself, how can you hope to be kind to others? Kindness originates in selfishness. Therefore, ipso facto, I am the kindest person imaginable.*"

"I will have to think about that."

"*What about me?*" Samantha asked, wriggling her stomach under the back of his head to get his attention. "*What of my qualities?*"

He turned around in the crowded bed to face her.

Samantha's breasts disappeared under Wallace's hands. A ridge of black down joined her sunken navel to the elastic of her knickers inviting his eye to follow the curve of the transparent cloth with tiny yellow flowers floating on its surface into the shadow between her legs. She raised her protruding hips from the mattress to allow him to pull her knickers over the bush of hair, and down over her downy legs.

"Shouldn't you shave those—?"

"*Women are hairy. Haven't you noticed?*"

"*I'm not,*" Progress said, butting in. "*I'll list your attributes,*" she added surveying Samantha's boyish frame with a sour expression. "*You are smelly, secretive, sneaky, nasty, moody, and hairy in all the wrong places.*" She ran her hands over her own ample breasts. "*Compared to my perfect figure, you are a collection of bones held inside a bag of pale skin.*"

Samantha aimed a punch at Progress, her extended arm flashing across Wallace's face. He woke up with the empty covers wrapped around his knees. A trickle of sweat ran down the centre of his back as he gasped for breath. I need a drink, he told himself for the five-hundredth-and-seventy-second time since arriving at Fortune Mansion.

In a room on the ground floor Samantha Spencer's forehead rested on the desk in front of her open laptop. The green and red pattern of the screensaver swayed over and back like a belly dancer in synch with her loud snores. Dolores O'Riordan was working herself up on the desktop speakers.

"I am interested in your work with computers," a naked Wallace said. She knew he was lying, but she wasn't angry. Why couldn't she be angry with him?

Now he was sitting beside her.

"Explain to me again how you built the algorithm for kindness."

She rotated the laptop on the desk to block the view of his pale, hairless, concave chest.

"Only if you get dressed!"

The screen flashed light-blue when she opened the KindFace application. She scrolled down through pictures to stop on a rose. Here is someone who has over seven million hearts, she said.

"Is that the highest number?"

"Thus far, it seems to be."

Rik lay back on the pillows that appeared around him, folded his arms behind his head, and raised one leg to rest it on his knee.

"Please dress. I can see much too much of you," she said, staring at his crotch.

"*What does it say? Read it to me.*"

Dear KindFace,

I was kind to my elderly neighbour. I put her in my car and took her on a picnic with my dog. That wasn't the entire kind act. Even though I was late for dinner, on the way home I dropped her off at the local A&E to have her broken hip fixed. The cow decided to fall over when she was with me. She didn't collapse last week when the Smiths – who are her neighbours on the other side – threw her from her front door into the back of their station wagon parked on the street. She didn't dare break anything when she was with the bloody Smiths. The doctor said it was brittle bones. She didn't have brittle bones last week. That's the last person I'm going to be kind to, so please heart this. Where can I collect my money?

"*Will Randy find that morally consoling?*" Wallace asked.

Samantha tried to ignore him to concentrate on searching the site for another leading example of kindness.

"Oh, here is one. It has almost as many hearts."

Dear KindFace,

I hope you don't have rules against historical cases of kindness because my example began over ten years ago. Back then I didn't approve of my sister's fiancé, so I lied to her that he had made sexual advances to me while she was undergoing surgery in hospital. I did it for her sake. They broke up despite his protesting his innocence. Well, he would, wouldn't he? Last week I confessed to her that I had lied. This was after seeing a counsellor who helped me realise that I stopped being jealous of her when I married and had three children. Now my husband is dead because my sister killed him in an act of revenge. Please heart me for my unselfish kindness to my sister – the one with the ex-fiancé and not the other one whom no one likes.

Perhaps it was the movement of her head as it came up off the desk a fraction of a second before her eyes opened that woke Samantha. She rubbed her face in her dry hands and ran her nose along the length of her arm to soak up snot that had leaked out. It's the cheese that causes such weird dreams, she thought. I should stop eating cheese.

Behind the wall, Eustis had nodded off.

Upstairs, Julie Progress was on her back, staring at the ceiling. She couldn't sleep. She was wearing a wetsuit. Beside her, Randy Fortune snored. She was thinking how easy it was to accomplish the big things such as saving the planet, recycling everything, or being a vegan when she was sober. It was the little things – for example, not smothering Randy – that were difficult. Between stentorian blasts she reminded herself she needed him alive because she wasn't certain if she was mentioned in his will. Surely, he would include her after all she had done for him. How would she find out? Could she ask him over breakfast? How would she start that conversation without raising suspicion?

She fell asleep while counting her possible inheritance.

XXIX

Dubois In Novissimis Dierum?
The Last Days of Dubois?

Jackson and the librarian stood outside the closed bedroom door in their tiny flat above the second-hand book shop. They were listening. A sustained silence following the sound of vomiting, interspersed with groans, offered hope that, at last, Ellen Dubois was unconscious.

"Are we doing the right thing?" Jackson asked.

"We need more time. She won't listen to a word we say about what she should tell Randy Fortune when we finally pluck up the courage to let her meet him. Besides, the general side effects of Temazepam are ideal for the hypochondriac."

"Apart from the unfavourable impression she is likely to make on Randy Fortune, I am starting to conclude she may not be the most suitable match out there for Rik Wallace. It wouldn't be fair on either of them. They are both too … *neurotic* … in incompatible ways. Individual eccentricities need to complement each other—"

"Shush. Will you shut up? I'm trying to listen," the librarian hissed, pressing her ear to the door.

Jackson continued regardless. "He is too thoughtful, and she doesn't think at all from what I can tell. He would be better off without her, though you can be sure he wouldn't thank us for the years of misery we would spare him if we found someone else."

The librarian removed her ear from the door. "I don't hear anything now. She makes more noise than a hippopotamus when she is asleep, and when she's awake all she does is demand we drive her to Fortune Mansion to collect her billions. Do you think she might have expired?"

"We are never that lucky."

"Your idea to make Wallace a widower with three darling children is not the worst one you have come up with."

"Thanks." Jackson blushed. He wanted to shuffle his feet but couldn't because a child had perched on each of his insteps, pinning them to the floor. The third child clung to the librarian's leg. The fate of their mother in the bedroom did not excite their curiosity.

"By the way, how did you know how much Temazepam to put in her tea?" he asked.

"I consulted the Internet. We can say it was an accident if it is detected in her system."

Now Jackson took his turn in pressing his ear to the door. "I can't hear anything at all. Do you think she is—?"

"Don't say that word in front of the children. You could traumatise them for life."

"You already said it."

"I didn't, did I?"

"She didn't," the tallest child confirmed. "She said *expired*."

Jackson almost fell into the room when the door opened.

Ellen Dubois was upright but clinging to the doorframe. The librarian examined her with the close scrutiny of an experienced physician assessing the decline of a patient presenting with a perplexing range of symptoms.

"We were … err … concerned for you," Jackson stammered, imagining he was explaining away the group in the doorway. He took a step backward. "You don't look so good."

Ellen Dubois had turned a shiny snot-green colour since her children had last seen her.

"I'm sick. Something is wrong," she gasped.

"Can you list your symptoms?" the librarian asked, bringing the tips of her fingers together.

Ellen Dubois vomited down the front of Jackson's ironed paisley-patterned shirt.

"Nausea," the librarian confirmed. "Anything else?"

"I am trembling all over. My pulse is going fast and slow. Feel that," Ellen said, clamping Jackson's hand onto her breast that bulged out over the top of the librarian's best nightdress that she had loaned her. Jackson used his free hand to cover his mouth while gagging from the smell of puke.

"Are you dizzy?" the librarian asked, pulling her husband's palm from the patient's bosom. She wondered if she could bring herself to ever wear that nightdress again once this unfortunate episode was behind them.

"I can't stand up."

"Ah. Weakness. Good. I mean, that's terrible."

"What is wrong with me?"

"You might prepare yourself for amnesia, headaches, depression, and coma followed by death." The librarian clamped her hands over the ears of the child clinging to her leg, just then remembering the sensitivities of her audience. "Sorry, children," she said, letting go of the child's head to clarify. "I mean, a coma followed by a restful, *permanent* sleep."

"What have you done to me? I am dying."

"Now, you have to admit dying is your default condition. You cannot blame us for that. Go back to bed and sleep. I will bring you another mug of soothing herbal tea."

"No. This is different. Call an ambulance. I can get them to stop by Fortune Mansion to collect my billions if I feel better on the way. I know most of the drivers."

"I'm sure you will be fine if you rest."

"Call a fucking ambulance," Ellen shrieked.

"Children, go and play in the kitchen," the librarian said, indicating the space behind her head by raising her eyebrows.

"There is nothing to play with. You have no toys," the tallest child complained.

"Your place is boring," the second one confirmed.

"Go and play with the pots and pans. We have gas. Play with that while we take care of your mother."

Ellen Dubois lay under a sheet on a trolley just inside the entrance to the A&E at Saint Drogo's General Hospital. The automatic doors slid open and shut with the constant stream of passers-by like a pair of lungs ventilating the building. Her arm hung down between two bars of the stainless-steel safety rail holding her in place. Jackson, sitting on a stool beside her, clung to her hand with both of his. A white-coated doctor stood at the foot of the trolley reading medical notes clamped to a clipboard. He was speaking, though no one seemed to be listening. Certainly not Ellen Dubois.

Perhaps his conscience or the chill air from outside

distracted Jackson. But, as with many who regret their recent behaviour, he hadn't yet resolved to make any major changes unless it was to employ a less messy method the next time. Nor could he make up his mind to move out of the draught. His will seemed to be paralysed. The librarian sat on the opposite side with a half-full bowl of vomit on her knees. She crinkled her nose in a futile attempt to impede her olfactory function. Apart from the smell. she was also struggling with a novel emotion. She was anxious about the children back in the tiny kitchen where she had left them with a frying pan, a bag of flour, and a dozen eggs with a stern order they make pancakes for their dinner if they didn't intend on starving to death while the adults were at the hospital. When the blue flashing lights bounced through the upstairs windows signalling the arrival of the ambulance outside on the street, the middle child had climbed into his coat in Pavlovian expectation that he would be coming along too. He was handed an eggbeater and told to stay behind with his siblings.

"I have seen this before: nausea, shaking, gasping for air, weakness, and dying. In fact, Ms Dubois, I saw it all last month when you were admitted here to Saint Drogo's A&E."

Ellen Dubois panted for air.

"You are exhibiting your habitual symptoms. Everything is familiar here apart from the diarrhoea that I grant is testament to your dedication to the general cause of hypochondria. I am confident you will be up and around in time to be back again next month. You have caught me in a good mood. You can stay here until, say, ten o clock, imbibe our hospital ambience, and then please go away. Okay? That is the limit of my compassion."

"Listen, you moron," Ellen Dubois wheezed. "I had

important business with a billionaire to attend to on the way here, but I wasn't up to it. That's how sick I am."

"Thank God," the librarian mouthed to herself.

"This time it's different," Ellen Dubois gasped.

"It always is," the doctor muttered.

"I swear to you I am dying."

"You have broken that promise so many times already. Without doubt, metaphysically we are all dying, you included; but medically – no. I cannot send you for a CAT scan every time you turn up here at death's door. Our hospital budget doesn't stretch that far. Those who are ill need—"

"I want to see a real doctor."

"For my part, Ms Dubois, I have real patients to see. I could send around our resident psychiatrist for a chat. How would that be?"

"No. No psychiatrists," Jackson pleaded.

"I'm dying," Ellen Dubois moaned.

"That would be the fourth time this year, and that's just counting this hospital," the doctor said, flicking through the pages of medical notes.

"I only have to be right once. Find me a real doctor. One who cares. One who takes their hypocritical oath seriously."

"We would be glad to take her straight home and care for her there, doctor. That is if you will sign off that nothing serious is wrong with her," the librarian said. She looked around for somewhere to put the basin of warm vomit. Before she could decide between pushing it under the trolley with her foot or placing it on top of a low dresser where she would pretend to forget it, Ellen Dubois deposited another half cup of fresh spew into the bowl.

"Yes, that would be great," the doctor confirmed.

Jackson stood outside the bedroom listening for the third time in twenty minutes. Meanwhile, the librarian applied a large plaster to the cheek of the girl whose hair was covered in a helmet of flour and mayonnaise. "You would have an eye patch if that fork had been one inch higher. You could have been a pirate for the rest of your life. Would you have liked that? You, yes, you, whatever your name is, stop skating on those broken eggs," she shrieked.

"At last, I hear snoring," Jackson confirmed, interrupting the librarian voicing her regret she had forgotten to stop on the way home for Lego. It's my own fault if they wreck the place, she was telling herself.

"The sleeping pills the doctor gave us must be working," Jackson said.

"You, yes, you with the frying pan," the librarian said. "Stop that racket. All of you - get out of the kitchen. I have to make tea for your mother."

"Wait to see if she wakes up again. In the meantime, I will order pizza for dinner," Jackson said. "Would everyone like pizza?"

The children squealed and ran from the tiny kitchen into the living room, knocking over the librarian's prized milk jug on the way, and back again into the kitchen. The girl skidded on egg yolks on the floor and smacked into the cooker. She began to cry, holding her nose in her hands.

"Jackson, you are driving them crazy. Shut the fuck up," the librarian screamed, but it was impossible to tell at whom the command was aimed: the children, or their mother behind the bedroom door, or Jackson, or her own hysterical-self inside her head.

The librarian was pinned once more between the oven and Jackson's pointy hip.

"I've been thinking," she said.

"About what?"

"What is best for the children!"

"So, you've decided not to smother them after what they did in the kitchen?"

"Not entirely. I thought we might keep them for, say, a month on a trial basis. Don't look at me that way. I can't turn my head, but I know you are making one of your faces. After that, we could review how we feel, and if we are not keen on them by then, we can still smother them."

"All three?"

"I haven't gone soft. I still hate children. It's just that I am getting used to these particular ones."

"I remember reading somewhere that parents aren't expected to like their children straight off, perhaps ever. I am sure most love their children, but I doubt you will find many who like them. What about Rik Wallace?"

"What about him?"

"We promised we would find him a family."

"He can wait a while."

"He needs them urgently."

"He is not a suitable role model for those children. He never stops thinking."

"There is that."

"He has no home; no proper job nor prospects; he can't offer them security. Those children need a stable environment after everything we have put them through."

"Even though I stood up for him at his trial, it strikes me now that perhaps he would be better off in Saint Drogo's Asylum for the Criminally Insane."

"That institution can give him what any wife and family can't: peace of mind."

"That's what I mean. He belongs there."

"Definitely."

"I was thinking it would be best for Rik if we tell Inspector Sullivan where he is hiding, because he will never find him without our help."

"For his own good."

"Definitely."

"Let's sleep on it."

"I can't sleep."

"Read a book."

"Not enough room to bend my elbows."

Sometime during the night, under the cover of darkness, the mysterious knot that binds family members together loosened before tightening again around a different formation. As Ellen Dubois slept, she was unaware that from now on she was on her own. Jackson and the librarian's new-found parental instincts would prove stronger than the bonds of friendship with Wallace. But that was natural, wasn't it?

XXX

Antiqua Serra
An Old Saw

Rik Wallace sat at the end of the table slurping the juice from a semi-sphere of grapefruit by clamping it between his front teeth.

"The machine over there can do that for you," Samantha Spencer suggested, pointing to a juicer standing on a long sideboard that ran the length of the smallest of the three spaces designated as dining rooms before the era of ennui.

"I know," he said, wiping pink liquid from his chin with the back of his hand.

"Barbarian."

Before he could think of a reply the butler distracted him by fussing over the presentation of his employer's breakfast. Eustis was confident the fried egg would meet with Randy Fortune's approval because it was in the exact centre of the plate, having measured the distance from three points on the circumference to the edge of the egg yolk as instructed. He had cooked it on a pan set up on a burner on the sideboard for that purpose. He placed the silver rack of equally sized triangles of uniformly beige toast beside the plate and positioned the triangular pat of butter in the round dish to the side. Looking down on the breakfast from the ceiling above a spider might be put in mind of a Miro painting.

Julie Progress sipped coffee from an oversized cup, lost in her own melancholic thoughts. She was confident she couldn't pass another night encased in rubber, but how was she to bring up the matter of her potential inheritance? It alarmed her to discover money was not a compensation for everything. In desperation, she had proposed marriage again to Randy at 4.12 a.m. She remembered the time because it was illuminated in green digital numerals on the music system in the bedroom. A legacy seemed her last remaining hope if a wedding was now out of the question. She would introduce it casually to avoid his questioning her motivation again.

"You must eat something," Randy told her, shocking her out of her reverie. He picked up a knife from where it lay on the crisp, white tablecloth with its edge towards the symmetrical egg. "Breakfast is the most important meal of the day."

What she wanted to say was, "Fuck you". Instead, she muttered that she wasn't hungry.

Randy sliced a wedge from the egg white, forming a triangle with an acute angle of sixty degrees and balanced it on a fork before depositing it on the pink tongue that he let hang out of his mouth with the deliberate movements of a forklift driver.

Progress considered picking up the knife by her empty plate and placing it at an angle of ninety degrees to Randy's face by driving it through his fucking eye socket. But she resisted the impulse – as she did every morning after a night in rubber.

"When can we expect to meet your family, Wallace?" Randy asked. "I have to say I am getting tired of waiting."

The grapefruit juice stopped on its way down Wallace's

oesophagus.

"Speaking of families, Randy," Progress butted in, "it's important I know what you are leaving me in your will before—I mean, *in case* anything happens to you?"

"You are not family. Anyway, nothing."

"What do you mean nothing? You selfish bastard," she screamed at him.

"I mean nothing is going to happen to me, because I plan not to die. I'm having myself frozen and thawed out when someone has invented a cure for death."

"The awareness of our mortality is the only thing that makes life tolerable," Wallace said, having at last managed to swallow.

"Isn't there a law against spouting philosophy so early in the day?" Samantha asked. Eustis was positioned behind her, holding an enormous coffee pot, anxiously waiting to pour.

"Listen to him, Randy. Listen to him," Progress hissed, pointing a fork at Wallace. "He knows better than anyone here that nothing could be worse than living forever."

Randy ignored her. "Where did you say your family were coming from?" he asked Wallace.

"The moon," Wallace answered.

"Where?"

"I said *soon*. They will be here soon."

"We are making such an unexpected breakthrough with KindFace, it would be a shame to abandon it just because its inspiration was a selfish loner, who thought of no one other than himself," Randy said. "I can't trust people who don't have families."

"Yeah, where are your wife and children?" Samantha asked

Wallace. "It's not fair to keep us all in suspense."

He was desperate to tell her that love was more important than the disappointment and multiple homicides that must surely follow his confession that he had no family. As Wallace shaped his lips – while contemplating the most poetic form of words he might use to confess, followed by his declaration of devotion to Samantha – Eustis saw his opportunity. Had he known the impact of the revelation before he interrupted, he may well have chosen to remain silent. Such moments mark the junction between the easy and the hard road. Eustis chose the latter without ever realising the existential impact of his not remaining silent. He cleared his throat as a prelude to an announcement of his own. "What everyone needs is cheering up. I have an idea for a wonderful distraction. Who wants to attend a magic show in the library?"

"I would rather drill a hole in my forehead," Progress said. She stirred sugar into her coffee in a vain attempt to sweeten her mood.

"A magic show," Randy repeated. "Have you lost your mind, Eustis?"

But the butler didn't catch these words because Randy was trying to dissolve the egg in his mouth without chewing while talking. Randy swallowed and added, "Magic would demand a level of naïve credulity I abandoned a long time ago."

"I am reliably informed that magic is a cure for depression," Eustis said, undaunted.

"Who is depressed now?" Samantha asked, taking her face out of her cereal bowl.

"Everyone in this fucking mansion," Progress confirmed.

"I am not accusing anyone in particular of being depressed.

I am speaking hypothetically," Eustis said, while leaning over Samantha's cup with the coffee pot that seemed large enough to topple him face-first onto the table.

"I love magic," Samantha said to annoy Progress.

"I can assure you this will be no ordinary show. A contemporary production. This magician comes with the highest possible commendation," Eustis said. He placed the pot down on the edge of the table with a shaky hand. "He does more than perform tricks. He is also famous for the accuracy of his predictions. And who doesn't want to learn what the future holds?"

"I don't," Wallace said between sucks on the grapefruit.

"He can also tell how long you will live," Eustis said, narrowing his eyes at Wallace. "Even those who plan to live forever." He now narrowed them at Randy.

"Having your fortune told is the last resort of the desperate," Wallace said.

"That would suit you then," Samantha said.

"I am desperate," Randy confirmed.

"He can make contact with your future self. Time and space are no barriers to his powers," Eustis said, voicing whatever words came into his head, having forgotten his prepared script. "All the celebrities love him."

"What is his name?" Progress asked.

"His name?" Eustis repeated the question out loud while thinking what a bitch Progress was. Tiberius and he had planned this conversation down to the last detail except for the fucking name of the magician he was going to play. "His name?" he repeated, vying for time. "He is called The Great Augustus," Eustis said, picking a title he imagined was at random, but which perhaps a Freudian could have argued revealed an unconscious megalomania. Consciously, he was annoyed that his twin brother hadn't agreed to just strangle Wallace and have done with it, saving him all of this palaver. Family could be so selfish.

"Never heard of him," Samantha said. "How great can he be? I'll look him up on the Internet."

"He's not on it. He is too … mysterious … for the digital world," the butler lied with unguarded energy.

"Augustus?" Wallace asked, having exhausted the half grapefruit. "I have an acquaintance called Tiberius. But he is not a magician. He is a madman. I wonder if they are related?"

"No, they are not," Eustis snapped. "The Great Augustus has no earthly relatives." The butler was on a lying roll.

"No family?"

"Wizarding and families don't go together."

"You seem quite agitated. What's wrong, Eustis?" Progress asked, sensing a chink in the butler's otherwise reliable performance of habitual calm. "Your anger seems to have made you stronger."

Eustis considered hitting Progress across the side of the head with the giant coffee pot, which he was unaware he had picked up again in his agitation. But acting school had taught him to channel his emotions towards the overriding dramatic goal that, in this case, was getting Randy to agree to a magical performance in the library. Besides, he wasn't a homicidal maniac like his brother, was he? While he was at it, he should have arranged for Tiberius to throttle Progress as well. Siblings are such selfish bastards; they consider no one's needs but their own. He took a deep breath. "The Great Augustus is wonderful," he said. "I guarantee you will have never seen an act like his."

"Every rational person knows that magicians are charlatans," Progress said.

"Happily, there are no rational people here," Wallace said. "Apart perhaps from me. Well, perhaps not."

"Once you work out how the trick is done it loses its appeal," Progress added, ignoring Wallace.

"In general, that is true, but with The Great Augustus, his magic is real," Eustis said narrowing his eyes again at Progress. "No tricks." I can't rely on my brother for the tiniest favour, he thought, studying her neck. "He can cut a man – or a woman – in two in front of your eyes and put them back together again."

"Anyone can do that with the appropriate kit," Progress said. "You can buy all that stuff on the Internet: a box with a hidden compartment. You make your victim squash into the top half and hire a small person or use false feet for the bottom half and—"

"Yes, on the Internet, but in the real world you need to be prepared to be covered in blood and deafened by screams."

"So, he is not that good then?"

Eustis inhaled and exhaled.

"On the contrary, *real* magic can go wrong, while trickery works every time. To demonstrate his superior skill, he will saw two people in half simultaneously, one on top of the other. I bet you have never seen that before." What am I saying? he asked himself, but got no reply. Has someone taken control of my mind? Still no answer.

Unknown to the actor, his character, Augustus, was beginning to take shape in his imagination. A plan was forming, the details of which were materialising in patches in response to Progress's contrariness. "Yes, two at once," Eustis confirmed. He was almost surprised he wasn't cackling.

"What do you say, Wallace? You are the philosopher. Do you believe in magic?" Randy asked.

Eustis glared at Wallace with an expression the meaning of which he could easily interpret.

"I dismiss no beliefs. I hold everything and nothing to be true at the same time."

"What a load of bullshit," Samantha said. "Reminds me of my father."

"Let's put it to a vote," Randy said. "All in favour raise your hand."

"I am not voting for it," Progress said. She folded her arms across her chest as if one of them might shoot above her head against her will.

"I am for it if she is against it," Samantha said. She raised her hand exposing a tangle of matted hair in her armpit.

Eustis remembered to rest the coffee pot on the edge of the table in time to extend his own hand, but slowly.

"I suppose I could vote for it if he promised to saw her in half," Progress relented, nodding at Samantha.

She unwrapped her arms.

"Can your magician turn this coffee into whisky?" Wallace asked.

"Easy," Eustis confirmed.

"In that case, I'm in," Wallace said. He ignored the second half of the grapefruit to raise his arm without regard for his future.

"It seems you can have your magic show, Eustis," Randy

said, raising his hand. Everyone at the table was staring at him when he looked up.

"What?" he asked.

After breakfast, the butler hid in a cupboard under the stairs. He needed to be alone.

"Two at once," he muttered to himself. "Am I fucking mad? Tiberius will kill me when he hears about this. What was I thinking? Think, for God's sake. Try to have wizardly thoughts. What would The Great Augustus do? You have to psych yourself into the role."

It was too dark for the actor to observe the scepticism on the face of a passing rat.

XXXI

Conjungens Punctis
Joining the Dots

Bentley Murphy found Bernard the security guard sitting behind his desk with a stack of cardboard-covered patient files in front of him when he arrived at his office ahead of schedule to steel himself against that day's therapy sessions.

"What are you doing?" the psychiatrist protested, while throwing his new tweed jacket onto the hook on the back of the door. "Those are confidential."

"I'm not surprised given some of the things I have been reading. Made the hair stand up on my wife's head. I will treat the inmates in this place with greater respect from now on."

"Close those files and get out from behind my desk."

Bernard ignored the order. "Since I still feel guilty over my part in Tiberius Lang's escape – though my wife blames you for not projecting the appropriate psychological gravitas on my first day: you just didn't look like someone in charge – I decided to read his file in search of clues as to where he might be hiding."

"You are going through all my files, not only his."

"I couldn't put them down once I started into one. This is gripping stuff, Prof. Have you thought of publishing? The story of the cat and the washing machine – readers love cats, but this is—"

"They are not stories. They are people's lives. Give me that," Murphy said as he reached across the desk for the file in Bernard's hand.

"My wife thought we might find a reference to some place with sentimental significance for Tiberius such as his parents' home," Bernard said. He pressed the file to his chest, beyond the psychiatrist's reach.

"Don't you think I already thought of that? It's a dead end! He burned that house down after strangling them." Murphy banged the ends of a handful of files into line on the surface of his desk.

"Were you aware his birth mother had another baby when she sold Tiberius to that pair of psychologists?"

"Only one of them was a psychologist. The other was an analyst."

"It's the same thing."

"It's not, Bernard. For Tiberius, it is the defining difference around which he constructed his entire psychosis. You must respect the obsessions of your patients in order to win their trust if you aspire to be a psychiatrist."

"My wife got thinking to herself – okay, so I am a lunatic therapist who breaks out of Drogo's, where can I turn for help?"

"To the one living relative I have – my twin brother," Murphy added.

"Yes. That was her first line of thought until she read in his file that Tiberius isn't sentimental."

"I know. I wrote that," Murphy said. "Oh, Bernard, I am an idiot. So is your wife. Listen." He brought a finger to his lips to signify the depth of his concentration. "Tiberius is a Freudian so, of course, because he denies it, we can tell he is obsessed with his family. Why didn't I see it sooner? I should be reading the subtext. The absence of any emotional reference is proof of his obsession with sentimentalism. In fact, strangling his parents was the kindest act he could have done for them if it ended their misery of having him for a child. He would consider that a normal response."

"I would never strangle my mother, and I am normal."

"I am sure you love your mother, Bernard."

"You make it sound so creepy. You never met my mother. I didn't say I loved her. I said I wouldn't strangle her."

"Shut up, Bernard. The point I am making is that if we find the brother, we will find Tiberius because family is the root cause of all madness for a Freudian."

"That's what my wife was trying to say," Bernard sighed.

"Yes, but she's not qualified to say it."

"How did you become a Freudian, Prof?"

"It's a long story. We don't have time for it now."

"Your first patient is not due for half an hour," Bernard confirmed looking at Murphy's diary open on the desk.

"I was hoping to have time to analyse my own thoughts before getting into other peoples'."

"My wife says too much thinking is detrimental for anyone. She says, if you're talking, you're not thinking. You should spend more time talking to me."

Murphy sat down and stretched out on the chaise longue. He rubbed his hands together, one over the other.

"Well, I suppose, if you insist."

"I do."

"After deciding to specialise in psychiatry because I never got used to the sight of blood in medical school, I needed an approach to madness. My journey through the forest of ideas was by trial and error. Once I thought I might even be a Heideggerian. Can you imagine? You are thinking how wild was I back then."

Bernard was wondering what his wife had packed for his lunch.

"I was confused, which is understandable because Martin Heidegger has had an influence on existentialism, hermeneutics, and even theology. One evening I was having dinner with my at-that-time research supervisor. We were in a cheap Chinese restaurant. She was both parsimonious and a highly regarded scholar. That was not as rare a combination back then as you might imagine. A dozen round tables covered with plain red oilcloths were spread out across the bleak yellow rectangular room. We sat at the first one, inside the large window; she was watching the rain running down the glass outside – Heideggerians can find something of interest in the most banal detail. It turns out she chose that place not only because it was inexpensive but also because she had proposed to the student who became her second husband at that very same table.

"I had just swallowed a mouthful of tepid, cloudy, green tea when I felt fingers gripping my knee, and attempting to crawl up my leg like a tarantula. I didn't scream. Instead, I looked around the room. Back then I was a rationalist, trained in the art of logical deduction. I observed that there was no one sitting within two yards of us. This allowed me to eliminate the possibility that someone from another table, even someone with long arms, was involved. Furthermore, my only other suspect, the sullen waiter, was at that time back at the service hatch picking up plates of chow mien, for which that place had a reputation. Therefore, I was able to deduce the fingers belonged to my supervisor sitting opposite me. My hypothesis was proven to my satisfaction when she confirmed, on my enquiring, that indeed it was her hand that I felt groping its way up the inside of my leg. Say what you like about phenomenologists, despite their commitment to obscurity, they will answer a direct question if put to them in a focussed way. I then enquired if the coherence of my potential thesis, not as yet written you understand, would be affected by my reaction. I suspected she was not being truthful when she denied the tarantula on my leg had a bearing on the future success of my research. In her defence, one must wonder how a phenomenologist, who doesn't know what they are saying half the time, would even notice when they are lying?

"I told her to remove her bony claw from my thigh. She dumped me before the chow mien arrived. But she was right. Even though I was starving, I could recognise we were not a suitable match. I was never a committed phenomenologist."

"Intriguing. Go on," Bernard said, nodding his head while doodling on the desk blotter. This was more distracting than security work, even if it was impossible to concentrate on what his client was saying.

"I found my ultimate supervisor at the breakfast counter in the hotel hosting a conference on human evolution. By then, I was thrashing around for anything in which I could persuade myself to believe. I came up behind him as he was jamming a butter knife, the base metal kind one finds in cheap cafes frequented by students and philosophers, into the toaster, in a vain attempt to retrieve a disintegrating slice of bread. He threw the broken sections onto a plate while muttering curses on the technology. 'Professor Woolf,' I said – I had seen his name affixed to a photograph on a poster in reception – pointing to a large sign above our heads, 'it says up there not to stick a fork into the toaster. You need to take care of yourself because you are a national intellectual treasure.'

"He waved the blade of the butter knife under my nose with one hand while pushing the long thin grey strands of his hair back over his oversized skull with the other.

'What is that?' he asked.

'A knife,' I said with rash confidence, because it seemed an easy metaphysical question coming from a professor with a head that size.

'What does that sign advise against using on the toaster?'

'A fork,' I confirmed.

'Exactly. A fork. So? Fuck off and mind your own business.' With that he turned his back on me and began to attempt the toasting of another slice of bread with the aid of the knife.

"I tapped him on the shoulder.

'What do you want now?' he snarled, without turning around.

'I am looking for someone to supervise my psychiatric research,' I told him.

'I am too busy to take on another sycophant who admires my books,' he said.

'I haven't read a single word you have ever written,' I stammered. Then I felt it would be polite to enquire what theory he followed.

'Freud,' he said.

'That suits me fine,' I said.

"Then he did turn around to scrutinise me with his huge watery eyes in which I could observe my reflection drowning. 'Okay, I will take you on,' he said. 'Now, fuck off.'

"Which I did, leaving him there at the breakfast counter with his back to me again. For the next ten minutes, from a table in the corner, I watched him struggle with the toaster as a queue formed behind him. I was not yet sold on Freud. Later, I stirred my coffee with a plastic spoon, working hard on an air of indifference, while he was being loaded into the back of an ambulance. I had nothing with which to reproach myself.

"That, Bernard, is how I found my way to Freud – who has the advantage of being a far less complicated thinker than Heidegger – when the professor was released from hospital the next day. Why make things difficult for oneself? Psychiatry is hard enough without picking on the most impenetrable people to make sense of it. Unfortunately for the progress of my career, if not my happiness, my formation remained incomplete when a truck ran over Woolf while he was arguing outside a school with a lollipop woman that her sign did not mean *all* of the children were slow-witted. But then, rationality is overrated. Don't you agree?"

"Interesting, interesting – but I'm afraid our time is up," Bernard said, looking at his watch and taking his feet down from the desk. "We will have to take this up again in our next session."

Bentley Murphy sat up and placed the soles of his feet on the brown carpet.

"Anyway, my wife did a little research. It turns out the brother's name is Claudius Steel."

"Whose brother?"

"Tiberius's twin brother. The one who was separated at birth!"

"Don't you mean Lang?"

"No, you idiot—I mean, Professor. Lang is Tiberius's adopted name. The brother is Claudius Steel."

"The actor?"

"My wife says he is currently playing a butler at the billionaire Randy Fortune's mansion following his critically acclaimed appearance in the sequel to the superhero movie. She knows these things because she reads *Celebrity Hermit Magazine*. His fans are unhappy because they don't get to see him perform anymore."

"I've heard of him. He played Macbeth in that all-nude production that was closed down when he sliced off Macduff's penis during a sword fight. It was in all the papers."

"Yes. That's him.

"Bernard, your wife is a genius."

The security guard turned red and shiny with pleasure. "She is? I'll tell her you said so, but I'm not sure she will be pleased," he said when he was able to speak again.

"Thanks to her we now know where we can find this Claudius, who will lead us to his alter ego, his twin brother, Tiberius, and we can be confident he is obsessed with this brother precisely because he denies it. Simple. I will pay Randy Fortune's butler a visit."

"You will need security going there. These super-rich people are as crazy as the patients locked up in here. Liable to try anything," Bernard protested.

"I'll go there on my own. This is psychiatric business,"

Murphy said.

"My wife will kill me if she finds out I missed out on the chance to set eyes on the inside of a billionaire's mansion. She will want to know what colour curtains he has, and how many carats are in the golden toilet bowls. I have to go with you."

"We can't turn up and risk startling Tiberius if we find him there with his brother. We don't want him running off again."

"I'll bring my Taser gun."

"No guns, Bernard."

"We could wear disguises, just in case."

"That's an excellent idea, Bernard."

"As you always say in these cases, Professor, it is the client who does all the work while you get paid."

"Who should we go as?"

"Phenomenologists?"

"You haven't understood a word I said, have you, Bernard?"

"I wasn't listening."

"We professionals never listen, but that doesn't prevent us understanding what's being said. You have a long way to go if you want to be taken seriously in psychiatry."

XXXII

Adparatio
Construction

Jackson and the librarian stood at the foot of the bed they hadn't slept in for ages, surveying their house guest, whose head hung over the side of the mattress at the other end.

"This looks like malice aforethought to me," Jackson said, picking up a hammer by the handle and dangling the evidence between his thumb and forefinger above the duvet.

"I poured enough Temazepam into her to knock out a mid-sized elephant, but she wouldn't shut up about her billions," the librarian said in mitigation.

"The hammer?" he asked.

"It wasn't premeditated. I was hanging up a framed poster of Eric Cartman for the children when I was overwhelmed by an impulse."

"Hmmmnnn?"

"She was sitting there, propped up against our pillows, droning on and on about when she was going to get her money. I couldn't take anymore. I snapped."

"How will you explain away that lump as a form of hypochondria to the staff at Saint Drogo's A&E?" Jackson asked, pointing the hammer at the purple third eye in the middle of Ellen Dubois's forehead.

"It turns out, by a stroke of luck that I hit her with just the right amount of force. Despite appearances, she isn't dead. She is in a coma, and that is where she can stay. Social services will leave the children here with us because their mother could wake up any minute: they wouldn't want them to miss out on that maternal treat."

"We should call an ambulance, again."

"We are not taking her to the hospital where they may revive her."

"I'm not sure they would."

"I am unwilling to take that chance."

"If anyone asks, let's say she fell down the stairs while rushing for an ambulance."

"That's credible. But what about Rik Wallace? He is expecting her to show up at Fortune Mansion any time now. What are we going to tell him?"

"I would think of something, but to do that I need one good night's sleep. I want my bed back. My spine is killing me from the kitchen floor."

"I'm not getting back into that bed again, ever."

"This flat is too small for our growing family."

"We are parents now. We have to make sacrifices."

The doorway filled with children.

"You can make whatever noise you want. Your mother is sound asleep."

"I've made up my mind. I'm calling Inspector Sullivan to tell him where he can find Wallace. We can't go on with this uncertainty. It's not fair on those children. I'm sure it's the right thing to do."

Jackson and the librarian believed in doing immediately what they could wisely postpone until tomorrow or, indeed, even forever.

The middle child spent an hour writing a note with three different coloured crayons on the back of a cereal box advising the few regular customers that the consumption of food and beverages was prohibited in the bookshop downstairs. The librarian taped this to the window, proud that one of the children was displaying her penchant for signage.

"Can I have a puppy?" the girl asked, catching Jackson's eye.

"A puppy? Never. Dogs shed hairs. Hairs aren't good for children."

"A hypoallergenic breed," her brother suggested.

"We'll see."

"Please. Pleeeeease."

"Let's start with looking after a goldfish."

"Goldfish are boring."

"Children must learn responsibility. We can consider a hamster if you manage a fish, and then maybe a cat, working our way up the hierarchy of species."

"How long?"

"How long what?

"For how long must we take care of a goldfish?"

"Until he dies. From natural causes," Jackson added for clarification. "There will be an autopsy."

Sergeant Jones was searching for possible clues she may have overlooked. Glancing up from the pages of the *Complete*

Psychological Works of Sigmund Freud, Volume VII: Jokes and their Relation to the Unconscious, she had never before seen Inspector Freddy Sullivan move so fast as he approached her desk in the middle of the crowded open plan office.

"This is the break I have been waiting for. I know where Rik Wallace is!" he announced.

"You do?"

"I got an anonymous phone call, but I know who it was from."

"Did you recognise the voice?"

"No. He used a foreign accent, but I recognised the mobile number. It was my old boss, Jackson. I should have guessed he would be involved somehow. He says Rik Wallace is at Fortune Mansion."

"The home of the billionaire, Randy Fortune?"

"The same. My mother subscribes to *Celebrity Hermit Magazine.*"

"But he is a recluse; he sees no one."

"He is seeing Rik Wallace every day."

"What is he doing there?"

"He is giving Mr Fortune moral advice. We should get over there and rescue him now."

"Who? Wallace?"

"No. Randy Fortune."

Sullivan was so excited he gyrated out of the office with Jones following close behind, her heaving bosom almost poking him in the back.

The librarian hummed to herself as she balanced the tray on the palm of her hand for the short journey from the kitchenette to the bedroom. In the doorway, her brain processed the scene. She would have been surprised but not shocked to find Ellen Dubois dead in bed, her swollen tongue protruding from between her cracked lips, eyes bulging from their sockets. But she wasn't prepared for this! The covers were thrown back and the bed was empty.

"Jackson, get the bicycles out. She has escaped. Children, stay here and play with the goldfish."

"I want a hamster, now," the girl whined, stamping her foot and dangling the fish by the tail between her fingers.

"Come on," the librarian said, dragging the sleeping Jackson out of his comfortable armchair. We know where to find her. We just have to get there first."

It seems everyone was headed to Fortune Mansion.

Part III

Trans Lignum Et Curculionem

Beyond Wood and Weevil

XXXIII

Potentia Magicae Cogitationis
The Power of Magical Thinking

As the lights dimmed, a murmur of anticipation rose from those occupying the rows of chairs arranged in the middle of the library in Fortune Mansion. When Rik Wallace, Julie Progress, Randy Fortune, and Samantha Spencer took their seats in the back row they were in time to catch the supporting act, which was the undergardener singing her own melancholic compositions accompanied by her father, the head gardener, on a guitar. He was made anxious by listening to her lyrics. At the end of the second song, when she seemed to be falling over a garden rake placed across her path by yet another unsuitable lover from the glasshouses, Samantha started heckling.

Bené, Maxine, and the popular physicist sat in the middle row flanked by the household servants. Gardeners, cleaners, and off-duty security guards squeezed onto an uncomfortable wooden bench in the front.

Professor Bentley Murphy and Bernard the security guard had arrived on their psychiatric mission just as the undergardener commenced the most depressing dirge in her cheerless repertoire. They were shoved into two empty spaces on the side of the stage by the underemployed chef hurrying to take his seat for the main event. These visitors from Saint Drogo's Asylum for the Criminally Insane wore T-shirts with coloured horizontal stripes, white pantaloons, leather waistcoats, eye patches and untidy nylon wigs topped with gold-trimmed three cornered hats. They had each blacked out several of their front teeth. It was Bernard's wife's idea that they disguise themselves as pirates.

Wallace didn't notice them come in, being distracted by the song lyrics. He was drawing parallels with his own misery. He was impressed at how the undergardener could capture his tortured feelings for Samantha, even if he couldn't compete with the metaphor of manure-spreading throughout his own pain.

How could this be love, he wondered? He hardly knew Samantha. They had talked in reality how many times? He couldn't tell. Had they kissed outside his fantasies? Could an emotion that caused his heart to beat so worryingly loud and fast be sustained by just a single sense: smell? What poet wrote of his true love's odour? God, he needed a drink. Perhaps it was anxiety he felt in his chest and not love. Maybe he was having a heart attack. Should he hope he was having a heart attack? He could hear his heart pounding above the whine of the undergardener's lament, keeping time with the melancholic rhythm. He wanted to go home. He had had enough! But where was home? He didn't want to be a moral advisor to a wretched billionaire nor any kind of philosopher. What else was there?

His melancholic reflections were interrupted when the lights came on, full blast. Someone said, "Ooops" in a stage whisper before the room went dark again. Who was he? He wanted to be himself, whoever that was. Could he go back to the asylum? Turn himself in? At least, it was regulated. He used to crave order back in the days when he imagined he was in control. Could he return to CAT College and revive his academic career? For a short time, he had been happy there. It was a very short happiness driven by the exhilaration of not being caught. Where to from here? If only he loved money? But he did love Samantha, didn't he? The undergardener was sure he did. She was singing to him alone. Then she stopped and departed the stage so suddenly she didn't give the spectators a chance to think about applauding, not even out of relief at their unexpected deliverance. Her father followed her off the stage, calling after her.

A hesitant applause did leak out of the compact audience when a spotlight trapped The Great Augustus holding a white rabbit by the ears in his right hand and a top hat in his left. As the creature struggled to break free, Claudius Steel regretted ignoring the prop-shop owner's advice that he buy the drugged creatures he kept under the counter for amateurs.

A plywood platform built by the otherwise idle carpenter improvised as a stage. Velvet curtains hanging from the ceiling at the rear and sides enclosed a space in which the magician looked as nervous as the rabbit. Several trapdoors had been built into the elevated stage floor under Claudius's instructions – if only he could remember where they were. He began to stamp.

Under his nylon wig, the psychiatrist didn't recognize the twin of his escaped patient beneath the heavy white grease paint, the black circular eye shadow, the eighteenth-century wig and pointed hat bent near the top. Waxing and waning moons and constellations of stars were scattered across the floor-length black silk cape with white fur trim.

Wallace was not surprised to see Della standing behind a table loaded with props. She wore a skimpy sequined monokini, smiling as she held her hands above her head in a banally dramatic pose. He had seen her wearing less. Blues and greens shimmered when she shifted her ideal weight from one long, sheer stockinged leg to the other.

Piped music of a genre that might accompany the upbeat funeral of an unpopular person came from somewhere behind the purple curtains.

"Predict something," Progress shouted, bored with the rabbit trick.

The Great Augustus, weary of his own performance, cast the animal over his shoulder into the dark recess behind. Della caught the rabbit as it sailed past her head.

"Ask me a question," the magician said, raising his arms and shuffling the large triangles of cape down past his elbows as if to prove his predictions were not hidden up his sleeves.

Della placed the rabbit down on the plywood where it squatted for a moment to recover its wits before she gently pushed it under the curtain with her foot: perhaps the most relieved creature in the room.

"When will I get married?" Progress asked, linking her arm into Randy's. She leaned against him causing him, in turn, to unconsciously lean away from her.

"Never!" The Great Augustus predicted, raising a cheer from the front row. "Anyone else?"

"In what year will mankind colonize distant planets?" the popular physicist from television whom no one recognised asked.

"Do you have a particular planet in mind?" Della enquired.

The Great Augustus muttered something inaudible under his grease paint as he aimed his two black-rimmed eyes at his assistant.

"Jupiter," the popular physicist suggested.

The illusionist rolled a glass orb down his broad sleeve and into his hand with a speed that would have surprised the sceptics in his audience had they been able to detect it; but the stage was dark except where spotlights lit the floor near his feet, and he had been practising, having at one time in his thespian career been an adherent of the Stanislavski system. In a single fluid motion, he hurled the orb onto the platform in front of his shoes with the rolled-up toes.

Everyone in the library, including The Great Augustus himself, jumped at the detonation. When the smoke cleared, the magician reappeared towards the back of stage beside Della where he had been trying to land a blow on her arm. He hoped the explosion would make his audience forget he had been asked a question about space travel. He had only four orbs left in storage up his sleeve. A rabbit strapped to his chest, impatient for his dramatic debut, kicked him so hard he pulled in his arms causing a squeal to emanate from between the long seam running up the front of his cape that only added to the growing mystical impression he was beginning to conjure from the semi-shadows of the stage. Some other creature was crawling up his spine with pointed nails. "Oh, God, I forgot the trick with the bloody hamster," he muttered.

But it was too late now. He was already deep into the fortune-telling part of his act. While shrugging his shoulders in what he hoped would be interpreted as an occult technique to summon supernatural inspiration and not the prosaic effort to redirect the path of the hamster, The Great Augustus scanned the audience for his brother who should be disguised as Eustis. While lying to the head gardener that he saw a handsome mentally-balanced man in his daughter's future, his black-ringed gaze moved from row to row. Where was Tiberius? He had put him into the butler's clothes himself and showed him the moves, over and over again.

The tedious billionaire two seats over from Wallace in the back row had his arm in the air. Claudius could not ignore him.

"Yes, sire, what is your challenge for my esoteric powers?" he asked.

"Have you seen my butler, Eustis?"

"We are psychically attuned, because at this exact moment I have been asking myself the same question. Where could the butler be?"

"He could be anywhere. Have you seen how slow he moves?" Progress asked.

The clairvoyant lifted his arms while contemplating the value of releasing another glass orb. "Sire, I am here to deal with metaphysical challenges and not your domestic staffing problems. Do you have another question to test my psychic powers?"

"Well, then, can I ask this question – will I always be unhappy?" Randy said.

On stage The Great Augustus was struggling with a creature that had broken free from the pouch sewn into the front of his underpants. "I'm a fortune teller, not a therapist. Where is the fucking butler?" he asked no one in particular. He executed a motion somewhere between jogging and jumping while pressing his arm hard against his ribs, squashing the rodent and causing him to scream when a claw pierced his flesh. "Why hold the rest of us responsible for your bloody misery?" he shouted in pain. "Why imagine you would be happy if you cut yourself off from the outside world?" The Great Augustus began to dance across the stage, trying to shake himself free of his most recent oppressor.

"He's good," Maxine told Bené.

"He could have read about Randy's desire to be left alone in *Celebrity Hermit Magazine*," the popular physicist said, resorting to the scepticism of the scientist. "Anyway, he never answered my question about Jupiter."

"When is Rik Wallace's wife going to show up?" Samantha blurted out.

Heads nodded to signify the general consent that this was indeed a good question.

"Think of a card, any card," The Great Augustus suddenly commanded the head gardener, who hadn't yet recovered his normal equanimity following his daughter's performance. He was unable to dislodge from his mind the image of her smothering in a manure heap, which was how she had closed the final verse.

"The ten of clubs," he said.

"Don't tell me, you idiot," The Great Augustus said. He was about to burst into tears.

Just then the butler appeared, shuffling his feet as instructed, as he moved behind the back row. "Don't run. Don't run," he was muttering to himself. "Small steps, the way

Claudius showed you. Tiny steps that will lead to greatness. Oh, to hell with this."

He ran.

XXXIV

Exitiom

Destruction

Della strolled across the front of the stage in her glittering monokini. "For our next illusion The Great Augustus will perform his notorious sawing of two people in half at the same time trick. For this we need two volunteers from the audience."

"Never heard of it," Bené told Maxine.

Della flourished a long saw over her head, gripping the wooden handles riveted to each end.

The audience rumbled their general approval of the proposed innovation on the standard sawing of one person at a time in half trick.

Unlike everyone else, Professor Bentley Murphy, under his eye patch and three cornered hat, didn't observe a hamster abseiling down the magician's left sleeve because he was distracted having at last hit upon a foolproof plan on how to kill himself. Della's words and the sharp teeth on the strip of steel had given him an idea.

"Our first volunteer, please," Della was saying.

Murphy raised his arm as high as it would go without his standing up.

The magician's assistant ignored him.

Murphy waggled his hand on the end of his wrist.

"Pick him," The Great Augustus muttered, stretching out a painted pointy nail glued to the end of a bony finger on the clenched hand on the arm that protruded from under the enormous cuff. His eyes flashed at Rik Wallace with mysterious intent before dropping to the floor as he aimed a kick with his rolled-up toes at the hamster passing in front of him, again.

"I'll do it," Murphy shouted from the side of the stage.

An unprecedented calm had descended upon him. His pulse slowed and the noise of the room retreated. He was alone with the swish of his blood coursing past his ears. It was the perfect solution. The fusion of his own passivity with the incompetence of this absurd wizard with a sharp saw would provide him with that elusive release he craved. The agonizing pain would surely last only a moment. He could simply ignore whatever instructions he was given for positioning himself in the partitioned box that the magician's assistant was then wheeling on a chrome trolley towards the centre of the stage and it would soon be over. Sweet oblivion.

The Great Augustus turned to his left to address the volunteer. If he showed surprise at finding a living pirate at the side of the stage, it manifested itself only as the slightest narrowing of his eyes. He cleared his throat.

"Who the hell are you."

"I am Black Beard," the psychiatrist said.

"Calico Jack," Bernard corrected. "We agreed I could be Black Beard. That's why I have the beard."

"Oh, yes. You are right," Murphy muttered. "I am Calico Jack," he shouted at the stage.

"Aren't you dead already?" the magician asked. "Never

mind. You won't do."

"Why not?" Calico Jack asked.

The Great Augustus pressed his fingers to his temple while staring in fake concentration at the darkened ceiling.

"Because your future is only a dream you haven't had yet," he intoned, remembering one of the few lines he rehearsed.

"He is good," Black Beard nodded.

"Shut up, you idiot," Calico Jack said, elbowing his brother pirate in the ribs.

Della shaded her eyes and looked to the depths of the room where the audience had hoped to avoid participating.

"We have a volunteer at the back. Stand up, please," she instructed.

"I said I'll do it," Calico Jack protested from the side.

"The gentleman in the back row had his hand up first," Della lied.

"To which idiot is she referring?" Rik Wallace asked, looking around him to see who was stupid enough to volunteer, apart from a pirate.

"You," Samantha Spencer confirmed.

"I didn't have my hand up."

"You did," she lied, smiling.

"What are you doing to me?" he hissed.

"Go on. It will be fun to watch you being cut in two."

"You can have the bottom half," Julie Progress said.

"At least that half doesn't talk philosophy."

"Are you sure?"

Samantha and Progress laughed, a fleeting shared moment of satisfaction at Wallace's distress.

Calico Jack's disappointment at failing to put himself in

danger turned to surprise when he saw Wallace mounting the improvised stage.

"What is he doing here?" he asked Black Beard.

"And why does he want to be cut in two?" Black Beard asked the psychiatrist, imaging that to be a question demanding psychological insight beyond his brief exposure to the discipline. "Cheer up, Jack. At least, we have found one of our loonies," he added. "I knew I was right to bring my Taser just in case," he said reaching under his leather waistcoat to fondle the gun.

"You will not zap him. After the show I will raise my eye patch to reveal my true identity and ask his forgiveness for my misguided therapeutic approach."

"Suit yourself but is that wise? I say, zap him first, and apologise afterwards."

Wallace hesitated when he reached what appeared to him to be an open coffin awaiting him on stage.

"Okay, you are first. Climb in," The Great Augustus told him. "No. I mean, wait! Damn it. I can't remember the order." He turned to his assistant for help.

Before Wallace could even begin to imagine what the pirates with their three cornered heads leaning together in whispered conspiracy were doing in the library, Della pushed him backwards into the oblong box.

Just as his head protruded from a hole in the topside a panel slid across to pin his neck in place. He struggled to stretch out his knees that appeared to be trapped against his chest by an obstruction somewhere in the middle. As he pushed down hard with the soles of his feet, he realized his mistake, and immediately drew his knees up again as his instinct took over.

He was on the point of being sawn in two so, he should squish himself into the top half, not lie out full stretch. At the other end Della had already grabbed ankles and clamped them in a stocks.

"Anyone can see what that assistant is up to," Black Beard told Calico Jack. "Those are someone else's feet at the bottom. There are two people in there."

"Which means the total will be four when the next volunteer climbs in," Calico Jack finished the line of thought for him. "Do they take us for idiots?"

"Did you notice what colour socks Wallace was wearing before he got in?"

"No. I did not. Did you?"

"No."

"Pity."

"Now for our second volunteer. Where is the butler?" The Great Augustus asked.

Before Calico Jack could even register this latest injustice, Eustis astonished the audience by jumping onto the stage. His brother had to place a palm on his chest to stop him leaping straight into the box on top of Wallace.

"Wait," he whispered. "My assistant has to make secret adjustments before you can climb in."

"I thought I am supposed to be on the bottom," Tiberius hissed.

"Are you sure?"

His assistant had rehearsed The Great Augustus as to what hidden buttons to press, and in what sequence, and where to position the blade of the saw. He was confused because she had insisted that he memorise the opposite to the instructions that

Tiberius had carefully taken him through earlier because, her logic was the standard trick had to be adapted for two people. Well, the innovation was his idea, so what made Tiberius an authority anyway? Now he couldn't remember what he was supposed to do. And his assistant in the monokini was proving to be all-round useless because all she wanted was to show off her fabulous legs. Everything was going too fast. Now she was nailing on the lid before he had time to think it through. Who was right: her or Tiberius? Who should be on top? Oh, fuck it. Who cares? It's a stupid trick anyway. He was supposed to cut the box along a pencil line on the lid, move the sections apart on the trolley wheels, and display the halves to the audience. That would give Tiberius enough time to analyse Wallace, wouldn't it?

Tiberius was stretched out flat mouth-to-mouth and eye-to-eye with Wallace. His ankles were jammed in a slot at the far end stretching his spine. "Get out and let me in the bottom," he growled at Wallace.

"You might notice you are lying on top of me, so you move."

"I demand to be on the bottom," Tiberius told The Great Augustus.

"It's fine, Tib—I mean Mr Butler. I think I know what I'm doing. Besides, my assistant knows more about magic than we do. She even had her own costume when I interviewed her for the job."

The audience looked on as a whispered argument broke out on stage between the wizard, his assistant, the butler's head, and Wallace's head sticking out the top of the box.

Claudius pressed the jagged blade and flinched when a

drop of blood appeared on his fingertip. He would give Tiberius two minutes to complete his therapy while he distracted his audience by removing creatures from his underwear. That would be enough time to hear something, anything that would trigger an impulse to make his brother strangle Wallace behind the curtains after the act. Saw over and back slowly on the pencil line on the lid, that's all; over and back slowly, he told himself. Whose idea was this? What had he been thinking?

Wallace thought he saw something familiar in those black pupils suspended over his. Perhaps it was his reflection.

Tiberius imagined running his fingernail across Wallace's throat. He was so near his goal, but his arms were confined inside the box. The head of his ideal client was literally at hand. And yet how far from his objective he remained. From his prone position Tiberius saw Calico Jack beside the stage. Did the professor imagine he wouldn't be recognised under that cheap wig, eye patch and hat? The fool who helped him escape was grinning beside him under an even cheaper beard. He had heard everything he ever needed to hear from Murphy. He wouldn't even bother to ask him how the cable tie was making him feel before tightening one around his neck after the show. But first he had to deal with Wallace.

"Your wife was right, Calico Jack. His brother, the butler, is here, right there on top of Wallace, but I can't see Tiberius anywhere."

"It's Black Beard, Professor. Are you sure Freud's analysis of sibling attachment is correct? You know, the way they can't stay apart because they hate each other?"

"Freud knows everything about families. They are trouble, Black Beard. Trouble. I will bet my psychiatric reputation on

Tiberius being around here somewhere."

Tiberius suddenly felt calm. Maybe now he would find the answer inside Wallace's skull: the solution to the meaning of his life. Then he could retire to his penthouse. But he would be out of options if Wallace proved to be yet another empty self-obsessed vessel. The thought of strangling his way to retirement exhausted him. It was best not to dwell on the possibility of failure. Tiberius was too near to Wallace to whisper in his ear, so he settled for talking into his eye. "We don't have much time. Don't you recognise me?" he hissed.

Maybe Wallace smelled rather than perceived something familiar about the butler.

"Don't you remember a fellow alumnus from your old asylum?"

On hearing the words, Wallace recognized Tiberius beneath the butler's make-up.

"Oh, God. Not you again. What do you want?"

Tiberius crinkled his nose.

"You were eating garlic before the show. How inconsiderate."

"I wasn't expecting to be this close to anyone, except maybe—"

"Listen. I need to analyse you. To make the story of a tediously long psychic journey short – by the time I realized you were the ideal client, you had already fled our asylum; so I had to take off after you. Oh, if only you had stayed locked up—"

"Don't you think I haven't had regrets?"

"Shut up."

Wallace rolled his eyes in concentration. "Let me get this straight. You have been pretending to be Eustis the butler since

I got here. But that would mean—"

"We switched places."

"But if you swapped with him that means he must be—"

"I don't have time to go into every little detail. I'm not Eustis. I'm Tiberius. And Eustis is Claudius, my twin brother, who is now a wizard. Okay? If you lie to me, my brother, The Great Augustus—"

"Who used to be Eustis?"

"Yes. Shut up."

Wallace wriggled in the box to get comfortable. "You have to agree, it's confusing," he said.

"It doesn't matter who the fuck anyone is: identity is totally overrated these days. Augustus is going to cut you in two with that saw in a few minutes," Tiberius said as Della brandished the blade beside his eye.

"It's a trick. I wasn't born yesterday."

"Claudius doesn't realise it yet, but I fixed this box backstage so that you will have a hideous death on the teeth of that saw. Do you imagine I would leave any aspect of our meeting to chance? I moved around a few springs, cut a second groove, and made a separate opening. That's why I was late getting around to the front. I'm supposed to walk slowly. Claudius is frightened to do his own dirty work in case he discovers he is the homicidal maniac that he imagines I am."

"Who did you say Claudius was?"

"I'm Tiberius. Claudius is Augustus." Tiberius waggled his eyebrows in frustration.

"Your parents must have been classicists."

"Oh, I would hit you if I could move my arms. Shut up and listen to me. We are running out of time. I'm going to analyse you, and then my brother will unwittingly saw you in half. Is that clear?"

"I'm not worried," Wallace lied. "This is some harmless trick you have come up with to scare me into allowing myself to reveal some dark secret I don't even know I'm repressing. You are as bad as Murphy. You therapists would do anything to get a client to spill their guts; though I might point out I hardly qualify as a client because there is a process you are supposed to go through governed by ethics in order to—"

"Shut up! Wait a minute; I don't care what that bimbo assistant says, I'm sure you are supposed to be on top!"

"You need to see someone urgently, Tiberius. I wouldn't recommend Murphy considering the situation both of us are in now following his treatment—"

The Great Augustus bent over the two heads sticking out of the top of the box and twanged the blade as he buckled the sheet of steel in proof of its solidity.

The audience cheered its approval.

"No one will save you because those fools will imagine your screams are part of the act." Tiberius cackled.

"What do you want with me?"

"At last, I have your attention. Listen without interrupting. You embody the archetypal human experience I imagined existed when I was in college. That was before the threat of nihilism began to erode my confidence in—"

"I hate to interrupt, but isn't that a Jungian concept? I thought you were a dedicated Freudian."

"Shut up."

The Great Augustus hesitated. He couldn't remember on which of the two pencil lines that ran across the top he was supposed to place the blade. The last time he looked there was only one. He sighed and picked the nearest one at random.

"Who are you, Wallace? I can tell you are hiding some important truth from me. I have an instinct for these things."

"Not this again, Tiberius. Just like Murphy. Don't you analysts care about anything other than who people imagine they are not? You are dribbling on my face."

"I should have anticipated this: what we spend our lives in search of will only prove be an anti-climax because it cannot be what we thought we were looking for otherwise we would have found it."

"Just accept that you are mad, Tiberius, and move on."

"Please, for my sake, talk faster and with more focus. Can you do that?"

The Great Augustus pulled the blade towards him.

The audience gasped.

"Don't you realise I am supposed to be a philosopher? What am I supposed to say?"

"That is the problem. I wouldn't fucking be here with my twin brother about to saw one of us in half if I knew what I wanted you to say."

The Great Augustus watched Wallace mouthing the word help to his assistant as he pulled the blade over and back slowly and carefully. Funny the way she had telephoned only minutes after his advertisement appeared in the classifieds. Still, she seemed to have a greater understanding of magic than he did. The sawing of two people in half trick was his idea, but she had arranged the props. Oh, God, he was sure Tiberius told him Wallace was supposed to be on top.

"I can't take much more of this," Calico Jack may have told

his alter ego, the psychiatrist to whom he wished to address his anxieties; or he may have been speaking to Black Beard. On this occasion he couldn't tell.

"Nonsense, this is the best magic show ever. So realistic, and look at his face. The Great Augustus is brilliant at conjuring up a sense of danger, that in my experience, is usually missing in these shows," Black Beard said.

"Not the magic. My life; life in general. I'm the one who should be up there, face to face with the butler."

"You need to lighten up, Jack."

Back on stage, Tiberius was talking.

"Claudius told me he overheard your friend Pandora telling Julie Progress that the ex-policeman Jackson discovered the wife and children you are waiting to show up here aren't yours. It seems, Professor Murphy was torturing you for nothing. Hah. That sort of shock should put you in touch with your true feelings."

"But this changes everything."

"Indeed, it does. Now. How do you feel? Eh? How does that make you feel?" Tiberius cackled, dripping saliva down Wallace's nostrils.

"Since everyone now seems to accept that they are not mine, I can live happily ever after with Samantha."

"Who is Samantha?"

"It is meant to be because I thought she was imaginary, and then I discovered she is real, and my wife, whom I was starting to think maybe was real, isn't. And—"

"Who is Samantha?"

"I'm not sure, but to me she is the ideal woman. She is smart and smelly. Did I tell you I have discovered the wonders of natural body odour? Who would have imagined the effect the smell of sweat would have on me? Especially armpits. It's as if smell is the one infallible sense. The money we spend on perfumes, sprays, deodorants, and – I appreciate it's not rational – but—"

"Claudius," Tiberius screamed. "Get me out of here."

"What is it now?" Claudius asked leaning towards his brother's head.

"You two are both in love with that smelly woman."

"I knew it all along," Claudius growled.

"That's it! That's what I have learned about the fucking meaning of life!"

Claudius was overcome with a jealous rage. The saw took on the rhythm of the dialogue between Tiberius and Wallace. The Great Augustus began cutting with reckless haste: over and back, over and back. No one would get in the way of his getting at Wallace. No one. He cackled, impressing his audience with his commitment to his character. But to his brother crammed into the top half of the box this act felt more real than anything he had ever experienced in his life of psychotic delusion.

"How is it that magical thinking is the final refuge for fools? We cling to fantasy when all hope in reason is gone," Calico Jack lamented.

Black Beard ignored him, watching the show with an open mouth.

"Reason is disappointing. Believe me, from the time I spend analysing lunatics at the asylum, I can see the limitations of rationality," Calico Jack told Black Beard.

"I am going to open a smell museum when I get out of here," Wallace told Tiberius. "What do you think?"

"What can I do now? No one has ever been able to sustain belief in nothing!" Tiberius gasped his final words.

"What do I mean by belief in nothing?" Calico Jack asked himself, despairing of a coherent answer from Black Beard. "Do I mean there is no truth is out there to apprehend?"

"Or do you mean nothing is meaningful?" Black Beard asked, surprising his brother pirate.

"Say something, Tiberius. I prefer when you are raving to this silence. You are dribbling on me again."

"I mean anomie. Life is pointless without some ultimate truth. Man has looked to science, religion, art, music, and mathematics to no avail. I have looked to the mind. My path has been internal. Taking me further and further into the caves inside my skull. You cannot imagine my disappointment with what I found at the end of that journey," Calico Jack moaned.

"I can," Black Beard replied, without turning his face from the stage.

Tiberius's dying thought was that he was everyone and no one if he only existed inside his own head. Perhaps he had achieved his great therapeutic goal after all, made all the more profound because it couldn't be passed on.

"Everything is false," Calico Jack confided to the psychiatrist or Black Beard. He hardly knew. "All the thoughts I have ever had are lies. This magic is a fraud. But yet I cling to the fantasy of life. Why am I still here?"

The saw flew over and back, the squealing timber drowning out the gasps from the audience. Claudius screamed in pitch with the biting blade.

Now Samantha felt something in the pit of her stomach. Was this a reflex at the sight of the cruel saw chewing through the flimsy wood or anxiety for those in the magician's box? She had no feelings for Eustis. He was only the butler. Could she be afraid for Wallace? Impossible. She hated him, didn't she?

"He is good, isn't he? Look at the expression on the face of The Great Augustus. He belongs in our asylum," Black Beard shouted above the squeal of the saw. "Terrific show. My wife won't believe me when I tell her."

"I can almost feel the teeth of the blade on my spine," Calico Jack said.

"We are insignificant insects crawling across the bloated crust of some monstrous imaginary pie," Black Beard said, not knowing where those words came from.

"Do you think two people who are attracted by their smell can be happy forever?" Wallace was asking Tiberius who was no longer listening.

"I am not a true nihilist like that butler or Wallace. Yes, I have an impulse to destroy myself, but only to clear the path to a fundamental truth," Calico Jack said.

"Tell your brother to stop, Tiberius. I feel something warm inside the box. Oh, you're not pissing on me, are you?"

"My life is a competition between numbing fear and existential despair," Calico Jack said.

Tiberius's forehead rested on Wallace's.

"This amount of despondency demands too much commitment," Calico Jack observed from the sideline.

"It is piss!" Wallace shouted, trying to dislodge Tiberius's forehead from his own by wriggling his head from side to side.

"Am I depressed, Jack?" the doctor shouted into the wigged ear of his brother pirate.

"I told you I'm Black Beard. Perhaps you are apathetic."

"It doesn't matter what I am. I blame Nietzsche for everything that has happened. He predicted we would arrive at this point of collective listlessness," Calico Jack murmured. "And you know what? I don't care."

"You are having an intellectual crisis? Ignore it, and it will pass. Stop reading books for a while, and you will be fine. Try to concentrate on what is happening on stage."

"There is only decay," Calico Jack said, just then sensing the chair leg bending beneath his buttocks.

"Come on, Tiberius. Cheer up. Wake up."

"I blame my parents for my existence. They should have read Nietzsche who believed marriage was the greatest banality after death and birth," Calico Jack said.

"Careful with that saw," Wallace shouted. "Something is happening in here."

"I am cutting you in two, you fool," The Great Augustus screamed, beads of sweat breaking through the white paste on his forehead.

"Tiberius. Tiberius! Do something about your brother," Wallace pleaded.

A red disc erupted from the cut down the middle of the box. Spinal cord shrieked when the blade hit bone. Gobs of blood flew through the air as the crate broke in two.

At this point, what there was of The Great Augustus's limited magical training took over. He dropped the saw onto the stage and rotated the top half of the box while his assistant turned the bottom half so that the two parts could be revealed to the audience. It was obvious even to those in the back row that the saw had cut all the way through hips releasing a sag of genitalia from one end and a pair of legs from the other.

Claudius knew little of anatomy. On those few occasions on which he met his brother, he was reminded that neither of them possessed a medical qualification. But he observed what looked to his thespian eye to be a cone of intestines forming on stage.

No one moved when the top half of a body slid out of a cunningly hidden compartment in the lid when lubricated by the build-up of blood and gore inside. It plopped onto the stage with the unique sound of severed bone coming in contact with plywood. When the half-cadaver landed upright facing the audience the eyes stared out of a gory mask while the backs of the hands rested on the stage. The legs followed the top half out of the opposing part of the apparatus. These knocked over the torso causing it to make an extravagant bow.

The library was as quiet as a crypt on a Wednesday evening. Several seconds passed in a dramatic silence of the kind that would have impressed a theatre critic. Just then a woman appeared through the split in the curtain in the wing. She was wearing a frilly nightdress several sizes too small for her. Her large right breast bulged over the elasticated collar pushing her elongated nipple within inches of her cracked lips. She staggered across the stage holding her hands out in front of her. Green snot ran from both of her nostrils, and her eyes seemed to have been refined with coarse sandpaper. She stopped when her instincts told her she had reached the limelight, lowered her arms to her sides, turned to the audience and said, "I am Rik Wallace's wife, Mrs Wallace. Give me my billions, Randy Fortune."

XXXV

Intestina Necessaria Sunt
It Takes Guts

The response of the audience that followed The Great Augustus's performance of sawing a lady in two with the innovation that this time it was two men – a butler and a moral philosopher – simultaneously was the most animated Claudius had experienced since his role in the nude Macbeth. It would be unfair to say who started the stampede, but it was probably someone in the front row. While there were several authorities on individual behaviour present in the library that evening, there was none with expertise in spontaneous collective action. Therefore, when the crowd reformed in the garden to exchange anecdotes on what it was they imagined made them run in the first place no one, if called on for an explanation, could say what had happened. However, if blame cannot be assigned to an individual, the general cause was obvious. Had they exercised restraint, the members of the audience might have lingered long enough to determine the identity of the corpse or, indeed, to whom the legs belonged if not to the same person. On closer inspection, the grey-striped cuff of the trouser leg would have provided a clue. But with Ellen Dubois's hideous debut, they had seen enough.

The mob had flowed as a mountain stream out the door of the library, down the corridor outside in the direction of the tall windows at the end of the hall, past the paintings of historic figures who looked out of their golden frames with revived curiosity, broke around the corner, and on, unhindered, towards the fall that was the main stairway.

The Great Augustus ignored Ellen Dubois, who was by then wandering around in circles, to study the two halves of the corpse.

"What have I done?" he muttered.

An unfamiliar feeling that had begun in his feet rose up through the back of his legs, past his knees and groin, before lodging in his stomach. He began to shake.

Della helped Ellen Dubois down off the front of the stage before shoving the separate halves of the box back together. She closed fasteners on the top and bottom that she had told Claudius were ornamental handles.

As Claudius had never had a feeling quite like the one he was experiencing now, it was understandable that he should take it for guilt. He had read about it, and his brother had talked at tedious length of his clients' experience of it on the few occasions on which they had met. "Guilt," he disclaimed to the improvised auditorium, now empty except for Ellen Dubois wandering amongst the chairs. "I feel guilt. I am guilty," he shouted. He strode to the front of the temporary stage with dramatic purpose, ripping off his wig and conical hat, and wiping a streak of the grease paint from his face with his sleeve. He raised his arms to deliver a soliloquy.

"Gaze with grief on our slaughtered hero," he commanded the empty overturned chairs, pointing to the corpse with the flat of his hand. Ellen Dubois ignored him. "He was calm to the end. He is gone, but not before I learned a monumental truth from Wallace – oh, not whether psychoanalysis can be reconciled with behaviourism," the ham said. His artificial nails sunk into the flesh of his forehead. "That was my brother's purpose, not mine. I have discovered that I still have it: what a performance."

"Run for your life. He's raving mad," a stampeding maid who had returned for her handbag shouted for her own encouragement.

Della wheeled the reassembled box through the same slit in the curtains through which Ellen Dubois had first appeared, and vanished from view as the heavy velvet closed on her role without applause.

Claudius was alone with the sound of retreating screams from the hall outside and the word "billions" being muttered over and over again in the dark at the back of the library.

"I may take this show on the road. I always knew I could achieve greatness. If my brother can kill people, so can I," he said. He executed a pirouette inside his long robe that almost overbalanced him. He straightened up and skipped across the stage. "I feel awful. But oh, I am so glad that I feel so terrible. I'm normal, ordinary, psychologically unremarkable," he shouted. "I'm not like Tiberius, who doesn't feel guilt. I am not a lunatic. I admit I was worried I might kill Wallace and discover that I didn't feel guilt. But I am not my evil twin."

The audience, had they stayed may have appreciated the comparative sincerity of this performance.

"Wallace died to set both my brother and I free," Claudius said while bending down to prop a gory torso on his knees, brace the head in the crook of his elbow, and knead the bloody hair back from the forehead. Ellen Dubois plopped down beside him.

"How can I thank you? I am sorry for what I put you through. Believe me, I am," Claudius whispered into a gory ear. "I didn't plan it this way. Here in front of everyone. Tiberius was supposed to kill you discretely behind the curtain. I will never hear the end of it from the cleaners. Mind you, they don't do much around here, anyway. It was an accident: a trick that went right or wrong depending on your point of view. But it was my hand on the saw." Claudius's words came quicker. "I want to talk about my feelings. Do you hear me? I can't shut up. Oh, God. I am normal. I am the same as my brother's boring clients. Now I understand how they feel. I realise, apart from being a famous actor, I have always wanted to be just *ordinary*."

Ellen Dubois took a gory hand in hers.

"Who should I cut in two next time?" Claudius asked himself. "No. No. Perhaps you are enough. You have achieved what all those damned reviews never could. I might have played my current role here forever, because I couldn't bring myself to face another audition. But this performance will throw the spotlight back on my talent. Directors will be queuing up, begging me—"

The backs of Claudius's legs were beginning to ache from squatting. He repositioned himself, elbowing Ellen Dubois out of the way, and crawling around on his knees in front of the corpse's face that he held between his palms. "Don't look at me that way," he commanded the glassing eyes gazing up at him. "Don't stare at me with those— Wait! With my eyes? You're not

Wallace! What have I done?"

He jumped to his feet allowing Tiberius's head to hit the plywood with a thump so loud it may have proved fatal had he not already been dead.

"You're my brother."

Claudius looked to the dark ceiling of the library and shouted with all the air in his lungs. "Wallace, you bastard. I'm going to kill you."

"I'm going to kill him too," Ellen Dubois shouted.

Meanwhile, outside, Maxine had pushed Bené aside by pressing her hand into the side of his face at the first turn in the hall, gaining the lead as the popular scientist crashed over a narrow table against the wall supporting a Ming vase. He scrambled back to his feet by grabbing hold of Maxine's slender ankle.

Samantha wanted to stop her legs running, but she had lost control of them: they needed to be outside. Wasn't there something she could have done? Was she responsible for what had happened to Wallace? She would reflect on it when she was safe. Her legs ran on carrying her thoughts with them.

In the middle of the pack, Calico Jack was asking himself why Black Beard was running. Those behind went past. Seeing Calico Jack slow, Black Beard reduced his speed in turn. They propped their hands on his pantalooned knees, and gasped for breath with their gold braided three cornered hats almost touching. The power of their disguises was starting to wear off.

"That was disgusting," Professor Bentley Murphy said.

"Rik Wallace didn't deserve to die like that even if he was a lunatic. I should have Tasered him when I had the chance,"

Bernard the security guard said.

"Poor Wallace. Did you see the expression on his face? He looked serene even as his guts spilled onto the floor."

"I read somewhere that being disembowelled doesn't hurt as much as you might imagine."

"It must be true. Wallace was the calmest person in the room."

"Who was that woman in the tiny frilly nightdress?"

"I don't know but she was terrifying."

"Do you think she could be his long-lost wife?"

"If she is, I don't blame him for running away."

At the bottom of the stairs the audience was gathering torrential momentum as it aimed itself at the glass air lock in front of which Inspector Sullivan and Sergeant Jones, having just arrived, stood rock-like.

"Damn it, Jones," Sullivan shouted as he braced himself for the impact, "we should have come straight here, sirens blazing. Why did I let you talk me into stopping for tea and scones? I told you Rik Wallace would be wreaking havoc. Tell me all these terrified people are not his victims," Sullivan managed to shout before being lifted off the black-and-white tiles and dashed against the glass box.

Randy Fortune had stopped running when he reached what he considered to be the safety of the hall. Julie Progress halted beside him, not out of any protective instinct, but because she worried he might meet someone else if she left him alone with so many people around. Randy shouted at her that he was calling the police.

"Are you sure that is necessary?" Progress shouted back.

"Either my ethical advisor or my butler or both have been

sawn into two distinct halves so, yes, I consider it necessary."

"It is Eustis's own fault. It was his ingenious idea to put on a magic show."

"You don't have to call the police because we are here already," the inspector said, getting up off the floor and flashing his badge at the billionaire. "Don't panic. I will restore order," he shouted over the stragglers jogging past the glass doors that were now hanging off their hinges. The head gardener's daughter screamed in F sharp as she went by, Bené behind her – perhaps in search of a record collaboration.

A week later, the television scientist appeared on a show demonstrating the potential domestic applications of nuclear fission. He had a black eye partly hidden under heavy make-up that he acquired running into the outstretched fist of a Roman statue in the garden of Fortune Mansion.

XXXVI

Onero Notitia
Information Overload

"You take upstairs while I check the ground floor," Inspector Freddy Sullivan instructed Sergeant Jones as he had helped her back onto her feet.

Halfway up the staircase Jones met a dishevelled celebrity limping down on a broken heel. "You're Maxine," she said. "I saw you in that video with the Pandas. I love your music. *What the actual fuck do you thiiiink?*" Jones sang, while rotating her backside in synch with the baton she was waving above her head. As she finished the chorus, she bumped Maxine twice with her hip and grunted, "Uh, uh."

"That wasn't me, but thank you, anyway," Maxine said, leaning against the wall.

"What happened?" the policewoman asked, remembering why she was there.

"There's blood everywhere. It was ghastly," Maxine sobbed, almost unable to focus on herself.

"Do you mind if I take a selfie? Jones asked, leaning into the star's shoulder while holding her phone at arm's length. She smiled instantly. When the phone flashed, she said, "Thanks. Where were we? Oh, yes, I was asking you what happened?"

"Randy Fortune hired a magician to cheer himself up because he has been depressed; though, I can't imagine why with all his money."

"Yes, I read that in *Celebrity Hermit Magazine*. My sister keeps a copy in her toilet."

"There was someone on stage in a tiny nightdress: a drug addict, or perhaps part of the act? I don't know. The wizard sawed one, maybe two, people in half. There was so much blood. The noise. Screaming. It might have been the butler or the philosopher, whose name I forget, but he was a founding member of KindFace. By the way, it's a cool app. I have the first account, and I already have a million hearts, which is one of the highest."

"Who is this wizard?"

"That's him, there," Maxine said. She pointed an arm, on the end of which was a jewelled fingernail, at the robed figure that just then appeared at the top of the stairs.

"That's Tiberius Lang, the escaped maniac," Jones shouted, shoving Maxine aside as she took the steps two at a time. "He has shaved off his beard, but I would recognise him anywhere."

"Who cares how many hearts knowing Randy is worth? I'm never coming back to this dump unless he sponsors my latest perfume range," Maxine complained to herself, hobbling down the staircase.

Claudius Steel turned on the landing and shuffled as fast as he could inside the long cloak back down the hallway in the direction from which he had come.

"Stop, police!" Jones shouted, running after him – a command that Claudius ignored. The sergeant reached the top of the stairs in time to catch sight of him disappearing through the third door on the left. At the other end of the corridor, a barefoot woman in a tiny frilly nightdress, holding what seemed to be a leg under her arm, opened a door, looked inside, closed the door, and turned back down the corridor muttering something about billions.

Jones kicked the door in, holding her baton in front of her in both hands. She saw Claudius in the middle of the room, halfway out of his robe. "Give up, Tiberius. You are surrounded."

"I concur if you mean surrounded by imbeciles. I will go quietly. But first let me take off this ridiculous costume. I am certain a flesh-eating guinea pig is still in here somewhere." Claudius sat down on an ornate armchair at the end of a four-poster bed in the otherwise empty room as soon as he had shrugged himself out of the hat and gown. Underneath, he was wearing a light-blue cashmere sweater and cream flannel pants as if he had prepared to play a round of golf after his performance. "Excuse me, while I remove the wildlife," he said, jamming his hand down the front of his trousers. Claudius's brain was racing through the possibilities. He had just killed his brother in front of witnesses, so being Claudius would be problematic. On the other hand, it would be tricky to revert to being the butler, who had been sawn in two in front of the same witnesses. But this policewoman thought he was his twin, Tiberius, who was on the run from a lunatic asylum: an understandable mistake. His dilemma reminded him of all the fun he and his brother could have had confusing their teachers if they hadn't been separated at birth. Should he be Claudius or Tiberius? Think. What to do? Who to be? I have it. I am an actor, he thought. With my talent how hard can it be to play the role of a therapist? As Tiberius, perhaps I could analyse my way out my current dilemma. Lull this policewoman into dropping her guard, hit her on the head with something, and make a run for it. Nothing as taxing as the time I played the back end of the— "Did you always want to be in the police?" he heard himself ask, as Jones drew nearer, still holding her baton out in front of her.

"Yes, since I was a child."

"Tell me about your childhood," Claudius said. He sank further into the armchair.

"Nothing to tell. It was all quite normal. Put your hands up."

Claudius ignored the command. "Normal is my favourite state of being, so I'll be the judge of whether or not it is normal. Many people lead fascinating lives without even realising it. Lie down here," Claudius said patting the smooth silk bedspread with the palm of his hand. "A little bit of complimentary therapy before you lock me up couldn't hurt, could it? I mean, who doesn't want to talk about themselves to professional listeners? I would. In fact, I can't wait to return to Saint Drogo's to resume my dialogue with my psychiatrist," he lied.

"Okay, what harm can it be but just for a few minutes? I have never been analysed. Does it hurt?" Jones asked, mounting the bed with her buttocks, one at a time, each in turn trying to take a grip on the slippery bed cover.

"That depends on how much pain you are able to dredge up from your past."

Jones shrugged and lay on her back on the silk counterpane staring at the ceiling through the opening between the four posters of the bed.

Spiders, who had gotten into the room through a spy-hole in the wall, gathered to eavesdrop.

"Start at the beginning," Claudius suggested, looking around for anything heavy he might use to stun his client. His eyes narrowed on a tall glass vase on the mantle over the fireplace. Could I kill again so soon, he wondered? Wouldn't so short an interval between homicides make me a homicidal maniac? Perhaps I should wait a few minutes? While he was trying to calculate how many steps lay between the bed and the door, Jones started talking.

"I was born at 10.16 a.m. on a Monday. My father said it was 10.10, but my mother said 10.16, and she was always a more reliable timekeeper. I wasn't there, so I can't say who is correct. I mean, I was there, but since I was just born, I wasn't able to establish the exact time for myself—"

"That's fine. Let's move on a few years to your first memory."

"I remember a trip to the zoo. My father said we were twenty-second in the queue when we arrived, and my mother said we were sixth, if you counted only the adults. It took us twelve minutes to get past the barrier that was—"

"Less detail, please."

"Oh, okay. I saw two adult giraffes, one baby and one adolescent. There were five monkeys of a variety of ages. I could tell which one was the oldest because he had grey hair on his—"

"That's fascinating, but tell me something psychologically relevant."

"I don't understand what you mean."

"For example, the first time you realised you wanted to kill your father."

"Kill my father? That's not normal, is it?"

"Trust me, it's normal."

Above Jones's head, the spiders, appearing to have lost interest, were already dispersing. Some were running.

Claudius told himself he mustn't kill her: he was normal; she was normal; everyone was normal; so he shouldn't kill her. And not after the sacrifice his brother made for his future career on stage. His eyes wandered back to the vase. What was she saying now? God. She was back at the zoo buying ice cream. She deserved to die.

"It came down to a final choice between chocolate and strawberry. I couldn't decide so I had both. I vomited onto the glass on the lion's enclosure. They were trying to lick it off from the inside. My mother said I was very naughty to eat so much. Is that psychologically interesting?"

"Aren't you lucky to have had such agreeable parents? Not everyone is so fortunate. Let me tell you about *my* childhood. I never went to the zoo," Claudius hissed, getting to his feet. "My mother wouldn't even let me look at a picture of a giraffe. She insisted I read the fucking racing pages. I didn't get to choose between ice cream flavours. No. I had to choose between nags."

"Whose session is this anyway? Aren't I supposed to be doing the talking part?"

As Jones tried to sit up Claudius pushed her back down. "You haven't shut up once since you lay down there," he said, digging the artificial nails still glued to his fingers into the flesh on his forehead. What to do? What to do?

"I'm not sure you are any good at this therapy business," Jones said, gazing again at the ceiling, trying to get back in the zone.

Claudius sat down.

"I'm sorry. It's been a difficult day. Go on. You were at the zoo," he prompted, making a tent with his fingertips in what he considered to be the acme of therapeutic poses.

"It took us two hours and forty minutes to go all the way around after the stop for ice cream—"

At this rate, we will be here for a hundred fucking years. These memories are going slower than real time, he told himself. Stop looking at that vase.

"My father said I should attend the school that was three-and-a-half miles from our house, rather than the one that was five miles away, because I would lose an average of thirty-six minutes coming and going each day. That all adds up, you know. Over a six-year period, he calculated that was five hundred and one hours. Tiberius? Tiberius?"

Jones sat up in time to catch the door closing behind him.

On the floor, a white and brown guinea pig sniffed the air before ambling off under the bed, where it imagined freedom lay.

XXXVII

Cogitans Ex Camera
Thinking Outside the Box

Rik Wallace opened his eyes. It was so dark he couldn't even make out the blood vessels on the inside of his eyelids. He may have lost consciousness after the show, but he couldn't remember. He could hear his breathing. When he raised his hands – that were folded in the manner of a reposing corpse – his knuckles bumped against a rough, flat surface inches from his face. His probing fingertips concluded he was inside a box. A shroud of icy sweat condensed on his skin despite the suffocating heat. Then, remembering the saw, he groped for lacerations across his stomach. His guts seemed to be in place under his unbroken skin. But hadn't he read somewhere people were always healthy after dying? He wondered who had come back to spread that rumour? Could he be alive but also dead? How would he know? Then he remembered the woman in the nightdress. Who was she? Perhaps she was the gardener's wife? That would explain a lot about the undergardener's lyrics. He banged with his fists, shouting for help. "Somebody, anybody! Get me out of here. I'm alive," he screamed.

Della gripped the steering wheel with both hands and hummed to drown out the noise from the magician's box nailed inside the crate in the back of the white van. She had stencilled the word "Fragile" on all the visible surfaces in large black letters. Should she pull over and let him out? But if she opened the crate, there would be questions. Endless metaphysical, epistemological, ethical questions, and she didn't have any answers. It was annoying when you knew people would criticise your plans when they didn't have anything constructive of their own to offer. Not that he would ever thank her for saving his skin again.

Despite what had happened in the library at Fortune Mansion she didn't consider herself to be a cruel person. It wasn't her fault. She had only handed Claudius the saw. How he chose to use it was his moral responsibility. She had learned that much from Wallace.

Anyway, she didn't have the time to face Wallace just now. She glanced at her watch. She needed to be at the port in under an hour. She was the one who had to go around saving those who had too much faith in humanity. Wallace just blundered along in the dark, heedless of the dangers around him.

She would have to find some place to leave him if she didn't open the box and let him go. But he was the most wanted lunatic in the country now that Tiberius was – well, physically separated. That was the best way to view his condition: somewhat appropriate after years of psychological separation. Despite all the planning she put into the act itself, as usual, she hadn't thought through what would happen when the show was over: a typical circus performance. Her brother reminded her on his rare sober moments that her problem was a fundamental immaturity. Maybe he was right. For Wallace's sake, she should find someone reliable to leave him with, unlike her. Who at no notice was the most sensible person she knew? She sighed. It was easier to rescue people than to know what to do with them afterwards.

Wait, she had it. Of course! She felt a fleeting pang of guilt at relying on them to help her out with Wallace yet again. Now where was that bookshop?

She pulled on the handbrake, as she swung the van into a one hundred and eighty degree turn on the slippery road. Wallace's cheek smashed into the timber panel beside his head. He stopped shouting to concentrate on swearing.

Della smiled at herself in the mirror at the thought that, at least, she had still managed to fit into the monokini.

XXXVIII

Oedipus Non Complexu
Oedipus Uncomplex

Claudius Steel slammed the door behind him and leaned his back against it, gasping for breath. He wasn't fit. He had run down the stairs, along several corridors, and into the kitchen, deserted except for Inspector Freddy Sullivan, who was just then bent over the abandoned cooking pots on the six-ring burner, probing for clues amongst their contents.

"Ah, Tiberius?" he said, straightening up. He had been caught in the act of licking tomato sauce from his index finger.

"Who are you?" Claudius asked.

"Inspector Sullivan," the policeman said. He flashed his badge at the brother he took to be the fugitive.

"I had no idea I was so well known."

"I have become quite an expert on you," Sullivan said while tapping the side of his nose with his now sauce-free finger. "Professor Murphy, your psychiatrist at Saint Drogo's Asylum for the Criminally Insane, told me everything about you. He thinks you are extremely dangerous, but if you ask me, that man is clueless. You might consider seeking a second opinion when you're back there. Murphy believes you have some sort of twisted obsession with Rik Wallace based on your childhood experiences. He thinks I have it too, so maybe we have something in common." He chuckled at the idea. "By the way, is shaving off your beard the best you could do as a disguise? Are you aware your face is covered in some sort of white goo?"

"It's make-up," Claudius said. He ran his sleeve over his cheek.

"I was hoping to find Wallace here at Fortune Mansion," Sullivan said. "Have you seen him?"

"As a matter of fact, I have been looking for him myself," Claudius said, trying to decide whether it would be more satisfying to kill Wallace or see him thrown back into the asylum. He concluded he wanted to exterminate him.

"Come, come, Tiberius. In exchange for your co-operation, I will make sure your life back at the asylum is more pleasant."

"How?"

"I could get you a flat-screen television for your padded cell. HD?"

"What form do you want my co-operation to take?"

"Tell me where Wallace is hiding?"

"I don't know where Wallace is, and if I did, I wouldn't tell you because I'm going to bash his fucking head in with one of those frying pans when I catch up with him."

Sullivan laughed again.

"Yes, I would expect you to say that, being a lunatic and all; except I thought you liked to strangle people? Professor Murphy did say you are incurably mad. But my priority is to find Wallace before *he* kills again. In my opinion, he is far crazier than you."

"Is that so? I resent unqualified people offering uninformed opinions on such delicate matters as who is the maddest. I suggest you go upstairs and check out the library before coming to such a hasty conclusion; though I admit, that might be as much my assistant's work as mine. I haven't worked out yet how she did it, but I will, and then I am going to bash her head in too."

"I don't understand a word you are saying, thank God – which is what I would hope when listening to a madman."

Sullivan unclipped a pair of handcuffs from the back of his belt and stepped closer to Claudius. "I studied psychology at the police academy. That is how I know you are the one who has a striking resemblance to Freud who was obsessed with having sex with his mother."

"Have *you* a mother, Inspector?" Claudius asked, playing for time. He was regaining his confidence in acting the therapist after his poor debut with Sergeant Jones. But it seems he was lucky that his first probing question pierced the thin crust maintaining the inspector's fragile emotional composure like a psychological fork.

Sullivan paused, with the handcuffs extended towards Claudius. What thoughts were these cascading from a fractured dam in his brain? He loved his mother, didn't he? No. Not *that* kind of love. The sort with which the Greeks were obsessed; Not Oedipus – the other kind. The type Plato invented.

"I hate my mother." There. He said it. Relief. The way she controlled every moment of his life from his first waking millisecond. Even before he woke, she appeared in his dreams sifting through his drawers, holding one of his large collection of bland shirts she bought for him up to the light for critical inspection before sniffing an armpit. She was beside the bed holding a cup of tea when he opened his eyes in the morning. It was normal for a busy son to allow his mother to dress him. He was normal.

She told him he was special. Yes, he was, but even he knew his colleagues didn't always share his mother's confidence in him. He heard the comments in the corridors that stopped when he came around the corner. The way they looked down at their shoes. Why hadn't he found another woman who thought he was special? Because he was the greatest love of his mother's life, even while his father was still alive. An unbidden memory. She could have called the ambulance, but she waited – as she put it – to see if her husband would rally when he stopped bleeding. Why hadn't he registered the delay before now? He allowed her to do everything for him. He had – what was the term he had learned in the police academy? – *enabled* her to disable him. But she started the dependency when he was born. It was her fault he was this way. What way was that? It didn't bear thinking about. But he couldn't stop the torrent of thoughts.

Oh, God. He did love her, but he also wanted to wrap his fingers around her scrawny neck. But all love is the same, isn't it? Without love, there would be few homicides, and the police would become redundant. By the logical deduction beloved of detectives, he realised he would be out of a job without his shameful love for his mother. She was the reason he had a career at all. She embarrassed him. He pressed his fists into his eyes to block out the image of her standing in front of him at graduation spitting on a handkerchief and wiping an imperfection visible only to her from his forehead. He couldn't stop his ears going red, glowing on the side of his head, twin beacons illuminating his humiliation at his classmates' smirks. That was why she did it. To remind him he was chained to her, if he had ever allowed himself to imagine for one moment that becoming a policeman would liberate him.

A mother's love should be free from sordid, emotional attachments. Why couldn't she be like those drug-addled mothers he encountered as a rookie in uniform? The ones where social services would come to the house and take the children away in the back of a car while the mother knelt on the floor with her arms stretched out towards the broken dirty windows shrieking how much she loved her equally filthy children. No one had taken him away. Not even for a weekend respite from the suffocating love of his all-too-sober mother. Why couldn't she have dabbled with crack cocaine?

He looked at his watch. His dinner would be mummifying in the oven while she paced the kitchen floor. The second he opened the front door she would tell him how she was certain he had been shot dead at seven thirty-five, two minutes before his usual time for getting home. And what time did he call this? She worried about herself, and how she would cope if he ever plucked up the courage to leave or, even better, got himself killed in the line of duty. Once he had screamed at her to fuck off and leave him alone before running into his bedroom and slamming the door behind him. But there he found himself in an emotional cul-de-sac without a television. An almost imperceptible tap from outside. The door opened a crack and a whisper that his favourite soap was starting brought them back together on the couch where neither exchanged a word for twenty minutes; a silence that ended in hugs. No, not gropes. Her hand was inside his shirt by accident. He was her human doll. He could see it now. A fucking doll! She always said he was the only light in her otherwise dark-as-the-tomb life. It wasn't his job to give her hollowed-out existence meaning, was it? Fear. Yes, that was it. She was terrified. Her terror explained the futile attempt to control the random meaningless acts that comprised a life. She tried to force the anxiety back into whatever dark hole in her heart from which it had slithered by managing every fucking single second of his miserable existence. But he knew control did nothing to abate the terror of living. He wanted a bit of that. A slice of life – living. Just once he wanted to be out of control.

"Inspector?"

"What? I think you have said enough, Tiberius. I don't want to hear another single word," Sullivan said, sinking onto the floor beside the ovens, sobbing with his face pressed into the palms of his hands.

"I still have it," Claudius told himself as he tiptoed towards the double serving doors that led out of the kitchen into a wide corridor beyond. "That was an Academy performance."

Once outside, he ran.

Inspector Sullivan pressed himself against Sergeant Jones as they passed in the corridor in a now-shared search for Rik Wallace. Perhaps it was to shield her from a woman in a shamefully tiny blood-soaked nightdress going past clutching an uncooked leg of something while muttering to herself about billions. Or maybe it was the inevitable consequence of Jones's unconscious pushing out of her breasts, and his unthinking complementary crotch thrusts. Whatever the motivation, a panel in the wall between a pair of matching gold-framed eighteenth-century racehorses opened, causing them to stagger into a narrow corridor lit from above by the light from the dining room streaming between the original ceiling and the new wall. Once inside the panel closed behind them on a spring.

Somehow Sergeant Jones's blue mohair cardigan was being pulled off over her head. But in the tangle of limbs and the poor light, it was difficult to tell who was pulling what. There was no time to undo those large fake brass buttons.

The instant her arms were free, she slammed the inspector against the original panelled wall and ripped open her blouse, reaching around behind her back to release her breasts from the sensible brassiere, bigger than anything Sullivan had ever seen at home.

The inspector used the opportunity to unbuckle his trousers and pull down one of a matching set of three-per-pack underpants his mother bought for him whenever she encountered discounts as she passed through the menswear department on a mission to buy a shirt for her only son. Did she ever pause to wonder if she had other children, whether Freddy would still be her favourite? He benefited from the lack of competition: if not psychologically, at least when it came to underwear.

Sullivan paused to stare open-mouthed at the maps of blue veins, twin deltas meandering from red nipples that were then springing into life like the speeded-up films of plants he saw on nature programmes on television with his mother sipping hot chocolate beside him, muttering disapproving commentary on the sexual habits of wildlife, unrestrained by social convention.

Now the top half of Jones and the bottom half of Sullivan

were unclothed. She pressed her bare breasts into his shirt while he ground his naked crotch into her navy, flower print A-line skirt.

This was the moment when they should have rationally reflected on the potential complications of their future working lives together. But reason never prevails against a hormonal revolution joining forces with years of pent-up sexual frustration.

Sullivan might have paused to consider if Jones was the ideal woman his mother pretended that she hoped he would bring home to meet her so that she could expire with an easy mind knowing he would be looked after when she promptly died, as she promised. If he had any thoughts at that moment, we can assume, or even hope, his mother was not amongst them.

Jones might have stopped to reflect on whether she could live with remembering every detail of what was about to happen, or consider how news of this liaison would go down in the staff canteen when she told her colleagues, which she must, being a dedicated gossip, even against her own interests. She didn't assess whether sex with her boss would undermine or improve her chances of promotion. But it is difficult to compose ones Curriculum Vitae while trying to drag one's knickers over one's bowed knees while one's lower lip is being held between one's boss's poorly maintained teeth.

The moment for possible sanity passed faster than it took Sullivan to hoist Jones's skirt over her buttocks.

They anatomically came together with a desperate plunge that caused them to fall sideways into a plywood trough containing a mound of dried plaster abandoned or mislaid behind the wall, the uneven surface of which did not stop their spasmodic lunges against each other.

"Fuck my mother," Sullivan grunted.

"What?"

"I said fuck my mother."

"Yes. Fuck her," Jones gasped.

They would have the bruises for weeks.

Whatever position it was, it was not one that allowed either of them to notice the reflection of light from the cornea pressed against the knothole in the panelling in the room outside.

They flapped together for a minute in the manner of fish smothering in air before their spasmodic struggle shuddered to a halt. The sound of their breathless gasps was audible outside in the empty corridor beyond the secret panel.

"Where are we?" Jones asked, sitting with her back against the inside of the new dining room wall, groping for her clothes with her fingers tasting the ground like the feelers of a black widow spider.

"I have no idea," Sullivan answered.

"What do you think?"

"I think we should do that again."

"The floor is flatter here," Jones said.

"And then let's go to my place. My mother would love to meet you."

XXXIX

Temperantia Exercentes
Exercising Restraint

Julie Progress and Randy Fortune walked as slowly as possible along the hall leading to the bedroom that they now both seemed to unconsciously acknowledge that they reluctantly shared.

"How can you think of food at a time like this?" Randy was asking.

"Maybe that little Italian place on the corner near—"

"The show ruined my appetite."

"You never want to go out anyway."

"I am a hermit."

"I'll order a Chinese takeaway."

"I should never have hired Rik Wallace to assist me in giving away all my money. I'm doomed to remain rich. Was that his wife on stage? She's not the sort I expected to marry a moral authority. I don't mean to be judgemental, but she could do something with her hair. Perhaps he is better off dead."

"Rik Wallace is alive," a disembodied voice beside them said.

They both jumped.

Claudius Steel stepped out of a crevice in the wall neither

had noticed before.

"Keep away from me, Eustis. You are a ghost. I saw you being sawed in two in the library."

"I regret to say I sawed my brother in half instead of Wallace. I suspect my assistant had a hand in it. I am sure she rigged something; though I can't work out what it was. Her skimpy monokini distracted me from what she was up to. One should always be suspicious of those who turn up serendipitously, don't you agree? But then, maybe Tiberius himself was responsible because he didn't believe in co-incidences. Perhaps he was right: maybe it was a miracle. After all, it is a miracle I am still free."

Randy backed away from the disturbing apparition in golf attire with his hair standing on end."

"Don't you recognise me? I'm your butler, Mister Fortune. That was my twin brother, Tiberius, who was cut in half in the library. We were separated at birth."

"Tiberius?" Progress asked, clinging to Randy's arm not out of fear, but from an unwillingness to let him go. "The madman Pandora warned me wanted to kill Wallace?"

"The very same."

"Identical twins?" Randy asked.

"Yes."

"Separated at birth? How fascinating. I funded research into—"

"Wait a minute, Progress interrupted. "How do we know you're not Tiberius pretending to be his identical twin brother, Eustis? That's the kind of stunt a homicidal maniac would try to pull."

"Are you speaking from personal experience?" Claudius

asked. "I can prove I am Eustis. Ask me any butlering question you like."

"Tell me what I have for breakfast," Randy said.

Claudius exhaled in relief.

"Oh, that's easy. First, I warm a plate to fifty-one degrees Celsius and—"

But his elaboration of the familiar breakfast routine almost immediately evolved into a low screech before he fell face down in front of his astonished audience.

"Got you," Bernard the security guard said having materialised out of the gloom in the hallway, blowing onto the barrel of his Taser gun. "This, Mr Fortune – by the way I recognize you because I saw your picture in my wife's copy of *Celebrity Hermit Magazine* – is the most dangerous lunatic in the country," Bernard said, pointing his gun at the twitching body on the floor. Bernard zapped Claudius again for good measure when he groaned. "Can't take a chance. He has been on the run from Drogo's with Rik Wallace. I would recognise him anywhere, even without the beard. I admit sawing people in two is an unexpected departure from his usual habit of strangulation, but lunatics will always surprise you."

"But he is my butler—"

"He would say that wouldn't he? We see it all the time in the psychiatric services – to which I belong, by the way. He fooled me once when I helped him escape, but he won't deceive me again," Bernard said. "I blame myself, but then it was my first day on the job, and no one had told me what to expect."

"But you are a pirate," Randy said, waving a hand at the security guard's costume.

"Black Beard. Sometimes when dealing with insane cases

on the run we have to wear disguises in case we distress our clients by appearing suddenly. It's all part of the job. I was terrified when I started at Drogo's. My wife was convinced I would go crazy. But, as I assure her now, you get used to it."

"I need air," Randy said. He wrestled his arm free of Progress's grip and ran down the hall.

"Have you seen Professor Murphy?" Bernard asked Progress, ignoring Randy's abrupt exit.

"Who?"

"The other pirate: Calico Jack. He is bound to have a straightjacket on him. Not wearing it, you understand, but amongst his possessions. I advised him to bring several to be on the safe side because you never know when you are going to run into a lunatic. He probably left them in the car. Typical. I have to take care of everything myself. Miss, would you mind grabbing hold of the fugitive's legs? I'll just give him another zap before we get going."

Progress knelt and held Claudius's ankles together. She was functioning automatically because she was distracted by Randy's abrupt departure leaving her alone with this Taser-wielding pirate. That wasn't proof of love. How dare he run away first! If anyone was leaving, it was she. She would be long gone if only she could afford to be, especially now that Wallace was dead. Or, was he? Who or what was she supposed to believe? As soon as she had something to eat – and a few glasses of wine – she would think about grieving for him, just in case.

"Now, Miss, do you know the way out of here?" Bernard asked, dragging Claudius along the floor by the arms.

Progress had never liked the butler anyway.

XL

Medice Aliis Mederi
Physician, Heal Others

Meanwhile, Tiberius Lang was still on stage in the library in Fortune Mansion dragging out his performance for Bentley Murphy, who was sitting on his own on a chair he placed right side up from amongst the overturned ones beside the antique globe. He had a mobile phone pressed to his ear under the three cornered hat.

"Hi there. You are through to Don't Do It support services. We are experiencing a larger than normal volume of calls."

"Typical," he muttered. "Yet another sign of the futility of my not killing myself. As if I needed one. Now I literally am in a death queue. My father moved to the front of the same line – how many years ago now? There was no putting that thought back from wherever it had suddenly sprung.

He saw his father turn in the doorway on his last morning alive. He ran to him and jumped into his dad's paternal embrace: his arms were made for wrapping around his infant son. Little Bentley pulled on the scraggly beard, stretching a laugh from the poet's kind mouth. Next in his child's memory, the vision of the policeman at the door bearing tidings that could never be untold. The image of his screaming mother kneeling on the floor, pushing him away in her grief. In the intervening years, he learned there was no psychiatric cure for a wound that deep. There was no therapeutic intervention to undo a random traffic accident. A second ahead or behind, and he would be occupying a different world now. It was the randomness of life to which he could not reconcile himself. He would pray all the time, if only he could believe in God. He envied those with faith and good knees.

The recorded voice on the phone reached him. *"Please stay on the line until one of our qualified counsellors is available to chat with you, because each desperate plea for help is important to us."*

He remembered his replacement father coming home every day at the same time from his cubicle surrounded by his actuarial charts and calculations, climbing out of his brown car, in his grey suit without a verse on his mind. His mother wasn't going to risk another poet. Over dinner, he would remind little Bentley and his sister of the potential impact smoking, drinking, driving, skiing, not taking enough exercise, taking too much exercise, foreign travel, sports, over-sharpened pencils, not sufficiently chewing one's food, talking while eating, and being alive in general had on one's life expectancy. There were unquantifiable risks of which he had first-hand theoretical knowledge. Every Wednesday evening when the food was safely swallowed, the plates cleaned and put away, and the glasses stacked on the draining board his father would dress up as a rancher in the costume hanging in the same place in the wardrobe. Bentley and his sister would climb into their sheep's clothing and pretend to graze the carpet, bleating whenever they felt the end of the shepherd's crook on their woollen backs. His memory retained a single still photograph of his mother at the top of the stairs dressed as Bo Peep, yodelling with a frantic grimace painted onto her face with red lipstick on the otherwise black-and-white image projected onto the inside of his eyelids whenever he closed them to indulge in the exquisite pain of recalling his childhood. Billie, the real sheep dog, cowering in canine terror under the television that was never turned on.

"Your call may be recorded for training purposes."

The two sheep, Bo Peep, and Billie the dog may not have admitted it at the time, but they were relieved when the rancher broke his neck falling down that carpeted hillside, a risk little Bentley was confident his second father had not factored in to his own actuarial calculations. He couldn't recall where each of them was within the tableau when it happened. He may have been on the landing or on the top step behind his stepfather's knees. Or that may have been his sister or Billie. But he resolved years ago that he would never remember. His mother decided she had had enough of the dangers of marriage. She would try alcohol instead.

Leonard Cohen came on the line singing that Suzanne takes him to her place near the river where he could hear the boats passing. "You can throw yourself out her fucking window and straight into the water," the psychiatrist improvised to the tune.

Suddenly, he had a novel idea: one of those thoughts that, having taken years to ferment deep in his unconscious, seemed obvious once its bloated form broke the surface. "Pills. I'm a doctor, for God's sake. Pills. Why didn't I think of that before now? Oh, I am so stupid. My scepticism with regard to medication blinded me to the solution to my problem. I will write myself a prescription for an overdose." Leonard Cohen broke off to allow a recorded voice to advise Murphy that he was fifth in the queue and to hang on in there. Leonard assured him he wanted to travel with Suzanne, and he wanted to travel without being able to see.

"Listen to all of the following options carefully before choosing. Press One to talk to someone who has been through what you are going through now. Press Two for life insurance. Press Three for—"

"Hi. My name is Imelda. How can I help you today?"

"Help me? You can talk me out of killing myself. What else are you supposed to do?"

"Oh, haven't you heard? We are no longer just a suicide counselling service. We also offer hotel deals in a surprising range of desirable destinations for those who need to get away from—"

The psychiatrist was on his feet screaming down the phone at Imelda, who was calm because she had been through a course on dealing with difficult callers. As he explained that he didn't want a weekend break in a relaxing fucking luxury spa, Randy Fortune, who had wandered into the library in search of air, cleared his throat.

Murphy hung up as he twisted his neck around to catch sight of whoever was behind him.

"That was … err … customer service," he said, raising his eye patch.

"They can be annoying. By the way, I'm Randy Fortune the billionaire." He held out his hand, forgetting his skin allergy.

"I'm Bentley Murphy the psychiatrist," the doctor said, shaking Randy's hand up and down.

"In that case, I feel I can tell you anything."

"Please don't."

Murphy sighed, sat back down and removed the wig and three cornered hat.

"I suffer from ennui. Complete lassitude," Randy said, turning over a chair and sitting down beside him.

"Not enough to stop you talking. Anyway, I have been suicidal for as long as I can remember, and it depresses me to think how many times my attempts to kill myself have come to nothing. In fact, just now I was on the phone to a suicide support—"

"Also, I am allergic to everything. Paint, soap, nuts, skin—"

"I hate my patients. My God. Did I only realise that now? I detest all of them."

"I'll miss my butler. I had come to rely on him to keep people away from me."

"Ah, yes. Bernard's wife told him that she read in *Celebrity Hermit Magazine* that the great Claudius Steel was acting as your butler."

"Bernard?"

"A security guard at the hospital. He is disguised as Black Beard or Calico Jack. I forget which."

"The one with the Taser?"

"Err, yes, that's the one."

"We've met. It's Black Beard."

"Did Black Beard tell you that your butler's twin brother, Tiberius Lang, escaped from our lunatic asylum? That's why we're here. We believe he came here to see his brother, because he told me in therapy that he has no interest in his family; but as a classic Freudian I am—"

"I believe you will find that Black Beard … err … Bernard

has the situation with Tiberius under control. He zapped him outside in the corridor."

"Well, then, with Tiberius safely apprehended, and poor Rik Wallace there cut in half that's my two most challenging cases resolved," Murphy said, pointing to the gory corpse on stage.

"Him?" Randy said, raising his eyebrows and lifting his chin. "That's my butler, Eustis. Look at his grey-striped trousers."

"Aha! I thought it might be your butler, but Bernard tried to persuade me it was Wallace. Two together, face to face in the box, and so much blood it was impossible to tell who was screaming the loudest. What an extraordinary act! If I hadn't seen it with my own eyes, I would never have believed it. He is gone now, but he will never be forgotten. What a legacy!"

Against his will, Murphy's thoughts drifted to – if not his maddest – definitely his most annoying patient: Wallace. He resented him the least of all the inmates at Saint Drogo's, and now he realised that was because – obviously – he was sane when he first met him. At least as sane as he was. Yes. Yes. Of course! Why didn't he see it? It was an act. He was engaged in some form of thespian philosophical experiment. "This is what happens when you read Nietzsche," he said, out loud.

"He read Nietzsche? It goes to show you can never really know people. He was very convincing in the role, which is the result of his dedication."

"He was very convincing. He fooled me."

"He fooled everyone."

"I'm sure it was metaphysics."

"He was a method actor—"

"I wondered what his motivation was?"

"I remember reading somewhere it was the Meisner technique."

"I was sure he would return to academia. But maybe the pressure was too much for him, because Nietzsche was the greatest actor of his or any generation of philosophers. This is all starting to make sense to me now. It was an act, and I should have seen through it at once. I knew he was sane. I knew it."

"I'm surprised you haven't seen his earlier work. His nude Macbeth established his reputation."

"Obviously he was accomplished in several fields. We had a famous actor in our asylum all this time, and I never knew it? Imagine that. My patients constantly surprise me. That's another reason why I hate them. You would be amazed how many celebrities need psychiatric help."

"Or fabulously rich people. Me, for example! I have tried everything imaginable to relieve the overwhelming torpor that has held me in its grip since I became stinking rich, but nothing works. Money, cars, yachts, racehorses, travel, marriage, hanging out with famous people, this huge house and gardens, and now magic. Nothing works."

"I have given considerable thought to gassing, hanging, or shooting myself; throwing myself off a cliff, provoking homicidal maniacs at the hospital to throttle me; and this evening I wanted to volunteer to have myself sawn in two, but *he* got in before me," Bentley said, nodding towards the stage. "So here I am. Still alive."

"That's nothing. I started a foundation to give away all my money, and I am getting richer."

"Have you tried pills?"

"What kind of pills?"

"Anti-depressants."

"Aren't they addictive? Besides, shouldn't I sort my underlying problems out rather than rely on medication?"

"Who cares, if they cheer you up?"

"Why don't you try them?"

"I wouldn't blame you for wondering what kind of a doctor I am. I didn't even consider taking pills myself until a few moments ago. Can you imagine that? Often, we can't see the obvious thing right in front of our noses. Maybe it was the suicide support service gave me the idea. They seem to know their business. Forget I said anything. I shouldn't medicate every little problem. After all, I support the talking therapies. At least I did for everyone, except Wallace. I really fucked him up. To compensate for what I did to him, let me write you a prescription."

"I will take your pills only if you will too."

"Deal," Murphy said on impulse.

Randy held the psychiatrist's hand in his and turned it over. Murphy began to massage the back of Randy's wrist. "Strange the way I am not allergic to your skin," Randy said. He placed the palm of his other hand against Murphy's cheek, allowed it linger there for a moment before holding it in front of his eyes, fingers spread out, to inspect the flesh. "It's a miracle. No inflammation. Nothing. You are the first person I have met since I became rich that doesn't cause me to break out in a rash."

"I'm starving," Murphy said.

"There's an Italian down the road on the corner. Right beside the pharmacy."

By the time Jackson and the librarian arrived on their bicycles at Fortune Mansion three ambulances, two police cars, and a fire engine were parked in front of the steps running up to the front door. Intersecting circles of blue, green, and yellow lights danced across the front of the house. As Progress descended the steps towards them, two paramedics in luminous orange vests went past carrying a body bag on a stretcher. "You're too late," she said.

"For what?" Jackson asked.

"For everything. My simple plan is in ruins."

She wandered off towards the garden.

Just then they both caught sight of Ellen Dubois climbing, perhaps out of instinct, into the back of the ambulance nearest the steps.

"She's ours," the librarian told the paramedic who was helping her in, pulling the fugitive back out by the arm.

They accepted a lift home in the ambulance, leaving their bicycles in the care of one of the more responsible-looking entrepreneurs whose improvised campsite outside the front gates had been flattened by the traffic. By the time they passed through the red telephone-box doors of the bookshop with Ellen Dubois clamped between them, they were too tired to notice the large crate sitting on the floorboards squeezed between two rows of shelves. Had they looked closer they would have observed it was marked "Interesting Books – Open Immediately" above where one of the words "Fragile" had been crossed out.

XLI

Prope Extincta Genus?
A Dying Breed?

The "No Smoking" sign in the waiting room was fixed to the wall at eye level opposite Pandora. She would ignore it, but the three mothers were glaring at her with such maternal fury she removed the unlit cigarette from between her lips and slid it back into the packet. She was getting soft, she thought. An infant who gripped the back of her mother's stockinged leg sneezed into the confined space. Pandora could imagine the microscopic viral mist floating on the air between them before landing on her skin. Such were the distractions in this place where one waited to learn if the world would start to revolve on its axis again. Even the studied meaninglessness of her life had somehow become pointless for Pandora.

It was imperative to prepare for what may lie ahead beyond that door, but she found it impossible to concentrate on her fears when a baby who was pinned to the floor by a full nappy, hurled the letter "N" at her head. She tilted to the side before the wooden brick could make contact with the left lens of her sunglasses.

Whenever she advised parents with infants she encountered in public spaces – where she felt they should be banned –

that she hated children, they imagined she was initiating a sentimental conversation on their darling progeny in her own quaint way. She had a theory she would share: the less valuable she believed their contribution to society, the more likely people were to reproduce themselves in some act of revenge on civilization in general, and on her in particular. "Pandora?" a voice called, causing her to stand automatically up.

The general practitioner gripped Pandora's hands. Or perhaps Pandora clung to hers, we will never know. Either way their fingers were entwined. The doctor's obvious emotion made Pandora uncomfortable. "The prognosis is – better than we could have hoped," the doctor blurted out. "I'm delighted—"

"What have I got? What is it called? I can look it up on the Internet when I get home."

"I cannot find anything wrong with you, which is a miracle considering your habits. Have you thought of donating your body to science when you eventually go – which from the look of things won't be anytime soon? Here," the doctor said. She unfastened her fingers to rummage in her desk drawer for a brochure depicting a half-skinned cadaver. "Read through this."

"So, I am dying?"

"Living is a form of dying, but you are not doing so at an abnormally accelerated rate."

"I know, you can't bring yourself to put it into words. You are thinking if you don't say it out loud perhaps it will … just … go away," Pandora said.

"That would be denial."

"What else is there?" Pandora asked. "How long have I got?"

"Have you thought of counselling? I can recommend someone who specialises in hypochondria."

"Man up, doc. Tell me what I have."

"You man up, Pandora. It's all in your mind. Physically, you are in perfect health. A medical anomaly perhaps, but you are as healthy as a horse. Makes me think that life is so unjust. Some people exercise, eat the proper foods, don't smoke or drink and wham, they're gone. What does it all mean when someone like you can—"

Pandora removed her sunglasses to treat the doctor to the full force of her penetrating bloody-egg-yolk stare.

"You should focus on the positive aspects of your test results," the general practitioner stammered.

"Which are?"

"Whenever a patient gets good news, it can be an appropriate time for them to reassess their habits and decide what changes to their life style they want to make. You might consider sticking to the recommended alcohol limits and quitting cigarettes while you are ahead."

"You're right, doc."

"I am?"

Pandora put back on her black plates to the relief of both. "It's not as if it's a surprise. I smoke at least a hundred cigarettes a day."

"The surprise is you are physically fine. Isn't there someone at home you could talk to if you won't go for counselling? Over a single small measure of wine in the evening?"

"Horse, but he has his own problems with his knitting

patterns. This would tip him over the edge."

"You are not sick, Pandora. Oh, I give up."

"Have you a gun I could borrow? I assume you hand out firearms on an occasion such as this? I had to drop my own in the river at short notice."

"No. God, no. You can't give up and shoot yourself. Where there is life there is hope, etcetera."

"I am planning to shoot someone else. Someone I cannot leave behind. He is precious to me, but at the same time he has annoyed me since the first time I laid eyes on him."

Those eyes! The doctor shuddered.

"Someone I want to take with me. Why not? Isn't that how people in my position behave? What difference does it make?"

"I can't give you a gun. Apart from the fact that I don't have one, you don't need to take anyone with you because you aren't going anywhere. There is nothing – *no-thing* – physically wrong with you. Besides, I must consider my Hippocratic oath. I am sworn to uphold ethical standards."

"Oh, those. You are worse than Rik Wallace. I am surrounded by ethics. I can't take any more. What will I tell Horse? He is not going to see this in a positive light. He booked our holidays for next year. I told him we should be spontaneous, but no, he likes to have everything organised in advance. I love Horse, but he doesn't repel me the way Wallace does. You would understand if you met Wallace. He drives everybody crazy. Sometimes I feel sorry for him. Most of the time I hate him. Sometimes I think … I even … love him despite all his non-stop talking. He is the kind of person anyone would want to kill just to make those feeling that drive a person crazy go away. Besides, I told him I would if he ruined my life at Candid Online College. I have to keep my promises or people won't fear me."

"For God's sake, get out of my office, Pandora."

Pandora gazed at the Glock 17 9mm pistol before hugging it to her chest.

"Thank you for the gun, Horse. For a moment in the doctor's office, I considered shooting everyone I ever knew – except you and Marley, of course – but that would take too long. Besides, that wouldn't be as ethical as killing the one person who most deserves to die. Don't make that face, Horse. Yes, I said ethical. Everyone else tries to be moral, so why not me? I have settled on one person: the true cause of all our troubles. I want you to go shopping when I do it – somewhere they have security cameras – to establish your alibi. Oh, don't cry, Horse. Buy socks or something. Wool. The blue alpaca you saw in the fabric shop last time. Blow your nose, for God's sake. You are getting snot on my jacket. I leave Marley in your care. No sudden movements around the house first thing when you wake up in the morning. Let him get warmed up first. And one chocolate-mouse a day because he is getting too fat."

Marlboro studied his reflection in the powered-off television screen with critical feline appraisal. If he felt the comment on his shape was unjustified, he didn't say anything. But then it is difficult for any cat to accept that he has become a fat cat.

XLII

Cogitans In Camera
Thinking Inside the Box

Rik Wallace was thinking how Julie Progress would never see him again. Beautiful Progress. He suspected she would survive because that is what she did. But he would never smell Samantha Spencer again. Fragrant Samantha. He could stretch out, but he couldn't feel his legs below his knees. He screamed and beat on the lid with the side of his fist while kicking his feet in his first tantrum since infancy.

"*Calm, you must stay calm,*" Wallace told himself.

"Why should I?" he asked, his personality fracturing under the pressure building inside the box.

"*Because it would be the philosophical thing to do.*"

"Who said that?"

"*I did.*"

"Fuck philosophy. I want to get out of here." He hammered on the lid again.

"*I thought you didn't approve of bad language?*" he asked when he had run out of energy.

"Fuck you. I do when the occasion demands it, such as now. Fuck, fuck, fuckety-fuck!"

"*Reason is more consoling than swearing; though. I admit*

I am struggling to remember the words of any philosopher that might offer you consolation in our current circumstance. I can't recall one who wrote with inspiration on being buried alive, can you?"

"You're the expert, not me. Oh, God, I could die happy if I could feel my fucking legs."

"Give me a minute, and I will think of someone."

"We don't have that much time. I can't breathe. I have a pain in my chest. I am having a fucking heart attack."

"You do realise we would be dead already if there wasn't air coming in some place?"

"You haven't measured the capacity of this box. I know more about woodwork than you do."

"I forget what the Stoics have to say regarding this sort of situation," he said, ignoring his irrational other half."

"Dying doesn't bother me, but spending my final moments alive with pins and needles in my legs and enduring your fucking pedantic bullshit is more than I can stand," he screamed. "That's it! I can't stand!"

"That is unfair. I am trying to offer you comfort in your—"

"Shut up. Listen. I can hear something outside. It's laughter. Someone is jumping up and down on the lid."

"She loves me, you know."

"Who?"

"Samantha."

"You're crazy."

"You're jealous."

"If she loves either of us it has to be me. She hates philosophy. She and I have that much in common. Don't you appreciate how that discipline has ruined your life – *my* life?"

"I am amazed you can bring it up now."

"I cannot imagine another person anywhere on earth who has suffered as much as me."

"Well, there's me!"

The librarian sat into the armchair opposite Jackson in front of the grate with the artificial coal in the tiny sitting room above the bookshop. Ellen Dubois was sound asleep in their bed. An almost empty wine bottle stood between them on the floor.

"Cheers," Jackson said for the twenty-second time that evening.

"Cheers," the librarian replied without feeling.

"What's wrong?"

"Our plans are in tatters. Rik Wallace has disappeared, and we are left with her on our hands."

"What are we going to do?" he asked nodding towards the door from where the sound of snoring came.

"She is no use to us now."

"We need her in case social services show up."

"I can't stand it."

"Having a family involves sacrifice. You knew that when we got into this. Focus on the rewards."

"Yes, I suppose. All three of them."

"I couldn't believe her timing, falling asleep just when we got her through the front door."

"I thought she was going to wake up again when you had her under the arms, and I was on the ankles hauling her up the stairs."

"So did I."

"And her –I mean, *your* nightdress catching on that nail."

They chuckled at the shared memory.

"What about television?"

"A five-foot screen is enough for any child."

"I meant for how long?"

"Ten minutes a day."

"But only educational programmes."

"No cartoons."

"Agreed."

"Where are they now?"

"Downstairs playing in the shop."

What was that smell? Rik Wallace sniffed the sour air. Amongst the stench of his farts, sweat, and other excretions, his olfactory receptors picked out an egg molecule.

"Egg sandwiches," he muttered, his fingers following blind directions from his nose as they sniffed out a package behind his back. He brought it to his face, peeled away the waxy paper with his teeth, and inhaled.

"*I* hate *egg sandwiches.*"

"Well, *I* don't."

"*I'm going to stop talking if you're going to carry on like this.*"

"Fat chance of that! Maurice Spencer warned you of the dangers of reading Nietzsche but would you listen? No. Not you. First you got us locked up in Saint Drogo's and now this."

"*No credible research has ever found a direct link between reading Nietzsche, going mad, and being buried alive.*"

"Well, you might undertake it, if we ever get out."

"*Besides, I was never mad.*"

"It's obvious to me you were, but don't ask me to prove it with one of your useless logical arguments. I just know it the way most normal people just know the obvious stuff. I refuse to be drawn into your world. You would love that, wouldn't you, if I gave in to philosophy?"

"You were also there when Spencer warned me about Nietzsche. You ignored him too."

"Doesn't he have something to say on death that might give us hope?"

He chewed on a corner of the stale bread while awaiting an answer.

"Well, sort of. According to him God is dead."

"Typical. While that is thought-provoking, it is hardly pertinent to our current predicament."

"It does rule out the value of prayer."

"Great. Now all hope is gone. Do you want to try half of this sandwich?"

"I told you, I hate eggs. They make me nauseous. Now, let me see. Nietzsche believed that by accepting death with courage one can rise above the herd."

"What herd? There isn't room for anyone else in this coffin besides the two of us. There isn't even space for our legs. I'll never walk again. Oh, God. I wish I were part of a herd now – a walking herd."

"Embrace suffering."

"How did I end up being buried alive with a philosopher? Why couldn't you have had to pass yourself off as a sports commentator or an accountant or a lawyer?"

"Or a poet?"

"Even a poet. I was better off before you became a

philosopher. I had control over my life. No one noticed me. I fitted in. I had my DIY at the weekends. Not like you. Always having some new fucking thought or other."

"*I saved you from yourself. You were boring.*"

"I was happy. I was living a quiet life. A lot can be said for boring. I wish I were bored now."

"*What difference does it make in the great scheme of things? Perhaps like Nietzsche who was exhausted by life, a coffin is as good as anywhere. At least, it is where most ordinary people end up.*"

"Help. Get me out of here!"

"*Get me out of here too. I have so much more to learn. Consider the opportunities that despair presents. You can behave whatever way you want, and it won't change how things turn out.*"

Silence. Then: "Fuck off. What does that mean?"

"*Heidegger.*"

"I am already sorry I am asking, but what about him?"

"*Maybe he can help.*"

"Does he know we are in here?"

"*He wrote on authenticity.*"

"Who am I supposed to impress in here with my authenticity?"

"*Yourself.*"

"Help! Help!" The sides of his fists were raw from beating against the lid.

"*Pull yourself together.*"

"Why should I?"

"*Because you cannot experience your own death.*"

"I don't know why I am saying this, but explain what you mean."

"*Okay. Those who remain behind perceive death as a loss.*"

"Why can't someone else be trapped in here with you listening to this drivel instead of me? Why did you volunteer for that fucking magic trick?"

"*I didn't volunteer.*"

"It's not fair. Tiberius should be in here with us."

"*There isn't room. Besides, you already experienced his loss.*"

"Did I?"

"*You saw him slither out of the box before Della grinned, shoved your face inside, and slammed the halves back together.*"

"Della. She did this to us. *Why would she bury you alive? She is supposed to be your friend; your guardian angel.*"

"She is a bit … flaky."

"*I have noticed that circus folk can be fickle. Lacking rationality, if you ask me. Not that I know anything about that subject other than what I picked up from you against my will.*"

"Why would she do this to me?"

In response to the question the fingers on his hand closed around a cylinder in his pocket: a flashlight. He fumbled to illuminate the inside of the box. He saw a note with his name taped to the sidewall. He almost dislocated his shoulder ripping it free.

Rik, don't panic. You are in the magician's cabinet nailed inside a shipping crate. If you are reading this then everything is going exactly to plan. I have packed a lunch for you.

Inside the box find a copy of *Celebrity Hermit Magazine* if you are bored.

Yours affectionately,

Della

"What an idiot," he muttered. "A fucking egg sandwich doesn't count as lunch."

His foot bumped against something.

"Wait. A bottle."

Now, how was he supposed to get it up from down there?

After a great deal of stretching and improbable contortions his fingers closed around the glass neck.

Good old Della. Whisky? Gin? Vodka? Anything would do.

He brought it up to his eyes and flicked on the light he was determined to conserve. A note taped to the side indicated it was for pee.

"Now she tells me". He wriggled his damp crotch.

"This is a great neighbourhood in which to raise children," Jackson said. "Good schools a bike ride away across only two dangerous road junctions."

The yellow pup raised his leg again against the edge of a shelf of cookery books.

"What's in that?" the librarian asked, sliding the dog away with her foot and pointing her toe at the end of crate marked "Interesting Books – Open Immediately" and festooned with the word "Fragile" sticking out beyond the end of the rows of shelves.

"I have no idea. I thought you ordered them."

"I could swear I heard noise down here last night."

"Mice."

"I'm exhausted from trying to sleep on the kitchen floor. Let's open it tomorrow."

Rik Wallace strained to hear sounds from outside. Once he was sure the box moved, but that had been an incalculable eternity ago. He imagined he heard a seagull. Della was sending him overseas with a smuggled family of penniless gorillas.

"I bet they have bananas and not fucking egg sandwiches."

"*The sandwiches are all gone.*"

"What do you mean gone? Gone where?"

"*Speaking metaphysically, you ate them.*"

"You ate them too."

"*I did not. You did.*"

"I ate one."

"*Who would put only one rotten egg sandwich in a coffin?*"

"I have no feeling below my waist. Can you feel anything below yours?"

"*Dampness.*"

"What will you do if you get out?"

"*It depends on where we are. What do you know about gorillas?*"

"Nothing, but how hard could it be to fit in? At least, they would not be interested in Nietzsche."

"*I was thinking of opening a museum of smells.*"

"Your darling Samantha could be the main exhibit. I wonder if she is searching for us?"

"*Times have changed. These days, being bust out of an asylum is no longer a convincing foundation for a career in philosophy, and as you keep reminding me, I have no proper qualifications. Randy Fortune will have to sort out his own moral problems without me. But how will we survive?*"

"I suppose we could help him finish his mansion. I could paint the walls, and you could advise him on furniture and fittings."

"An enormous crystal chandelier would look good in the hallway."

"And I would remove those airlock doors."

"An eggshell blue."

"Too cold. Green."

"Yes, green."

"At last, we are agreed on something."

The crate remained unpacked because Jackson and the librarian were distracted by their new life as responsible parents.

"Have you noticed the rash on the middle one's arm?" the librarian asked. "It wasn't there yesterday. I didn't want to say anything in front of him this morning, but I just might pop him into Saint Drogo's A&E tomorrow if it hasn't cleared up by then. The girl looked a bit green yesterday, so I might take her along with us. Just in case."

"Don't worry about them. They are fine. Children take a little getting used to, that's all. You'll feel calmer when they get back from school. I'm dying to learn how their first day went." Jackson sighed and studied his watch, before lifting himself from the chair by pushing down on its arms. "It's my turn to change Ellen Dubois's drip. It's your turn with the incontinence pads. Are you sure keeping her alive is worth it?"

"Until the youngest is eighteen."

"Shouldn't we unpack the crate downstairs?" he asked.

"I'm exhausted. We will deal with it tomorrow'.

"Let's not be one of those families who don't unpack for ten years."

"Tomorrow."

XLIII

Normalis Usus Est Reddita
Normal Service Has Been Restored

Bernard grabbed the railing on the gangway leading up from the afterdeck to the lounge area with one hand, while balancing a circular steel tray of margaritas on the palm of his other hand. He tilted into the mild swell running out of the mouth of the broad harbour. He was proud of how quickly he had found his sea legs, even if he had not yet been beyond the line between the lighthouse on the distant hill and the buoy marking the entrance to the bay. His wife in the galley below the waterline had told him yet again how she didn't approve of anyone, even those who didn't need to work, drinking alcohol so early in the morning and especially those cocktails she had to look up how to make online. She had punctuated each word of her disapproval with a blow of a meat mallet on a bag of ice.

Bernard had stood with his back to the lace curtains in their sitting room, hands clasped behind him in imitation of the most authoritative person he could imagine – an old-style admiral – while explaining that her presence on board wasn't based on her approval. He said that he was quite willing to leave her on shore if she refused to come with him. Besides, he reminded her, she had confessed the day before to a curiosity to observe how the other half lived. He pedantically pointed out that it was the other zero-point-nought-nought-one part who were living on yachts and not half of the population at large. Even though she was certain he would never abandon her, she agreed to join him. In truth, she was as excited as he. But first she had to protest because she believed a sound marriage was built on a strong foundation of fake dissent. For his part, he hid his overwhelming relief when she caved in.

Up on deck, a naked Randy Fortune lay face down on one of a pair of matching white lilos. A nude Bentley Murphy was slathering sun tan oil onto Randy's buttocks. Bernard closed his eyes and tried to serve the drinks by remembering where the low glass table was because he didn't want to see anything. His eye fastened on a triangle of black pubic hair when one eyelid involuntarily lifted. Then both opened. Through squinted eyes he was relieved to realise the fuzz emerged from between sunburnt cheeks. But when Murphy stood up and turned around Bernard's gaze was fixed on his round protruding stomach. Is this the first pregnant man, he wondered?

"Your margaritas, Prof," he announced, reversing towards the low rail.

"Thank you, Bernard."

Murphy handed a drink to Randy who stood up. They banged the heavy crystal glasses together.

"Fuck the poor," Randy said as a toast.

"And fuck the mad," Murphy said.

"Yes, fuck them both. What have the poor and the mad ever done for anyone? The mad poor or even the poor mad."

"They are the worst because they can't even pay to see a psychiatrist."

They laughed as Bernard slinked back down the gangway.

Randy and Murphy sat down side by side on the nearest lilo.

"Imagine you cured me with a pill," Randy said. "A teeny-tiny pill." He held up his index finger almost touching his thumb to illustrate the insignificant size, trapping the sun between his fingerprints. "Swallow, wait a few minutes and wham," he said, slapping his palm into his chest, causing Murphy to jump. "My ennui is gone, and with it my desire for poverty. You are a genius, Prof, restoring all of this to me," he added as he stretched out his arms to take in the boat, the harbour, the blue cloudless sky, and the lifestyle. "How does that make you feel?"

"I feel fucking fantastic, because don't forget, I have been taking those tiny pills too," Murphy laughed.

"Does it bother you? Your life's work replaced by a pill?"

"Not at all. Bernard here – oh, he's gone – could zap me with his trusty Taser and it wouldn't trouble me. I have never been so happy." If he was lying, he couldn't tell now that he was wasted. "Imagine, no need for therapy," he added.

"And I have gone back to being a normal, selfish bastard, same as every other billionaire. I used to be obsessed with who the people around me were – family trees and celebrities. But look at me now. I don't care who anyone is. I don't care who you are, or Bernard, or his wife below deck."

"Huh, what a brilliant example you are for anyone sceptical about the efficacy of modern psychiatry."

Randy picked up the folded newspaper from the round glass table and tapped an article with the knuckle of the hand unburdened by the crystal glass.

"I sold KindFace," he said. "I'm out of the altruism business forever, because it's not a good fit with the rest of my portfolio. God, I feel great."

Bernard had returned with a tray of caviar blinis. "My wife says there will always be a need for existential angst; for misery that gives dialectical meaning to the good times," he said. "Without experiencing despair, how could we appreciate the nature of happiness? She has been reading some of your books that I borrowed from your office, Prof."

"I thought I told you to throw them overboard. Nouveau philosophers like your missus are jealous of psychiatry because we have worked out a way of solving the meaning of life with a pill."

"But what of phenomenology, Heidegger, Freud and the rest of them?"

"The person that they meant something to is gone, Bernard. G-O-N-E."

"What's next?" Bernard asked Murphy.

"Next I will swallow another one of these little pills. Chemistry, Bernard, is superior to abstract thinking. Heidegger wouldn't have written a fucking word if he had been on medication."

Randy and Murphy roared with the kind of laughter Bernard last heard from Mother Theresa back at Drogo's when he deposited the still-protesting Claudius Steel in a padded cell, before handing in his notice.

"I meant, when we weigh anchor? Where are we going, Mr Fortune?"

"I haven't had time to plan my future. For years I enjoyed my misery too much to do anything about it. I was addicted to melancholy. But now I am determined to be happy. Live in the moment. Look at me, Bernard," the naked billionaire said as he spread his arms wide.

"Do I have to? I'd rather not."

"For the first time since becoming mega rich, I have neither cares nor anxieties."

"Me neither," the psychiatrist concurred. "Not one. Except – no, it's not important."

"What? You can confide in me," Bernard told him.

"I was wondering who stuck that syringe filled with poison in the duty nurse's neck the day Tiberius Lang and Rik Wallace escaped. That tiny question has been buzzing around inside my head like a bluebottle getting louder and louder these last few days, and I haven't been able to swat it away," he said, rotating an invisible whisk beside his temple. "I know the asylum is filled with maniacs, but it had to have been either Tiberius Lang or Rik Wallace. But we know Tiberius strangles people, and if it was Wallace, then my entire understanding of the human condition is flawed. And if it wasn't them, who else could it be? So, you see, Bernard, I'm worried I may have missed something."

"My wife says that in one of your books—"

"Bernard, for God's sake, shut up," Randy said.

"Randy's right. Let's just leave that life behind us. Let there be an end to psychiatry, or I'll go crazy again. I have spent too many years surrounded by lunatics. From now on I'm socializing only with sane people. Do you agree, Randy?"

"Definitely."

They clinked their glasses together.

"Pass me some caviar, Bernard. I am determined to enjoy

myself. Cheer up. You look too serious for a trainee steward. After all, what can go wrong?" Murphy asked while smacking the side of his head with the palm of his hand to squash the buzzing that had started up again, louder than this morning. "What's that noise? Can you hear a whirring sound, Bernard?"

"It's the engine," Randy said. We're off on our great adventure."

As the boat moved forward Murphy ran to the rail and vomited a caviar blin into the azure water where it was gobbled up by a school of multi-coloured fish of various lengths who seemed to have been circling the hull in anticipation.

XLIV

Audition
An Audition

While Claudius Steel was pondering if an actor pulled off the greatest performance of their lives at Saint Drogo's High Security Asylum for the Criminally Insane and there was no one there to witness it, would it count for anything, the door to his padded cell opened. A woman in a brand-new white laboratory coat stepped inside. She was also wearing a nervous smile. She held out her hand in greeting before retracting it when she observed the straightjacket.

"How are you feeling today, err … Tiberius?" she asked glancing down at her notes pinned to a clipboard.

"My name is Claudius. I'm Tiberius's identical twin brother."

"Oh. That's nice. You're my first case. I've just started working here at the asylum. Not that I approve of the term – she glanced down at the notes again – 'insane'. It's so judgemental don't you think? I prefer to consider the guests here our emotional clients."

The doctor took a step backwards when Claudius struggled to free his arms.

"I've read your file, Tiberius."

"I am not who you think I am. My name is—"

"I hope you're not," she broke in. "Otherwise, what would be the point in psychiatry in the first place? It's such an exciting discipline, don't you agree? My friend Carol is specialising in brain surgery. She believes psychiatry is a complete waste of time. Where were we? Oh, yes, sorry for interrupting you. You were saying? As I said, it's essential for me to shut up and give the client – *emotional guest* – a chance to say something and not to be talking all the time. It's a skill I have to perfect. Go on. I bet you were going to ask me who do I imagine you think you are; or was that who do you believe you are? I should take notes, shouldn't I?"

"I'm a famous actor, Claudius Steel."

"Oh, yes. That was a tragic accident with the saw. He was playing a butler at the time. I read about his nude Macbeth in the obituary in the newspaper. I didn't see it myself but—"

Claudius groaned.

"So, Tiberius, in order not to raise unrealistic expectations, I must tell you I am not planning to cure you or anything. You are a hopeless case. However, I do plan to write a paper on you. You might even become infamous."

"What do you need to know?"

The doctor squatted on the rubber floor and stretched her legs out in front of her. "Could we start with your celebrity victims?"

"There were so many. Most of my clients were celebrities. Don't you agree life is too short to spend on the troubles of ordinary people? You will have to refresh my memory. What ones did you have in mind?"

"The opera singer."

"Opera singer?"

"Milan."

"Oh, yes. That opera singer. Of course. Now let me see. Why did I strangle him?"

"Her."

"Ah yes. Her. That was the point. He thought she was a he! That's why she came to me for help in the first place."

"Wait. Wait, Tiberius. I have to write this down."

The doctor took a pen from the breast pocket of her crisp white coat and cracked open a new notebook she took from a side pocket. "Okay, I'm ready. Wait. First, I will write my name and contact details on the inside cover in case I lose my notes. I am always mislaying stuff. I wonder what that means?" She smiled at the pleasure of some possible insight into herself.

Claudius looked to the ceiling for inspiration where the fluorescent tube flickered under its wire cage. "Do you approve of shock therapy? For example, using electricity on your guests?" he asked.

"Gosh, no."

"Pity. Now why did I strangle him – I mean, her? There were so many reasons. I should put them into some order. Would alphabetically suit your research purposes?"

The doctor nodded as she removed a packet of mints from yet another pocket and popped one in her mouth. "Mint?" she asked, pointing the cylinder at Claudius.

"Maybe later when my arms are free. Ideally, I need my hands to articulate my emotions. Waving them around aids my memory."

"And strangling people," the doctor said with a disappointing display of common sense.

"Where was I?" Claudius asked, determined to play the long game. "Ah, yes, in Milan. I had a wonderful book-lined office off the Piazza Cordusio. It all started one morning with a loud knock on my door. If I knew then what I know now, I wouldn't have been so enthusiastic in shouting, "*Entra!*" But here was my first client since moving my practice so suddenly to Italy."

XLV

Ethicis Spiritus In Machina
An Ethical Ghost in the Machine

Samantha Spencer linked her fingers together and stretched her arms in an arch above her head until her joints cracked. She was now well into her fourth day in front of a computer screen at her father's house where she had come after Randy Fortune vanished without warning. She left the desk to refuel from whatever substances remained in the fridge and kitchen cupboards since her father's time and to pee into an empty bean tin on the floor rather than walking all the way to the toilet at the end of the hall and back. She didn't know if it was day or night outside because the heavy beige curtains were closed. She waggled her fingers over the keyboard and hit the reboot button. The screen went black before turning green, painting her face an alien hue in the darkened room. A line of text above an empty box appeared half way down the screen.

"Yeeeessss. It works," she said, clapping her hands together. "I am a bona fid-e genius."

In the box under the line that read "Please Enter Your Moral Question" she typed "Should I kill Julie Progress?" and clicked on Go. A rotating circle of dots indicated that the computer was mulling over the matter. A blue page replaced the green one, in the middle of which was a text box contained the answer in tiny white font. Samantha leaned into the glass screen.

> From the data available in the profile of Julie Progress entered on our system, it is not possible to conclude she is not evil. However, you should not kill her.

"Pity," Samantha said out loud.

> Take consolation from the fact that she will be more miserable in her bleak future than if you take her life. Besides, according to Heidegger, she would not be able to experience her own death.

"I knew I should have omitted him from the algorithm. Damn my father's books."

She read on.

> However, against this would be the satisfaction of watching her suffer if you devise a painful and long-drawn-out method of execution. Something medieval, perhaps, involving a garrotte. Nietzsche has little to say on this matter. But, according to Kant, who is sensible, in his Metaphysics of Morals written in 1797 that is surprisingly still relevant today, he distinguishes between a public and a private crime where a public offence impacts on a greater number of people than just you. Sometimes we imagine we have a right to avenge a private insult, but this would make our act one of vengeance rather than justice. Revenge is emotionally satisfying, but unfortunately, not ethically justifiable. If you are frustrated that the law is too weak to punish Julie Progress for transgressions not strictly illegal, you could consider campaigning to have—

Samantha broke off reading to nibble on the upturned corner of a sandwich. She peered between the slices to acquire a visual aid as to what the flavour of the filling might be before swallowing. Bored with Kant she clicked on the Ask Another Moral Question button at the bottom of the screen. On an impulse, she typed "Should I sleep with Rik Wallace?" and pressed Go.

A list appeared. She was asked to clarify by sleep did she mean hibernate, doze, repose in the same bed, or copulate. She made her choice and pressed Print Answer. Then she had to search for the source of the noise as the printer whirred into life. She found her father's obsolete machine behind a pile of clothes under a table in the corner of the room.

She sat on the floor waiting for the paper to make its slow passage onto the roller. At last, there were three pages of close type face down in the tray. She picked them up, stood up, and returned to the desk. "It's tuna," she said of the substance in the sandwich, her brain having finally processed the chemicals. "Or vomit."

She took a breath, turned over the pages, and held them under the circle of yellow light from the desk lamp. As she read the text, she exhaled. "Oh, God," she groaned.

It was three days before Della could get a mobile signal at sea, so until she rang Jackson to enquire if Rik Wallace was all right, the crate remained unopened. Jackson lied when he promised he would open it that very instant. Instead, he and the librarian had an existential crisis over the possibility of losing custody of the children to their fake father. Jackson rang Inspector Freddy Sullivan to ask him to come and pick up the crate containing Wallace. But Sullivan told Jackson he didn't care any more about Wallace. Murphy was right. He was an obsessive personality, but now he had a new obsession. He didn't explain before hanging up.

Next, they rang Julie Progress, suggesting that Wallace and she were made for each other, and that she should come and take him to a remote tropical paradise where they might live together happily ever after while he was conveniently confined to a crate, a proposal Progress denied held any attraction for her before she too promptly hung up and then spent the rest of the evening regretting not making further enquiries.

What could they do now? Who else could they ring? There must be other women out there who might distract him! Think. Think.

XLVI

Incipiens Videre Lucem
Beginning to See the Light

Pandora threw her cigarette through the open window of the white taxi waiting on the road outside when Julie Progress came out the main gate of Fortune Mansion and past the entrepreneurs dismantling what was left of their encampment. "That's her. Come on, get going."

The driver straightened up in his seat and turned on the engine.

"Don't lose her," Pandora growled.

"She's on a bicycle," the driver protested to his passenger.

It wasn't just any bicycle. It was the librarian's large black model with the basket that one of the entrepreneurs had rented to Progress for a very reasonable sum.

"It's time you learned the difference between right and wrong," Jackson told the three children standing side by side in front of him in a descending row watching him jam the flat end of the crowbar between the horizontal and vertical boards of the crate marked "Interesting Books – Open Immediately" in which Rik Wallace remained entombed. "Della phoning after thr—five days is an example of something that is bad. Della ringing at all is good. Can you understand the difference? No? My point is, morality is often a question of timing."

"I know the ten commandments," the tallest one volunteered.

"I know three of them," the middle one said.

"Never mind those. My commandments are clear and practical. Who covets anything these days? Have you heard of any coveting in this neighbourhood? No? My commandments apply to the real world. First," he said, suspending his weight on the crowbar to hold up a finger. "Never ever tell lies. Under no circumstance is it morally justified to lie. Simple."

"Ever?" the tallest asked.

"Never? Always tell the truth no matter what the consequences. There are no exceptions. Once you go down the road of compromise, there is no end to the complications. I have seen too many people destroyed by compromise." The wood splintered as he leaned again on the lever.

"Except, of course, when you have to tell little lies," the librarian put in. She was standing behind Jackson, biting her nails. "White lies are acceptable, if used to avoid gratuitously hurting someone's feelings."

Jackson stopped prizing off the lid.

"Or to avoid getting into trouble yourself," he added as clarification. "That's the only other exception."

"No. That's not a good reason," the librarian said.

"What I meant to say was, you could tell a lie if it was preferable to telling the truth. Is that clear?"

"Like telling my teacher what you told me – that mummy had a stroke?" the middle child asked.

"Exactly," Jackson said, pleased at how the complex life lesson was going. "But apart from a few tiny exceptions – such as your apposite example of your biological mother, who, remember, is not your care mother like the librarian here – always tell the truth."

"Or Santa Claus," the librarian added.

"What about him?" the smallest child asked.

"He doesn't exist. Grown-ups made him up because it is impossible for an adult to deal with the existential abyss that is the contemporary mid-winter festival of Christmas without recourse to myths and alcohol."

The little girl burst into tears as the top came off the crate. The nails came out of the side panels with a low screech.

"It's quite exciting. I hope he is alive, though we got no response when we knocked earlier," Jackson said.

"Who's in there?" the tallest child asked, shrugging free of the line-up to peer inside, hoping whoever it was had sweets.

More panels were removed, and the librarian shrieked when Rik Wallace sat up suddenly as if propelled by a spring under his spine. It was impossible to tell from his cadaverous appearance whether it was the philosophical or the DIY Wallace that rocked over and back – or both reunited, having survived their incarceration. His audience waited to see if the apparition could speak.

"Where am I?" Wallace asked, studying the rows of books running up to the ceiling. "Oh, I'm back here," he said, recognising the faded interior of the bookshop. "Have you considered a green for the walls?"

"It was painted sometime in the last twenty years," Jackson protested.

"Nevertheless, a green would go well with the book spines."

"I think he has lost his mind," the librarian said. "Probably oxygen deprivation."

The children giggled and made faces at the smells rising from the crate as they helped the adults lift Wallace out and prop him on the high stool at the counter, where he sat with his legs dangling uselessly.

"It's Della fault. She said to apologise to you for not ringing earlier to check if we found you, but she couldn't get reception on her phone at sea. We didn't know it was you in the crate because she left you here when we were out trying to stop Ellen Dubois confronting Randy Fortune. She is the woman who agreed to be your wife in exchange for some of Randy's billions. She is in a coma upstairs," the librarian said, trying to cram everything into her excuse.

"I thought I was headed for South America in her animal smuggling ring. How long did you leave me locked up in there? It must have been weeks ago I heard laughter. I was sure I was going to die—"

"Look what I found when we were tidying up to make room for the interesting books we thought were in your crate," Jackson said, to change the topic away from their neglect, lifting the glass lid on a turn table. "And my collection of records. I haven't heard this one in years."

He slid the vinyl from the sleeve on which there was an image of a banana. "The old technology is the best, don't you agree?" he asked.

"No," Wallace said.

"Listen to this. It will cheer you up." On his first attempt he missed the groove between songs with the needle. "I love the way you can hear all of the imperfections. It's more real than the digital world."

The record crackled before a harsh voice warned him that he should run, run, run, run.

"Well, maybe not that," Jackson said. "We don't mean to be inhospitable."

"How long are you planning on staying here?" the librarian added, still irrationally worried he might want to pursue custody of his fake children.

"As soon as my legs work, I'll be on my way. Who are these?" Wallace asked, for the first time taking notice of the three children silhouetted in the window who stared at him with the admiration only children can have for a rancid adult. A sleeping yellow pup sagged at each end where the girl looped her arm around its fat stomach. He felt them as a source of unidentified anxiety.

"Oh, don't worry. They are not your children. We did find them when we were searching for yours, but it turns out they are ours. What a co-incidence," the librarian said. By now her laugh had more than a tincture of hysteria.

"Yours? I wasn't aware they were missing."

"Neither were we." More hysterical laughter. "Anyway, you are in no condition to fret over family matters. We would love for you to stay here with us until you get your strength back," Jackson lied, "but you see, we are running out of space for everyone."

As Wallace gazed at the six shoes on the children, the bell over the red telephone-box doors interrupted his blank reverie.

He saw Samantha Spencer standing in front of him when he looked up. He felt he could fall into her arms if he could only get to his feet. "You look wonderfully awful," he said as he smiled at her.

"You too," she said. "You stink."

"I assume the same as you, but I can't smell anymore." He tried to raise an arm and apply his nose to his armpit. He pinched the bottom of his trousers away from his crotch with two fingers as a gesture towards tidying himself up. "I was thinking of opening a museum dedicated to smell."

"Thank God she turned up," Jackson told the librarian. "I was beginning to think no one wants him."

"When Randy Fortune suddenly lost interest in KindFace and fired me, I locked myself up in my father's house to design a cool computer application that solves moral dilemmas. I thought maybe we could work on it together if you like. You do the moralising, and I'll design the algorithms. I brought this for you," she said to Wallace, holding out the now crumpled pages, blushing red under her white make-up. "It's about you. No. It's about us. You see I was surprised how upset I was when I thought you were dead. When I found out it wasn't you that The Great Augustus cut in half, I asked the computer if it was right for me to continue hating you and—"

"That's a great idea. I'm surprised no one has thought of that before." Wallace took the pages, but before he could even move his eyes over them the bell above the red doors clanged again.

"Oh, my, we are popular today," the librarian said as she turned around to see who had come in. "I should put up the 'Closed' sign."

"I'll find something upstairs stronger than tea to drink," Jackson said. "Something to get your legs working again,

Wallace, so that you can walk out of here with Samantha."

"I have discovered liking someone involves commitment beyond just pressing a button," Samantha was saying as Julie Progress appeared from behind a shelf.

"Rik," Progress said, pushing Samantha out of her way and throwing herself at him where he balanced on the stool. "I was sure you were dead. It was a whole day before the police confirmed it was the actor, Claudius Steel's body in the library. A nude Macbeth in tribute to his career is opening in the—" She stopped talking and held him at arm's length. "Your hair. Your eyes. What have you done? This look doesn't suit you at all. You're not a drug addict, are you? I'd kiss you, but you stink. Almost as disgusting as her," she said inclining her head in Samantha's direction.

"Seems Rik and I have much in common," Samantha said as she pushed Progress aside.

"Don't worry about anything, Rik. I will take care of you from now on," Progress said, shoving Samantha back again.

"Let's drink to this unexpected reunion," Jackson interrupted, appearing in the doorway carrying a tray of glasses and a bottle.

"Progress! You told me on the phone you never wanted to see Rik again."

"Children, go upstairs," the librarian said.

"We don't want to," they chorused.

"Go up and stare at your mother. Shout down the stairs if she opens her eyes."

The children filed out of sight behind a shelf where they remained hidden, their hair visible over rows of books at different heights.

Nico sang that she would be their mirror, reflect what they were, in case they didn't know, which was probable.

"Obviously, I was lying! What kind of a moron are you?"

"What about your relationship with Randy Fortune?" Wallace asked Progress as Samantha grabbed her in an armlock around her neck.

Jackson was bitten twice before he got them separated. "Oh, Randy," Progress panted. "That worked out wonderfully. Before he ran away to sea with your psychiatrist Murphy, he gave me a rucksack stuffed with money and told me to get lost. Since I am free, I thought you and I might become a philosophical item again, just like old times."

"And what about Pandora? What about her stay-rich scheme at Candid Online College?"

"She can sleep with that creep if she wants to. I have principles."

"Not according to my computer programme, you haven't," Samantha said, shoving Progress backwards by slamming her palms into her chest.

"Don't worry about Pandora. I can take care of her—"

The librarian raised her eyes to the ceiling when the bell jangled again. "I'm definitely putting up the 'Closed' sign."

"I told you that 'Book Sale' notice done in crayon in the window was a mistake," Jackson called after her.

At the front of the shop, the librarian told Pandora to come in. "What a lovely surprise," she said without feeling.

Pandora walked behind the librarian down the corridor formed by two shelves. She took the Glock from her handbag as she reached the open space in front of the counter.

"Ah, Pandora. We were just talking about you. You will

never believe what Randy Fortune did," Progress said. Then she saw the gun. "What are you doing here?" she asked, pushing Samantha in front of her.

"I followed you."

"Why?"

Progress was now behind Samantha who stood to the left of Wallace, who was teetering on his weak legs that he was just then testing so that he could leave as soon as possible, preferably with Samantha holding him up. It was always good to be liked, and Progress had a bag of money, but unfortunately, he had never been motivated by wealth; which was a pity because getting rich must surely be easier than philosophy, and his other self was right, it was time to stop thinking, if only he could. Next in line, Jackson was pouring whisky into glasses perched on an improvised drinks cabinet made from cardboard boxes.

"Just in time to toast our reunion," Jackson said, not seeing the gun because he was distracted counting glasses.

Pandora raised the pistol holding it in both hands at arm's length, her index fingers resting along the sides of the barrel.

"What are you doing?"

"You look terrible, Rik, but I have no time for chit-chat. In fact, it is essential you don't speak," she said squeezing the trigger.

Nico was still singing.

Nothing happened.

As Pandora searched the unfamiliar weapon for the safety, Progress dived behind the counter. The librarian jumped in front of Jackson to protect him. Meanwhile, Wallace was tilting forward, allowing himself to fall towards the floor. It occurred to him that his final thought should not be on Kant, or Nietzsche. It should be on love – his love for Samantha. Or Progress. No, definitely Samantha. But what was it Heidegger said about not feeling the bullet when it hit him? Pandora took aim again at her moving target. This time the gun did go off.

XLVII

Certamen
Struggle

Rik Wallace raised himself on his elbows and dragged his legs behind him between a pair of shelves. He crawled over the floorboards, through the red telephone-box front door, before subsiding face down, exhausted on the uneven granite paving stones outside. Pandora walked behind him holding the pistol upright at her shoulder, pointed at the sky.

"You can't slither away from me, Rik. Turn over, and take what's coming to you, because I don't want to shoot you in the back."

Just then the three children emerged from behind the shelf to get a better view of who was shooting whom.

"Quick. Help me find my service revolver. It's around here somewhere," Jackson said. "Come on, everyone, start looking now."

"Didn't you hand that in when you retired?" the librarian asked.

"I meant to, but I forgot. Here, you take those," he said, pointing the children to a row of drawers and shoving a box into Progress's arms. "And you two search those shelves over there," he told the librarian and Samantha.

Everyone began to throw things into the air: the children throwing them higher than the adults.

Outside Wallace turned over on to his back and raised his arms in surrender.

Pandora aimed the gun at his face, but changed her mind and redirected it at his chest, because she assumed, he probably planned to freeze his head like all the other philosophers.

"I swear Pandora I am cured. I had an existential crisis in a crate when I thought I was buried alive, and as a consequence, I have emerged free of abstract thoughts. I promise you I will never have an idea again. I want to open a museum to smell. I'm a changed person."

"No, you're not." This in a high-pitched growl.

"Who said that?" Pandora asked, looking around her, the plates of her dark sunglasses scanning left and right.

"I did," Wallace said.

She focussed the black lenses on his face. She knew this was the moment when she should squeeze the trigger, but curiosity got the better of her. What is it about curiosity even when we have heard it all before?

"Shut up, for God's sake. Can't you see she has a gun?"

"Who are you talking to?" Pandora couldn't resist asking.

"It's me. The moral philosopher inside me."

"I swear, Pandora. I thought he was gone."

"I'm still here."

"Don't listen to him, Pandora."

"You really are crazy," Pandora said as she rummaged in her pocket with one hand for her cigarettes.

"It's not my fault. I told you I was crazy, but you bust me out of the asylum anyway. I begged you to leave me there."

"Well, you are definitely as sane as Nietzsche."

"Shut up," he screamed at himself.

"You shut up," he screamed back.

Wallace wrapped his hands around his throat and began to strangle himself. His face turned red as his eyes bulged. He rolled from side to side on the footpath.

Pandora lowered the gun and raised her sunglasses to study the example of a dissociative identity disorder writhing on the granite paving under the shop window. She placed a cigarette between her lips.

Between gasps for air, Wallace was shouting something about Heidegger.

Pandora raised the gun and took aim at Wallace. He stopped struggling and clenched his eyes closed, pulled his legs up to his chest, and waited for the bullet.

He heard the shot, followed by the sound of glass falling around him on the concrete like crystal rain.

Silence. He felt nothing. No pain. Nothing. Heidegger was right after all! He opened his eyes and blinked.

Pandora's face hit the granite inches from his. The right lens of her sunglasses was missing. Wallace saw a bloody hole where her varicose eye should have been.

Ellen Dubois's face came into view through the bottom of the shop window. Then Jackson's head appeared beside Ellen's before disappearing again.

"I want my fucking billions," Ellen Dubois shouted.

Jackson prized his gun from her fingers which were wrapped around the grip. He handed it to the tallest child. "Don't give that to your biological mother, again," he said. "Even if he has a new obsession, we had better phone Freddy Sullivan."

XLVIII

Spe Quae Ex Frigore
The Future of Frozen Goods

Horse sat on his own up front with Marlborough in his arms at the service for Pandora at the Frozen In Time Cryogenics Centre. It was his wish that she be preserved for future generations. He was crying to his choice of music. The centre allowed just one verse of Nick Cave & The Bad Seeds to assure the audience that people are no good because there was a queue of bodies forming outside waiting to get in.

Rik Wallace was in the second row studying his shoes. Since he had first gone down the road of doing good, he had lost count of the number of funerals he had had to attend. Perhaps trying to do the right thing and death were somehow inextricably linked. Disguising himself as Nietzsche hadn't been his idea. From two feet away, you could be forgiven for thinking he was the unstable philosopher. But it seemed an unnecessary precaution because both the police and psychiatric services seemed to have lost interest in his case. What was it about him, he wondered, that prevented his holding people's attention, even while resembling a nineteenth-century genius?

He goggled his eyeballs into what he considered to be an intense stare worthy of Nietzsche. He would have stroked his luxuriant moustache, but he couldn't move his arms. Julie Progress on one side squeezed his hand at the same moment Samantha Spencer gripped his other one. He couldn't tell whether they were consoling him or pinning him in place!

416

Intermissio
Intermission